KATE CANTERBARY

Editing provided by Julia Ganis of Julia Edits
Editing provided by Erica Russikoff of Erica Edits
Proofreading provided by Jodi Duggan, Marla Esposito, and Nyla Lillie
Cover illustrations created by Qamber Designs

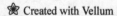 Created with Vellum

about shucked

His best friend's little sister is *not* an option.

No one ever accused Beckett Loew of being the nice Loew brother,
especially not Sunny Du Jardin.
Stuck back home in the quirky town of Friendship, Rhode Island,
Beckett is scrambling to save his family's oyster bar and take care of his
teenage brother.
He doesn't have time to deal with the beautiful, sunshine-y owner of the
new vegan cafe next door too.
His best friend's little sister may be all grown up, but Sunny's still a
distracting pain in his side.

No one expects much from Sunny Du Jardin, especially not Beckett
Loew.
She's not worried about her older brother's tall, dark, and broody best
friend or the battles he insists on waging with her every day.
She's not the same kid he teased years ago.
Now, she composts his type for breakfast.

They're all wrong for each other.

Bitter rivals.

Complete opposites.

Off limits.

Except they can't keep their hands off each other.

They tell themselves it's nothing more than a steamy summer fling until secrets spill and real trouble comes their way.

CW: chronic illness (epilepsy), mention of childhood bullying, putting the fun in dysfunctional families, parents who turn into accidental criminals, incarceration, open door spice, drug and alcohol use, suspense and moments of peril.

For my grandmother, who told unbelievable stories that I still believe after all these years.

And for all the fixers who fix everyone else first, second, and always.

chapter one

Sunny

Today's Special:
Disaster over an Herb Salad

I WAS COMPLETELY out of control. That was one thing I knew to be certain.

There was no other explanation. I mean, if I was in control of *anything* at all, would I be the newest resident of the same small town that I'd plotted to escape as a teenager? No. Hard pass. But that was the problem with big plans and the rate at which spinach went bad in my fridge and the whole damn world: I couldn't control any of it.

Another thing I knew was that this messy, chaotic universe loved to hand me things I didn't see coming and didn't know how to handle. But the joke was on the universe because I loved mess and chaos, and I was an expert at figuring it out as I went. I could even pretend it was part of my plan all along.

My present chaos was a series of mostly happy accidents that forced me to push the far limits of figuring it out. There was no pretense of a plan. No one could've anticipated any of this and I was still impressed at how I was tap dancing my way through these flails and flops.

Exhibit A. Last summer, I won the deed to an abandoned bait shop on a random piece of waterfront in a poker game with a bunch of real estate moguls. As one does. Imagine the jump scare at realizing this property was located in my small hometown of Friendship, Rhode Island—and was the meeting place for all the area raccoons. I was hoping one of those real estate guys would be happy to win the bait shop back the next time they played poker at my tavern but the universe swooped in with a hearty chuckle of "You fucked around, now it's time to find out!"

Exhibit B. My boss Murtagh—the crustiest, curmudgeoniest man on any planet—decided to close up The Soggy Dog, the tavern he'd owned forever and a day. While Murtagh was a complete grumble bucket, he'd let me run the tavern for almost two years, kept his complaining about my regular time off for travel adventures to a low snarl, and only threatened to fire me once or twice a week. Losing that job was my least favorite kind of mess, and seeing as I'd spent the past handful of years following my moods from New York to Boston to Maine to Rhode Island, I didn't have a solid next step lined up. But crusty old Murtagh made out like a bandit when he sold the building he'd owned since around the time of the Louisiana Purchase, and he gave me a small chunk of change from the proceeds for, as he put it, "not being useless."

Exhibit C. One by one, all of my favorite people suddenly experienced big changes in their lives. Within a month or two, my best friends and I all lost jobs, partners, or promotions, and we now had unscheduled wiggle room to come together and have fun with this chaos. Our version of fun was hatching a plan to rehab the old bait shop and open a vegan café that also dabbled in book clubs and sunrise yoga and full moon ceremonies. As one did. If it was weird and wonderful, we wanted it. The wonkier, the better.

The past few months had been like juggling knives on a roller coaster while tequila drunk. I knew there would be more juggling to come though the roller coaster would be different, but I couldn't believe this was the mess the universe had made for me. If I'd asked the sixteen-year-old version of myself if I'd be opening a vegan café with three besties when I was twenty-eight, and doing it in the Rhode Island town that had felt more like a cage than a cozy, quirky, seaside enclave, I would've laughed. *Hard*. But that was the whole thing about chaos. You had to take your mismatched parts and soul-sucking career prospects and the childhood epilepsy you never outgrew, and build a life out of it. Create a path that didn't make you dread Monday and every day after that. Construct a world for yourself, even if you had no idea how to do it.

Fuck around and you'll find out.

So, here I was, turning off Friendship's main road and down the narrow side street leading to Naked Provisions. We were ready to put the finishing touches on this weird brainchild of ours before opening the doors and serving our first customers today. The only things left to do were fill the window boxes and pots lining our freshly refurbished patio, and wait to discover the multitude of things we hadn't planned for.

From the looks of the crushed shell parking lot, two of my partners were already inside the café, prepping for the day. Since I was useless in the kitchen, I headed straight for the patio on the back end of the building, my fold-up wagon loaded with potting soil and plants.

It wasn't hard to love the old bait shop now that it was clean, airy, and raccoon-free but I especially loved the patio. We were on a knobby outcropping of land known as Small Point, at the edge of Friendship Cove where it became Narragansett Bay, and something about this in-between spot—thick with old trees that bent at breakneck angles from wind howling in off the water, and marsh grasses along the rocky shores —felt like a secret kind of magic. Every time I saw the sunlight sparkling over the waters of the cove, I reminded myself that mess could be the best.

Another thing I loved was that we were only a few minutes' walk from the town center though it felt like we had our own private world out here. Private except for the semi-famous oyster bar on the other side of the parking lot. I'd almost perfected my ability to ignore its existence.

My service dog Scout sniffed at a pot overflowing with lavender, rosemary, oregano, and hardy geranium, then sneezed and stalked away as if repulsed. The two-year-old chocolate Lab settled in a sun-drenched spot beside Jem, the German shepherd who refused to accept that he'd flunked out of service animal school. "A bold statement coming from someone who spent five whole minutes licking rocks this morning," I called as I started on another pot. "Come over here. Just give it a chance. I know you'll love this."

"I cannot see a single reason why that would be the case."

I snapped my head from the plants to find *him* glaring at me.

Even if I had a hundred chances to guess the nightmare from my past who would stomp out of the oyster bar next door and across the small parking lot we shared, I never would've named *him*.

Before I could get my hands out of the soil or make sense of the irritable man and his expensive-looking dress shirt rolled up to the elbows, he continued. "I'm not sure who you are or what you think you're doing but this is private property. You need to take all of this"—he motioned to the pots and garden supplies with a quick *what the fuck* shake of his head that I remembered all too well—"and leave immediately."

It was him and *he didn't remember me.*

I wasn't self-centered enough to assume anyone would remember me after twenty-ish years, but when it came to this guy, there was nothing I wouldn't hold against him. His entire existence was a problem for me to the point that I'd built an iceberg of resentment for him. A massive, fatal, frozen mountain I'd forgotten about until seeing his face again and now I could feel frost swirling around me like I was made of things that only existed in subzero conditions.

Still kneeling on the patio, I glanced down at the soil and flowers, and brushed my hands together. So this was the thing we hadn't planned for. It would've been so much better if we could've blown some fuses running six juicers at the same time or got locked out of the point-of-sale system. This could not be solved with a hard restart.

It stood to reason that I'd run into him sooner or later, what with his family's restaurant being *right there* and all. But by all accounts he hadn't set foot in this state for years. I'd hoped for later. A lot later. "Actually, I don't have to go anywhere. This isn't your property."

"That's inaccurate." He slipped a phone out of his pocket and thumbed in a code. "I know who owns this building and it's not you." He raked an impatient glare over the maxi skirt pooled around me, up to my sleeveless top, and eventually settled on my face.

I was older now but I still had a baby doll face with the same round, rosy cheeks as ever. Everyone remembered these cheeks. *Everyone.* Even if they forgot my name, they'd smile and point to their cheeks in a makeshift sign language of *I remember your face!* Not a single flicker of recognition in those dark eyes of his.

"Let's move this little flower cart operation along before I have someone do it for you."

Of course it was him. Of course the universe would fling this insufferable ass my way at the exact moment I thought my life was finally coming together. Of course he'd be just as rude and arrogant and dismissive as he'd always been.

I felt Scout settle beside me as I drank in this man who was roughly the size of a garden shed. Shoulders like he put the ox out to pasture and pulled the cart all by himself. Legs like an old-growth forest, cruelly wrapped in the kind of trousers that whispered of wealth and taste. Forearms kissed with enough sun and strength to suggest he did more than bark orders from behind a desk all day. And that ever-present scowl, the one that teetered into a half smile and tottered into a half frown when he found it in him to express an emotion beyond his usual sludge of gloom and grump.

The years had changed him. He was just as tall and dark as always but there was a polish to him now. Cleaned up, smoothed over, ironed out. Those unruly waves of his had learned some manners and he wore the kind of scruff that was only a few days short of declaring itself a proper beard, and it all fit together in a way that made me think he woke up in the morning and checked off items on his Wickedly Successful Businessman Style Guide.

Time had treated him with a lot more generosity than he deserved. With more kindness and comfort than I would've extended him.

Beckett Loew.

Heir to an oyster empire.

Bane of my childhood existence.

My older brother's best friend.

Chaos, and not the happy accident kind.

And here he was, back home after all these years, towering over me and hoisting the insufferable douchebag flag on my café's opening day as if it was his preordained right to ruin my life all over again.

Ah, but he knew nothing about my iceberg. Me and the 'berg, we were a goddamn force of nature. There was nothing we couldn't do and no one who could stop us. We could move mountains and take down ocean liners without a hair sliding out of place.

We were our own kind of chaos, baby.

I knee-shuffled over to the next pot of herbs, giving him my back as I reached for a flat of citronella. After a minute of fussing with the leaves and ignoring him, I called over my shoulder, "Thanks, but I don't think that's going to happen, so why don't you just turn yourself around and stay on your side of the street."

chapter two

Beckett

Today's Special:
The Meet-Argue, Medium Rare

I DIDN'T KNOW which time zone I was in. I was only superficially aware of which continent I was on. I had no fucking clue what day it was or the last time I'd changed my clothes. I smelled like airport bars and jet exhaust. My contacts had fused to my retinas about sixteen hours ago. If I could focus on one thing for seven seconds without encountering another disaster, I'd figure it all out. But as it stood, life was fucking me in ways even the most adventurous porn had not prepared me for.

This white girl with her flowerpots hardly ranked with all the other bullshit on my plate. I'd flown thousands of miles, been awake for three (four?) days straight, and had to fire most of the staff of Small Point Oyster Company this morning.

I didn't have time for anyone's fucking flowerpots.

It didn't matter if her cherubic face was familiar. Everyone in this town was familiar and I forgot their names all the same, just the way they forgot about me before the door hit me on the ass on the way out.

I gestured to the pots eating up the already limited space of this area but she didn't notice. "These things can't stay here."

She spared me a quick, cool glance as she arranged a plant in the pot. Dark hair with golden highlights spilled over her shoulders, thick and wavy where it brushed her bare arms. Round, pink cheeks and a cute little nose, like a doll but the kind of doll that would kick your ass while smiling at you with that heart-shaped mouth. She was young, probably mid-twenties. And beautiful. Like, *drop everything and stare because how is she even real?* beautiful.

I knew she was just following orders and didn't want to get her in trouble with her boss but I really couldn't spend all morning explaining to this young woman that her flowerpots wouldn't survive the weekend if she left them in the middle of my delivery unloading zone.

"And why is that?" she asked, her hands deep in the soil.

I checked my phone for new messages and shoved a hand through my hair. There were at least ten very good, logical reasons why this woman couldn't drop a half dozen flowerpots in this precise location but my brain was running on empty and I could only manage to say, "It gets busy here on weekend evenings. People park right there, in that spot, all the time. And we have frequent deliveries. If you leave these things here, your flowers will be roadkill before Monday morning rolls around. Not to mention blocking fire lane access." I glanced up the impossibly narrow driveway, the one that necessitated a valet team of four on the busiest nights of the summer, and remembered the most important point. "And you're on SPOC property."

"You might want to check your info because that's not correct."

There was an air of authority in her words, one that woke up my last functional brain cells and promised I'd enjoy this fight if I stuck around long enough to get in another shot. A shocked laugh cracked out of me because it was amusing to think anyone could fight me on this topic. I knew the business of Small Point Oyster Company backward and forward, and I'd known it for the past twenty years. There was no doubt in my mind that I was right about this. That simply was not possible. "No," I insisted, "*you* are mistaken."

"Amazingly, I am not." She didn't bother looking up from her plants to say this.

The bold dismissiveness, it was killing me. She didn't give a shit what I had to say and she wanted me to know that more than anything else. And—I liked it? Or I experienced something that resembled mild amusement at this hole-in-the-head conversation. It was vaguely fun to play this pointless game with her while my family's business crumbled by the second. Kind of like playing Tetris while getting fired or hearing you had six months left to live.

"I have to be honest here and say you're overreacting in a significant way," she continued. "A few flowerpots on the perimeter of the patio are not trouncing anyone's property lines and they certainly aren't creating fire lane issues. Of all the things to get fussy about, this is a silly one."

I blinked. Maybe she was a mirage and I was just extra fucked-up from—well, everything. Because no one spoke to me like that. No one aside from my brothers but wasn't that the whole point of brothers? Not that either of them talked to me much as it was. "The property lines run from there"—I pointed to the dock extending out into the cove—"to there." I swung my arm in the opposite direction, toward Market Street. "As you can see, you're encroaching on my property. I'm sure there's plenty of room on the other side of your little patio for this whole situation."

I wasn't positive about her being a real person and not a figment of my sleep-deprived imagination, though it seemed like she muttered "such an ass" under her breath.

Rather than responding, I reached for one of the pots. It was ludicrously heavy and cumbersome, and moving it really did require another person or heavy machinery, but there was no way in hell I could admit defeat. I was committed now. I had to get this overflowing monstrosity out of my way and prove my damn point to this imaginary yet very mouthy and *very* beautiful woman. Even if I gave myself a hernia in the process.

I craned my neck to avoid getting a face full of flowers and found her glaring up at me. Soil spilled down the front of my shirt. I could feel some leaves or petals sticking to my beard scruff. It was horrible. I hated this. But I hated backing down even more.

"I'll thank you to stop this nonsense now." She pushed to her feet as she spoke, and her dogs—fuck, those dogs did not look happy—closed in on either side of her. Her hands were dirty and her stare was dark, like she had no trouble imagining me crushed under the pot.

I had to give her credit. Most people found me intimidating, especially when I issued orders, and this woman seemed to find me as intimidating as a gnat. Probably because she was a hallucination. Was it normal to have conversations while hallucinating? Did it always feel like being plugged into an electrical outlet and fully alive for the first time in forever? Would I remember any of this when it was over?

I hoped so. She really was breathtaking, even while being an endless headache.

"I'll put it down over there," I said, jutting my chin across the patio and away from my loading zone. "Off my property and where it's not interfering with the flow of traffic."

"Just because you say something over and over doesn't make it—" She took a step toward me, a warning expression carved into her lovely face, but her sandal caught on a loose stone and she pitched forward.

When panic flashed across her hazel eyes, I realized there wasn't time to catch the woman and keep a hold on the flowers. Had to make a split-second choice. While one was an increasingly annoying problem, the other could be replaced within the hour.

Decision made. The pot hit the stone and cracked. I caught her by the wrist and she slammed into my chest. Her dogs closed in around us, whining and nosing at her as she gasped.

If this was a mirage, a hallucination, a goddamn nightmare—it was a good one.

Instinct took over and I flattened my hand between her shoulder blades as she stared up at me, her lips parted. There was a streak of soil on her cheek, four studs climbing up her left earlobe, and no hint of a bra under my palm. She was *so* beautiful. Stunning. If I'd met her before, I'd remember. I wouldn't forget a face like this. I couldn't. I *wouldn't*. I wouldn't forget anything about the way she felt in my arms. Small though soft. Curved in the most lovely ways. All I wanted to do was hold on.

She was on the short side. I hadn't realized that until I watched her tip her head back and—and *scowl* at me. Why was she scowling at me? I saved her from eating rocks.

"You didn't need to do that," she said. "I tripped and would've recovered just fine. Even if I didn't, the dogs wouldn't have let me fall."

"The *dogs*?" I snapped. As if waiting to be invited into the conversation, one of the dogs nudged between us while the other thumped his tail against my leg like a warning.

"Yes, the dogs," she said, pushing away from me. "Just because you haven't had to put up with a neighbor for years doesn't mean you can come over and yell about anything that comes to mind and break a pot in the process."

I couldn't believe this response. I'd *saved* her. "I think what you're trying to say is thank you."

"Once again, I think you're confused." She crossed her arms over her chest and shook her head at the broken pot. I worked very hard at keeping my eyes on hers rather than dropping to study the bra-free situation.

I thought about wiping the dirt off her cheek. I thought about reaching for her again to steal one more moment before coming to my senses from this stress-coma. Though I knew it was no hallucination, no mirage. This was real and I was fucked as per usual because I had too many problems and she was too young and—by the grace of a good attorney—I wouldn't be here too long. But that bra-free thing, I had some thoughts on that.

Instead, I did the only thing I could reliably do for anyone, and pulled out my phone and shot off a few messages. "I wouldn't be so quick to make those kinds of declarations," I said.

"I can be whichever speed I'd like when I'm right."

Yeah. I liked arguing with her, I really did. It was fun in a dangerous kind of way, like the looseness that came from a good whiskey or too much soap on the shower floor, and it made me want to throw out every preposterous thing I could come up with just to hear her reaction. "Then power-walk yourself over to the Town Hall and take a peek at the property lines."

"If you think I don't think I already have a copy, then you—"

"What kind of shenanigans have we started back here?"

I looked up from the screen to see a trio of women coming around the side of the building. They shared a silent conversation over the ruins of the flowerpot and my soiled shirt before my clumsy friend with the dark hair and all the unjustified glaring said, "The neighbors aren't a fan of our herb garden."

"Now wait just one second." I glanced over my shoulder to find Hale Wooten, my oyster alchemist and one of the few people I wouldn't be firing, pushing a dolly stacked with crates of this morning's harvest up the dock. "We love herbs. We love gardens. Don't let this guy tell you otherwise. He doesn't like anything."

"Yeah. I've noticed that," the dark-haired woman said.

I stared at her as if to say *Really? You're doing this to me after I saved your pretty little face?*

Hale strolled over, barely suppressing a laugh at the soil all over my shirt and the wreckage at my feet, and held out a hand to me. "Figured you'd show up today. Holdin' up all right?"

"Fine." I wasn't interested in discussing this in front of these people. I nodded to the crates on his dolly and gave him a pointed look. "Good catch?"

"You know my answer to this, man." He yanked off his cap and ran a hand over his forehead and the hair tied in a short ponytail. "There are no good days, no bad days. The water knows what to give us."

Though it wasn't a response that made any sense to me, and it ignored the considerable resources I poured into predicting oyster harvests, I didn't argue with him. Hale's family and their Narragansett ancestors had been raising oysters in this area for at least five hundred years. I'd defer to generational wisdom here.

"Doesn't the place look good? Hard to believe it used to be the old bait shop," he said with an elbow to my ribs. "They've put a ton of work into it this winter."

"About that," I started, glancing at the women who looked like they wouldn't mind taking a shovel to my head. It was obvious I wasn't going to make any progress here and shouldn't waste any more time when I could resolve matters with the people in charge. "Is your manager here? Can I speak with them? Or would you give me their number so we can get to the bottom of this?"

I knew I'd made an enormous mistake when the dark-haired woman seemed to buzz with evil glee. She looked like she was prepared to torture me to my death and she was really fucking happy about it too.

"Yes, the manager is here." She stepped around the broken pot and held out her hand. "Sunny Du Jardin."

My life, it really was an endless series of getting fucked in new and unsatisfying ways. No end. No stopping point. Not even a lull in the action where I could contemplate throwing myself off a cliff simply to avoid the next round of fuckery.

This woman—this adult woman who was old enough to make her own decisions about piercings and flowerpots and bras was *Sunny Du*

Jardin. And that would've been fine under any other circumstance except for the minor issue of her being my best friend's little sister. And by *little sister*, I meant that she existed in my mind as a child. Not that she was much taller than the last time I'd seen her but this woman—the one I'd had flattened against me a few minutes ago, the one with the sadist's smile, the one I would've considered pursuing if not for my entire life—was so far off-limits, she might as well be a mirage.

When I left this town for good after college, she'd been ten or eleven, a kid with short, curly hair, braces, and an obsession with horses. She loved to get her brother Lance in trouble and his parents always believed her since they hovered and doted on her because of her seizures and—

I snapped my fingers at the German shepherd beside her. "Wait. Is that Buster?" I knew it was a dumb question the second it was out of my mouth and I knew I was an idiot for asking about her old service dog, the one Lance had called Buster Nuts because we'd been stupid, *stupid* children, even as teenagers. Especially as teenagers. But somehow that was the first thing to push through the collision in my head of the Sunny I'd known twenty years ago and the one I'd had pressed up against me moments ago.

The Sunny who wasn't wearing a bra and had the kind of wide, sumptuous hips that were meant for dragging into laps. For gripping hard and holding on tight. For—

Fuck, she's Lance's little sister and I am a pervert.

She rolled her eyes and I had to swallow a groan. Pissing her off tickled at something deep and uncivilized in the back of my skull, and there was no way for this to get any worse. I needed to stop with all these feelings. They weren't doing me any good and they were quite likely to land me in a world of hurt. But goddamn, I liked the prickly side of her. Too much. Way too much.

"Buster died fifteen years ago. Now I have Jem"—she patted the dog's head—"and that's Scout. And I have Naked Provisions, a vegan café sharing this cozy little area with Small Point Oyster Company."

I nodded at the renovated saltbox-style building. I'd missed the black-and-white sign along the side of the building due to the stress-coma. And the skirt that almost hid the curves my hands itched to explore. As if that would ever, could ever happen. Lance would detonate, to start, but then Sunny would kill me. Chop me up and bury me in her flowerpots. And I didn't have the time to chase a skirt or the exceptionally smart-tongued woman wearing it. Not when I was now managing an oyster company and also the guardian to a seventeen-year-old.

"This is your place?"

"It is. This weekend is our soft launch."

"Then why aren't your parents here? Or Lance? Why isn't anyone helping you?" I asked.

She gave a slow shake of her head, that evil glee still shimmering in her eyes. "This might be difficult for you to understand but I'm not the eight-year-old I was when you moved to town, although it does seem as though you're permanently stuck with the maturity and temperament of a sixteen-year-old."

This was not my finest hour. I was an actual mess—dirty, tired, mentally toasted. My mouth was moving much faster than any portion of my brain. The rest of me was still reeling from the feel of Sunny in my arms, which was a noteworthy problem that compounded every time she threw a glare in my direction because she was my best friend's little sister and there was no set of circumstances in the universe where knowing the status of her bra was acceptable. If I had any sense, I'd shut up and walk away. Take the loss and put an end to this supremely confusing interaction before life could find a new way to fuck me.

Then again, holding Sunny Du Jardin before knowing she was Sunny Du Jardin *was* a whole new way of getting fucked. If we wanted to talk about unsatisfying, this was it. Front and fucked-up center.

"Aside from the fact Lance lives in *San Francisco* and wouldn't be useful for much more than setting up the wi-fi, I don't need his help. Or my parents'. I'm sorry that I have to be the one to explain to you that I'm capable of running a business without the assistance of my parents or brother. Not when I have extremely competent partners." She motioned to the others. "These are my partners and very dear friends. Partners, this is Beckett Loew. He and his family own the oyster company."

A tall white woman with a pair of dark braids spilling over her shoulders crossed her arms over her black dress. "Meara Monahan," she said. She looked like Wednesday Addams' twin sister. She'd take the shovel to my head first and then she'd sign my tombstone like she wanted the credit.

An Asian woman with bright pink lipstick waved, saying, "Hi! I'm Bethany Shawpscock."

"Shawps...cock," I repeated.

"Yep!" she said with a bubbly nod.

"I run the kitchen. I'm Muffy McTeague," a Black woman wearing a denim apron and thick gold hoop earrings said. She had intricate tattoos all down one arm and lime green glasses. She'd also kill me but she'd do it with knives and make a stew from my bones.

"I'm sorry. Did you say your name is Muffy Mc...Tease?"

"McTeague," she repeated with a tolerant smile. She'd heard that one before. I'd make a fine stew.

Hale chuckled beside me while I blinked at them. I was in a real-life delusion. Any minute, Hale's oysters would break into a song and dance routine and a mermaid would surface in the cove. That was Friendship, Rhode Island for you. "Is this some kind of skit?"

"I don't know what the hell is happening here," a voice called from across the parking lot, "but it looks like it's long past time for Beck to stop talking."

I turned to find Melissa Salcedo walking toward us. Mel was an expert mixologist and managed the front of house, and somewhere in her give-no-fucks heart found the time to give many fucks to my parents. She was another one of the people I wouldn't be firing today. That brought the count up to three if I included my seventeen-year-old brother Parker who bussed tables and washed dishes. With any luck, he hadn't been involved in any of the counterfeiting or money laundering schemes. I could depend on him to sleep through most things. Speaking of which, I'd need to find out *where* he was sleeping seeing as I was his new guardian and he refused to answer his phone.

"I don't know what happened here"—Mel swirled a hand over the flowers I'd destroyed—"or what happened here"—and the soil on my shirt—"or any of this"—a wide-eyed glance at the women of Naked Provisions—"but I'm not about to let you dick around all day. Woot would allow it but I won't." She gave the oysterman a withering stare. Not a single fuck given. "I see you laughing into your elbow, sir. Not helping."

"I have no idea what you're talking about," Hale said, chuckling.

"You are a troublemaker and you know it." Mel returned her gaze to me, saying, "Wrap this up."

Something in Mel's tone cleared away the fog of the mirage, the stress-coma, the braless holodeck. I had to pull myself together and stop being dick silly over the most untouchable woman in the world, who happened to be a kid (fuck my life) in my head. I was here to clean house and put my family back together, and I didn't have time to spar in circles about some flowerpots.

"I'll wrap it up just as soon as our new neighbors agree their decorations are blocking our traffic flow and they move them to a more suitable location," I said.

"Your traffic flow," Sunny said, all ice and sadism, "is not our problem."

"It will be your problem on Saturday when this place is mobbed and we're stopping traffic on Market Street because a vendor is trying to back their truck down here without sideswiping every car they pass. It will be your problem when the police implement a parking ban and your customers have to walk down from Market Street to get"—I waved toward the building—"vegan things."

Hale shook his head. "I don't think you need to worry so hard over it, Beck. Nothing has really changed. It just looks different because they cleaned this area up."

Okay so maybe I was firing him. It couldn't be that difficult to find someone else with five centuries of oystering in their blood.

"It gives me no pleasure to agree with Woot on anything," Mel started, "but he has a point. It only looks like they're cannibalizing our driveway because this area seems much bigger now that it isn't covered in overgrown beach grass and abandoned lobster traps."

It looked like I was down a front of house manager too.

Sunny crossed her arms and shot me a triumphant grin. "Does this make any more sense to you now that two other people have explained it?"

I didn't try to withhold my eye roll. It was perversely entertaining to argue with her. It didn't matter that I urgently needed sleep, several gallons of water, and to yell at my attorney until I lost my voice. Didn't matter that my clothes had seen four continents or that my contacts were dangerously dry. I wanted to yell at Sunny and I wanted her to yell back, and that was a serious fucking problem. "My point still stands and you're ignoring the fact—"

"All right." Mel clapped me on the shoulder. "Meet me inside when you're finished here. For everyone's sake, please finish quickly. We have business to discuss."

"Hello there," Bethany said to Mel, extending her hand. "I'm Bethany. Everyone calls me Beth. Or Bethany. Either one is great. Or Bea. No one calls me that, but I wouldn't mind if you did. Or anyone else. Hi. Hello. I don't think we've met."

Mel froze on the spot. She stared at Beth's outstretched hand but made no move to accept it. After a pause that had everyone looking at the ground to get away from the awkwardness, Mel said, "We haven't met." She clasped Beth's hand for a split second and then shot me a side-eye glance. "I'll be in the office."

I watched as Mel sprinted across the lot and into the restaurant without a backward glance. Another in the greatest hits of *what the fuck is happening here?*

"I gotta get these babies inside." Hale knocked his knuckles against the crates. To the women, he said, "I'll stop over this afternoon when I'm done for the day. You have my number if you need anything but I know you're going to kick ass. Everyone in town is pumped for this. Save one of those spicy cinnamon rolls for me, Muff?"

"I save nothing for no one," she replied. "But I might forget a few rolls in the walk-in. It happens. I'm very busy, Woot. I've explained this to you many times. Go away now."

"Damn right you're busy," he said. "Can't expect you to keep track of every spicy bun."

With Hale heading toward the restaurant, the women turned their attention on me. I couldn't remember the last time I'd spoken to Lance though I knew he hadn't mentioned anything about his sister managing a new café in Friendship—and one in throwing distance of my family's restaurant.

We'd fix that real soon. Right after I got my brother out of bed, fired everyone, and yelled at my attorney. Then, I'd tear into my best friend for failing to share any of these important updates.

I watched while the chocolate Lab nosed at the soil spilling out of the broken pottery. Why did she have two dogs now? "I'll have the flowerpots taken care of."

"That's not necessary," Sunny said. "We know how you feel about our flowers. We're not interested in seeing how you 'take care' of them."

Rather than respond, I pulled out my phone to move things along.

Before I could fire off another message, a pair of landscaping trucks rumbled down the drive toward us. When they stopped, a crew of six poured out of the trucks and immediately reached for rakes, shovels, and leaf blowers.

"Over here," I called to Rainey, the guy who looked after the grounds at SPOC. "This pot needs to be replaced and everything cleaned up. There's also the matter of a loose paver stone. It's a hazard. Do whatever you need to do to secure it."

Rainey zeroed in on the wobbly stone, pressed the toe of his boot to it, and nodded. "Oh, yeah. This needs to go."

"Excuse me," Sunny started, a hand held up, "but what do you think you're doing?"

I turned toward the one place I thought I'd never have to visit again, the place I'd maneuvered myself out of once and for all. "I'm looking after your liabilities," I said, forcing myself to keep my eyes fixed on Small Point Oyster Company and as far away from Sunny Du Jardin as possible. "Someone has to."

chapter three

Today's Special:
A Hash of Locally-Grown History

"THAT WAS INTERESTING," Muffy said as she wandered into the kitchen.

I leaned back against the front of the counter while Meara gathered an armful of vases filled with rosemary and daisies and started setting them on tables around the café. My dogs tucked themselves into a cozy corner near the windows where they hung out while I was working. Near enough to help me if I needed them but far enough away from the close quarters behind the counter. "I'm not sure I'd call it interesting when terms like *obnoxious tool* and *needlessly aggressive* and *excessive penis wagging* exist."

"Excessive penis wagging implies the existence of an appropriate amount of penis wagging," Bethany said as she rearranged the bottled juices and kombucha for the hundredth time.

"An inadequate amount too," Meara added. "I can tell you from experience that the right amount of penis wagging can be difficult to land on but you'll feel it when you're there."

"So much to unpack from so few words," Bethany said.

"It's one of my many gifts," Meara replied.

"It might be difficult for us, but I bet we can agree he's a strong personality without making it about his gentlemanly business," Muffy called from behind the kitchen pass-through.

"With that big bossy bossman vibe? His business isn't gentlemanly," Meara said with a slow nod. She shifted to gaze out the long wall of windows facing Small Point Oyster Company. "That I can promise you."

"He's a jackass," I said.

"This isn't like you, Sunny," Muffy said. "Breathe it out. Shake it off. Let it go. I'm going to need the sweet to my sour back if we're opening the doors in eighty-one minutes."

"He's a jackass," I sang as I curved my fingers into the shape of a heart and tap-danced across the café.

"Speaking of his ass," Bethany said, "did you see those trousers? Or those tree-trunk thighs? Is his tailor an actual angel or what? How is everything so—" She gestured like she was squeezing two handfuls of Beckett's backside. "*Mmmm*. Between the buns and the rolled-up shirt-sleeves, I didn't hear a word he said the entire time."

"Since when do you even acknowledge the existence of men?" Muffy asked her. "What are you doing noticing buns and tree trunks, madam?"

"I'm not attracted to men but I'm still aware of when they are attractive," she replied. "Like how Meara thinks I'm hot and will tell me that my boobs look especially juicy sometimes but she doesn't want to get me naked."

"You are gorgeous," Meara said to her.

"Thank you, lovebug," Bethany said with a blushing grin.

Meara tossed her braids over her shoulders. "Anytime, baby."

"Can we get back to the jackass at hand?" I asked. "Because I think he's going to be a real problem."

Bethany set to organizing the carrots and apples behind the juicing counter. "I don't think so. Maybe it started off rocky but Beckett made everything right. He didn't have to get a crew to fix the patio. You have to admit that was really nice of him."

"Nice," I started, seesawing my hands, "or aggressive, unnecessary penis wagging?"

"You girls need to work on keeping penis out of your mouths," Muffy called. "Not an hour goes by that I don't question my life choices with you three, I swear."

"I've never had a penis anywhere near my mouth," Bethany said, "and I intend to keep it that way."

"Wow. I opened the door for that one," Muffy said to herself. "I really am doing this to myself."

"If you're going to question your life choices," Meara started, "you'll need to go back to the moment you took a blowtorch to your bridges in New York's fine dining world. A couple of girls who get mouthy about dick are not where your problems started. And I wouldn't even call it a problem."

"A feature," Bethany said. "Not a bug."

Meara pointed at her. "Exactly."

"Anyway." I grabbed the chalk and went to work on our sidewalk sandwich board. "All I'm saying is that being the big, bossy bossman—"

"With the angel-tailored trousers," Bethany added.

"—who shows up and creates chaos but then fixes it with a wave of his hand and an on-call maintenance service is not my favorite thing in the world," I said.

Meara turned to face me, her head cocked to the side and her dark eyes narrowed. "Do you have history with him? Is there something about Beckett Loew you haven't mentioned? Muff's right, this isn't like you at all."

"Of course not!" I didn't intend to yell but that was what happened. A smile tugged at the corner of Meara's mouth and Bethany abandoned the fruits and vegetables to study me. "We do not have *history*. Not what either of you are thinking. He's a friend of my brother's. That's all. They were close in high school—and he was a jackass back then too."

Meara gave a thoughtful bob of her head as if this explained everything. "Ah. I see."

"Nothing to see," I said, returning to my sign.

After a moment of Meara and Bethany carrying on a silent conversation over my head, Bethany said, "Even if he's a grumpy, growly one, I want to get to know those folks. They're our neighbors. We're practically family! Maybe I'll grab a drink there after we close up tonight. I wonder if Mel usually works days or evenings. Who wants to come with me?"

"I'm not going anywhere near that shellfish haven," Muffy called. "Not without five EpiPens and a team of paramedics."

Muffy was uniquely suited to be a vegan chef as she was allergic to damn near everything. She held the record as the chef requiring the most calls to emergency services in her culinary school's history. She'd worked in some of the top restaurants in New York City until she was passed over for a well-deserved and long-promised promotion. That was when the blowtorch entered the picture.

"The husbands have expressed some interest in testing out the oysters-as-aphrodisiac hypothesis." Meara watched me for a moment. "But I can talk them out of it. I'm always on your side, you know."

I erased a few lines with my thumb and set to correcting the shape of my *N*s in *Now Open!* Why was I the only one fuming about Beckett Loew and his high-handed antics? Didn't everyone else see how much of a know-it-all ass he was? Asking to speak to the manager *and* wanting to know why my family wasn't helping me do my job? Unbelievable.

Although the truly unbelievable part was that, after all these years, all it took was a word out of Beckett's mouth for me to go flying into ice queen mode. I didn't have to let him bother me this much. I could just let it go. I didn't have to drag a whole damn iceberg around. This thing was heavy.

And yet—

"No," I said. "If the husbands want to experiment on you, I don't want to stand in the way." I pushed to my feet and wiped my hands on my skirt. The chalk would blend in with the print. "My problems with Beckett don't have to be everyone's problems."

"But that's where you're wrong," Bethany said. "Like Meara said, we're always on your side, even if it means giving up oyster-induced sex and badass babes in leather jackets."

"Oh my god." I groaned at the ceiling. My anger at Beckett had blurred out her obvious flirtation with Mel. "You already love her, don't you?"

"A little bit," Bethany admitted. "I can't help myself around girls with short pompadour hairstyles and lots of black eyeliner. And the ripped jeans and the leather jacket!" She pressed her fists to her mouth. There were actual hearts in her eyes. "But I won't go there with her if it bothers you."

I hefted the sandwich board and pushed open the door. "Beth. Honey. I would never do that to you. I'd worry that you'd spontaneously combust into a swarm of pink killer bees."

As it was, I was likely the one to combust here, though it would be for entirely different reasons.

chapter four

Beckett

Today's Special:
Slow-Roasted Loyalty over a Bed of Lunacy

THE INTERIOR of Small Point Oyster Company—SPOC to those who knew—was the same as it had always been. Dark, shiny wood. Weathered bronze. Water views as far as the horizon stretched. It was quiet and cool, the faint scents of lemon wood polish and vanilla extract lingering in the air. The raw bar was scrubbed to a shining, sterile clean. The white and stainless-steel kitchen gleamed.

It was the exact change of state I needed after my encounter with Sunny. No humidity curling around my neck, no sunlight to blind me from common sense. No gorgeous hazel eyes or wicked grins. This place was a blast from the mentally suppressed past and there was nothing sexually confusing about it. Perfect and perfectly fucked-up, just the way I liked it.

As I made my way up the back stairs to the offices hidden there, I tried to remember the last time I'd visited. It had been years, and I'd lived comfortably with that distance because I'd hired the right people to maintain order and keep this place running the way my great-uncle had wanted. Excellent local food and drink with top-notch service. Simple, honest, and exceptionally good.

Easy enough, right?

Not quite.

I ripped off a strip of yellow police tape barring the general manager's office door and stepped inside. The computer was gone, the desk emptied and drawers strewn across the floor, chairs overturned.

Mel appeared in the doorway as I righted the furniture. "Before we handle any of this nonsense, would you care to explain the nonsense I walked into outside? You wouldn't like it if I filled in the blanks on my own."

"Nothing to explain," I said, fighting a drawer to get it back into the desk. "You know how bad the traffic can get in the summer. We've been cited by the cops enough times to know better than to fuck with them."

"Mmmhmm."

"I didn't realize the old bait shop had changed hands. Would've been nice to hear about that before now." I shot a meaningful glance at Mel. "Would've been nice to hear a few other things too."

She held up her hands. "I've never withheld my feelings about Marty sitting in the general manager's seat and you know it. If I'd known anything about money laundering, I would've been the first one hollering at you. I would've dragged you back here by the ear if I had to and you damn well know it."

I picked up the desk chair and pushed it in. I stood behind it, my arms folded. From here, I had a clear view of the bait shop and the crisp new Naked Provisions sign painted on the long side of the building in black and white. I could see Sunny and the others moving around the café, and Rainey's crew scouring the patio. And I could see the crushed shell driveway sticking out like a bright white line which I was not to cross under any circumstance. As if I needed that reminder.

"We have to clean house," I said.

Mel let out a huff. "Yeah, I'd say so."

"How far does this go?" I asked.

She shook her head. "I don't know for sure but let me tell you what I do know. I have a lot of single moms driving shitbox cars and squeezing tips to cover daycare and doctor's bills. There's no way in hell they're in on an operation like this. Not with the miles each year puts on them."

"Let's not make single moms squeeze tips to cover basic needs, okay? If we need to revisit the pay structure, we'll do that. Minimize opportunities for people to feel like they need to get in on a scam to get by."

"Consider it done." She picked up a framed newspaper clipping about SPOC, leaned it against the wall with several more. "Some of the others? Maybe. I can see it if I look for it."

"When the FBI raided this place"—saying it out loud made my stomach hurt—"they questioned everyone, right?"

Mel nodded.

"Do you think that was enough to scare off anyone who might've had a hand in this? If they weren't arrested, why come back and risk it?"

She eyed me for a minute. "Yeah. I can see that."

I turned away from the windows into the snow globe that was Sunny's world. Who the hell had given her permission to grow up? And how the hell was I supposed to put this place back together, save my parents, and look after my brother while Sunny was *right there*? Not only was touching off the table but looking would end one of the longest-running relationships of my life, though I couldn't tear myself away from those windows.

"We'll need to hire replacements immediately," I said.

"When are you expecting to reopen?"

I ran a hand down my face. I was so tired I'd come out the other side into wired. I didn't feel like I'd ever sleep again. It was horrible.

Everything was horrible. "Tomorrow would be good," I said, knowing it was unrealistic and Mel was going to blast me for it.

She cocked a brow. "Not sure how you expect me to pull that off but okay."

"We've been down three days and that's three too many. We can open tonight. Put me and Parker on the schedule. We'll cover tables."

"As much as I enjoy watching you on the floor, I think we've lived through enough trauma this week. Let's keep you in the back offices where you can't scowl the shit out of our customers."

"But Parker you'll take?"

She shrugged. "People like that kid. He's a clusterfuck but he's cute."

That could be the Loew family motto. Translate it to Latin—if anyone knew a clusterfuck, it was the Romans—slap it on a crest with some oysters, a janky old RV, and a bucket of dirty baseballs. There it was, everything the Loews stood for. Grand, wasn't it?

I drilled a knuckle into my temple. "Go clean out your team. Keep only the ones you trust."

"What about Devon? Your dad hired him. He's been here for *twelve years*. He's a grade-A asshole but customers love him."

I paused. My instinct said slash and burn, but many of our customers were loyalists. They'd been coming here for decades. They noticed when we changed linen suppliers or replaced the wineglasses. For them, SPOC was an institution. The place they celebrated birthdays and anniversaries. A required stop on their seaside vacations each summer. A destination for marriage proposals involving elaborate desserts.

We drew the line at hiding diamond rings in oysters. Too easy for that one to go sideways.

"Can we trust him?"

Another shrug. "I don't know. Last weekend I would've said yes, but Marty, your dad, two servers, and our lobster supplier are in federal custody. I don't know what to believe anymore."

"Don't forget my mother evading arrest in Central America," I added. "That part's important."

Mel laughed. "Not sure if Sandy's evading arrest so much as lost. The only things she knows how to evade are organization and structure."

"Explain that to the FBI," I grumbled. "They're under the impression she and Dad are criminal masterminds."

She picked at the shreds of police tape hanging from the doorframe. "Your father doesn't know how to cheat at bingo. I don't think an illegal thought has ever crossed his mind." She balled up the last bits of tape. "They'll come through this, Beck. You'll get them out of this just like you always do."

I stared out the window as Mel headed downstairs, her boots thudding on each step. She was right about me getting my family out of these crises—and it not being the first or last time.

FOUR CUPS of coffee and three billable hours on the phone with my attorney later, I slammed my laptop shut and pushed away from the desk. My back and shoulders gave a snap-crackle-pop and I grunted at the ceiling. When I was finished feeling every one of my thirty-six years, I paced to the windows to get a closer look at the line stretching out the door at Naked Provisions.

I'd noticed it about half an hour into my call with Adrian Pineda and his legal team, and watched it steadily grow as morning shifted into afternoon. That damn patio was a huge hit. It had been packed from the start, with customers filling the small tables as they sipped coffee and shared saucer-sized cookies.

I tapped Lance's number with an eye still fixed on the busy café.

Where were all these people coming from? And for what?—*vegan* things? I needed a lot more information about this place Sunny was running.

"Loew!" Lance boomed. "It's like two in the morning for you. Is this your one call from a jail cell?"

I didn't enjoy how close to home that hit. "Not in Singapore today. Not in jail either."

He blew out a laugh. "There was a point in time when any call from either of us was probably coming from a jail cell."

"More you than me," I said.

"Where the hell are you if not home in Singapore?"

"Home in Rhode Island," I said.

He made a strangled noise. "Why the hell are you *there*?"

The goth girl with the braids swept through the patio collecting dishes and mugs. I'd heard her say something about publicity. I wanted to know what kind of PR strategy had a line out the door and halfway to Market Street on the first day of their soft launch.

"Long story," I said, "but the better question is why did I have to find out that your sister is running a café fifty feet from the oyster bar by catching her before she took a header on the patio?"

"Wait—what happened to Sunny?"

"Nothing. She's fine. She just…tripped and I was nearby." *Because I was debating property lines and parking requirements and the curve of her waist before realizing she's your very grown-up sister.* "No injuries to report."

"Oh, okay. Good."

When he didn't go on, I said, "So? About this café?"

"I didn't realize you wanted the play-by-play on my sister's life. Or anything happening back in Friendship."

"Well," I said on a sigh, "I'll be hearing about Friendship for the foreseeable future. I'm on a leave of absence from my firm."

"What the fuck? Why?"

I leaned against the wall to get a better look at the foot traffic outside. "Because the feds busted a money laundering and counterfeiting ring at the oyster bar. My father was arrested along with the general manager and a couple of servers. The lobster guy was picked up for ferrying cash in and out of Canada. Oh, and there's a warrant out for my mother's arrest but she never got on her flight home from a last-minute girls' trip to Belize. The assumption is she was tipped off about the raid and went into hiding."

"When in reality she probably got distracted by a stray dog and missed her flight."

My mother was one of the best people in the world. The very best. She'd give you the shirt off her back and every last cent to her name, and she'd also forget that she turned on the garden hose a week ago and wonder why the backyard had become a swamp. "Basically."

"Holy fuck, man," Lance said.

"Yeah. My firm isn't in love with the idea of a partner managing billions in private equity while having a business he co-owns facing prosecution for money laundering. They were in favor of some time out of the office and away from the finances."

"But you're good, right? They're not investigating you?"

From this angle, I could see straight into Naked Provisions *and* watch the black sedan that had followed me here from the airport. I was guessing FBI, SEC, or US Marshals. That they were content to stay in the sedan for hours suggested they weren't here for me but they wanted to keep tabs. That was a nice bonus to the excitement of the day.

"Based on everything my attorney has learned, yeah, I'm good. It seems like it was an on-the-ground operation."

"Okay. At least we have that," Lance said. "So, what's the plan?"

"I don't even know," I admitted. The exhaustion was catching up with me again. "Turn over most of the staff. Weed out any remnants of the previous management. Make my attorney earn his hourly and keep my parents out of prison. Figure out where in Central America my mother is." I glanced at my watch. Where the fuck was Parker? "Wake my brother up and put him to work."

"Which brother?" The sarcasm in his question had me rolling my eyes.

"The baby," I replied. "The last thing Dex would ever tolerate is me making him work, let alone doing it in Friendship."

"Life of a major league ballplayer," he mused.

I needed to call Dex and update him on this before he was blind-sided in a locker room interview, but I was more interested in harassing Lance at the moment. "Why is your sister opening this café all by herself? Why aren't you or your parents here?"

He murmured to someone before answering. "Sunny doesn't need me standing around being useless, and by her standards, I'd be extremely useless. She doesn't need anyone's help, man, and she has no problem saying so."

"Yeah. I noticed that."

Lance barked out a laugh. "Remember all the shit we used to give her? I can't believe she never tried to kill me in my sleep. It would've been justified."

"We weren't that bad," I said.

Sunny came out of the café with a tray full of small cups that she distributed to the people waiting in line. She had her hair pulled up on the top of her head now, leaving her shoulders bare. It was nearly inde-cent. I was never leaving this window. I rubbed my eyes.

Fuck, I couldn't stare at her like this while talking to her brother. Lance was my rock. My person. We hadn't lived on the same continent since college and we could go months without talking now but we were always there for each other. Loyal to the marrow, not counting this present conflict of interest.

"We were merciless shitheads, Beck. Remember when we dismem-bered all of her dolls and then Frankenstein'd them and put them back like nothing had happened? She fucking hated us for that."

"She hated you," I said.

"Remember how we'd mess with her service dog by stuffing bacon in our pockets and walking into her room every few minutes? She screamed the roof off when she figured that one out. My parents were so pissed."

Ah. So that was what Sunny had meant about me not maturing past my sixteen-year-old self. I had to believe I was better than the bacon trick. And the doll dismemberment. I just fucked around with other people's money now. Much more civilized, at least on the surface.

"We were terrible," he said. "My mother got drunk at Christmas a few years ago and told me that we were the reason Sunny refused to show any weakness and wouldn't take anyone's help for anything. Not the disability but a pair of high school dirtbags." After a pause, he continued, "She's living at home, at my parents' place. She's been there —what, maybe a year now? A little more? I'm not sure but she doesn't say much about this new business. Mom thinks she wants it to succeed before involving us, or something along those lines. She's independent like that." He cleared his throat. "Keep an eye on her, okay? I'm sure she's kicking ass and all but she's still a kid, and since my parents moved, she's kind of on her own—even though no one is ever alone in that town."

My entire life was an endless sequence of keeping an eye on people, but keeping an eye on Sunny seemed like a much more complicated undertaking. Rather than telling my best friend that it was a disastrous idea, I went hard for his favorite topic: dunking on the weird little place where we'd grown up.

"There were signs announcing an asparagus festival when I drove into town," I said. "It's small-town charm on acid. It's the kind of thing you read about in travel guides. I would not be surprised to find a goat presiding as the official master of ceremonies."

"Friendship loves to be friendly," he said. "They'll invent reasons to socialize, even if it requires celebrating some fucking asparagus. Good luck with that, man. I couldn't do what you're doing."

I had many more questions about his sister, but Lance muttered, "Shit" and there was a flurry of conversation on his end. "I gotta go, Beck. Keep me posted on the criminal activity at home."

"It will hit the national news soon enough once it's connected to Dex," I said.

"Hey, listen. Don't tell Sunny I said anything about you watching out for her. She'd hate that I asked you to do it and I'd get an earful about how she doesn't need a babysitter. And don't give her too much of a hard time. You'll regret it," he said with a laugh.

The only thing I'm going to have is regret.

I forced myself down the stairs. Mel was out on the deck with a few servers. She was patting them on the back and looking like she was about to pitch herself over the railing and into the cove. Most of the kitchen staff was busy inventorying the contents of the walk-in fridge or cleaning already-spotless prep counters while casting cautious glances at the chef. For his part, Bartholomew was muttering to himself in French while sipping cognac out of a ramekin.

Good to see we were all well on our way to a breakdown this afternoon.

The black sedan was still parked out front.

Since I wasn't prepared to deal with the remaining staff yet, I went outside. A Black man sat in the sedan, aviator sunglasses low on his nose, his dark tie yanked loose, and a folded newspaper resting against the steering wheel.

After a minute of glaring at each other, I knocked on the window. He paused for a long moment before rolling it down.

"This cove is an ecological preserve home to dozens of species which rely on clean air and water to survive," I said. "It's bad enough we have ocean temps rising to a level that interrupts entire life cycles of critically endangered species, but we have microplastics and carcinogenic chemicals seeping into the groundwater at an alarming rate too. At the very least, turn off the gas guzzler. We don't need you pumping exhaust directly into the oxygen supply of my oyster farm and this food chain for hours a day."

The agent nodded slowly as he studied the cove. He turned off the car and stepped out. "It's a pleasure to make your acquaintance, Mr. Loew. I'm Special Agent Naeem Price."

"Given the circumstances, you'll understand that I can't say the same."

With a broad grin, he dipped his hands into his pockets and leaned back against the sedan. "And you'll understand that I have to tail your ass until we locate your mother or confirm beyond a doubt that you are not concealing her whereabouts."

"I don't have a damn clue where my mother is or how she became separated from her friends. But if I did, I'd arrange for her to turn herself in so we could get those charges dropped as soon as possible." I flung an arm toward the restaurant. "Now that we've cleared that up, are you hungry? Need a cold drink? I have a chef who is going to pop a blood vessel and filet the first person to cross him if he doesn't cook for someone soon."

Agent Price inclined his head toward the crowd at Naked. "I was thinking about checking that out. They were offering samples of basil lemonade earlier. It looked like seaweed water but it was really good. Weird but *good*."

I jabbed a finger toward SPOC. "If you're going to be up my ass until we get my mother back home, you're going to do it without polluting this cove or stepping foot in that café."

He pushed away from the sedan. "It doesn't work that way, Loew. You call none of the shots. But I'm hungry so I'm gonna let it slide."

"Smart choice." I held the door open for Agent Price as he stepped into the oyster bar.

At the same moment, Sunny emerged from Naked Provisions,

another loaded tray in her hands. She caught me staring and held my gaze, tipping her chin up. The challenge came across loud and clear. She wasn't backing down today or any other day. I arched a brow in response but that only seemed to strengthen the steel in her spine.

Our wordless exchange grew thick and heavy like a summer storm. Her stare cut straight through me and lifted the hairs on the back of my neck. I wanted to march right over there and resurrect our argument from earlier in the day or invent an entirely new argument just to tease out that wicked grin of hers again, and I was ready to step away from the door to do exactly that when my phone vibrated in my pocket. I blinked down and this battle was over.

Her lips pulled into a smile as she shifted away from me, moving through the line and handing out more green lemonade.

My life, it never stopped fucking me.

chapter five

Sunny

Today's Special:
A Salted Spread of Big Dock Energy

CALL me crazy but I thought soft launches were supposed to be soft, not the championship round of an ultimate fighting competition. The good news was that we survived, even if my feet hadn't hurt this much after climbing Machu Picchu, and we'd sold out of everything hours earlier than our most ambitious projections.

Meara Monahan, folks. Her marketing magic was real.

The biggest win was getting through the weekend with unbelievable crowds and doing it without waking the troll next door. The troll being Beckett Loew of course. Though we did see him pacing the parking lot on several occasions, usually while yelling his way through a phone call or eyeing the line outside the café like it was about to morph into a dragon and swallow the whole town in one roaring gulp. I was certain nothing would make him happier. Drama and destruction had to be his favorites.

As for me, I loved waking up early on bright May days, especially when I got to set up the café for our first Monday in business. I did not love turning down Succotash Lane and slamming into a massive traffic jam.

In all our months of planning for Naked Provisions, we'd never devoted more than a few moments of consideration to parking issues, and somehow, that was now the source of all my problems.

Today's crisis was courtesy of all manner of construction equipment including a *crane* clogging the space between the café and Small Point Oyster Company. There wasn't a single parking spot to be had, barely even room to weave my bike between the trucks and equipment.

Whatever this was, it couldn't continue.

When I let myself into the café, I found Meara and Muffy there, staring out the windows. "What's going on?" I asked.

"I wish I knew," Meara said. "Was hoping you had some idea."

I joined them at the window to get a better look at the center of all this activity. "Why would I know?"

"Let's see," Meara started, holding up a finger. "You're from this town, you know the people here, and you have a complicated history with our neighbor, who seems to be directing this project."

"I wouldn't call it a complicated history. I haven't seen him since I was a kid."

"Doesn't matter," Muffy said. "Having history with the guy automatically volunteers you to go find out when the crane will be leaving."

"Me?" I yelped.

"Customers didn't mind finding parking on Market Street this weekend because they knew we were open and enough people were waiting in line to serve as the social proof that hoofing it down here would be worth it. But if customers can't see past the dump trucks and backhoes to the café, they're not bothering with us today." Meara glanced at me. "Find out what's going on and when it will be over."

"I made extra cookies because they were the first to sell out," Muffy said. "So many cookies. But now this." She waved a dish towel at the window. "I'm gonna cry in the walk-in if we end the day with three hundred double-chocolate olive oil cookies."

"Go," Meara said to me. "And try to be nice this time."

"I'm always nice." I shuffled toward the door, more than a little outraged. "He's the one who's not nice."

"Beth will tend to your feelings when she gets in this afternoon," Meara said. "Until then, we're focused on outcomes."

She didn't give a shit. She'd throw me to the teenage bully wolves if it served her marketing strategies.

Ugh, that wasn't true. Meara was like that one strict teacher everyone dreaded but who ended up being the unquestionable best. She gave a shit but only when you earned it.

It didn't take long to find Beckett. He stood near SPOC's main entrance, phone glued to his ear as always and wearing another fancy vest with a dress shirt rolled up to his elbows. A Black man in a suit leaned up against the building as he read a newspaper. I waved to them, saying, "Good morning" as I approached.

Beckett glanced over his shoulder at me with a scowl before pacing away toward the dock.

"Any idea what's going on here?" I asked the guy with the paper.

"Not a clue." He frowned at the headlines then asked, "Is basil lemonade on the menu today?"

"All month."

He pumped a fist. "Excellent. I'll be over when this guy stops being so interesting."

"Interesting?" I repeated.

He was shorter than Beckett the Broody Beast but then again, everyone was shorter than him. But this guy, he was attractive. Nicely dressed. Dapper, if that word still existed. Great smile too. And he liked our lemonade. I liked this one. I approved.

He shrugged. "In a manner of speaking."

Behind me, a throat cleared. "I see you've met Agent Price," Beckett said.

"Agent Price," I said to the man, smiling. "It's lovely to meet you. I'm Sunny Du Jardin."

He tucked the newspaper under his arm. "I know."

That froze the smile on my face. It was weird that he knew my name, right? Super weird. "Oh." I glanced at Beckett, who seemed mildly amused. "Okay."

"Agent Price is with the FBI. He's following me around in case I let slip my mother's location or any other stray details of the money laundering operation that was based out of the oyster bar. All of this is unlikely to occur since I know nothing. That has yet to deter him."

I opened my palms at my sides, expecting to find a dog waiting there before remembering I'd felt well enough to leave them at home today. "What—um—sorry, what are you talking about?"

Beckett crossed his massive arms over his chest and flicked a bored glance between me and his phone as he took a few steps away from the restaurant's entrance. Even though I wanted to dig in my heels and make him come to me, I followed him across the driveway, edging around lumber and steel rods and workers in hard hats.

"The crime ring with my parents as the masterminds," he said. "The arrests. Certainly the news made it across the way to the land of vegan delights."

"In case you haven't noticed, I've been a little preoccupied with opening that land of vegan delights. Speaking of which, what is this all about? And when will it be over? And why didn't you tell us this would be taking place?"

He turned around, the same old disinterested scowl carved into his features. The fact he was obscenely attractive was truly regrettable. It was unfair at an outrageous level. What was nature tripping on to make a man with *so much*. Good hair, huge hands, tall as a redwood, jaw sharp enough to peel potatoes. And the scowl situation, it should not have worked for him the way it did. It should've marred this otherwise perfect portrait of a troll who had everything and then some. But it didn't, not at all. All of these pieces added up into a man composed of hard edges and impossibly long limbs and a scowl that reminded me he was made of stone and had the emotional depth of quick-dry cement.

"I didn't realize I had to run capital improvements on my property past you."

"A little notice is all I need," I fired back. "If you're going to have a crane"—I flailed my arms toward the massive thing—"parked outside my café, I'd love a wee bit of notice."

"The next time I call for a crane, I'll see that I do that. Until then, this is the reality we're working with. We can't wish it away and there's no sense in debating it either. Run along to your café and play with your vegetables and nut milks."

His dismissal knocked me back a step, then another. He didn't have to make everything so difficult. I was being perfectly nice and *he* was the one being hostile.

Annoyed, I took another step away from him. "Can you at least tell me when this will be—"

I didn't finish the thought because Beckett darted forward, grabbed me by the elbows, and threw me up against the building. "What the fuck was that?" he roared over his shoulder, his broad chest heaving against mine. Each breath rumbled like a steam engine. "You could've killed her! Watch where you're going!"

Just a few feet behind him, a forklift sped past, it's arms loaded with lumber and bags of concrete mix. The driver shouted, "Good reason to stay outta the way."

With a growl, Beckett stared down at me. He dragged his hands up to my shoulders. His paws were enormous and surprisingly warm. He watched me, each fingertip pressing into my skin, lingering there long enough that I didn't know what was happening or how to respond. Did I seize the opportunity to knee him in the balls or grab that tie and give him a good yank? Or did I stare into his eyes and try to find an explanation as to what was happening here, what was going on inside me in this hot, prickly moment?

In the end, I didn't have to do anything because he ruined it all by opening that damn mouth of his.

"I assumed the situation last week was an accident but now I'm wondering whether you're simply careless with yourself."

His hold on my shoulders was relentless. Once or twice it seemed like he was stroking his thumbs over my collarbones in the kind of psychotic foreplay that preceded him wringing my neck. I reached up, closed my hands around his wrists. My thumbs settled on the pulse points there. "If you're thinking about strangling me, I should remind you that there's an FBI agent watching."

Something in his dark eyes sparkled and I realized they were more green than brown but only in this light and only up close. I'd never have known that if I only looked at him from a polite distance. And this was anything but polite.

This was war—and something else I hadn't figured out yet.

"Are you encouraging me to strangle you? Is that what's happening? Are you giving me pointers?"

I tried to shrug but his grip didn't allow it. "If you're going to do something, at least have the self-respect to do it well."

"Perhaps we could apply that logic to you not walking in front of heavy machinery."

"Perhaps heavy machinery should slow the hell down because I'm not the only person walking here and it's a narrow space to begin with."

He didn't release my shoulders and I didn't release his wrists. We stared at each other, locked together in this battle embrace, and I detested myself for marveling at the thick, corded muscle under my grip though the real outrage came when I realized I was tracing that muscle with my fingertips. Taking a thorough inventory and cataloging it for future reference, as one did in neck-wringing moments.

I stopped, remembered myself and my trusty iceberg, and that was when Beckett dropped his gaze to my hands. The smallest fraction of a smile moved across his lips.

Such a jackass.

"You need to be more careful," he said.

"I know all about careful. I've dedicated entire decades to being careful. You don't get to tell me anything about it."

I squeezed his wrists until he released me. He dropped his hands to his waist and allowed his gaze to travel over my face like he was entitled to examine me. For a long beat, he did. Then, "You've grown up to be quite the storm cloud, Sunny."

"And you're still an asshole." I crossed my arms to force a bit of space between us but he didn't back up. My forearms brushed that ridiculous vest. As if anyone needed to wear a vest here, on the seacoast, in May. He probably did it because someone told him the angel-tailored vest-trouser-shirt triumvirate made him look like a corporate wet dream when in reality he was a grizzly bear dressed up in stupidly expensive clothes. "What's the deal with the construction?"

He glanced toward the dock ramp, saying, "Some kids took a boat out last night and didn't know what the hell they were doing. They plowed into our dock a little after two in the morning. When the Coast Guard showed up, they tried to tow the vessel out from under the ramp and succeeded in damaging it beyond repair. Since we use this dock as the primary port for harvesting as well as receiving deliveries from local fishing co-ops, we needed a functional dock more than we needed to worry about equipment getting in anyone's way." He swung his attention toward me and the heavy weight of it pressed down just the same as his hands. "I'm paying a premium to have the work completed today."

This had to stop. We couldn't stand here like—like whatever the hell this was. It was tense and uncomfortable and we weren't getting anywhere. Time to push back on the bear. I stepped around him, forcing him to follow me this time. "Okay, so, first of all, you should've led with that. There was no need to make me squeeze info out of you."

"Like I said, I don't need to run capital improvements past you."

He rocked back on his heels with an unkind smile and I wanted to do more than push back. I wanted to push him off the remnants of the dock and watch while he splashed in the water and flung jellyfish out of his designer suit.

"That brings me to my next point," I said. "While operating this way might've been cool when you didn't have any neighbors, that's not the case anymore. I'm sorry you're dealing with messy family and business stuff, and that you have an FBI agent as your shadow, but that doesn't entitle you to be a jerk. You don't own all of Small Point. You have to play nice."

"For fuck's sake, Sunny." He shot an arm out over my chest and forced me to take several steps back as the speed-demon forklift rolled by again. His fingers flexed on my bicep several times before he released me.

He retreated, shaking out his hands. "I've noticed you don't like looking out for yourself," he said.

I put real effort into killing him with my eyes. I was all about peace and love, and live and let live, but this iceberg of mine was a frosty bitch. "And I've noticed you're an outrageous douchewaffle."

His scowl deepened. His brow creased. He seemed authentically shocked to hear his behavior was out of hand. As usual. "I beg your pardon?"

"You can beg all you want," I said, bold and frigid and completely unlike my usual self. "You're not getting anything from it."

"I am getting whatever I—"

"Hello there!" a voice boomed.

Beckett and I turned away from our glare-off to find an older white man dressed in athletic gear cutting through the construction and heading toward us. At his side was a thin man with golden coloring and a wide straw hat perched on his head. But that wasn't all.

A group of people followed, emerging from the paved trail that snaked along the edge of the cove and out onto Small Point, the rocky peninsula jutting into the bay, past the narrow strip of beach belonging to Friendship, through several residential areas, and emptied out behind the library in the center of town.

The man leading the group approached, a hand outstretched toward me as he said, "Ranger Dickerson. Pleasure to make your acquaintance." He gestured to the man beside him. "My partner Phil Collins."

"Sunny Du Jardin," I replied, smiling. I'd noticed these two walking the trail over the past few months, but our paths never crossed at the right moment to stop and talk. It was nice to finally meet them.

"Phil...Collins," Beckett echoed. "Am I in a skit? I really think I'm in a long, complicated skit."

"Ah. You're thinking of the English singer-songwriter. That often confuses people. This Phil Collins is an actuary. Not a musical bone in his body," Ranger said.

"I'm definitely in a skit," Beckett murmured. "Or a really long stress dream."

The group from the trail filed in between the heavy machinery and congregated behind Ranger. Not a single forklift blazed out of nowhere to nearly pancake them.

Ranger held out his hands, saying, "We planned today's expedition of the Friendship Walking Club through the cove to visit Naked Provisions though we didn't expect to run into such a calamity. Should we come back another day?"

"No," I said quickly, thinking of double-chocolate cookies. So many cookies. "No, not at all. We'd be happy to serve you." I pushed up on my toes to get a better look at the group. At least fifteen people. Probably more behind the crane. Enough to make Muffy crack a smile and allow Meara to fully inhale for the first time this morning. "All of you."

"You don't mind?" Ranger asked. "We don't want to impose, what with this project under way." He eyed Beckett, a knowing set to his mouth as he nodded. "I hope the Faro kids learned a valuable lesson about maritime safety. It's a good thing they're strong swimmers."

"And the water is barely eight feet deep at high tide in this part of the cove," Beckett added.

"Grown men can drown in a ten-inch bucket of water, Loew. The depth isn't the factor."

"We have plenty of room for everyone," I said, placing myself between Beckett and Ranger. "Our chef made a special batch of her secret recipe double-chocolate cookies too." I caught sight of Agent Price looming nearby. "And our famous hand-pressed basil lemonade."

Ranger pivoted toward his group. "Refreshments," he called with a sharp gesture toward the café, part drill sergeant, part team mom. "Thirty-minute break before we roll out for the final leg of the trek." As the walking club marched toward Naked's front door, he surveyed the work on the new dock and ramp. "The crew's making good time. They'll be finished before sunset."

"Yes," Beckett replied, sliding his hands into his pockets. "They will."

Ranger noticed the cool cut of Beckett's response but he didn't react. Instead, he turned an affable grin in my direction. I liked this guy's style. We were going to get along just fine. "We'll see you at this weekend's asparagus festival?"

Beckett audibly rolled his eyes though he made no move to exit the conversation. He stayed there, the whole hulking lot of him in shoes that probably cost more than my car, and stared at us like a sigh.

"You will," I said. "Bethany, another one of Naked's partners, used to operate Roots and Shoots Juices. She registered for all the local events before we came together. We decided to keep those events and attend as Naked Provisions with our baked goods and her juices."

"How serendipitous," Ranger said, and that word sounded strange coming out of a man who seemed to be the human definition of *rigorous*. I had the impression he ate plain oatmeal every morning and topped it with half a banana as a "treat." He studied the freshly painted exterior of the café. "Bait shop no longer!" To Beckett, he added, "Isn't change wonderful?"

"It does make me wonder," he said under his breath.

I restrained myself from elbowing him in the ribs. Barely. I'd probably break my arm on his titanium body and he'd give me that smug half smile of his and say something jackassy about how I didn't make good choices for myself. And then he'd call a yard crew to cart me to the ER in the back of their lawn mower trailer.

Ranger tipped his hat and motioned for Phil Collins to go ahead of him into the café. Then he raised a hand in greeting and called, "Good morning, Agent Price."

"Do you two know each other?" Beckett asked.

Ranger lifted his broad shoulders. "I make a point of knowing when law enforcement agents invite themselves to my town."

Once we were alone again, I asked, "Is Ranger his name or his title?"

Beckett frowned at his phone, saying, "It could go either way."

We watched as Agent Price strolled into the café. He offered a quick wave and a sheepish grin that didn't make too much sense given his enthusiasm for basil lemonade but then I caught Beckett's glare. It seemed I wasn't the only one on the receiving end of the troll's moods.

With a contemptuous glare at his phone, he continued, "As I said, the work will be finished today. Should any future inconveniences arise, I'll see that someone from SPOC notifies you or a member of your coven. Is that sufficient?"

"Don't you think you're being a little—"

"*Goddammit*, Sunny." He stepped into my space and forced me back against the side of the building, though this time he did it without touching me. He kept his hands raised as if he was prepared to drag me out of the forklift's path but he'd rather do it with the indomitable force of his will.

Somehow, this shook me harder than both of his hands on my body.

Breathless and more unsteady than I'd admit to anyone, I stared up at him, all green-brown eyes and sea-swept dark hair and broad shoulders, and I almost forgot that I despised this man. That I'd tolerated the intolerable from him, and I wasn't going down that road again. I was stronger now, and smarter too, and he had no idea what was coming to him.

I took a step sideways, out of his invisible hold.

As I walked toward the café, not bothering to look back at him, he called, "Be careful, storm cloud. I can't look after you all day."

chapter six

Beckett

Today's Special:
Soft-Shelled Skirt

I DIDN'T OPEN my eyes as I reached for my phone. I knew where it was without looking and I wasn't willing to leave the last fragment of this dream behind for anything. It was a distant, watery vision of a gorgeous woman with dark hair, and her hands were everywhere. I couldn't see her face, thank god, but I *wanted* her and the unknown made it deniable enough for me to want her without feeling like a back-stabbing pervert.

But I had to answer my fucking phone. "What?" I grumbled.

"Oh, Beck! This *is* your number! I'm so happy I remembered it!"

I forced my eyes open and my mind away from that hair and those hands. I squinted at the read-out on the screen. "Mom?"

"I lost my passport, Beck," she went on, "and I missed my flight because I was looking for it. The girls had gone ahead of me because I wanted to give your dad a buzz before going through airport security. You know how he gets so distracted when he hears flight announcements over the phone. But Melissa had his phone and said the police were at the restaurant? I had no idea what she was talking about. What's going on, Beck?"

"Well," I said with a sexually frustrated yawn, "Dad was arrested along with a couple of servers, Marty, and the lobster guy."

I'd never not be pissed that Marty, the person I'd handpicked to run the restaurant so my parents could focus on things that fell in line with their interests and talents, turned out to be a crook. Not only had I selected him, but I'd defended him too. Mel had long insisted the vibes were off, and Hale was unusually cautious with him. And I'd ignored them.

"For what?" she yelped. "I tried to call Melissa again but I dropped my phone in a toilet and none of my credit cards worked when I tried to get a new one."

I paused to add up the days since Mel called me with the news. "Where have you been staying, Mom? It's been almost two weeks."

"I got a ride to a cute little island. It's called—"

"*Don't tell me.* Easy on the identifying details, unless you want the FBI agents surveilling me to show up within six hours and arrest you as a coconspirator."

"But what did *I* do?"

"They're claiming you and Dad ran a money laundering and counterfeiting scheme out of the restaurant."

"Why would I do that?" she cried, as if I'd come up with these charges on my own. "*How* would I do that?"

"I don't have those answers for you," I said. "But you're okay? How are you surviving without any money?"

"Babysitting," she replied simply. As if it was the most obvious answer in this very logical shit circus. "I ran into an American couple outside the airport and they were headed to this island. They offered to pay cash if I could look after their little boy and not tell anyone about their business. I'm sure they didn't mean I couldn't tell you. Not that I know what they're doing anyway. It's all computers and busy things like that. No matter. I have plenty of money but I can't get a new phone without a credit card so—"

"What do you mean, not tell anyone about their business?"

"Oh, I don't know. They're just trying to be anonymous, I think. Not drawing too much attention to themselves."

Awesome. That was just awesome. I was sleeping on the bottom bunk in my childhood bedroom and she was babysitting for people who were paying in cash and trying to stay off the radar. Couldn't get any better than that.

"This trouble with the restaurant will sort itself out," she said with a confidence I didn't share. "Just give it time."

"And until then?"

"I'll hang out here. Everything will be okay. Oh, and make sure Parker gets to school on time!"

I couldn't help myself from asking, "Are you sure you're okay?"

She huffed out a laugh. "Of course I'm okay! I'll make my way home, you'll see, and everything will be back to normal."

My mother always landed on her feet. She had countless stories about sticky situations working out in her favor or circumstances changing at the last minute. But I believed that had more to do with the people around her cushioning those landings than anything else. My mother didn't possess a magical supply of safety nets and, the last time I'd checked, she wasn't a cat.

"I hope you're right," I said. "I should let you go. If the feds haven't tracked your location from this call yet, they'll have it soon."

"Okay, okay. Give Parks a big squeeze for me and tell Dad I miss him something fierce. Thanks so much for taking care of everyone, Beck."

The call cut out before I could respond, and that was a good thing. I didn't know what I'd say if I had to acknowledge that I was the one who dropped everything to solve all the family problems every damn time. I'd been doing it for as long as I could remember and now it was costing me *everything*. I'd left my home in Singapore, I'd put my entire career on hold, I'd left every shred of the life I'd built away from this town.

And it was all because I'd thought I could leave. I'd thought I could snag the best general manager in the restaurant business and take a job in London—then Geneva, Zurich, Monte Carlo, Dubai, Tokyo, and most recently Singapore—and my great-uncle's legacy would live on exactly as he'd intended. I'd thought my years of parenting my parents were over. And yet here I was, learning my lesson the hardest way possible.

Instead of dwelling on that, I hauled myself into the shower. A call from my mother was enough to deflate the remnants of that dream, though being alone with warm water beating on my shoulders brought it all back. The feel of her hands, the slide of her hair between my fingers. She smelled like a garden, and if I held myself quiet and steady, I could pretend she was a mystery to me. A fantasy cooked up by the stray bits of my subconscious. A nameless, faceless manifestation of stress and proximity, and it had *nothing* to do with her. Yet I couldn't resist brushing all that long, dark hair away from her face and cupping her jaw while she took me—

"Hey, dickbag." The door banged against the wall as Parker barged in. "Do me a favor and don't park behind me anymore. If you're going to yell at me to wake up and tell me that getting to school on time is the name of the game, you can't add obstacles to the course."

I wasn't getting that dream back again. Not the way I wanted it. That was probably for the best, all things considered. Wanting it didn't mean I was allowed to have it. And I *really* wasn't allowed to want it.

I cranked the water to cold and groaned as the change hit me. It was going to be a rough day. "No problem," I said. "Now get the hell out."

I WAS HALFWAY through a protein shake and an endless scroll of my email when Reyna, my attorney's legal assistant, called. Reyna had no time for nonsense such as small talk or pleasantries, which was refreshing since her boss seemed intent on dragging every last conversation into a full billable hour every time he called.

"All right, Mr. Loew," she started, her thick Bronx accent booming in my ear. "I researched the title history for the property you requested. If you still want to go forward with writing up an offer, I can get that submitted to the owner today."

"Do it," I said between sips. It was a dick move. I knew that when I sent Reyna to investigate the property and I knew it now. But I needed to regain some control. I couldn't turn around without coming face-to-face with a new layer of unbelievable and crazy, and all I could do was take a machete to the chaos. At least now I'd always be able to fix the loose stones and whatever the hell else was wrong with the place before they turned into serious problems. "Offer ten percent over fair market value."

"Figured as much." I could hear her typing. "Escalating to fifteen if they counter?"

"Fifteen, but I'll go as high as twenty if they're aggressive." Reyna murmured in agreement, still typing. "Are you sure I can't hire you away from Adrian? I'm much easier to work for."

"Somehow I doubt that," she said.

"Better hours," I added. "Work from home, if you're into that."

"The devil you know and all," she replied. "Okay. Very good. I'll call you as soon as I have an update."

That was how Reyna ended conversations. I admired the hell out of it. Every time I hung up on someone, they told me I was an asshole. Reyna did it and she was a boss.

Before returning to emails, I made the call I'd put off for two weeks.

I knew Dex's team was on the West Coast for a five-game swing this week but my brother hadn't been on the field in a month. I didn't know if he was traveling with the team, at home in his Camelback Mountain mansion, or fucking off somewhere else. As the call went to voicemail—as it always did—I debated how much energy I could devote to Dex with everything else going on. Honestly, it wasn't much but I'd never been one to pay attention to my limits.

"Hey, Dex," I said, noticing for the first time that the wall calendar on the back of the kitchen door was two years out of date and there was a reminder scrawled on the message board about Parker's eighth grade end-of-year field trip. "I need you to give me a call. Dad's been arrested and Mom is—technically, she's a fugitive but, you know, it's Mom. If you haven't been asked about this yet, you will be soon. Anyway, I'm back in Rhode Island, looking after Parker and SPOC. Call me. I don't care what time it is. Texts work too. Just…get in touch."

I ripped the calendar off the wall and erased the chalkboard. Sunlight had baked the letters in, leaving behind the ghosts of *Friday, June 14* and *Beavertail Lighthouse hike + picnic.* A quick survey of the kitchen cupboards revealed entire shelves of food that had long since expired while others were crammed with cereal and microwavable macaroni and cheese cups. Another held spools of yarn, phone bills, and cans of dog food.

My parents didn't have any pets and, as far as I knew, they didn't knit.

As I shoved it all in trash bags, I placed a call to Adrian. He picked up immediately, saying, "Stop trying to poach my staff. It's not helping your case."

"Your hourly rate is all the help you need," I said, trashing an assortment of takeout containers. "Any news for me?"

"A truck showed up this morning with sixty-two boxes from the prosecution. To say we have some evidence on our hands would be a massive understatement."

"Fantastic." I dropped four empty bottles of dish soap into the bag. No need to wonder why they'd kept four empty bottles. The explanation was always irrelevant. It was just how we did things around here. "Let's schedule a day to get out to the federal facility where they're holding my dad and see what he can tell us about all that evidence."

Because there's no way in hell he did any of this.

Adrian snorted. "Just as soon as we read it all."

"Right."

"My crew will get some motions cooking. If this goes the way I'm thinking it will, at least half of it will be circumstantial. Unless they have him on tape, carrying a bag of cash out of the restaurant and handing it over to the lobster guy with the explicit, spoken directive of sailing it to Canada, it will be hard to nail him on the big counts."

I blew out a breath. "Okay. Let's hope there isn't a video."

"Let us pray." He laughed. "Any word from your mother?"

"She called," I said with a sigh. "Didn't say where she was but that she'd lost her passport and that's why she missed the flight."

"Just like you said." There was a touch of skepticism in Adrian's comment.

"Yeah, well, I've known Sandy Loew for thirty-six years. I've been to a lot of her rodeos. They usually involve her losing shit, getting lost, or losing shit while lost and making friends with strangers." I edged around the refrigerator to get a look out the front windows. Agent Price was parked at the curb. "If I was conspiring with her, I sure as hell wouldn't say that on a phone line that's more than likely under surveillance."

"With respect to that, let's keep our conversations offline. I'll get back to you once we put a dent in all this discovery. Talk soon."

I pulled a cabinet open only for the door to fall off and knock me on the head. "Thanks, Adrian."

I LEANED against the door to the kitchen, half listening as Chef walked the servers through tonight's specials. Ninety percent of these servers were new to SPOC, though Mel swore they could hack it. Even the two who were entirely new to food service.

I had no choice but to trust her.

My phone buzzed with a message from a local number I didn't recognize.

Unknown: Good to see you back in town! Can I count on you to sponsor some of the Grad Week events for our high school seniors? We sure could use your help.

"Hey." Mel nudged my arm and jerked her chin toward the front entrance. "Something tells me she's here for you."

I glanced over Mel's head to find Sunny Du Jardin flinging the door open, her dark hair loose and streaming over her shoulders in waves. It was the first time I'd gotten a good look at her since that morning at the dock, though it was far from the first time the sight of her hit me like a gulp of too-hot coffee, burning its way down my throat while I stood there, incrementally dying until I learned to swallow around the discomfort.

She wore another one of those long, flowy skirts, though, and as she marched toward the kitchen, I realized this one was held in place by a knot at her waist. This seemed unwise. It also did terrible things to me. If the only mechanism securing that skirt to her body was one little knot, I would never survive. I would perish if I had to think about her walking around in a loose scrap of fabric hastily gathered at her waist.

And that certain death didn't account for her shirt. It was a little sleeveless thing with the words *GET NAKED* emblazoned across her chest. This did nothing good for my mental health. Not a single thing.

"Are you even listening to me?" Sunny yelled.

I shook my head. No, I was too consumed with the crisis that was this skirt on her all-grown-up body to hear a word she'd said. Didn't she know she wasn't allowed to turn my world upside down with a *skirt*?

And that shirt. Holy fuck, that shirt. "What problem are we having today, Sunny?"

She held up a piece of paper. I didn't look at it. "You tried to buy my building."

I crossed my arms over my chest. It did nothing to slow the riot behind my ribs. The entire staff was watching, even Chef, who'd been known to fling spoon at anyone who gave him less than their complete attention.

That evil grin fixed on her inconveniently beautiful face, Sunny said, "Before you come back with another offer, you should know I'm not selling. I own the bait shop free and clear, and that's not about to change."

She *owned* the building?

Little Sunny Du Jardin owned commercial real estate and she did it in a shirt that commanded me to get naked and a skirt that would hit the floor with one good pull. And there was something very wrong with me because I couldn't understand how I had these thoughts about someone who, in my mind, was still in elementary school and screeched every time Lance and I so much as walked by her bedroom.

"Why can't you be a normal, decent human person?" Sunny asked. "If your solution to everything you don't like or can't control is to buy it and make it go away, you have a lot more problems than I thought. You need to find a good therapist because none of this is *my* problem."

She slapped the paper—the purchase offer, by the looks of it—against my chest.

"You tried to buy the bait shop?" Mel asked under her breath. "Really?"

"We need the space," I said. Pathetically. "For outdoor seating."

"The bait shop was vacant for at least a decade," Sunny went on. "And now—today—you decide you *must* have it? That you need to expand your empire right this instant? Does that even make sense,

Beckett? Because it sounds like you don't want any other businesses down here and decided to throw some money around to get your way."

"I made a strategic assessment since returning to Rhode Island," I said, as detached as I could manage while *GET NAKED* burned behind my eyes. "That it coincides with the opening of your little outpost is irrelevant."

She glared at me, her gaze viciously cold. God, this girl *hated* me. Which was excellent, considering my immediate reaction to her was complete depravity.

"What did you think you were going to gain from this stunt of yours?" she asked. Her voice was low and soft in a way that tiptoed across the back of my neck and gave me the impression she'd take pleasure in strangling the life out of me. "What did you think was going to happen, Beckett?"

I gave a disinterested shrug and glanced at my phone. "As you've already stated, expand the so-called empire." I paused to read a new text from that unknown number and cement my status as an ultra-premium asshole. "This has nothing to do with you. Business is never personal."

"My business is really fucking personal and yours should be too."

I didn't hear half of what she said because I was staring at her lips, which were only slightly more inappropriate than her shirt. And that pull-off skirt. I slipped my hands into my pockets to steady myself. "We'll agree to disagree on that. Now, unless there's more thunder and lightning you wish to unleash on my kitchen, why don't you run along. Certainly there are some flowerpots for you to rhapsodize over or some carrot water to sell."

To my mind, it made perfect sense to give her all the reasons in the world to hate me. The more she hated me, the farther away she'd stay. Skirt out of sight, skirt out of mind.

But I didn't expect to feel like fresh garbage when my words hit her like a slap across the face.

I didn't expect to hate myself right along with her and I didn't plan on wanting to snatch those words out of existence and promise I hadn't meant any of it.

Thankfully, Sunny saved me from acting on those reactions.

She propped her fists on her hips and squared her shoulders, and part of me braced for impact while the other was so fucking proud of her for refusing to take my shit that I almost smiled.

"I'm a kind person," she said. "Actually, I'm very kind. Most everyone agrees. I'm also really tolerant and accepting. I let people live their lives and respect that everyone is going through something I'll never understand. But you're being outrageous and unreasonable. I don't know what your problem is with me but I'm not going to put up with it any longer. If you want a war, Beckett, I'll give you a war. I just hope you know what you're asking for."

With that, Sunny turned from the kitchen and stormed out the door, her skirt billowing around as she walked, her sandals echoing off the hardwood floors.

No one made a sound until the entrance door rattled shut behind her. Only then did Mel murmur, "Holy shit."

I collected all the scattered pieces of me in time to look like I had everything under control when I turned back to the staff. "I believe Chef was discussing the second of tonight's entrée specials. Let's not waste any more of his time."

Beside me, Mel pressed a hand to her mouth to conceal a laugh. "She's scary as fuck. I think I like it."

Yeah. Join the club.

chapter seven

Sunny

Today's Special:
Tossed Salad, Raccoon-Style

MEARA SIGHED as she laced her fingers around her mug. "It's not that I didn't like it," she said carefully. "I wasn't right for the book. It was me."

Muffy dropped her head onto her upturned hand. "I know, and I see the things that probably didn't work for you." She blinked several times as if she was fighting a rush of tears. "I just loved it so much. Like"—she pressed a hand to her chest—"I felt that book in my bones. It did things to me. And I needed you to love it the same way I did." She slipped her fingers under the frames of her glasses and rubbed her eyes. "I know that's not fair. You're allowed to love or not love whatever you want."

"No, no, it's fair," Meara said. "We love nearly all the same books. I don't think there's ever been a time when our vibes were this far off. But now that it's happened, it probably won't happen again for years. If ever."

I caught Beth's eye from across the table and gave her a *what do we do now?* glance before returning to my hibiscus tea. We'd dedicated part of this morning's meeting to discussing our plans to launch a Read Naked book club this summer but that quickly dissolved when Muffy and Meara found themselves at odds over the book choice.

Thank god Beth and I were mood readers to the highest degree and too out-of-step with the reading list to have an opinion on the matter. The last thing I wanted was to take sides. A divided vegan café could not stand.

"I just don't trust my recommendations for you anymore," Muffy said. "I'm second-guessing all the other books I wanted to propose for Read Naked."

The moment Meara shifted from patient and empathic back to her usual commanding self was obvious. "We aren't doing that, Mathilda. We are allowed to experience a book differently without it changing the flow of recs between us."

"I know, but—"

"But nothing," Meara interrupted. "You saw demisexual and ace love on the page—and saw it done well—and that hit close to home for you. What I needed from the book is irrelevant because the book wasn't *for me*. More importantly, my experience takes nothing away from your experience. And *that* is what we'll take away from this."

We'd had plenty of disagreements, the four of us. We had a lot in common and shared many of the same perspectives but we were quite the variety pack. Maybe that was why we worked so well together. It was also why we'd slam into walls on occasion.

"Next on the agenda," Beth sang, "is the housewarming party! I'm so happy we decided to do this. I can't wait to have the local food service fam over for a little get-together." She grinned down at her notebook. "I talked to the fancy cheese shop people and the couple that runs that crazy burger place and most of the Little Star Farm folks too." She pointed her pen in my direction. "Don't forget to invite the oyster company crew."

I nearly dropped my mug. "I don't think so."

A full week separated me from my dramatic performance in the Small Point kitchen, and my nemesis hadn't pulled any new stunts in that time. I hadn't seen much of him, save for all the pacing he did in the parking lot while talking on his phone and pulling at his hair or rubbing the back of his neck. Why he insisted on doing that with his shirtsleeves rolled to his elbows was still a mystery to me.

Though I'd been riding high on my iceberg of resentment when confronting Beckett, it turned out the people working at Small Point lived for icebergish monologues. We'd made a lot of new friends in the past week and it was nice to know that not everyone over there begrudged our existence. In fact, most of them loved that we didn't bow down and kiss the oyster.

"You are the right person for this job," Muffy said. "The broody bossman is probably still burnt from the roasting you gave him, but Hale and Mel will spread the word well enough. Talk to them."

I made a grumbling sound and scowled into my tea.

"If it's a problem, I can do it," Beth said.

Meara shot her a curious glance. "Many a night you've parked your sweet little bottom over there. Any updates for the group?" When Beth responded with only a slight shrug, Meara continued. "Nothing you'd like to share about a very pretty, very aloof front of house manager?"

Beth stared at her notebook for a long moment, her expression giving nothing away. Then she erupted into giggles and joy and a face-splitting grin. "She's ignoring my entire existence and yells at the bartenders about not overserving me. She never speaks to me and refuses to make eye contact. It's absolutely glorious. I'm dying."

"I think it's imperative we give you a reason to talk to Mel," Muffy said.

"Probably best to wear the most outrageously pink lip color you can find," I said. "It will make her head explode."

"Don't be surprised when she mauls you in a dark hallway," Meara warned.

"Oh my god, I can't wait," Beth whisper-shrieked. "I haven't been mauled in months!"

"That sounds unpleasant but I'm happy for you." Muffy tapped the face of her watch, saying, "As much as I prefer the six a.m. team meeting to the nine p.m., I have dough to get in the oven."

"And I need to get the juice bar prepped," Beth said.

"And I need to take pictures of all that and post on socials," Meara said.

I tucked my notebook under my arm and stood. "That leaves me to take care of the sidewalk signs and set up the patio."

"Teamwork makes the dream work," Beth said.

After stowing all our used mugs and dishes in the wash bin, I made my way down the wonky hallway leading to the patio. As with everything in this old building, it was narrow and not entirely straight or level. With the high ceilings, it felt like a secret passageway. We'd wanted to blow out these back walls to have a more expansive view of the water, but that kind of overhaul wasn't in our budget.

Maybe someday, if we continued selling out and—

I opened the door and found the patio in disarray. All the flowerpots had been overturned. The furniture was tossed all over the place. The tabletop lanterns we'd ordered for evening events were shattered. Even the umbrellas were ripped.

My hands shaking, I reached for a chair and set it upright. A storm had blown through last night. That must've been it. High winds, rain, some lightning. I knew the conditions on the coast were more intense than where I lived a mile inland, but I never would've expected this.

But—

The flowerpots weren't just overturned. They were cracked open, the soil and plants strewn all over the patio.

And the furniture hadn't simply blown over, it was banged up and dented all over.

Wind alone couldn't have pulled the lanterns out of the old lobster traps we used for storage.

The patio had been ransacked.

Someone had done this—and I could only think of one person who hated my flowerpots enough to cause this kind of destruction.

The thought hadn't even solidified in my mind before I started stomping across the driveway to the oyster company. I was well on my way to the iceberg danger zone when Hale called my name. I turned in a full circle before realizing he was coming up the ramp from the dock.

I liked Hale. He came into the café every morning and usually again in the afternoon, and he always stopped to talk with us. He was a good guy and I knew he'd be able to handle it when I yelled, "Where the hell is Beckett?"

Hale laughed as he pushed a cart up the ramp. "He'll be along anytime now. What seems to be the trouble?"

I flailed my arms toward the patio. "Something happened last night and my entire outdoor area is trashed."

He took in the mess of furniture and flowerpots, his eyes widening as he made sense of it all. "Oh, shit," he muttered. "Let me get these oysters on ice and I'll help you out."

"No, you're busy, but thank you. Did you see anything last night?"

He shook his head. "I'm only around in the daylight if I can help it. I'm up early and in bed early. Beck will have the late-night report for you. He's here all hours. He might be a vampire."

"I can believe that."

He pointed to SPOC's roof. "We might have video. There's a camera aimed at the dock. It might get a section of your outdoor area."

"That would be great. Can you access it?"

Hale turned as a luxury SUV cruised down the lane and parked close to the oyster company entrance. "Not exactly."

Beckett climbed out of the SUV dressed to kill. His navy blue suit was so crisp, I was convinced I'd cut myself if I touched him. His blood-red tie screamed out against his white shirt like proof that he was in fact a vampire. Dark sunglasses concealed his eyes but there was no hiding that granite-carved scowl of his.

It was completely unfair that I was A) often attracted (though not exclusively) to men, and B) Beckett had to be an insufferable, antagonistic jerk while also walking around with all that moody, broody, *come over here and rescue me from my feelings with your magical vagina* vibes.

Things could've been different for us if only he wasn't an expert-level asshole.

Beckett slammed the car door shut. "What's going on here?"

"This should be fun," Hale said under his breath.

"I don't find destructive pranks amusing," I said.

Beckett stared at me for a moment, the muscles in his jaw ticking. "And I don't find asinine riddles amusing. Either tell me what problem you have with me today or leave. Some of us don't have time to chat with the townsfolk all day."

The arrogance on this man. Made me want to hide musty old onions in his car. It just had to be an eco-friendly model too. It would've been so much simpler to hate him for driving a tone-deaf gas guzzler. "You trashed my patio. There's broken glass everywhere."

"I did *what*?"

I waved in the direction of the carnage. "You're hell-bent on getting rid of us, you hate that we've taken an inch of your precious parking, and you despise my flowers."

Still scowling, he glanced at the patio for a second. "Like I said, I don't have time for this." He pulled out his phone and started typing. I could feel the iceberg freezing over and bulking up inside me by the second. "If you think I have the kind of time or energy on my hands to fuck up your playground, you know less about running a business than I thought."

"Oh yeah? That's how it is? Then you must know a lot less about pulling frat boy pranks than I thought. Did Lance just make up those stories?"

Beckett eyed me over the rims of his sunglasses. I got the sense he regretted not saving at least one flowerpot to crack over my head. Eventually, he said, "I had nothing to do with this, Sunny. You should have learned by now that my brand of activism involves buying things rather than throwing things."

Hale whistled up at the sky.

Still dicking around on his phone, Beckett continued, "More to the point, Sunny, you need better security. Rather, you need *any* security. You cannot have a seating area that isn't visible from the interior and not expect to have problems. Especially when you're situated on a stretch of coastline that takes the brunt of all the wind and water that comes this way. Not to mention the wildlife in this cove." He pointed his phone toward a trampled heap of lavender. "It's more than likely some raccoons and deer came through and made this mess."

"Remember when those deer ripped the shit out of our new awnings?" Hale asked. "Damn, that was wild. Wouldn't have believed it if not for the video."

Beckett nodded. "One particularly strange year, a bear toppled the dumpster and forced his way into the kitchen. It was a disaster. You want to talk about destruction? I'll show you the images we submitted for the insurance claims. But at least I had the footage to know what actually happened instead of blaming the first person who happened to be in the area."

He went on typing while I stared at him. I was not a ragey, angry person. I did not lose my temper. Hell, I'd bartended through Super Bowls, World Series games, and many years of March Madness basketball. I knew how to keep my cool in the face of exasperating men.

But there was something about *this* man that had me boiling over every damn time he spoke.

Hale drummed his fingers on the side of the cart. "Try as I might, these oysters still haven't learned how to put themselves on ice. Catch you cuties later."

As Hale strolled inside and Beckett occupied himself with his phone —he was probably writing a list of perfectly delightful things to ruin tomorrow—my frustration grew. It was like blowing a bubble gum bubble and watching it grow bigger than you thought possible and knowing it would pop all over your face any minute but doing it anyway.

"Look." He held up his phone. While his arms were sprawling old oak branches, I still had to move closer to see the screen—and him. Such a dick. "There you go. There's your culprit."

I cupped a hand over the screen to block out the sunlight. A dark, grainy surveillance video showed eight or nine big raccoons hauling ass away from the patio only to creep back a few minutes later. They seemed to repeat this song and dance several times over the course of the night.

"That only shows them running back and forth." I took a step, away from Beck and the faint scent of vanilla that seemed to cling to him. It couldn't be vanilla. My brain had to be misfiring. "That isn't proof of anything."

With a rough, rumbly noise that seemed to start in his toes and vibrate all the way up through his body, Beck shook his head at me. Like there was no creature more aggravating in his universe than me and he needed me to understand that as deeply as he did. When he was finished with that, he asked, "Where are your dogs?"

I stared at his dark sunglasses, wishing I could see what was happening behind those frames to make some meaning out of his hard stare and harder tone.

"Please tell me your war games don't include harming animals."

"For fuck's sake, Sunny." He whipped off the sunglasses and rubbed his brow. "Aren't you supposed to have them with you at all times? For your own safety? You know, in case something happens."

"There are days when I leave them at home," I said slowly. I was still trying to work out why he wanted to know.

"And you're telling me that's a good idea?"

"Not that it's any of your business but I know my body and how it works, and—"

"Oh my fucking god," he said, back to kneading his brow. "Please stop talking."

A truck pulling a trailer filled with landscaping equipment turned down the lane and we watched as it pulled to a stop in front of us.

"About time," Beckett called to the driver. He circled the front of the truck while several workers climbed out. "Listen, I don't care what it takes, I need your guys to get all the broken glass. Replace the pots and whatever the hell was in them. Straighten it all out."

I stood frozen in place while the crew sprang into action with dust-pans and tiny brooms, along with several shop-vacs. Beckett went on talking to the driver—the same person who'd handled the patio stone I'd tripped over weeks ago—and I didn't know what to think.

Beckett was terrible—he'd told me to *run along* last week. He'd condescended all over me this morning. And he had his on-demand maintenance team putting my patio to rights once again. I didn't know how to make this make sense.

When he returned to my side, he said, "They'll need a few hours to finish this."

"I didn't come over here for you to ride to my rescue. I wasn't looking for that and I don't need it."

He shrugged. "Seems to me that you did."

"Why are you even doing this?"

"I can't have this kind of disarray right in front of my restaurant."

I glared at him as hard as I could manage. "The bait shop was all kinds of abandoned disarray for years. You didn't have any problem with that?"

"It was rustic, charming disarray." He tipped his chin toward the patio. "That is not charming. It's also another liability, and since you're not doing anything about it, I stepped in to get things done."

"I never once suggested I needed you to call up a crew to pick glass off my patio with tweezers. I came over here because I suspected you had something to do with this after last week's stunt." I crossed my arms over my chest. He glanced at my shirt and then away, frowning at the cove. Of course he'd hate our branding. "I am capable of running my business without your interference and I'd really like to go a full week without having to remind you of that."

He glanced back at me, a slight smile tugging at his lips. It was like his features had been written in a stately, serif font. The smooth expanse of his forehead bisected by a pair of deep, even grooves between his brows. The crisp, high fullness of his cheekbones and the aristocratic square of his jaw. The brackets at the corners of his lips that made every expression a bit more polished—and a bit more severe.

Leaning in close to me, he said, "I think what you're trying to say is thank you."

"That's not what I'm saying at all."

His gaze dropped to my mouth. He tucked some hair behind my ear. A single, pounding heartbeat passed, and then—"Would it be so bad?"

Without any forethought at all, I blurted out, "You're not my type."

Beckett laughed and took a decisive step back. He slipped his hands into his pockets and pulled on the cool, stoic expression he enjoyed so much. "That's an odd way to say thank you but probably what I should expect from a storm cloud."

He turned and walked into the oyster company without another word.

That bubble gum bubble popped all over my face.

MEARA SLUNG an arm around my shoulder and hummed to herself as we watched Beckett's maintenance crew rehabilitate our patio once again. "Is this okay?" she asked after a moment. "You'll tell me if you need to be in your body bubble, right?"

I nodded. "I'm fine."

"You're sure? You're feeling a little rigid."

"It's nothing. I know how to ask for space when I need it." Another nod. On my other side, Muffy shoved her hands in her apron pockets with a sighing laugh. Bethany held up her phone to snap a selfie of us. Something about this being the perfect girl band album cover.

"It's nice that you have a rich boyfriend," Meara said over the hum of shop-vacs. "It's really convenient to have someone who can snap their fingers and produce minions."

"And pay for them too," Muffy added.

I laughed so hard, I cried. "Definitely not my boyfriend."

"Your admirer," Bethany said.

"Can we really call him that when he's a complete pest?" I asked. "Seriously? This isn't second grade and he isn't pulling my pigtails."

"A pest in finely tailored Dior," Meara said. "It's happened before and it will happen again."

"Let me think about that." I tapped a finger to my lips as I pretended to consider whether Beckett was anything other than an infuriating, egotistical thorn in my side. "Yeah, no."

"You know, he's done a lot for us, Sunny," Beth said.

"He's fixed our problems on the damn spot twice now," Muffy said. "If we look past the whole drama of him trying to buy the building out from under us and probably putting us out of business, I can see the appeal."

I turned to face her. Her box braids were twisted up in a bun, her glasses sat low on her nose, and she had seven markers clipped on the bib of her apron. She looked entirely serious, not even a touch of her bone-dry humor sparkling in her eyes. "You can *see the appeal*? You find approximately no one attractive but you can see the appeal of Beckett Loew, the guy who wants to buy our building and get rid of us because he's annoyed about sharing a *parking* lot?"

Muffy waved a hand. "I will acknowledge that he comes on strong—"

"He comes on strong like a bull through the streets of Pamplona," I muttered to myself.

"—but I've had several perfectly reasonable conversations with him. Just the other day, a beer distributor was trying to make a delivery but this dude would have a hard time parallel parking on a football field and he blocked the espresso machine repair guy's truck—along with everyone else in the damn lot. But before I could start directing traffic and move things along, the bossman was tearing a stripe off that boy's ass. I heard him say he'd stop selling their beer if they couldn't deliver without causing problems for the neighboring businesses."

"We are the only neighboring business," I said.

"Yes, I know, and it's good that you're catching on," Muffy said. "When he was finished scaring the life out of the beer dude, he came over and apologized."

"A man who apologizes and pays for things," Meara said with a lusty sigh.

"I'm having trouble believing this," I said.

"Well, it's true," Muffy said.

"He's a very decent boss too," Bethany added. "I've been watching him—among others—when I hang out at the bar."

"That seems unlikely. He's a yeller. He yells. He probably throws things. Like, oysters. I'm sure he wings oysters at his staff all the time," I said.

Bethany stared at me for a moment. "I haven't witnessed any oyster throwing—"

"Can you even see through those heart eyes you have for Mel?" I asked.

"—but he shucks a lot of them. I can't believe how fast he can slide the knife in and bust those shells open. It's rapid-fire shucking, one after the other, no stopping."

"I do appreciate that sort of thing," Meara said under her breath.

"And *we* appreciate that sort of thing? We are talking about *oysters*. In the best of lights, they are briny, slurpy vaginas on a plate."

"And *I* enjoy that sort of thing," Bethany said under her breath.

"And *I* enjoy staying the fuck away from all that mess," Muffy said. "The shellfish and the shucking, if you know what I mean."

"I know that Beck is a pain in my ass though somehow I'm the only one who sees it," I said.

Bethany bobbled her hands in front of her. "I don't know, sunshine, he did fill in for a server who had to leave because her kid was sick. And last Friday he escorted a customer out after he got handsy with a busser. It was really hot. I could tell he was *this close* to grabbing the guy and tossing him out on his ass."

"Okay, so he meets the minimum criteria for being an acceptable person and boss. We are not required to throw a parade in his honor," I said.

"I have it on good authority that he personally covered wages for the entire staff while they were shut down for those couple of days after all the FBI stuff," Meara added. "And we ended up talking about college ball last week."

"Wait," Beth said, "do you know his brother? The baseball player?"

Meara shook her head. "I know I met some of the men's team when

U of A was at Vanderbilt for a tournament but I don't remember Decker."

"Six degrees of Division One college softball," Muffy said.

"Something like that." Meara glanced back at me. "He had legit opinions on some of the women's teams and the match-ups he wanted to see this year. I was impressed."

I didn't want her to be impressed. I wanted her to see that Beckett was a tyrant who used money to get his way. Money and cold, serif stares. I glared at her. I'd counted on Meara to be on my side.

"I have nothing else to contribute other than to reiterate that he solves problems for you. It's not the worst thing in the world, even if he is heavy-handed about it," she went on. "You're no doormat so it's not like you'll let him steamroll you." She shrugged. "See what happens. You might discover that it's not that bad to have an arrogant man around who takes it upon himself to help you."

"And pay for it," Muffy said.

"Don't remind me," I said.

"I don't know why he's doing any of this for you," Bethany said, "and I don't want to invent motivations for his behavior. But have you considered the possibility that y'all started off on the wrong foot and now you can't stop pushing each other's buttons?"

"That's a good point," Meara said. "We know he can be a functional human so why does Sunny send him over the edge?"

"I don't think I'm the one pushing any buttons," I said. "All I want is to avoid him. I don't like anything about the guy."

Muffy shifted to face me. "Why not?"

"What?"

"Why don't you like him?" she asked. "You like everyone. Always. You can find something redeeming and special in everyone. You don't do this—you don't hate a guy simply for existing, even if he is bossy and broody and a bit of a piranha when it comes to protecting the family business." She peered at me and I could feel heat rising in my cheeks. "What's that all about?"

Suddenly, everyone was staring at me with a whole lot of interest. I didn't have an answer ready to go so I watched the crew as they unloaded a dozen new lanterns.

Eventually, I said, "I don't know. He's my brother's best friend. They decapitated an entire stable of My Little Pony figures and hid the heads in my bed when I was nine. Last I checked, I'm legally entitled to hate him for life."

Muffy started to respond but stopped herself to shake her head at the sky. Meara put a hand on her shoulder, saying, "Allow me." She crossed her arms over her torso and rocked back on her heels. "My dear. My love. My sunshine. Is it possible that you're clinging to some very old bullshit and holding it against the broody bossman despite his obvious attempts at not being the kind of little rascal who might behead ponies mafia-style?"

"I just don't like him," I argued. "In this whole wide world, I think I'm allowed to dislike one guy. I mean, if things had been different before, they'd be different now. But they're not."

"Mmmhmm." Meara tipped her head to the side, considering me.

"Why can't they be different now?" Bethany asked. "What would happen if you decided to just stop fighting him?"

"I will *not* do that," I snapped. "I'm not the one who needs to change. He's the one who has treated me like an incompetent little girl from the minute he walked up to this patio. I'm not about to let any of that shit slide."

And I wasn't giving up my iceberg. Not that they needed to know about my iceberg.

"And you shouldn't," Bethany said. "But maybe you should stop *fighting* him. Stop giving him all your emotional energy, your firepower. Your attention. See what happens then."

Muffy clucked her tongue. "And that's why Shawpscock is the real genius here. I've never met anyone who looks so pretty and fights so dirty."

"It's a gift," Bethany said with a beaming grin.

"It's your attention he wants. He thrives on it. Craves it, I'd bet." Meara bobbed her head, sending one of her dark braids sliding over her shoulder. "We'll be here for you when the bossman loses his mind because you haven't yelled at him enough."

"We'll also be here for you when you realize you don't hate him at all," Muffy said.

"That won't happen." I watched as the crew pushed open the new umbrellas. I loved my friends but they were wrong about this one. They had to be. "Trust me."

chapter eight

Today's Special:
Hand-Pressed Problems

"I'M SORRY, but if you think I'm going to be able to keep Emily, Everleigh, and Evyanna straight, you don't know me very well." I pushed the report across the table to Mel. "Do you have to schedule them all for the same shifts?"

Mel toyed with the barbell through her eyebrow. The dining room was otherwise empty, the only sound coming from the first of the kitchen crew prepping for the day's service. "And who would you like me to schedule in place of them? Do you have a secret supply of competent servers? Or would you prefer I load up the other servers with more tables and hope for the best?"

We stared at each other while Hale slurped up the last of his iced coffee. Determined to get every last drop, he loudly sucked on his straw and then tore off the cup's top and went to work on the ice.

"You have a problem," Mel said to him.

Shrugging, he said, "It's really good coffee."

When he set the cup down, I spotted the Naked logo. I didn't try to hide my eye roll. "You've been over there every day this week."

"Because it's really good coffee," he said. "You guys should try it."

"I don't need anything special in my coffee," Mel argued. "Whatever they're doing is too much frouf for me. All I need is a good, basic black cold brew."

"I get cold brew every day," Hale said. "It's better than any of that drive-thru garbage you drink."

Mel looked at me. "We've lost him to the Naked girls."

Hale held up a finger. "Just a thought, but maybe we shouldn't refer to them as *the Naked girls*. I understand what you mean but it could be misconstrued and—"

"Yeah, yeah. We get it," Mel said. "I still don't need their coffee."

He folded his arms on the table and leaned in. "Why not?"

Mel started to respond but stopped herself to shuffle her schedules and reports. I tapped a pen to my lips as I waited for her. I needed to hear this. It would help me make sense of my own issues.

It had been days since the incident on Sunny's patio and I still didn't know what had happened there. I wasn't her type. She'd said that as if I didn't already know. As if all the reasons why she had to stay as far away from me as possible weren't already engraved on my brain. As if one wrong move toward Sunny wouldn't ruin twenty years of friendship with Lance.

With an impatient huff, Mel said, "Because I put milk—*real* milk from cows—in my coffee, and everything there is vegan so—"

"But you said all you want is cold brew and never once in five years have I seen you put anything more than whiskey in your coffee so what's the real problem?" Hale asked.

"I have no interest in their coffee," she snapped. "I don't want to know about anything they're doing. I don't care about them. Especially not the one who keeps parking herself at the bar and slow-drinking lemon drops." She looked up from her paperwork and speared Hale with a glare. "Why do you like them so much, Woot? You're always talking to the chef and the one who lurks at my bar and the little one who drives Beck crazy. Can you help us move this conversation along and just tell us if you're trying to get with one of them? We have more important things to discuss."

I swallowed a growl. Hale was charismatic as fuck and he had a lot of game when it came to romance. And Sunny—well, Sunny was a goddamn pain in my ass. She was impossible. Everything about her, impossible. He'd have a fucking field day. I had a lot of experience with silent suffering, but something about Sunny and Hale made my head pound in a way that had me thinking I'd sooner drown myself than stand by while it happened.

A smile pulled at Hale's mouth. "You just said you don't want to know about anything, Mel. I'm terribly confused."

Mel pushed up from her seat and started gathering her papers all over again. "If you want to date one of them or all of them, I don't need to hear about it." She hugged a few folders to her chest. "Beck, if you have a problem with Emily, Everleigh, and Evyanna, you have to figure out which is which first. Until then, let's see if we can survive a week without firing anyone. It's not been great for morale."

"Unless you're talking about firing Devon," Hale added. "Because he's a nightmare."

Mel glared up at the ceiling. She was really phenomenal at grudges. Even with the smallest grievance, she could refuse to make eye contact for entire days. Weeks if she put her back into it.

"What's the problem with Devon?" I asked. "I thought he was one of the few we wanted to salvage from the old crew. Customers like him, right?"

"They request him by name," Mel said, now staring at the water. "He's always the top server of the night, regardless of whether it's a slow Wednesday or full-house Saturday." She let out a lengthy sigh. "But he's a bitch to schedule and his behavior is questionable."

"Hmm." I held out my hand and she passed me last week's sales report.

Devon's numbers *were* good and I needed all the wins I could get. We were working with barely enough staff, Decker still hadn't returned my calls (and I didn't count a text reading "ok" as a real response), and my attorney called every day to tell me how bad the evidence looked. One less problem on my roster would be awesome.

"He's a nightmare," Hale repeated.

"Yes, and if we can hang on to him a little longer, that would make my life less of an ongoing train wreck. It's summer on the seacoast, Beck. We're booked solid for the next three months. Unless you're putting Woot on the schedule, I don't think we'll be able to replace Devon anytime soon."

"Walk over to Naked with me for a cold brew and you can schedule me every night this weekend," Hale said. "I'm going regardless of your non-arguments and I'll bring drinks back for both of you but it would be a lot more fun if you tagged along."

"Please explain to me why my presence would change a damn thing," Mel said.

"Because you light up my life, Melissa." He beamed at her. "And I need to visit with Sunny. We talked about going to the festival together this weekend so—"

There it was. That was the line. The point of no return.

"No." I leaned forward and flattened both hands on the table. There was a noise in my head like a swarm of bees. "Not for a damn minute you're not."

I reached for my water bottle and drained the contents. There was a ton of bricks on my chest. I couldn't breathe. Couldn't even think past the idea of Hale strolling around the high school football-field-turned-festival-grounds with Sunny on his arm. And I liked Hale. A lot. He was a good guy—a *great* guy. But, fuck, I wanted to throw him into the water for hinting at an interest in Sunny. It was spectacularly unreasonable. There was no defending that reaction, especially given that Sunny was as good as barricaded behind heavily reinforced lines. She was not an option, not for me, not for a fucking minute.

"Should I interpret that to mean you're interested in her?" Hale asked.

"That does seem to be the implication," Mel said.

Hale nodded. "Definitely the implication."

"I did not imply—" I stopped myself, shook my head. "That's not the case. Okay?"

"She's very nice," he went on. "Pretty, one might say."

"I mean, sure," I conceded, desperate to wrap this up. "She's cute."

"Cute," he repeated.

"Yeah, she's a cutie, I guess." I glanced between their blank stares. "Just a real cute...cutie pie. She's a cutie pie."

"She's a cutie pie," Hale said, bobbing his head like the caffeine had just hit his bloodstream. "And you're not interested in her at all?"

"Why would I be?"

Hale pressed a fist to his mouth, holding in a laugh. "I don't know, man, but I've known you a long time and never have I ever heard the words *cutie pie* come out of your mouth. That's gotta count for something."

Mel pressed both hands to her temples and groaned. "Seriously, Beck."

"Can we get back on topic? Please?" I held up last week's numbers. "Maybe we should cut Devon and be done with it. Schedule the Eliana-Evette-Emma troop for all the nights they'll take."

"You're firing Devon because you don't want to talk about the Sunny situation?" Mel glanced between me and Hale, apparently finished with today's grudge. "Is that what we're doing?"

"No, I'm responding to feedback about him." I glanced at my phone. "But if you'd like to give it another week or two, I'll defer to your judgment."

Hale snapped his fingers and motioned to the windows facing Naked. "I need more coffee. Who's coming with me?"

"Shut the hell up," Mel said.

"I need some fuel before I get back out on the water." He wagged his empty cup between us, entirely too amused with himself. "Does this mean y'all are skipping the Naked housewarming party?"

Mel seemed to choke on air. "The *what*?"

"I wonder if they know what they've done with that name," Hale mused. "Anyway, yeah, they're hosting a little party for industry folks. Monday because most of us are closed Mondays."

"We aren't," Mel grumbled.

"It's fine." Hale waved us off. "Since you don't have any interest in anything happening at Naked or any of their people, there's nothing for you to miss. Though I am surprised you hadn't heard about it. Sunny said one of her partners invited you."

Mel played with her barbell again. "The perky one with the lemon drops said something about a party the other day."

Hale pressed his lips together as he studied her. "And what did you say to that?"

She ran a hand over her hair. "I didn't say anything. I just...I don't know, I think I walked away."

"Wonderful." Hale nodded slowly. "Maybe next time, try for a word or two. We'll work our way up to full sentences."

Impatient, I asked, "When the fuck is this thing supposed to be?"

"Monday night. After sunset," he replied.

Five full days away. I'd see Sunny before then. It was only a matter of time until she stomped on over here to yell about some new problem for which I was tangentially responsible. If she wanted me anywhere near this little gathering—and I had my doubts about that, seeing as *I wasn't her type*—she'd let me know. Sunny wasn't afraid to tell me exactly what she was thinking.

Even more impatient, I asked, "And what the fuck is it all about?"

"Housewarming. You know what that means, Beck. It's when you move to a new place and invite everyone over to have some drinks and show off what you've done. Like that but for food service people. Very low-key." With a smile that said he was enjoying my annoyance, he added, "You can come too. Sunny said we're all welcome."

Even if that was the case, I knew better.

"We'll see about that," I said.

"COME ON." Mel barged into my office, motioning for me to follow her. "I need you."

I pushed away from the desk—and my premium view of the Naked Provisions patio—and trailed behind Mel as she descended the stairs. "What's on fire now?"

"Nothing. Stop talking. Just follow me."

"Should I call my attorney?"

"No. The more plausible the deniability, the better."

"Nothing about this sounds good, Mel."

When we reached the dining room, she beckoned for Zeus Castro, the assistant manager and backup bartender due to the present staffing situation, to come out from behind the bar. Agent Price was parked there with a mug of coffee and a hardcover novel. He gave me a quick nod before returning to his reading.

To Zeus, Mel said, "Beck and I are stepping out for a few minutes. You're in charge."

"How exciting for all of us," Zeus drawled. "Enjoy pretending that you're not sneaking over to the Naked party."

"We are not sneaking anywhere," Mel snapped. She grabbed my elbow and yanked me toward the door.

"Bring me a cookie," Zeus called behind us.

Once outside, Mel blew out a breath and skimmed her palms down her thighs. "This isn't a big deal. We have to stop in because everyone is over there and we'd look like cuntmuffins if we didn't."

"Cuntmuffins?"

"Very much."

I glanced between her and the group gathered on the Naked Provisions patio. I'd spent the past two hours trying to clean up a cost projections spreadsheet but managed only to open the file and stare out the window as Sunny and her partners set up for the party.

I learned that Beth took every opportunity to dance, and Muffy shoved her hands in her apron pockets and shook her head a lot. Meara liked to give directions but Sunny was quietly, *clearly* in charge.

She was also a complete hazard to herself. On three separate occasions, I watched her bunch up her skirt and climb on chairs to adjust the string lights crisscrossed above the patio. It was like she really wanted to find out how hard the stone would bite back when she fell on that sweet, cherubic face of hers.

Each time, I found myself standing at the window, a hand outstretched like I could catch her from here. Growing up, there'd been one rule in Lance's house: don't let Sunny fall. We were allowed to do anything we wanted so long as Sunny made it through the day without an injury. Somehow, after all this time, it was still the one rule that mattered most to me.

The other rules mattered too. They kept me up at night. They curled around my throat every morning when I woke up, choking on the unsatisfying fragments of dark-haired dreams. They were the cause of the knot between my shoulders and the dread I felt every time Lance's name appeared in my text notifications. They were front and center at all times.

But panic-watching as Sunny pushed up on her tiptoes *on the chair* to get the lights just right made me realize that if I turned all the way toward her and let her blind me, I wouldn't see any rules.

I knew this would blow up in my face. I knew I'd walk away with nothing but regrets. But I also knew I couldn't stop. Even when I told myself I didn't want this. I didn't want *her*.

With that cheerful thought lodged somewhere in my esophagus, I watched as Bethany flitted around the group, passing out cookies and shot glasses. "And she had nothing to do with your change of heart?"

"No," Mel said flatly. She shot a pointed glance to where Sunny stood surrounded by people. They hung on her every word and I was irrationally angry about it. "We're making an appearance. Nothing more."

"Because we don't want to be cuntmuffins."

"Not tonight," she said. "Not on purpose. You do enough of it just by existing. We can't add to the tab."

I reached into my pocket for my phone but realized I'd left it on the desk. "Fuck. All right." I jabbed a finger at her. "Five minutes. That's it."

She glanced in Bethany's direction. "We'll stay as long as it takes. We don't want to be rude."

"A second ago, we didn't want to be cuntmuffins. *That* was the bar. Now we've escalated all the way up to not being rude?"

"We'll leave when we leave, Beck. No need to bust out the stopwatch."

I huffed out a groan and walked across the driveway with Mel, who was doing a solid job of pretending she wasn't tracking Bethany's every breath. We stopped to say hello to everyone we passed and I did a solid job of pretending I didn't notice all the uncomfortable silence that descended when they caught sight of me.

I thought people were bad at talking about death but it turned out they were so much worse when it came to talking about your family's criminal enterprises. Who would've guessed?

Mel filled the awkward moments because she knew everything about these people and their businesses, but it served as a reminder that I wasn't part of this town in any true way. Farmers markets and festivals were not my way of life, and small-town politics annoyed the hell out of me.

We'd moved here when I was sixteen and my dad's uncle Buckthorne wanted him to take over the oyster company after building it up over sixty years. Lance Du Jardin had been my first friend—and arguably my only true friend since everyone else had long since selected their circles. For reasons I hadn't understood at the time, Lance belonged to all of those circles while also belonging to none of them. He was a happy stray who made a habit of smoking weed and getting kicked off various sports teams within a few weeks of making the roster.

Amazingly, none of this disqualified him from being tasked with babysitting his sister all summer long.

The same sister who'd grown all the way up and wouldn't get the hell out of my mind.

A swift elbow to the flank tore my attention away from the golden highlights running through Sunny's long hair. I swung a glare toward Mel as she whispered, "Be cool. Be fucking cool, okay?"

"Then keep your elbows to yourself."

Bethany swayed toward us. That was how she moved, as if she was at least partially possessed by salsa music. She had some kind of shimmer on her lids that made her eyes look enormous and her lips were painted watermelon pink. I could understand why Mel was losing her shit.

"Hello, hello, neighbors," Bethany sang as she approached. "Isn't it a gorgeous night? So gorgeous. And so happy we could steal you away from the oysters."

Mel made a sound like she was choking on a rock.

"It's easier to get away on a Monday," I said.

"Yeah, I bet." Bethany held out her tray, her gaze trained on Mel. "Could I tempt you with a taste of my juice?"

Mel wheezed so hard I started to think she was actually choking.

"I press it all by hand," she continued. "The yellow one is my Firepower shot. It's apple, lemon, ginger, and cayenne. It heats you up from the inside out."

At this point in Mel's grunting and huffing, it seemed like she was a second or two away from tossing the tray and throwing Bethany over her shoulder. And if Bethany knew what she was doing, she was playing it real cool. That was *talent*.

"I call the red one Sailor's Warning. It's beet and pineapple, and it makes you feel bright and alive."

I reached for that one and knocked it back. "Oh, that's fantastic." I grabbed another while Mel went on staring at Bethany. "I thought the beet juice was going to taste like dirt but it's excellent."

Bethany grinned. "If you liked that, you're going to love these cookies."

I took one of each of the plate-sized cookies. "Did you make these too?"

Bethany laughed and I could feel the intensity rolling off Mel. Her discomfort made this field trip worth it for me. Ten out of ten, highly recommend watching a friend torture themselves over a woman.

"I don't," Bethany said. "Muffy is very particular about who she allows into her kitchen. But sometimes, if I make her coffee just the way she likes it, she'll let me scoop the cookie batter onto the baking trays." She leaned in close, still swaying, still possessed. "I never let her see me lick the batter off my fingers though."

"Right." Mel took the juice tray from her and handed it to someone passing by. "Okay." She handed me the cookies. "That's enough. You're coming with me." She took hold of Bethany's upper arm and towed her around the far side of the building.

Alone, I bit into one of the cookies. It was rich and outrageously chocolatey, and it gave me something to do while watching Sunny tell a story with her whole body. I couldn't hear her from here but it was better this way. I could watch her without wondering why she didn't have her service dogs nearby or mentally compiling a list of issues to address around the café. Better exterior lighting came to mind immediately.

It also gave me a chance to watch the people listening to her. I had to imagine people liked her when she wasn't running around and screaming at them about real estate mishaps.

She was open in a manner that drew in people who enjoyed that sort of presence. She was warm. Engaging in an honest, authentic way. If I looked at it from a certain angle, I could understand the appeal. For other people. I didn't see it. I didn't care. And neither did she.

I didn't think anyone else noticed when her eyes landed on me and the pause between her words consumed an extra beat, but I saw every ounce of it. Right beneath that warm surface was a cold shoulder that froze me from all the way across the patio. Yeah. She was as honest as the fucking ocean, wide open and crystal clear.

The group around her swelled and I ended up staring at the back of the burger guy's head which interested me not at all. As I devoured another cookie, this one composed of chocolate and cranberries and corn flakes, of all the ridiculous things, I moved closer to the circle surrounding Sunny. She was talking about an issue they'd had with tile installation, and when she glanced around her audience this time, her gaze settled on me for a moment.

She rubbed her temple, flipping me off in the process, and the small, petty part of me rejoiced in forcing a real reaction from her. I'd nearly died waiting on a taste of that fire.

With that victory in hand, I shifted away from her legion of adoring fans. There was no reason to expect another round with Sunny, and I knew she didn't mind handing me my ass in front of a crowd. It was time for me to get the hell out of here.

On my way to the edge of the patio, I found Meara flanked by two men and I passed the cookies to her. "I don't think I should be left alone with these," I said.

Laughing, she took the tray and handed it to one of the men. "So, you're a fan of the salted chocolate cookie?"

They both eyed me warily. I'd seen them around the café many times but hadn't connected them with Meara until this moment. One was tall and deeply tanned, and wore a pair of sunglasses on top of his head. He reminded me of the kids from high school who went to yacht club camp in the summers. The other man had deep bronze skin and a ton of thick, curly black hair. His button-down shirt was open at the collar and tattoos ringed his neck. If he didn't have a history playing college or pro football as the defensive line, I'd be shocked. The guy looked like he could snap necks with his fingertips.

"It doesn't make any sense," I said, "but it's incredible."

She grinned. "That's pretty much our mission statement."

With a bit of grudging hesitation, I said, "I can see why you have a line all the way to Market Street most days."

She scanned the crowd, nodding slowly. "We've had a good start but —and I don't have to tell you this—the start doesn't matter if you don't keep the momentum going."

"Yeah," I said. "I do know that. If you're open to it, I'd love to grab some time with you to hear more about your social media strategy."

"That depends." She shot me a measured look before continuing. "Did you get all the shenanigans out of your system or should I be on the lookout for another purchase and sale agreement? Or are you trying to get our liquor license revoked? Maybe calling in the health department? Where are we with the games, Loew?"

Neck Tattoo crossed his arms over his broad chest. Yacht Club flexed his jaw. I could handle myself but I had no interest in getting on their bad side. For any reason.

"That was a misunderstanding," I said.

"Mmm." She nodded. "Let's not have any more of those." She glanced toward Sunny as those surrounding her burst into laughter. "Have you been inside yet?"

I blinked at her for several moments. "Have I—what?"

She pressed her lips together to fight off a smile. "The café, Loew. Have you been inside the café?"

I glanced at the building, once gray and slumped, now fresh, gleaming white with black trim. She was talking about the café, not the perverted noise in my head. "No, not yet."

"Buying sight unseen. Risky," she murmured. "And your efforts have been concentrated on the patio. Thank you for lending us your maintenance crew, by the way."

I dipped my hands into my pockets. "The least I can do."

"Yes, about that. It seems you have some issues with my girl," she said.

"Me? No. I have no issue with Sunny." I had many issues with Sunny, none of which I could express without sounding deranged. And none I wanted to share with this woman or her guard dogs.

"Then she has issues with you," Meara said.

"That…is possible, yes."

"Hmm. You should fix those issues." Meara studied the crowd for a moment. "I'm guessing we have another thirty, maybe forty-five minutes until winding down. I'm going to mingle and move these folks along. You should take a look inside. You can sneak out the front door and back to that office of yours." She glanced to the top corner of Small Point Oyster Company and then back at me with a knowing grin. "I won't tell on you."

I snagged a cookie off the tray for Zeus and nodded at the men on either side of her. "Thanks for having us." I glanced around. "I came with Mel. She is around here somewhere—"

"Oh, I know where Mel is," she said, laughing. "Remember what I said about the misunderstandings."

I needed to get back to SPOC so I headed toward the café's back door. Cool, complete silence hit me. I followed the narrow hallway into the heart of the café. It was bright and clean with tall windows, white-washed walls, and pale wood tables. It was small but they'd made the most of it. I turned in a slow circle, taking in the transformation and then gazing up at the exposed beams and industrial ceiling fans. The original bait shop sign had been refurbished and hung high above the letterboard menu. The place looked amazing.

"If you're doing reconnaissance for your next prank, I should warn you that Muffy has knives and she won't be afraid to wield them if you so much as breathe the wrong way in her kitchen."

I dropped my gaze from the old sign to find Sunny leaning against the butcher block counter. Her dogs sat on either side of her and she wore another one of those long, loose skirts held together with a knot, though this time it was paired with a button-down shirt also knotted at the waist. Always tying up her clothing. Almost like she wanted someone to unravel her.

"Seeing as I'm not a raccoon, I don't think I have anything to worry about," I said.

"We never proved it was raccoons," she argued.

"We never disproved it either. All this time, you're running around and letting people believe that—"

"Excuse me but I am not running around anywhere."

"—I had the time and inclination to come over here and bang up your patio."

"You come over here and growl quite often. It stands to reason you'd do other things."

"I do not come over here and growl," I said.

"In fact you do."

I held out my hands. "And that's somehow worse than you coming over to SPOC to yell your ass off?"

"I have never once yelled my ass off. I've had—"

"You yell like a fucking banshee."

"—plenty of reasons to have serious conversations with you but I've never raised my voice."

I held her gaze for a moment as I took a step toward her, then another. This place was small enough that it only took one more step for me to reach out and scratch her Labrador between the ears.

"I didn't see them outside," I said, still staring into her dark eyes.

"They were in the office." She arched a brow up. "You know, you're not supposed to pet them. They're *working*. You know better."

I let my gaze drop from her eyes down to her lips and then lower, to the skin exposed where the top buttons of her shirt sat open. In my mind, she was still a kid, the way Parker would always be a gurgling baby who belly-laughed anytime someone tried to steal his toes.

But being here with her, close enough to touch, to catch the fresh scent of her skin, I couldn't convince myself I knew this woman. It was almost enough for me to believe this wasn't completely wrong. *Almost*.

"I like your cookies," I said.

She tipped her head back, her eyes narrowed. "What does that mean?"

I lifted a shoulder. "It means I like your cookies."

She watched me for a moment before that adorably evil grin spread across her face. "You didn't think you would, right? It's killing you to admit it."

I stared at her mouth. *God,* those lips. "There are a lot of things killing me right now."

Sunny looked down to where I stroked the German shepherd's head. His tail thumped against the floor. "Tell me two of them."

Sunny was beautiful. I'd known that since the first morning, but seeing her up close like this turned my heart into a racehorse and that was enough to sweep every rational thought from my mind. I didn't need self-preservation and I didn't need to know better when I was *right here*. I didn't need a damn thing.

I brought my hand to her jaw, pressing my thumb to her top lip. "One," I said, groaning at the feel of her against my skin. I dragged my thumb to her bottom lip and died a little when I felt her tongue flick over me. "Two."

"You're unbelievable." She reached for me, grabbing a handful of my shirt and yanking me flush against her.

A breath puffed out of me as I tilted her head back to get a better angle. I leaned in and—

The back door opened and all the noise from outside rushed in. We sprang apart as one door slammed and then another. I was halfway across the café before I caught Sunny's eyes again. She pressed her fingers to her lips and stared at the polished concrete floor.

I ignored the pull in my gut, the blindness I felt when I stared directly at her, and spoke the first words to enter my mind. "That was a mistake. I-I shouldn't have and—"

She stretched an arm toward the front door. "You should go."

The German shepherd beside her growled. I nodded once. My legs were unsteady as I walked to the door like I was being carried by a wave. I stopped there long enough to glance back and find her gaze still fixed on the floor. I watched her mouth the words *Oh my god.*

That was all the proof I needed to know I'd crossed every conceivable line with Sunny even if the warmth prickling inside me insisted otherwise. Even if the pressure in my chest seemed to demand I go to her right now.

But I couldn't do that.

I pushed the door open and didn't look back in Sunny's direction until I'd reached the confines of my office.

chapter nine

Sunny

Today's Special:
Lust-Brined Mistake

WELL, that was humiliating.

I had to stop showing up in these situations with Beckett. The second I spotted him, I should've turned around and walked back to the party, and skipped the ritualistic beatings we liked to serve each other. Never, not for a single second, should I have given him the tiniest hint that I liked having his big, broody hands on my body. And that near-miss kiss? My god. What had I been thinking?

But that was just it. I hadn't thought at all. I didn't think when I was around Beckett Loew and I never made smart, sane choices. I just ran headfirst into fresh, new chaos every time I saw his annoyingly gorgeous face.

"Everything okay, babe?" Meara brought her palms to my cheeks. "You're looking flushed."

"It's nothing. I'm just a little warm."

She glanced around the empty café as if she expected to come across an explanation. When she didn't find one, she arched a brow at me. "Okay. I'm going to take your word for it even though it's rather chilly and there's a touch of fog rolling in. I came in here to grab my blazer."

"I'm fine," I said with a fairly convincing laugh. "Beth and I can take it from here."

"I like that idea though Beth might be preoccupied. I think she teased her grumpy friend from the oyster company a touch too hard, and, if the noises I heard are any indication, she's getting every ounce of it back."

"I can manage without her. There isn't much left to do."

She linked her arm in mine and guided me toward the back door, out into the crisp air. "You're sure you're good? I'll stay as long as you need me." Meara nodded toward the edge of the patio where her husbands stood with arms crossed and gazes fixed on her. "Ignore those pouty faces. They won't mind."

I sucked in a breath, nodding. I was fine. I could handle making colossal errors in judgment. I could go on without skipping a beat. I was *great*. "Get out of here."

"Promise me you won't stay too late?"

I grinned. Meara was the best mom anyone three years older than me could be. "Promise."

I took a pass around the patio after Meara left with her men, collecting stray crockery and making noise about having an early start in the morning to anyone who would listen. I was heading into the kitchen when Beth stepped out of the bathroom, hair wrecked, makeup smudged beyond repair, and lips swollen.

"Hey," she croaked.

It was my turn to bring the maternal energy. "Are you all right? You look like you just fell out of bed or—"

"—or had a religious experience? Because I think that's what happened. Religious experience." She waved a hand over her skirt. "In my vagina. Mostly. I think I just got shucked, maybe."

I nodded. "Yeah. You should take care of that. Why don't you head out?"

"Thanks." She pushed a hand through her hair. "I'll take one of your opening shifts next week. I swear."

"Don't stress. We'll figure something out." I stared at her visibly shaky legs. She looked like a newborn colt. "Are you sure you're safe to drive?" The back door opened and Mel from the oyster company stepped in. She arched a brow at Beth. "So that's how it is. Okay. Text me when you get home."

"She will," Mel said, crooking a finger toward Beth. She obeyed, shuffling toward the door. "Good girl."

I slumped back against the wall, pressing a hand to my chest. The lust in here was thicker than the fog outside and it did things to me. Stupid things. Irresponsible things. *March over to SPOC and tell Beckett that I'd show him what a real mistake looks like* things, which was crazy even among the crazy choices I'd made tonight.

But I went a little crazy around him. More like grossly immature and exceedingly feral, but I didn't see a reason to put too fine a shine on it right now. Not when I could still feel the pressure of his thumb on my lips, and a significant part of me wanted him to finish what he'd started.

Whatever the hell that was.

Though another part of me wanted nothing to do with that nonsense. Beckett was an annoyance—and a temporary one at that. Once all the drama with his family was settled, he'd be on the next flight out of here. Much like my brother, Beckett made no secret of his distaste for this town. He'd pick up his scowls and his broody bossiness, and he'd leave without a backward glance.

Yet he wouldn't give me the pleasure of disappearing entirely. He'd always be Lance's best friend, forever bound to pop back into my life and then flit away to his far-off existence. I didn't need to saddle myself with any constant, unpleasant reminders of a lust-drunk (and deeply misguided) night.

So, I didn't march over to the oyster company. I didn't turn his words over in my mind. I didn't even let myself think about what might happen if I pushed him—*really* pushed him—and let him push me right back.

Instead, I loaded the dishwasher, straightened up the kitchen to a level that wouldn't send Muffy into a tizzy, and joined the handful of people still lingering around the patio. Some of the kitchen staff from SPOC had made their way over and most of the group was gathered around the low stone bench that formed a half-moon along the water's edge.

The dogs in tow, I plopped down beside Hale Wooten. A woman sat on his other side, Nyomi from Little Star Farm. She gave me a quick wave.

"Did you always know you wanted to name this place Naked Provisions?" she asked. "Because it's a great name and I'm kind of jealous I didn't come up with it for my nonexistent vegan bakery café first. Not that I'd ever be able to bake vegan but jealousy doesn't really care about those details."

"We went through a lot of name ideas." They probably didn't notice the shakiness in my words but I felt it. I didn't think I'd get rid of this buzzy energy for hours. Without thinking, I glanced over at Small Point, half expecting to find Beckett standing by the door. He wasn't. He didn't care. He'd made his mistake for the day. "We tossed around ideas like Muffy's Muffins—"

"Oh my *god*," Hale drawled. "I love that."

"Then we went full English tea shop with Shawpscock and McTeague's, but that is a whole mouthful—"

"I am dying," Nyomi said, both hands pressed to her chest as she laughed.

"—and Meara thought we'd have trouble with social media because people would misspell or garble the names."

"And your initials would be S and M," Hale added, "which is also very special."

"So special," I agreed. "We thought about sticking with Roots and Shoots, from Beth's previous gig, but we didn't want people who knew that juice and kombucha business to think we only did that." I held up several fingers as I mentally checked off our old brainstorms. "We played with a lot of Green this or Coastal that names but in the end, Naked felt right."

"Does it ever," Hale crowed. "What a tagline. Whew. 'Naked: It just feels right." He ran a hand down his face, laughing. "Can you tell I'm up past my bedtime?"

"Not at all," I said.

"The dawn waits for no man," he said. "And it will be here before we know it."

"With that cheerful reminder, we should get going soon," Nyomi said. "Baker's hours and all. But we didn't want to leave in case you needed help getting rid of these people."

Hale tipped his head toward some of the oyster company's servers. "They'll hang out here all night if you let them."

As if we needed to test this theory, one of those servers strolled over and parked himself on the bench beside me. There wasn't enough room though that didn't stop him from pressing right up against me and jostling the dogs as he did it.

Breathe breathe breathe. Don't freak out yet.

At my feet, Jem gave him a low growl. The server didn't notice.

"Hey," he boomed, louder than anyone needed to be at such a close distance. "Sunny, right? I'm Devon. Killer setup you have here. Prime location for parties."

My eyes wide and smile pinched, I glanced between his grin and the many places where his body touched mine. *Set a boundary. Push back.*

Don't freak out yet. I forced a few inches between my legs to edge him away. "Thanks."

Devon swung his arm behind me and dropped his hand to the stone as if I'd given him any indication that I was interested. I could hear my heartbeat, and since the dogs could sense that, they sat up and gave me *we don't like this for you* eyes.

"The last time I was out here was when a bunch of guys bought out the oyster company for a bachelor party," he said. "They were doing lines off one of the old boats. Now, that was a fuckin' night. Those guys were throwing hundreds around like it was nothing. I walked away with five large that night. Legends, man. Fuckin' legends, all of them."

"I wonder whether the marriage lasted," Hale said under his breath.

"I wonder if the engagement lasted," Nyomi murmured.

I pressed my elbow hard into Devon's side. No mistaking that message. When he didn't take the hint, I said, "I could really use some space."

"We're all friends here," he replied, leaning in even closer. The tang of beer and cigarettes lingered around him, and my chest tightened.

An impatient noise rumbled out of Hale. "Come on, Devon. It's time for you to go."

Devon laughed. "Maybe you were leaving but I'm getting to know Sunny."

He ran that wandering hand up to my waist and I shot off the bench, hopping as best I could to avoid stepping on a paw or tail. "Excuse the fuck out of you—"

"Don't be like that," Devon said, his palms out and his brow crinkled like he was genuinely disappointed in me. "What? We're friends. We're *talking*. Can't we talk?"

Hale stood, crossing his arms over his broad chest. "Let's not have a problem, Devon."

Devon pushed to his feet with a groan. "You know what the real problem is, Woot? You don't know how to lighten the hell up." He grinned at me in a way that felt like the slimy slip of rotting celery. "Don't you think he needs to lighten up, Sunny?"

"Actually, no, I don't," I said. "It's not cool to hunker down into someone's space when they ask you to stop."

"Oh my god, you're one of *those* people. You're what's wrong with the world, you know that? Can't even sit down next to someone without it turning into an ordeal." He pushed to his feet and aimed a sneer at me. "Thanks for telling me now and saving me some time. Enjoy the stick up your ass, sweetheart."

Devon stalked to the parking lot while muttering insults and suggesting others follow if they knew what was good for them. To the credit of everyone else, no one took him up on the offer and few even paid him any attention.

I couldn't decide whether that meant they were used to his outbursts or I was overreacting. Years of therapy had shown me that a childhood loaded with hospital stays and invasive procedures left me very sensitive to any moment where I felt an intrusion on my personal space or loss of autonomy. There were times when that sensitivity pinged harder than required and I had to work through those reactions to figure out where they came from and why.

But instinct told me this wasn't an overreaction.

When I was certain Devon wasn't coming back for an encore, I turned to Nyomi and Hale, asking, "Who does that? I mean, at this point in human history, who is out there forcing themselves on people and playing the 'What's the big deal?' card?"

"Assholes," Nyomi said.

That was all it took for me to fall in love with her.

Hale pointed at Nyomi. "That would sum up Devon."

"Ugh, yeah," I said. "If Meara had been here, she would've neutered him and made him thank her for the service."

"On that note, if you decide to tell Beck about this, can I be there while you do it?" Hale asked. "I just want to watch."

"Why would he care?" I asked. Yes, I was still salty about him calling me a mistake. No, I wasn't ready to explore the reason he brought out the biggest reactions in me. "Other than finding perverse amusement in my discomfort, I can't see why it would matter to him."

He reached a hand out to Nyomi and she took it, gaining her feet. "I could be wrong but I don't think Beck would want me answering that for him."

I laughed. "What is that supposed to mean?"

Hale studied the last few guests as they made their way to the parking lot at a lazy, meandering pace. "Are you ready to close up? We'll walk you to your car."

That was a fun way to dodge the question—and a really exciting way to tell me that I needed to keep one eye open where that douche Devon was concerned.

"We can also hang for a little longer if you need it," Nyomi added.

I glanced between them. "Is this guy going to slash my tires or something? Did I just pick a fight with the mafia?"

"No," Hale said, laughing oof the question. "No, nothing like that. I just know Beck would—" He stopped himself, exchanged a glance with Nyomi. "We like to look after our friends down here on the Point. That's all."

I wasn't going to argue with that so I motioned for the dogs to follow me. "I just need a minute to lock up."

"Then we'll meet you out front." Nyomi leaned into Hale's side and he looped an arm around her shoulders as I headed into the building.

I grabbed my things, double-checked that the kitchen was in order, and switched off the lights as I went. The dogs hurried along, knowing a proper dinner and time to run free in the backyard awaited them at home.

"Thanks for staying," I said as I fumbled with the locks.

"Happy to do it," Hale said. "You should know that Devon is all about the noise. He's obnoxious, but that's the extent of it."

"In other words, he's a little bitch," Nyomi said.

Seriously, I *loved* her.

"Good to know." I held my Jeep's rear gate open for the dogs to climb inside. "Now, why don't you tell me what you meant by those comments about Beckett. You know, the ones you thought I'd forget?"

Hale barked out a laugh. "You should ask him yourself. Give him a call. He'd love that. He's a vampire, you know. Up all damn night."

I laughed at his comments but they stayed with me on the short drive home, while I fed the pups, and when I finally flopped down onto my bed. I was tired and should've prioritized sleep since I was due back at the café early tomorrow, but that tiredness plus the leftover energy from another run-in with Beck—not to mention Devon—left me edgy.

And reckless.

That was how I ended up texting my brother.

> **Sunny:** Can you give me Beckett's number?

> **Lance:** Sure. Why?

> **Sunny:** Nothing important.

> **Lance:** Cool. Everything good?

> **Sunny:** Great. You?

> **Lance:** Another day in paradise.

I didn't let myself think too hard about the message I typed out to Beck. No need to overanalyze here. All I wanted was the facts.

> **Sunny:** Someone from your staff came over after service and got a little frisky.

> **Beckett:** I beg your pardon?

> **Sunny:** Oh hi, it's Sunny by the way.

Beckett: I figured that since your brother just messaged me with a warning to be nice to you. May I ask what you've told him?

Sunny: Do you know how to be nice?

Beckett: Who was it and what happened, Sunny?

Sunny: Hale was right. This is amusing.

Beckett: You're saying I should wake up Hale to find out for myself?

Sunny: Nothing happened. One of your people just likes to run his mouth and doesn't know how to keep track of his hands. I handled it.

Beckett: Give me a name or I'll fire everyone.

Sunny: Why would you do that?!?

Beckett: Because someone can't keep their hands to themselves and that's a problem for me.

Sunny: I don't want to get anyone fired. THAT would be a mistake.

Beckett: And yet you made a point of telling me that it happened so you must be looking for some reaction.

Sunny: You know...I've been told you're capable of carrying on civilized conversations.

Beckett: Your point being?

Sunny: Why can't you do that with me?

Beckett: I could ask you the same thing.

Sunny: I think you're a bit worse. It's like you can't help but revert to being that heartless bully who traumatized me as a kid.

Beckett: I think "traumatized" is an exaggeration.

Sunny: Must I remind you of the My Little Pony incident?

Beckett: Fuck, I haven't thought about that in a million years.

Sunny: Funny, I think about it every time I drive past the Castros' stables.

Beckett: We were deranged. That's all I can say.

Sunny: You're still deranged.

Beckett: I believe that's another of your exaggerations.

Sunny: You just floated the idea of firing your entire staff because I said one person ignored my personal space boundaries and let's not forget how you tried to buy my café out from under me.

Beckett: I never said my approach was conventional and you'd be better off waiting for a bus at this hour than an apology.

Sunny: You were not only not nice to me when we were kids but you were actively hurtful. You and Lance were horrible that summer when I had to wear the helmet because of that super tiny skull fracture.

Beckett: Oh my god.

Beckett: Yeah. Shit. We were horrible.

Beckett: There's no excuse.

Sunny: Now you're getting it.

Beckett: Is that why you go thermonuclear every time I open my mouth?

Sunny: It usually has something to do with the noise coming out of your mouth but yeah, the history doesn't help.

Beckett: To be fair to our deranged, pathetic, hormone-addled minds, you did attach doll hair to that helmet and insist it was your real hair. We were helpless.

Sunny: You used my head as a Nerf gun target.

Beckett: What are you talking about?

Sunny: You guys would hide upstairs and shoot at me whenever I went out in the backyard. And that was the only place I was allowed to go that summer when my parents were at work. Because of the skull fracture.

Beckett: Shit.

Beckett: Would it help if I apologized?

Sunny: We've already established that you have no interest in apologizing so let's not pretend this gesture would be anything other than an end to the conversation.

Beckett: I'm not going to apologize for wanting to get rid of someone who, as you stated, can't respect personal space. We've been over the matter of buying your building backward and forward. Let's be done with that, please.

Sunny: I can't promise I won't bring it up again in the future because it was an expert-level dick move but yeah, sure, we can be done with it.

Beckett: I'd like to apologize for the inexcusable things I did all those years ago.

Sunny: When you say you'd like to apologize, I assume that means the maintenance crew will be out bright and early tomorrow?

Beckett: It means that if I could go back and punch my teenage self in the teeth, I would. I am sorry.

Sunny: Did you really like the cookies or was that a mistake too?

Beckett: I liked the cookies very much.

Sunny: That part wasn't a mistake? You don't have any regrets about the cookies?

Beckett: I stand by everything I said tonight.

Sunny: So...the maintenance crew won't be coming?

Beckett: Not unless you have an urgent need but I'm going to send my security company out to see about getting a system installed so you don't blame me the next time a raccoon goes wild on your precious flowerpots.

Sunny: It was not a raccoon.

Beckett: Tell yourself what you want, Sunny. Whatever it takes to keep you from yelling your ass off at me.

Sunny: I don't yell.

Beckett: You do and you get this wicked gleam in your eye when you do it like you're about to start blowing things up with your mind.

Sunny: Now who's exaggerating?

A minute went by without a response from Beckett. Then another. I flipped through my social media apps before rereading the text thread. By now, fifteen minutes separated me from the last message sent.

Maybe he was busy with whatever he usually did at one thirty in the morning. Maybe he'd fallen asleep. Or maybe—and most likely—this was how Beckett ended conversations. He wasn't one for hello or goodbye as it was, and I couldn't imagine him caring whether I was waiting on a response.

Or maybe he was with someone.

That thought sank in my stomach, murky and thick. And completely unnecessary. It didn't matter to me whether Beckett was in bed with someone. He was welcome to it. I didn't care. It was none of my business.

Except for the spike of curiosity that tempted me to ask what—or who—he was doing tonight. *Gahhhhhh.* Why was I like this? He'd confirmed—*twice!*—that the moment we shared was a mistake so why did I care? Why did I let myself be curious about his private life? I'd learned exactly zero lessons from today's experiences.

The phone buzzed with a notification and I woke up both dogs as I bumbled it out of my hands and it smacked against the hardwood floor.

"Sorry, sorry. Nothing to worry about," I said to them.

When I'd retrieved my phone and settled back against the pillows, I swiped open the message.

> Beckett: You should be in bed.

> Sunny: I am in bed.

> Beckett: For fuck's sake, Sunny.

> Sunny: What?

> Beckett: You should be asleep.

> Sunny: I'm getting there.

> Beckett: Are you going to tell me who it was? Who bothered you tonight?

Sunny: I don't want to get anyone fired. Assholes are allowed to have jobs.

Beckett: I'll find out. I have my sources.

Sunny: I bet you do.

Beckett: Good night, Sunny.

Sunny: Good night, Beckett.

chapter ten

Beckett

Today's Special:
A Brûlée of Apples Fallen from a Far-Off Tree

"YOU SHOULD PUT TOGETHER a short list of schools," I called to Parker as I surveyed the house siding. "Some top choices and a few safeties. Then you can figure out what you'll need to do in order to be a competitive candidate. I'm sure I can find a consultant to help with the process if you'd like."

He emerged from the garage, an orange surfboard tucked under his arm and a backpack over one shoulder. "That doesn't sound like something I'd want to do on the first beach day of the season but thanks anyway."

He pulled the garage door shut and the entire structure creaked like it was about to collapse. Not unlike the rest of my parents' house. I added "garage" to the list of urgent renovations.

The most cost-effective renovation would involve knocking this place down and starting over though my mother would hate that. If she found her way back here.

When. When she found her way back here. *If* was not an option for us. She'd come home and my life would resume. That was the only way.

"If not today," I said as Parker strapped the board to the roof of his car, "soon. You don't have much time to waste."

"Time is a social construct." He tossed his backpack through the open car window. "It cannot be wasted. It simply is."

I stared at the roof. Moss grew in a few shady spots. Shingles were missing in others. I clicked my pen and added it to the list.

"Okay, but—*fuck*," I called, tripping over yet another garden gnome. These fucking things were everywhere. Gnomes and grass-stained baseballs. *Everyfuckingwhere*. One of these days, I was going to break my neck and then everyone would have to solve their own damn problems. "You need to get going on that list."

Parker flashed a peace sign and dropped into the driver's seat. "Don't wait up."

"Where are you going?"

He gestured to the surfboard. "Surfing."

"Yeah, I got that," I called. "Where?"

"The ocean."

I rolled my eyes. "Could you be a little more specific?"

Parker draped both arms over the steering wheel and let out a long sigh. "I recognize that you're in this strangely parental role but you of all people should understand that I haven't had any conventional super-vision in a solid decade and I don't need any now. Don't invent prob-lems for yourself when we have enough for everyone to have second and third helpings."

"Okay," I managed. "Don't forget you're working tonight."

"Maybe." Parker shrugged. "Say hi to Dad for me."

I watched him back out of the pitted, pot-holed driveway and added that to my list too.

THE DRIVE to the federal detention center where my father was being held took ninety-seven minutes and I rehashed last night's conversations with Sunny for every one of them. I wanted to know who the hell had bothered her but I'd have to source that information elsewhere.

I was beginning to understand the mix of cold shoulders and hellfire she sent my way. Not that I could blame her. I didn't remember my teenage days with much clarity but I'd hurt her and the details didn't matter.

Then I'd gone and put an offer in on her building and made sure she knew that almost kissing her was definitely a mistake.

Of course she hated me.

But also, she didn't.

I didn't know whether she was a natural flirt or she was aiming that energy at me for a reason. Regardless of the origin, I was powerless in the face of those evil grins and those smart-ass comments. All she had to do was smile and tell me to go to hell, and I was fucked.

Considering I was already fucked in forty different ways, I didn't really have the time or brain space to let Sunny finish the job.

But I wanted it—even if my best friend would drown me in the cove for so much as suggesting that I was aware of his sister as a woman.

Lance wasn't protective or violent in any spectacular way but he was linear. Friends existed in one box, family in another, and he didn't manage blurred lines too well. He'd turn into a human error message if he found out his best friend was involved with his sister and he'd stay that way until we stopped being involved.

Which we would, and sooner than later.

My life was not in Friendship, Rhode Island. I'd stay as long as my family needed me, but I was pulling together contingency plans for the oyster company and Parker in the event that I couldn't find some resolution to this situation before the end of summer. Even if Lance wasn't part of my mental calculus, flirtation was as far as it could go with Sunny. Flirtation and driving me fuck-all crazy while she walked in front of forklifts and verbally assaulted me while the entire kitchen watched.

This was the way it had to be and it would be fine. It was always fine.

There was no other option.

———

"YOU WOULDN'T BELIEVE ALL the characters I've met in here," Dad said.

Everyone was a character in my father's world. It was always "that guy's one helluva character" and "what a funny character that one is!" and "would you get a load of this character over here?" and most people enjoyed being one of his characters. He was good at engaging with people and noticing the little things that made them unique.

So, of course he'd find himself a cast of characters while in jail. Nothing about that should've surprised me and yet I hadn't expected him to face incarceration with this much enthusiasm. It was like I'd shipped him off to summer camp and now he was brimming with stories about his exciting new friends from all over the country.

"Yeah, I bet," I said, motioning for Adrian to get started.

"I don't mind it," Dad went on, leaning back in his chair and lacing his fingers together over the front of his gray jumpsuit. "I'd rather be back home of course but this isn't bad as far as adventures go."

Summer camp. Seriously.

I rubbed my forehead. This was not an adventure. It was not another one of his journeys bred from naïveté and happenstance. We weren't hitting the open road in the old RV. It was the possibility of decades in prison and—once again—leaving me as the only adult in the room.

"I met a fella who used to be a trail guide through the Appalachians. The stories he can tell! You wouldn't believe it!"

Adrian tapped a stack of papers on the metal table. "Yeah? What's he in for?"

Dad gave that familiar shrug, the one that said he was unbothered by such details. "They say he's a serial killer but he really is the nicest fella I've met in here."

And that, my friends, was why my dad was in jail. Even when the facts stared him in the face, he turned his back to pay closer attention to his shiny, glimmering characters.

It was the reason I'd toilet trained Decker and managed the family finances by the time I was ten.

"We should get started," Adrian said. "We have a lot to get through." He spread documents out on the table, each marked with highlights and annotations. He added a few photos and diagrams until every inch of the surface was covered. "This is the core of the prosecution's case and, at this point, it's mostly circumstantial. But it's the kind of circumstantial that could cruise to a conviction."

"Well, that won't happen," Dad said.

I rubbed my temples. I didn't have a headache but I was certain one would find me before the end of this visit. "Let's hear what Adrian has to say before jumping to any conclusions."

Dad shrugged. "If you say so but I know the truth."

"Listen, Rabbit." Adrian slipped into his *I'll charge you extra for wasting my time* tone. "I need you to explain some of this evidence from your perspective so I can argue it. I need you to tell me why it doesn't hold water because a jury won't care if you're a friendly guy who swears the charges are bogus. They won't care that everyone loves you and they all say you're as honest as they come. They'll care that the prosecution has a motherfucking mountain of evidence that seems to point directly at you."

My father—born Roger but baptized Rabbit by the Guns N' Roses roadies who'd become our extended family in the years we'd traveled with the band and lived on the road—studied the papers for a long moment. Eventually, he said, "As long as we're finished by lunch. I'm supposed to talk to that Appalachian fella about his favorite trails today."

Adrian laughed to himself before tapping his finger against a document. "Let's start here. On this day, the restaurant received a delivery of lobsters and, according to this invoice, paid the vendor in cash on the spot. This is the first time any vendor had been paid in cash with the exception of small purchases using petty cash. From this point forward, the lobsterman was always paid in cash and the amounts increased exponentially without any correlating increase in market prices or volume. The prosecution will argue this was the start of the money laundering activities. My job is to dismantle that argument piece by piece and your job is to give me as much information to do that as possible."

My father scratched the back of his neck. "I can't tell you how much lobster we went through. Or what it cost. But that lobsterman is one helluva character."

For the next two hours, Adrian walked through each document and image, detailing the ways it would be used to implicate my father and the holes he intended to poke in the evidence. Dad didn't say much. By design, he didn't know the inner workings of the oyster company. I'd made sure of that right from the start. Where Uncle Buckthorne had seen his nephew as a jack-of-all-trades and my mom as a get-it-done powerhouse, I'd known that putting my parents in charge of a multifaceted business would result in its complete destruction within a year.

But now that meant my father couldn't answer basic questions about the day-to-day operations of the business he'd inherited. He knew the patrons and their families like they were his own, but he had no idea why several employees were taking their wages in cash or whether bar expenses on certain nights were ten, twenty, even fifty times higher than the same point in time years prior.

"We can work with this," Adrian assured me, holding out a hand to quell my rising frustration. "We can take depositions from a hundred people who will all attest that Rabbit isn't the numbers guy, isn't the logistics guy. He's the face of Small Point and we'll build on that. He didn't know this was going on because why the hell would he know? He's not in the back office, cranking out numbers and counting cash. He's the heart and everyone knows it."

"I'd argue Sandy is the heart," Dad offered.

"I get what you're saying and I think you get what I'm saying," Adrian replied.

"I'm fortunate enough to get what everyone is saying," I muttered.

Ignoring me, Adrian continued. "Like I told your son, unless they come up with video and audio of you carrying a takeout bag full of counterfeit cash to one of those lobster boats, they don't have a smoking gun."

"But they have the sound of the gunshot and a body with a bullet in it," I said.

Adrian nodded. "Yeah. That's a fair assessment."

Dad swept another gaze over the documents, his brow furrowed and his lips turning down into a frown. He looked closely at some of them, pausing to read and putting them on the table again with a shake of his head. He was quiet for several minutes and I prayed the gravity of this was beginning to settle on his shoulders.

Then—"I'll tell the judge I didn't have any part in this and I'm sure they'll see it's all a big misunderstanding."

Adrian cut a glance in my direction while I blinked at Dad. Once he decided something, there was no shaking him from it. On any other day, it was a great quality. He told the truth and believed in his bones that everyone else did too. He was as loyal as a golden retriever and his values were ironclad. But it spiraled into a real problem when his beliefs clashed with reality.

"It will be more complex than simply stating your innocence," Adrian said. "As we discussed when we went through all of this, we'll have to refute the prosecution's entire case."

"That's why my smart boy hired you," Dad said. "You're more than capable, I'm certain of it. You already have a fancy schmancy plan cooked up too. Now it's a matter of putting it into action."

I pulled out my phone to distract myself from the cold, sinking sensation in my gut. I really needed to get those contingency plans lined up.

THE MINUTE I turned off Market Street toward the oyster company, I knew many things were wrong. The Twisted Barn Breweries truck sat directly in front of Naked Provisions' entrance. Despite the hell I'd promised to rain down on Twisted Barn if they blocked the café again, this was the least troubling of the issues I'd cataloged by the time I climbed out of the car.

The presence of multiple firetrucks and police vehicles was a big concern but there were also two dozen people milling around the parking lot, and they were all soaking wet.

Not *caught in a sun shower* wet but *walked into the ocean* wet. And everything around me was wet. Cars, firetrucks, Naked's front windows.

By comparison, SPOC was dry and unscathed.

"What the actual fuck," I muttered to myself as I headed for the café.

When I made my way around the beer truck, I found Muffy sweeping a ripple of water out Naked's main door. Behind her, Meara and Bethany sloshed through ankle-deep water to carry a table outside and stack it alongside a half dozen chairs. I didn't see Sunny. Maybe she wasn't in yet. Hopefully.

I tugged off my necktie before setting to work on rolling up my cuffs. "What the hell happened here?"

Muffy pushed another wave out the door. It was dark inside, the lights off. "Your beer dude clipped the fire hydrant." Her glare sliced through me. "The good news is the water pressure is strong as hell. The bad news is a tidal wave came right through the front door and we're going to have to shut down for the rest of the day."

I hooked two chairs under one arm, two more under the other, and followed the women outside. "You don't have to shut down," I said, going back for one of the remaining tables.

Muffy scoffed. "That's nice of you to say, but unless you have your minions here with a quickness and I manage to resuscitate today's entire menu based on whatever we didn't lose in the tsunami *and* get the cops out of here, I don't think—"

"You."

I pivoted toward her voice. I didn't know how it was possible but I'd know Sunny's voice in a dark, crowded room and it wouldn't even take me that long to find her.

"You and your beer person! And your fucking fire hydrant!"

Sunny advanced on me and I was thankful for the tabletop flattened against my torso because she looked like she wanted to reach into my chest and rip out my vital organs.

"He's calling minions," Muffy said with a meaningful glance toward me. "They'll be here very soon."

"I don't care about minions." She had her long skirt gathered at her knees and held in place with a thick rubber band. "Everything was beautiful chaos and perfect imperfection until you showed up and now we have been flooded and ransacked and flowerpot-destructed! We were wonderful and dry before you came along and tried to buy the building!"

"We said that was in the past," I yelled.

"You said that," she cried. "I said I'd bring it up in the future because you're an expert-level dick! Guess what? It's the future and your fire hydrant exploded on us."

"I really do not think we can blame him for the location of the fire hydrant." Muffy pointed out the window, toward the police cruisers. "Considering that beer dude is submitting to a *second* field sobriety test right now, I'm not sure we can pin this one on Beckett."

"I don't care." As Sunny spoke, the dogs circled her, nudging her legs and whining as they went. "I want my happy accidents back. I'm done with the disasters."

"Babe," Meara said, wading toward her, "we need to get you away from all these flashing lights. I know the firefighters are hot but we don't want to have to call them in here for you."

"I'm all right," Sunny argued. The dogs continued fussing. The chocolate Lab bit at her skirt, trying to tug her to the floor.

I glanced back at the firetrucks and police vehicles. Those lights. They'd trigger a seizure—if she wasn't already on her way to one.

"Get her out of here," I barked. "Go to the office or patio. *Now.*"

"Do not come in here and tell me what to do," Sunny roared. "I do not need—"

I put the table down and crossed the narrow space toward her. "If you think for one second that I won't pick you up and carry you out of here, you're dead wrong and I fucking dare you to test me."

Meara looped her arm around Sunny's waist and pulled her backward. "As much as I'd like to see that," she said, "we've had enough drama for today. Come along, babe."

I pulled my phone out and tapped Rainey's number while Meara guided Sunny into the windowless office behind the kitchen. The call went straight to voicemail and I hung up. It took everything inside me to stay here when I wanted to follow them into that office and rage at her about taking better care of herself. This was out of hand and she knew it. She *had* to know it.

But I also wanted to go in there and rest her head on my lap and tell her I'd keep her safe as long as she needed, and that confused the hell out of me. If I was being honest, *that* was the reason I couldn't tear my feet away from this floor. I could vent my frustrations at her for a few minutes and risk nothing, but offering her comfort would change everything.

It would also prove that I was a goddamn liar because the only mistake I'd made was that I hadn't kissed her last night. Even if it upended everything, complicated everything, ruined everything.

"So about those minions," Muffy said. "Sooner would be a lot better than later, if the offer still stands."

"Yeah," I said, still staring at the office door.

"Meara will tell us if there's a problem," Muffy said. "We'd know."

"Right." Another moment passed but I couldn't look away. My stomach was on the floor. I had half a mind to yank some of those firefighters in here and send a medic to check on Sunny. "Beth? Can you— would you just make sure—if there's anything or—I don't know. Could you—"

"You got it," she said, splashing down the dark hallway.

I fired off a message to Rainey while keeping one eye on the office door.

"I'm gonna bake bread for you," Muffy said, pushing more water out the door. "Is there a certain kind you like best? Never mind. Everyone loves my sweet oat bread. I'll bake some sweet oat for you and you'll love it."

"You don't have to do that," I said.

"Yeah, I do. My mother has never once allowed anyone to do anything for her without thanking them with copious amounts of food. I don't know if that's a Cape Verdean custom or simply the way she interacts with the world but it's ingrained in me too. As far as I know, the only Scottish custom my dad carries on is an aversion to sunlight."

Bethany peeked her head out of the office and gave a thumbs-up.

My whole body sagged in relief.

"Aside from my obsessive need to acknowledge and appreciate every little thing, you're a nice guy in sneaky, low-key ways and you need some fresh bread for breakfast."

I glanced at her as I hefted another table. "I'm not."

"Yeah," she said, starting another pass with the broom. "I guess you're right. You probably have minions all over town, just waiting around for things to go sideways so they can swoop in and clean it up for you."

I carried the table outside, saying, "Look, Muffy—"

"You probably help out at the cheese store and the burger place too. Right? Since you're not a nice guy and you definitely do not jump in to take care of the people who are important to you, I have to assume you're hauling damp furniture around for everyone." She waved me off when I started to respond. "Don't try to argue with me. I know I'm right."

With that, I moved another table outside. Because she wasn't right.

Not in any way that I was prepared to accept.

chapter eleven
Beckett

Today's Special:
Diver-Caught Desire with Mashed Stress

"WHAT ARE THE ODDS?" Mel asked.

I pressed my palms to my eyes. "I don't fucking know."

"This is the sort of thing your dad would've known. Graduations, school plays, soccer tournaments. He always remembered the most random events. He'd pop into the office to tell us about a pharmaceutical conference in the city or a big book signing convention coming up and how we'd probably have large groups reserving tables at the last minute—and that they'd be rowdy as fuck. He'd be spot-on about it too. I still don't know how he did that."

"And full moons?" I snapped. "We can give him all the credit in the world but I don't think he would've clocked that one." I nodded toward the people gathered around a cauldron—an actual fucking *cauldron*—on the Naked Provisions patio. "Or that our new neighbors would need to celebrate them."

"Please. You know as well as I do that Rabbit would have four new besties in those girls and he'd be hopped up on their cold brew. Hell, he'd be over there with them. Sandy too."

The group had started small—maybe five or six people standing around—but then they'd started a *fire* in that cauldron and it ballooned to more than thirty. This would've been fine, even the goddamn fire, but the wheels were falling off at the oyster company tonight. We were running more than half an hour late on all reservations and the kitchen was taking a short eternity to get orders out, and the delays compounded with each passing hour.

This meant we had sixty increasingly hungry and impatient people packing the area between the oyster company and the moon ritual. Not five minutes went by without someone coming in to ask what was going on over there and why didn't we have picnic tables and drinks outside like we did last summer.

No one told me we had picnic tables and drinks last summer and no one told me there'd be a full moon festival the exact same day as graduation at both Friendship High School and the nearby university, and everyone's wedding anniversary too. No one told me a fucking thing.

"Why didn't Pink Lipstick mention anything about this to you?" I asked Mel.

"You damn well know that Pink Lipstick has a name." Mel scoffed. "And that was a one-time thing, not that it's any of your concern."

"Then you've been buying coffee there twice a day since last weekend because…?"

Mel turned away from the window to face me. "I'm sorry, do we not have an overbooked house full of people requiring the perfect graduation and anniversary evenings? Plus a massive backup in the kitchen, short staff on the floor, *and* girls chanting around a bowl of literal fire? Because I think all of those things are more pressing than where I'm getting my caffeine fix."

I studied the patrons crowded near the front door, silent and sullen as they checked the time on their phones and glared at the purple beverages and moon-sized cookies coming out of Naked. This was going to get much worse before it got better.

"I'm just saying, your *friend* could've mentioned that they'd be open late and—oh, I don't know—having a moon bonfire. If we'd known both places would have overflow tonight, we could've—"

"What, Beck? We could've what? Because short of succeeding in buying the bait shop, I don't see a solution in there." Mel ran a hand down her face. "You have a *friend* too. She has no problem coming over here and telling you how it's gonna be."

Except Sunny wanted nothing to do with me. In the four days since the beer truck debacle—and five days since nearly kissing her—Sunny had been scarce. She hadn't responded to any of my texts checking in and I couldn't ask Lance if she was okay without looping him into this whole situation, and I didn't care to do that.

According to Muffy, who'd delivered five loaves of fresh bread to the door but refused to breathe "shellfish air," as she put it, Sunny had avoided all seizure activity but was still mad that I existed.

I hadn't figured out how to solve that problem for her. Or myself, for that matter.

"We can't watch them throwing stuff into a cauldron all night. What's the plan? What do we do?" An uncomfortable thought crossed my mind, and not for the first time I longed for the cool, sterile quiet of my corner office in the Singapore Financial District. I was *excellent* at my job and I missed that sense of complete competence more than anything in the world. I used to have my shit together. I didn't wake up in a twin-sized bed, wondering whether the incessant *drip-drip-drip* was from the leaky roof, the leaky pipes, the leaky shower, or an altogether new leak I had yet to locate. I didn't argue with vegans or try and fail to set limits with an old-soul teenager, and I didn't resort to shucking oysters to work out my frustration with the whole fucking world. With a groan, I asked, "What would my dad do?"

Mel tipped her head to the side as if those memories only existed off-kilter. "Yeah. That's what we need. Go to the kitchen. See what you can do to move things along in there. I'm gonna start pouring the emergency champagne."

"We have an emergency supply of champagne?"

"The last general manager had a trick or two worth keeping," she said, shooing me away. "One of them was popping the bubbles when the shit hit the fan. Now, go."

The kitchen was humming like a hornet's nest which was great but also terrifying. I ended up expediting orders and jumping in to shuck oysters on the raw bar when they got overwhelmed. Every time I scanned the dining room, I caught sight of Mel floating between tables, armed with a magnum of champagne.

"Good call on the bubbly."

I glanced up from checking an order to find Devon loading dishes onto a tray. "It was Mel's call."

"Well, it was the Hail Mary we needed. I don't know what the hell those weirdos are doing over there but they're a real fucking problem."

I set the ticket down and stared at him for a second. Aside from the basic *hey, how's it going*, Devon and I didn't talk much. This was neither the night nor the topic for us to start. "What, exactly, is the problem with them?"

Devon waved a hand in Naked's direction. "They're fucking up the whole service with this shit! When we finally get guests seated, they're pissed and taking it out on us in shitty tips. It's total bullshit. This is usually one of my best weekends of the year and those woo-woo girls are screwing it all up."

Another server—one of the Emilys or Everleighs—grabbed her order, saying, "If you spent less time complaining to anyone who'd listen and more time keeping the drinks filled, you wouldn't be having that problem."

It was a damn good thing we hired her. Whatever her name was.

"You know I'm right." Devon glared after her. "You know all about it," he said as if we'd shared some confidence on the matter.

I didn't really trust myself to continue this conversation but that didn't stop me from asking, "What is it you think I know?"

"You know they're totally psycho. You've seen it firsthand. You know their whole nice-and-friendly thing is bullshit."

I folded my arms over my chest. "Let me invite you to watch your mouth."

"Hey." Parker sidled up beside me, a warning glint in his eye. "I don't know what's going on but I spotted that throbbing vein in your forehead from across the room."

"*My* mouth? Have you heard the shit that comes out of them?" Devon asked, jabbing a finger toward the café. "Since you don't know, I'll tell you. They're two-faced bitches. They act sweet as can be but they're cold, miserable cunts the minute you turn your back on them." His eyes gleamed as he went on. "You know how it is with them. The little one is always getting in your face like a fucking nag." He shook his head like he was truly exhausted by the café's existence. "Someone needs to shut her up."

I blinked at him as adrenaline spiraled through my body. As much as I wanted to grab him by the throat and throw him off the deck, I had three hundred people in the dining room and an FBI agent parked at the bar. Dunking this asshole in the cove would not help the Loew family reputation. And it needed all the help it could get.

I leaned close to Devon. "Get the fuck out of here. Now."

"So, we're doing this," Parker murmured.

Devon laughed as he lifted the tray. "You have a strange sense of humor, man. What are those girls to you anyway? Everyone knows that coffee place will be out of business by the end of the summer. Believe me, I have it on good authority that it's gonna go down that way. Then you can bulldoze the whole place."

I handed his tray to Parker. "Take this to forty-two," I said without looking away from Devon. "I meant what I said. You're finished here."

"What the fuck?" he sputtered. "What's your deal?"

"There's no deal. You're fired."

It took a second for the words to land, but when they did, fury burned in his eyes. His hands balled at his sides and he squared up as if he was ready to let those fists fly. "Who the fuck do you think you are?"

I brought my hands to my hips. "You know precisely who I am. There's no confusion about that or whether I have the authority to clean this house from top to bottom. Now, you ignored my first recommendation to shut the hell up and that was a mistake of your own choosing. Let's not do that again. You're leaving and you're going to do it without being a misogynistic jackass if you have any intention of ever working in another restaurant on this end of the Atlantic."

I registered too late the quiet in both the dining room and the kitchen. Everyone was staring. Both Zeus and Mel moved toward me, *what the hell* in their eyes. Price stood near the entrance to the kitchen, a hand extended toward a server as if to tell her to stay put.

"It's the middle of the fucking service," Devon said loud enough for all to hear. "Get over yourself and let me get back to my guests."

"What did I just say about that?" I motioned Zeus over. "That won't be happening because I fired you. Zeus is going to walk you out and you aren't going to give him any shit. Take that advice, Devon. It's the last thing you'll get from me."

I wasn't the only one amazed when Devon stalked out of the kitchen without a word. There was plenty of sneering and glaring but at least he was quiet about it.

"Hey." Mel came up beside me. "I'm sure you have some watertight reasons for everything that just occurred in front of all these people and I'm gonna want to hear about it later but I need his tables covered immediately. We're stretched too thin to redistribute and we're cranking as hard as we can so—"

"I'll take them." I reached for the dishes now waiting on the pass. I didn't know where they were going but I'd figure it out just like everything else in this damn place.

"Are you sure you can do this without inviting anyone to fuck off?" Mel asked. "Because I feel like that's where you're at right now."

"I got it." I met Parker's gaze from across the room. He rolled his eyes and made a jerk-off motion, which allowed for many interpretations. He'd have to explain that one to me back at home. "Maybe I'll finally learn a thing or two."

THE EVENING FLEW by but it was the longest service I'd ever worked at the oyster company—and that was saying something because I'd worked a whole lot of nights in this place.

It was late, about an hour after seeing our last party out the door, but I had a cold beer and sales reports to keep me company while my mind unwound the day. Mel had left with an empty threat about never returning and Chef had yelled at me in French for ten minutes between gulps of Bordeaux. I was this close to asking how his parents were doing back home on the ranch in Montana, where he was known as Bart and had grown up speaking English, but I'd chosen enough violence for the day.

There was a knock on the window and it took me a long second to swivel toward the sound. Sunny waved and motioned for me to join her on the covered deck ringing the restaurant on three sides.

I closed my laptop and grabbed the beer. If I was going another round with Sunny, I required fortification.

I stepped outside and immediately appreciated the fresh evening air. It was a perfect June night.

"I want to apologize," she said, her words spoken as if she'd practiced them a hundred times. She dropped into a chair. Forced a smile. Reached in and twisted my stomach into a knot. "We didn't expect such a huge turnout for the full moon ceremony, and we didn't plan on it running so late." She spread her hands over the table and I got the impression she was working hard at staying on-script. "I know it made things complicated for you tonight and I'm sorry. We'll do better at communicating our evening events to you in advance."

I sat across from her and sipped my beer. "Can I ask, respectfully, what the fuck a full moon ceremony is?"

She laughed and I'd swear the sound electrified the night. At the very least it electrified me. "It's all about setting intentions and charging your crystals and burning your shit."

I bobbed my head. "Right. Of course."

She tucked some hair behind her ear and glanced away. "From what I hear, you burned some shit of your own tonight."

"I don't know what that means."

She hit me with an indulgent smile as she propped her feet on the chair beside me. Her toenails were painted blue like the Caribbean. I wanted to scoop her up and shift her feet to my lap so I could run my hands up her legs. I also wanted to understand where the fuck those thoughts were coming from so I could attach them to a rocket and shoot them into outer space.

"You fired someone mid-service. Devon, was it?" When I nodded, she went on with a wide, knowing smile. "Good call."

I watched her for a second until understanding cracked like an egg over my head. "He was the one who bothered you?"

She shrugged in a way that could mean anything. "Is there any chance you broke the lock on our dumpster this morning? Or late last night? Have you been playing with crowbars, Beckett?"

I was too tired to respond with any heat. "No, Sunny, I did not."

"Yeah." She hummed to herself. "I didn't think so."

"Could've been kids," I said.

Nodding, she said, "Very possible. Or those notorious raccoons are wielding tools now."

I pulled out my phone and scrolled through the motion-sensitive alerts from last night. Save for a couple of coyotes and some of the large birds that nested around the cove, I didn't see anything remarkable. I added a reminder to my running list about installing more surveillance cameras. The items above that read *set up a meeting with Parker's guidance counselor, schedule medical and dental visits for Parker, find Parker's vaccination records, passport for Parker.*

I was so fucking behind on everything. It was a wonder this kid was still alive. And that he had any teeth.

"So, what do you do for fun?" she asked.

I stared at her through a sip of my beer. "Why aren't you yelling at me? Isn't that how we do this dance? I don't know what to do with you when you're not yelling."

She lifted a bare shoulder. It didn't seem like she owned shirts with sleeves much in the way she didn't seem to have any skirts cut above the ankle. Maddening. "You're going to have to figure it out."

"Is this some kind of cease-fire? I'd say surrender but I don't get the impression you do much of that."

"Ah. He's learning." That sadistic grin appeared. "Just answer the question."

"Living in Singapore was pretty fun."

"I'll grant you some leeway there but I asked what you *do* for fun."

I studied the beer label. "I...I do fun things."

She rolled her hand for me to elaborate. "For example?"

"At the moment, I'm managing an oyster bar, parenting a teenager —badly, I should note—and buying a criminal defense attorney several summer homes. If that's not fun, I'm going to need a review of the definition."

She leaned back, crossed her arms over her chest. "Ah. You're one of them."

"One of who, storm cloud?"

Her lips tipped up as if she enjoyed the nickname. "One of those people who think adventure is ordering the soup of the day instead of the reliable favorite. That spontaneity is hitting shuffle on the playlist. Someone who believes living somewhere interesting is the same as experiencing everything that place has to offer."

"That is"—I would *not* give her the satisfaction of reading me like a book—"some very profound armchair psychology. If carrot juice doesn't work out for you, I'm sure the FBI has an opening on the profiling team. I can ask Agent Price when he tucks me into bed tonight."

Sunny reached across the table and picked up my beer bottle. She took a long pull. I gripped the armrests to keep myself from leaning in close to study the way her throat bobbed. She set it down and took a moment to look me over. I felt the warm lick of her attention everywhere. "Let yourself live a little. You're not going to get another chance."

I stared at the bottle. *Fuck it.* I knocked it back, draining the contents. "Did you get that pearl of wisdom from your moon worship event?"

Before she could respond, Muffy bounded toward us. "Hey," she said, slightly out of breath. She pushed her glasses up her nose. "Saffire and Gayathri asked me to hang with them tonight at an art installation in Providence and—"

"Go," Sunny urged. "Have fun!"

Muffy glanced between us. "I can wait a little while if you need some time to finish up before I take you home."

Sunny waved her off. "Don't worry. I'll figure something out."

"I'm not leaving you to *figure something out* at this hour," Muffy said.

"I'll take her home."

"Beckett saves the day once again," Muffy said. She turned a stiff smile on Sunny as she passed a woven basket to her. "Isn't that great? Here. I got your things ready."

"I cannot believe you orchestrated this," Sunny said, all trace of our strangely amiable conversation gone as she snatched the basket and slumped back in the chair. "I'd rather walk through haunted woods and hope the full moon falls in my favor than go home with this guy."

I couldn't help it. I belted out a laugh so hard I almost knocked my chair over.

Sunny gave me a bland look. "What's wrong with you?"

"Sounds like a conversation y'all should conduct in private." Muffy backed away. "Good night! Text me when y'all get home to tell me you haven't killed each other."

Sunny grumbled as Muffy disappeared into the night. Again, I found myself noticing that the shadows cast by the café nearly consumed two sides of Naked Provisions in complete darkness. "You really need to invest in better exterior lighting."

She followed my gaze. "You might be right but that's not a conversation I can have with you tonight."

I pushed to my feet and held up a hand. "I'm going inside to lock up. Don't get any ideas about the woods."

Not waiting for her to respond, I headed in to the restaurant to grab my laptop and turn off the last of the lights. When I returned to the deck, she was right where I'd left her. It was a small miracle.

"Come on, storm cloud. I don't have all night."

Sunny stared up at me. Eventually, she said, "I'm only agreeing to this because there are no on-demand car services in this area and Meara picked me up this morning so I don't have my bike."

"Like I'd let you ride a bike home at this hour."

She arched a brow. "You don't have any say in whether I ride a bike in the middle of the night or not."

"Yeah, that comes as a real fucking shock." I motioned for her to stand. She didn't move a muscle. "As I've mentioned before, I have no problem picking you up so unless you want me tossing you in the back seat of my SUV, I suggest you get moving."

She considered this for an eternity, her gaze skimming over the inky surface of the cove as she drummed her fingers on the armrest. Then, without so much as a glance in my direction, she hooked the basket in the crook of her arm and strolled toward the parking lot.

I studied the sky, muttering to myself, "She is nothing short of impossible."

"Did you just call me short?"

"No," I said, following after her. "But even if I did, it wouldn't be inaccurate."

"Yeah, Beckett. That is an excellent point," she drawled.

We settled into the car in silence but I was immediately and uncomfortably aware of her mellow, earthy scent. It was green and organic, like a garden or a bunch of fresh herbs, and it wrapped around my throat and clouded my vision. I gripped the wheel hard and my fingers squeaked against the leather.

When I turned onto Market Street, I knew I'd die if we didn't break this silence soon. This was what Sunny did to me. Whenever she was around, she generated all this energy inside me and it grew and grew until we found something new to argue about—or I lost my mind and almost kissed her.

I didn't have enough steam in me to fight tonight and it didn't matter whether I wanted to—I couldn't kiss her. Or even come close. "What's with the basket?"

"The—what?"

I poked a finger toward the basket on her lap, the one holding a water bottle, several zip pouches, one of Naked's bakery bags, and a few other things I couldn't identify. "The basket."

"It's a palm leaf tote. I bought it from an incredibly talented collective of weavers in Dhaka."

"You—you've been to Bangladesh?"

"I have."

When she didn't elaborate, I asked, "When? And what were you doing there? And how——"

She glanced at me, her eyes narrowed and her expression tight. "I've been to a lot of places, Beckett. I enjoy traveling. Many people do."

I stopped at a light. "Lance didn't mention that."

"And he didn't tell me you lived in Singapore. Let's accept that my brother is not the best source of information on anyone other than himself. Even that could use some improvement."

"No shit." I laughed as the light turned. "I only knew he'd moved in with Chantal because she answered his phone once when he was in the shower."

"*He moved in with Chantal?*" she cried. "When?"

"End of last year? I don't know. He's shit with specifics. I don't know how he holds down a job."

"Believe me, I have the same questions. I was heading up to Alaska and Canada last summer, and planned two days in San Francisco to visit him. When I asked for his address, he just said the Mission District. Like it was self-explanatory or I should have some internal navigation system to deliver me to his front door."

"Sounds like Lance." I passed the high school, a shiny new multi-level structure in place of the low-ceilinged relic we'd attended. "May I ask—without you unhinging your jaw and biting my entire head off—why you don't bring the dogs with you every day?"

Because it was stressing me the fuck out.

She fiddled with the items in her basket for a moment. I didn't care what she called the thing, it was a basket. "Do you remember when you and Lance teased me about not being able to do anything alone and how I couldn't even go to the bathroom without a dog watching me?"

I stifled a groan. "I remember being an asshole and I'll apologize again for that."

"Past tense?"

"I-I'd like to think so."

"What about all the times when I was on a highly restricted diet and you guys would gorge on candy? Do you have any idea how much worse that made it for me?"

"To be fair, that one was mostly Lance—"

"You were there too!"

"Okay, yes, you're right," I said. "I was there. I gorged on the candy. I didn't tell him to stop terrorizing you. I'm sorry. I shouldn't have let him be such a fool."

"The problem with your apologies is that I have to accept them and that's kind of a bummer because I've built up a nice little iceberg of resentment toward you."

"Yeah, that must be terrible." I turned into her neighborhood. "Do you have an iceberg of resentment for Lance?"

She tapped at the smartwatch on her wrist. After a moment, she said, "I've had a long time to work through Lance's iceberg. You scowled your way back into my life last month. There's a difference."

I nodded. I'd have to accept that. "So? Why are Jem and Scout at home when they could've been worshipping the moon and Satan and whatever the fuck else you did tonight?"

"I don't need to worship Satan. She's already on my side."

"You say that as if I'm not already well the fuck aware of your sadistic tendencies, storm cloud."

She continued digging around in the basket and I heard the jangle of keys. "My epilepsy is much better controlled now than it was twenty years ago. When you knew me, it was really bad. Seizures all the time, injuries all the time. No warnings, no control. It took *years* to get the meds right and keep them calibrated as I grew and developed. But it's different now. I know my triggers and the best ways to respond to them. I can go months without so much as a prodrome or an aura. I can travel and work and even clean up after a flood without flying into a full-out episode. I'm more in control of it now." She pointed at her wrist. "Constantly tracking vitals helps predict patterns and alerts me to when my body is dysregulated, in case I don't notice. And I don't need around-the-clock supervision like I did when I was a kid. If I fall, my watch calls emergency services when I don't respond within a certain amount of time. But I haven't fallen in years. It's kind of disappointing to the dogs. They like riding to the rescue."

I pulled up in front of Lance's childhood home, a small Cape Cod with gray shingles and a bold red door. "But you still have service dogs. *Two* of them."

"The German shepherd is something of a rescue. Jem flunked service dog school. He can alert and intervene if I have an episode but he has little interest in meeting most of the behavioral requirements."

"You figured, what's one more member of the security detail?"

"Pretty much. Scout likes having a friend. Or, more specifically, someone to boss around." She glanced at the house. Red flowers spilled out of the window boxes. "Thanks for the ride."

"Anytime."

She closed her hand around the door handle but didn't push it open. "Another thing."

"Yeah?"

She glanced in my direction and then back to the house. "I've spent *my whole life* being treated like an issue. My parents, my doctors, they'd all talk over me, talk around me like I was nothing more than a passive ball of irregular electrical activity."

I watched as she climbed out, her long skirt swirling around her as she settled the basket on her arm. She paused, blinking at me.

"There is nothing more upsetting to me than being treated like a diagnosis. You might think you're doing the right thing by insisting on dragging me away from a trigger but I am the only one who decides what I can and cannot handle. Don't ever do that to me again."

"I won't. I'm sorry."

She gave a hesitant nod like she didn't trust my words. "You can go now."

"Get in the house, storm cloud."

"You're not waiting until I get inside. That's ridiculous."

"Tough shit." I shrugged. "You're lucky I'm not walking you to the damn door."

I'd thought about it but I knew I'd do something I'd regret if I went up there with her.

Shaking her head, she stomped up the front steps and unlocked the door. The dogs crowded around her, each jostling for her attention. She glanced back at me, waved.

I looked ahead and drove away.

chapter twelve

Sunny

Today's Special:
An Array of Freshly Foraged Mushrooms

"THIS WAY," I said to Jem, directing him to the back door. Jem was up for any adventure while Scout was perfectly content to continue sleeping under the desk in the office. "I'm not going out there alone."

I didn't mind closing, not even when we had special events that ran late—or, in tonight's case, a meeting of a local writers' group—but we'd had enough weird incidents around here that I'd succeeded in spooking myself. I knew I didn't have anything to be worried about but it put my mind at ease to have a growly German shepherd by my side when it was time to close up the outdoor area for the night.

The day had been blisteringly hot and only the bravest of souls had ventured outside to eat on the patio. Still, I had to take one more pass and drop some scraps in the compost bin before we could head home.

"Do me a favor and scare off any rogue raccoons. They might have tools," I said.

Jem sniffed the air and gave me a glance that seemed to doubt my concerns about the wildlife. But then his ears pricked up and he took one step toward the dock ramp, a low growl rumbling out of him.

I really, *really* did not want to meet the reason for that growl, not even with the growler by my side and a bucket of apple cores and carrot tops in hand.

Jem growled once more—and then the squawking started. My dog advanced another step and I mentally kicked myself for not listening to Beckett about getting more lights installed out here. SPOC was already closed for the night. Tuesdays were often slower for them and only the masochists wanted to sit on the deck and slurp raw seafood in this weather.

WITHOUT WARNING, Jem wagged his tail and bounded toward the ramp. I realized then that the squawking was a painful rendition of an old Britney Spears song and the source of the noise was surprisingly human.

Jem stopped at the top of the ramp, tail flying and tongue lolling as he waited for me. "This is going to be great," I muttered.

He barreled down the ramp ahead of me. I found him lapping the face of Parker Loew, who happened to be starfished on the dock.

It was worth noting that my primary reason for adopting Jem along with Scout was that he treated every rescue situation as a game. As far as I was concerned, if I was going to wipe out in the middle of a grocery store, I wanted a dog that enjoyed every damn minute of it.

This was also part of the behavioral issues that led to him failing his service dog tests. Fortunately for me, Jem's behavioral issues had him pounding on Parker's chest like the kid required resuscitation.

"Down, boy, down," Parker yelped between full-face slobbers and paw chest compressions.

I snapped my fingers and Jem retreated to my side but he was thrilled with himself for coming to Parker's aid. There was nothing better than a smiling dog.

"No one told me the party was down here," I said.

Jem thumped his tail in time with the music playing on Parker's phone. I spied a backpack and a half-empty bottle of tequila beside him.

"What do you think is worse?" he asked, the words slip'n'sliding together. "Not knowing what to do with your life or not knowing why you keep getting dumped? Or not knowing what happens when you die?"

"Oh, honey." I set the bucket down and offered him a hand. He had the same long, angular body as Beckett at that age, all knobby knees and knife-sharp cheekbones. Parker had let his hair grow into a curly mop, which was nothing like Beckett's preference for everything in an orderly fashion. "You can tell me all about it inside."

With Parker sandwiched between me and Jem—who was excellent at keeping wobbly people upright, just ask me how I knew—we slowly made our way to the top of the ramp. He insisted on dumping the compost bucket for me and even made some Beckett-like grumbles when I tried to wave him off. It was funny how that gruff insistence was baked into the Loew boys.

Once the compost was sorted, Parker flung himself into a chair inside the café, his entire torso sprawled over the table. I set a big glass of cucumber water in front of him and busied myself with straightening up one more time. "What's the story, friend? What were you trying to find at the bottom of that tequila bottle?"

"There are days when I feel like I know what I'm doing," Parker started, his head in his hands, "and then there are days when the universe tells me I know fuck-all about anything."

"Yes. I think that's the trouble with being aware of yourself and the world around you. I don't think it ever goes away," I said. "What happened today?"

"I just—" He shook his head, rolled his eyes at the ceiling. "First things first, I got dumped, which was fantastic. Then I had to pick classes for next year, and everyone acts like I'm supposed to know what I want and where I'm going in life. Like, how the hell should I know, at seventeen years old, whether I want to take calculus, which would open me up to take an assload of classes in college, or statistics, which doesn't do shit for college but actually sounds useful? And how should I know if I want to take four years of a foreign language? I don't know where I'm going or what I'm doing. I can't plan around the grab bag of requirements at all these different colleges. Fuck, I don't even know if I want to go to college."

He chugged half of the water and set it down with a thud loud enough to draw the attention of both dogs away from the broken peanut butter and jelly cookies I was feeding them from today's discards.

"You know who does want me to go to college?" he asked, stabbing a finger in my direction. "Fuckin' Beck."

I loved that. I wanted to change his contact in my phone to "Fuckin' Beck" because it was so accurate.

"He has *consultants* and *coaches*, and this whole big thing about making lists and visiting schools. This morning he hands me a printed-out page from a *spreadsheet* and tells me he has friends who are alumni at all these universities. He can schedule calls with them so I can ask questions about the schools." Parker tried to slap the tabletop but his hand went wide and he ended up connecting with his thigh. It sounded like it hurt. "*Schedule calls*. What would I even ask these people? 'Hey man, what's the food situation there?' What did I do to give him the impression I wanted conference calls in my life?"

"It's his love language," I said. "He means well."

"He means to give me a mental breakdown." He dropped his head into his hands again.

I nodded. I understood the tension of Beckett wanting to solve every problem he encountered, and everyone else's desire to exist without that kind of interference. Or conference calls. "He tends to give and help to the max, and ask questions later. If at all."

"You're right. That's the shitty part. Not that *you're* right but that the explanation is obvious." Parker drained the last of the water and burped loudly. Scout put her head in his lap. "Sorry for dropping all of my problems on you like that. I should've asked if you were up for it first."

I wiped down the counter and started reorganizing the Sharpie jar. "I would've said so if I wasn't."

Parker nodded and spent a minute scratching Scout's head. "Is there any way you could drop me off? Or drop me in the general vicinity of my house? The cops like to stop kids who are out late at night, and let's just say"—he cut the kind of nervous look at his backpack that yelled *I've got some real shit in here*—"we have enough legal trouble in my family right now."

I swallowed a laugh. This kid was too much. "It's on my way."

GETTING Parker into my Jeep was far more physically demanding than I'd expected. He tripped over his feet on the way out the door and spent five solid minutes cry-laughing while the dogs slobbered all over him. Then he was certain he was going to vomit, and since that wasn't going to happen in my car, we leaned against the bumper until it passed, at which point he admitted to mixing some magic mushrooms with his liquor.

There was a moment where I doubted those mushrooms were of the hallucinogenic variety but then he insisted the passenger seat was made of soft-serve ice cream and the highlights in my hair were sunbeams giving off UV light.

Parker ran his fingers over my hair as I drove, saying, "I wouldn't admit this to anyone else but it's kind of nice not having my parents around. Even though I love them—I *love* them, Sunny—it's like they're always running with scissors."

I murmured as he started braiding a chunk of my hair.

"I never would've gotten wasted tonight if they were home," he continued. "Not because I'd get grounded or anything. They wouldn't notice. They never notice that sort of thing. They pick random things to focus on, like whether I'm marked late for school, and that's their pet project but nothing else matters. I didn't go to phys ed *once* last year. I failed the class. They didn't fuckin' notice. Maybe they didn't care? I don't know. But they never stopped talking about getting to class on time."

"That must be tough."

"The tough part is when they almost burned the house down because they went across the street to have drinks with the neighbors on their porch but forgot to turn off the grill. There's a scorch mark on the back of the house. I showed it to my dad after it happened and he wasn't worried. Like, 'oh, well, no one got hurt, everything's fine.'"

"I'm sorry, honey."

"I don't need you to say that." He dropped my hair and gazed out the windshield, his head craned at a weird angle. "I'm used to it."

"That doesn't make it better."

"My dad could go to prison for the rest of his life and my mom might be a fugitive forever," he said, "but it's all good because at least I don't have to worry about them starting fires. That's fucked up and that's why I don't need your sympathy."

"It's not sympathy. I just know what it's like to feel as though you're living in a straitjacket."

With a gusty sigh, he said, "I read an article that said drinking pineapple juice makes your semen taste better but I don't think that's true because I drank a ton of pineapple juice and the person I was dating said he wanted to focus on himself this summer."

"I—hmm." I was not prepared to discuss semen tonight. Or any night, really. "I can't help you with that one."

"It's always the same. They need to focus on themselves. Four times since last fall. All different people. Girls, guys, folks still figuring themselves out. And none of them want me. Even with all that pineapple juice." He glanced over at me. "What am I doing wrong?"

"Nothing, sweetheart. It's just not your moment. The time will come. I promise."

With the help of both dogs to nudge him along, I escorted a very loose-limbed Parker to the front door. For his part, Parker did little more than wobble and insist he lived inside an oyster shell, not a regular house, but he did ring the doorbell at least fifteen times.

Just as the bolt turned in the front door, Parker threw his arms around me, saying, "I love you, Sunny."

Two things happened when the door swung open. First, I got an eyeful of Beck wearing jeans, a t-shirt, and *glasses*, none of which I'd spotted on him before. The jeans were sublime, of course, and the t-shirt proved the importance of t-shirts to society, but it was the glasses that threw me for a loop. The frames were a simple tortoiseshell but the effect forced me to fully and completely admit that he was attractive and *I* was attracted to *him*.

And second, Beckett pried Parker off me by the backpack straps like his brother was a venomous snake. "What the fuck, Park? Hands to your fuckin' self," he yelled. "Did you not notice you were a second away from knocking her over?"

"I'd be careful with that one if I were you." I held out a hand to steady him. Not that Beckett would let me be the one to do the steadying. "He's a little shaken and stirred, if you know what I mean."

"Dude, look at her hair," Parker said, calling on all his shroom power to break away from Beckett's hold. He shoved his fingers into my hair, pointing at my highlights. My stylist was going to die laughing when I told her this story at my next appointment. "It's like sunshine is trapped in her hair."

"As you can see, we've had some fun tonight." I gave Beckett a *you have no idea* smile. "There was tequila and—"

"Don't tell him about the drugs," Parker loud-whispered to the side of my face.

Beckett ran both hands through his hair. "Do I even want to know how you came to be in possession of this kid?"

"The usual way. Heard noises when I was closing. Thought it was an animal. Turned out it was a drunk teenager down on the dock."

"I took one of the boats to Jamestown," Parker said. "But I didn't get drunk until I came back."

"Thank you?" Beckett replied. "If there's a more appropriate response, you'll have to share it with me."

"Beck, my legs feel like spiders." Parker abandoned my hair to tiptoe around the porch. "Why is this happening to me?"

"You need to go to bed," Beckett said. "And you need to take the puke bowl with you."

"But it smells like popcorn," Parker whined. "Because it's the popcorn bowl."

Beck slipped his fingers under his glasses to rub his eyes. "Either you get the bowl or you sleep in the backyard."

"Fuckin' Beck," he grumbled. He dropped down on the floor, scooting on his belly to meet the dogs at eye level. "Your ancestors told me they're proud of you. Sing the songs of your people with honor."

Parker got to his feet, gave his brother a smacking kiss on the cheek, and disappeared inside the house.

Beckett shook his head after him. "I know I've said this already but what the fuck?"

I laughed. "Yeah, it's been a night for him. There was a lot he needed to get off his chest. He's really stressed."

Beckett glanced inside and then back at me. "Can you stay for a minute? I need to make sure he isn't actually in the backyard or asleep with his head in the refrigerator."

I looked down at my dogs. They thumped their tails and blinked up at me like they were cool with this place. So, sure, I could hang out for a bit. Since I was already here. That was the only reason. The real *reason*. Not that Beckett and I weren't screaming at each other for the first time ever. And it had nothing to do with him wearing glasses *and* jeans. "Yeah, no problem."

He pointed at the porch swing, the bossman stare dark in his eyes. "Sit down. I'll be right back."

For once, my first instinct was not to argue with him. Probably had something to do with the glasses. They sealed the deal for me in a way I could only express through hungry noises usually reserved for nature documentaries. This attraction was terribly inconvenient given the many issues I had with this man. He wasn't nice to me, for one. Not in the way normal people were nice. And he appeared to fundamentally dislike me. Not even the best pair of secret glasses could wipe that away.

But then he came outside with two beers, a glass of water, and a large bowl, saying, "I didn't know what you wanted, and since you're driving, I brought options." He set the beverages on the small tree stump table next to the swing and put the bowl in front of the dogs.

He brought water for my dogs.

"But we also have soda and sparkling water. And Parker has been stocking up on pineapple juice for some reason."

"You don't want to know about the pineapple. Trust me," I murmured.

Beckett blinked at me for a second before a disgusted look crossed his face. "Oh god, don't tell me it's the—no." He started to make a vague gesture then thought better of it. *"Fuck."*

"Pretty much." I laughed as he grimaced.

"Beer or water?" he asked.

I reached for one of the bottles. "Will you make fun of me if I only have a couple sips of beer?"

He sat down beside me, a beer bottle in hand. "Why would I make fun of you?"

"Because you make fun of everything," I said, laughing. "You never, ever stop criticizing me. It's like your favorite thing to do."

"I won't say a word. After what you've been through tonight, you've earned a free pass from me and my comments." He tapped his bottle against mine. "I was on a conference call with my partners to handle some issues that've come up since I've been gone. It went two hours longer than intended." He blew out a breath and took a long pull of his beer. "Lost track of time. I should've noticed he wasn't home yet."

"Eh, it's fine. What's the point of being seventeen if not to sail to Jamestown and wander the docks alone at night?" I took a sip. Alcohol was not a friend to my brain, but a small amount on certain occasions didn't bother me. "Though he really is overwhelmed. School and relationships and your parents. He's..." I rolled the bottle between my palms. "He's having a hard time with the college stuff. The pressure seems a little overwhelming. Maybe ease up on him?"

Beckett leaned back, the shift causing the swing to kick into a gentle roll. It was nice. Relaxing. Peaceful, even. If I could be peaceful while sitting next to my iceberg.

"We had a *conversation* about that this morning. I was informed that he's not me and he doesn't share my interests or, as he put it, achievement-obsessed perfectionist compulsions."

I pressed my lips together to hold back a smile. "I will not comment on that."

"And I will appreciate that." Beck pushed his foot against the porch floor, starting the swing on a steady rhythm. "I'm an idiot. I should've known he was feeling the pressure of all this shit even if he's been strangely philosophical every time we talk."

"How are *you* juggling all of this?"

Beck gave a hard, brittle laugh. "I'm clearly *not* juggling it. I'm dropping balls left and right."

I shifted, turning to face Beckett and folding my legs in front of me on the seat. My knee pressed against his thigh and I decided to leave it there. He could scoot over if he didn't like it. "I need to pause here and tell you that the teenage version of you would've turned that comment into something lewd."

He took a swig of his beer. "I still have an opportunity to do that."

"Happy to hear you haven't given up all your delinquent ways." We shared a laugh but it was plain to see that he meant what he'd said about struggling. "What's happening with the family?"

"*Everyone* knows what's happening, Sunny. Everyone in this town talks about it all the damn time."

"That's not true. Not even a sweet corn kernel of truth there." I held up a hand to stop his protest. "From what I've heard, no one actually knows what's going on but they're positive your parents had nothing to do with it." I leaned in. "But they're not surprised to hear the lobster guy was involved. Apparently he's shady as hell."

He arched a brow and gave me that same stoic look as always. "You really don't have to protect my feelings."

I brought a hand to my chest. "I cannot think of a single reason to concern myself with your feelings."

That wasn't strictly true but he didn't need to know that.

"Well." A sigh rumbled out of him. "My dad is facing a load of federal charges and he's approaching it with an *I just hope both teams have fun* attitude. Thank god for ruthless criminal defense attorneys." He scoffed. "And the fact I can afford him."

"Yeah. How did that happen?"

He eyed me as he shifted the beer bottle to his other hand. The newly free hand rested on his jeans, his pinkie barely grazing my knee. Probably an accident. "I manage other people's money. If I grow it well enough, I keep a bigger percentage of it. The percents add up."

"From the looks of things, it's a lot of percents."

He lifted his shoulders. "I do all right."

I had to give him a ton of credit for taking the truly humble path when he could've whipped out a bank balance or last year's bonus check. "I'm happy for you. Even if you aren't happy to be here."

His finger swept over my kneecap. Not an accident. "You have to admit the circumstances are not ideal."

I nodded. "Of course, although you have to admit that messing with my café is not a healthy form of stress relief."

He dropped his entire hand to my knee and squeezed. "Are you fucking kidding me right now? Because—"

I burst out laughing. Beckett glared at me like he wanted to strangle me but he didn't move his hand.

"I never thought—" He stopped himself, shook his head. "I figured you'd leave Friendship."

"I did. Several times. I've lived in a bunch of different places."

"But you came back." He said this like it was unfathomable.

"The universe brought me back—and before you roll your eyes about that, you should know I won the bait shop in a poker game. If that isn't the universe sending me home, I don't know what is."

"You won—*what*?"

He set his beer down and shifted his arm to the back of the swing, his knuckles brushing my arm. In the depths of my mind, I registered that he was claiming more of my personal space than I usually preferred to share with anyone but I didn't want him to stop. It didn't feel like he was taking anything from me. It felt like he was giving something and that made all the difference.

"I managed a tavern in Newport, The Soggy Dog, where a bunch of real estate guys from all around would get together every few months. They always played for big items. Properties, boats, cars. Stacks of cash. There's a reason they bought out the back room and were picky as hell about who served them, but they left incredible tips. Sometimes, after closing up, I played a hand with them. One night, I walked away with the bait shop."

He trailed his fingers along the edge of my sleeveless shirt, right in that tender spot where my arm met my shoulder. A breath caught in my throat and I had to fight off a shiver.

"That's amazing," he said. "And you knew you wanted to turn it into a vegan café?"

He leaned in and dropped his other hand to my leg, right above my knee. His thumb stroked in small circles, edging my skirt up with each rotation. There was no oxygen left in the world.

"That wasn't my first reaction, no." I tried to sound as even as possible considering my brain was splitting its focus between my shoulder and knee and nothing else mattered. "It's a long story, actually, and—" And I didn't know what I wanted to say next but I knew I had to make a decision. Either this continued or it didn't, and I had to be willing to accept the consequences no matter what. I had to make the right choice because I wasn't getting another go at this moment.

If this stopped right now, I had to brace myself for months of awkward tension between us. I had to be willing to shove down this attraction and cling to the last chunks of my iceberg.

But if it didn't stop, I had to acknowledge that I was risking a spider web of relationships. This wasn't just about the two of us, not when he was my brother's best friend and forever entwined in my world. Not when his family restaurant was on the same edge of Friendship Cove as my café and we lived in the same cozy town. And not when his life was up in the air—and based on another continent.

"I have the time," he said.

I blinked at him for a second. I couldn't make this decision with his hands on me. "Could I step inside and use the restroom?"

He bobbed his head, his fingertips sliding just under the edge of my shirt. He glanced at the dogs. "Yeah. Do they need anything? Oddly enough, we have a few boxes of dog biscuits. Plenty of tennis balls too."

My iceberg was little more than an ice sculpture at this point. "No, I gave them cookie scraps while Parker went on about your desire to set up some conference calls." I climbed off the swing and ordered the dogs to stay. "But thank you. That was...really nice."

"I cannot take the credit. My parents must've bought them. I haven't gotten around to getting rid of them."

He led me inside and motioned to a door carved into a nook under the staircase. I loved that kind of quirky stuff so hard. It took a lot of discipline to stop myself from gushing about the wonky shape of the door.

"I guess I could keep them," he said with a shrug. "In case you come by again."

This ice was melting *fast*. Ocean levels were rising here, people. "Yeah, maybe." I pointed to the door. "Just give me a few minutes."

I watched him stride into the kitchen, shaking out his hands and muttering something I couldn't hear as he went. He could be reciting dark magic for all I cared because that t-shirt stretched across his shoulders in the most perfect way. I was in big trouble.

Once I was alone in the bathroom, I gave myself some time to properly panic in between deep breathing exercises. It was all about balance. After a minute of running cold water over my wrists to calm everything down, I dried my hands, fixed my hair, and said to my reflection, "Stop trying to control everything. It won't work. Enjoy the chaos."

When I slipped out of the powder room, Beck was waiting—and he looked about as conflicted as I felt. But then he reached behind me, flattening both hands on the door and crowding me up against it. He stared down at me for a moment that passed in hard, pounding heartbeats.

"Sunny," he said, his chest heaving. He took my hands, pressed them to his shirt. Pushed against himself. "Tell me to stop. *Please*."

"I'm not going to do that."

"Sunny, I *need* you to say it."

"I won't."

"Why the fuck not?"

"Because I don't want to," I replied. "And I don't think you want it either."

He closed his eyes like he was in pain. Like he was being twisted apart, drawn and quartered.

"Make sure," I whispered. "No mistakes."

He skimmed a hand over my shoulder and up my neck. "It wasn't a mistake before. It's not a mistake now."

My lips parted as he leaned in, and though I knew it was weird I couldn't bring myself to close my eyes. I wanted to remember every detail right down to the way his glasses slipped on his nose and how the scent of vanilla lingered around him.

His fingers were in my hair when his lips brushed over mine and I wrapped my arms around him because it was the only thing I wanted to do. My back connected with the solid plane of the door as he pressed into me, hard and rigid and right where I wanted him, and—

Retching sounded from upstairs.

We broke apart on a shared shudder, both of us staring up at the ceiling in horror as it continued.

"I'm gonna kill him. That's the fastest solution to all of this." Beck dropped his chin to the top of my head and sighed. "Or I'll take away his phone. That's probably worse."

I rested my forehead on his chest and let him hold me close for a minute. It was comfortable and that was almost confusing. If you'd asked me an hour ago, I wouldn't have guessed that I'd find comfort in Beckett Loew. Attraction, some sexual tension, long-simmering resentment, sure. But comfort? No. That was the last thing I'd expected from this troll.

Another round of vomiting started overhead and we groaned. There was no unhearing that sort of thing and there was no quicker way to ruin a good vibe.

"You have a lot on your hands," I said. "I should probably go."

"Are you okay to drive?" He dragged his hands from the back of my neck down to my hips and it felt like every pass edged me closer to him. "I can drive you home."

"I had three sips of beer at the most. Or is there something else you're implying?"

A thunderous crash sounded overhead and Parker swore loudly.

"Maybe the question isn't *can you drive* but *can I ignore my responsibilities at your place tonight?*"

"I mean..." My body was cooking up some big, spicy ideas, and if the throbbing erection pressed against my belly was any indication, I wasn't alone in that. I tipped my head back to get a look at him. I found him staring at me, smiling. It was so strange to see anything other than a deep scowl on his face.

That smile faded when Parker called, "Beck? Are you there? Hello? Is our reality nothing more than a simulation? Or is it our consciousness experiencing reality after it's occurred?" He paused to empty his stomach again. "Or is our perception of reality nothing more than that—our perception of one iteration of the world? And billions of other universes existing all at once, separately, and rarely—but not never—glimpsing each other?"

He kissed my forehead. Who would've guessed Beckett Loew was a forehead kisser? In all of Parker's billions of universes, I wouldn't have tagged that. Even now, with his lips on my skin, I wasn't sure this was real. I wasn't sure it wouldn't end in the blink of an eye.

"What time will you be in tomorrow?" he asked.

"Later. Two-ish." I had the overwhelming urge to lick his neck. Just get right in there and taste him.

He nodded. "I'll walk you out." His gaze dropped to my chest like he had a similar idea. Instead, he banded his arms around me and held me in a way that felt like a promise. Like he wanted to infuse words into my skin and keep them there.

I really wanted to hear those words.

The shower turned on upstairs and Beckett called, "Try not to drown yourself. That would really fuck up the simulation."

"I don't have a ton of experience with people getting rocked off their asses on shrooms but I can't imagine it's a good idea to add to the existential paranoia," I said. "It's bound to backfire on you."

"Lance experimented with everything in college, and I fucked with him the entire time," he said, still holding me tight. "He turned out fine."

Ah. There it is. We were never far from a reminder of Lance and his role in this thing Beck and I had going. "That truly is debatable."

He murmured in agreement. "I guess you're right."

"*What* did you just say? Isn't it against your religion to allow me to be right at any point in time ever?" I looked around the hallway. "Will lightning strike you down?"

"You're funny, storm cloud. Real fuckin' funny." He ran a hand down my spine. "You're not wearing a bra—"

"Why would I torture myself that way?"

"—and that's doing *terrible* things to me."

"Oh, please. It's not like I have enough going on for it to matter."

"It matters to me. Everything you do matters to me, in case you haven't noticed." He skimmed a hand up my flank and drew his thumb along the underside of my breast. I tried and failed to withhold a soft gasp. "And believe me when I say I *love* what you have going on."

I brushed my fingers over a wavy lock of hair that'd fallen to his forehead. "Everything I do drives you crazy."

"Once again, you're right." He squeezed my backside like he wanted to leave his fingerprints behind. "If you have any real intention of going home tonight, I suggest you do it now. I'm about thirty seconds away from keeping you."

"And what exactly does that—"

"Beck? What do I do if I puke in the shower?"

A laugh snorted out of me as Beck groaned into my hair.

"I should've made him sleep outside." After drawing a deep breath, Beck stepped back and laced his hands behind his neck. "Come on. I'm walking you out."

Jem and Scout led the way to my Jeep, and Beck kept his distance while I ushered them into the back seat. He walked around to the driver's side with me, that stiff, scowly expression fixed on his face like always.

"Good luck in there," I said, tapping my keys against my palm.

He arched a brow and stared at me as if I'd said the most idiotic thing in the world. Then he rolled his eyes and grabbed my hand, saying, "For fuck's sake, Sunny. Get over here."

My head bumped against the window as he kissed me but I didn't care. It didn't matter. Even if everything was different tomorrow and we never managed to get back to this strange, messed-up night where we were perfect together for a few perfect minutes. Even if he sat me down to explain that we were in different places and it would never work and what about Lance? Even if I woke up and remembered I was hot garbage when it came to sex and romantic relationships, and I didn't want that stress in my life right now.

Beck brought his hand to the back of my head while he dropped kisses over my jaw and neck. "I've got you."

My vision swam. Where was the guy who'd tried to buy my building because he didn't want to deal with neighbors? Where was my iceberg? What the hell had happened here tonight?

"I-I should go," I managed.

He nodded, his head tucked into the crook of my shoulder as he kissed a tender spot behind my ear. "You keep saying that but I don't see you leaving."

"Probably has something to do with the, ah"—I ran a palm over his thick bicep—"very large, very *athletic* man pinning me to various surfaces."

He pulled back just far enough to catch my eye. "Is that a compliment?"

"Is that the sort of thing you need? I would've guessed you exist on protein shakes and the bones of those who dare to cross you."

"If that was the case, I would've eaten you weeks ago."

Our eyes locked and the slightest smile curled at one corner of his mouth. I planted a hand on his chest, pushing him away. "But I'm right about the protein shakes, aren't I?"

His gaze never leaving mine, he reached down to adjust the bulge in his jeans. "Stay the night and find out, storm cloud."

I opened the door. I had to go home. There were several reasons for this but chief among them was my urgent need to make sure I wanted this as much, if not more, when my body wasn't humming along in harmony. "You know as well as I do that Parker is going to come running out that door naked any second now," I said.

"It wouldn't be the worst thing this town's ever seen. More exciting than an asparagus festival." He crossed his arms over his chest. "I'll see you tomorrow?"

I settled into the driver's seat. "Around two-ish."

He bobbed his head. "Text me when you get home."

I smiled but I didn't agree to those terms. We'd see what happened with that. "Good night, Beck."

He watched while I drove away, standing in the middle of the street until he blended into the darkness.

ONCE I WAS HOME and the dogs were rolling around on the floor to celebrate the joy of taking off their service animal vests and finally being naked again, I glanced at my phone, knowing I'd find at least one mildly outraged message from Beck.

I found five.

It was kind of fun pushing his buttons when I knew what kind of bark to expect—and that I'd like the bite.

> Beckett: Tell me you're home.

> Beckett: If you think I won't drive over there at this hour to check on you, you're wrong.

> Beckett: I'd drive over there just to find out whether it's as easy to untie that skirt as I've imagined, and not just because I want to avoid being stuck here in the vomitorium.

> Beckett: For fuck's sake, Sunny, where are you?

The final message was a pic of Beck wearing yellow rubber gloves, a mask, and the glariest, grumpiest expression in the world.

> Sunny: Love that color on you. It goes so well with that murderous glint in your eyes.

> Sunny: Good night!

chapter thirteen

Beckett

Today's Special:
Port-Wine Poached Pretenses

PRECISELY FIVE MINUTES after Sunny parked her Jeep outside Naked Provisions, I barreled down the back stairs, buzzing past Mel on the landing and ignoring whatever she was trying to tell me. "Later," I called. "I just—I need a minute."

I needed many minutes, and I'd needed them since Sunny left the house last night. I'd barely slept, and not only because Parker learned the hard way that it wasn't wise to mix and match mind-altering substances. Between cleaning up after my brother and finding new closets of chaos in need of purging around the house, I'd spiraled down deep into every moment with Sunny. I relived the words, the laughs, the touches—innocent and otherwise—and obsessed over what came next.

I didn't have the answer to that.

I always knew what to do but I had no idea right now. And I *wanted* to know. I wanted a game plan, a strategy. I wanted to do everything in my power to avoid fucking this up. She'd said as much last time—there wouldn't be any more chances coming my way.

"Where are you going?" Mel asked. "We're supposed to go over budgets."

"Later," I repeated, flinging the door open and jogging toward Naked Provisions. I didn't know what I wanted to argue with Sunny about today but I'd figure that out when I found her. I'd figure all of this out when I found her.

"Hello there, Beckett!"

I stopped midstride and glanced in the direction of the booming voice. Sure enough, Ranger Dickerson, his partner Phil Collins, and the rest of the Friendship Walking Club spilled out onto the driveway from the path around the cove. "Fuck," I muttered to myself.

"Ranger." I pivoted to face him and fussed with my cuffs. They'd lasted a full twenty minutes before I'd rolled them up this morning. "Nice day for a walk."

"Excellent day," he replied. "Good to get a break from the heat."

I nodded, leaving it at that. It would be good to get a break from this conversation since I had to put eyes on Sunny and I didn't have time to dick around with Dickerson.

"I take it you heard about the disorderly conduct down the bay at Docksie's Tavern last evening," he said. "It's not every day the Coast Guard gets called in for a bar brawl. Quite remarkable in my experience."

With much regret, I said, "No, I didn't hear about that."

"The local police called for reinforcements when they couldn't control the fight. Seems the trouble spread to the marina and some of the boats. They must've had a team nearby," Ranger mused. "Seventeen people arrested. Thousands in damages, including two sunken skiffs and damage to a speedboat."

I bobbed my head. "Wow."

"In any event, word spread quickly as it does along the bay, and now the town council is voting tonight on changing the legal hours of operation for food and beverage venues in Friendship from eleven o'clock to ten and—"

"The fuck they are," I said.

Ranger chuckled. "Nice to see a strong fighting spirit in you, Loew."

"If you think this is strong, you're going to love Sunny's reaction."

Ranger herded his crew into the café while providing me a thorough overview of the council members and their voting records. The man had a lot to say, but the café's interior was too small and his group too loud for him to continue without screaming directly into my ear. Which he did for a minute.

After skirting around jogging strollers and climbing over a few chairs, I finally spotted Sunny. She was behind the counter, pouring cold brew with one hand, iced tea with the other, and calling out orders to the kitchen.

"I need to talk to you," I said.

She caught my eye and shot back a slightly manic glare. "A little busy here."

There were at least twenty people in line and that was on top of the ten or twelve already seated. I glanced around for reinforcements and found Bethany working multiple juicers at once and Muffy plating orders at lightning speed in the kitchen. Sunny shouted several drink orders before turning her attention to the espresso machine.

"Where's Meara?" I asked.

"Not in today," she said. "Really don't have time for a Q and A right now, Beck."

Since I didn't know how to observe a problem without jumping in to solve it, I circled the counter and posted up behind the point-of-sale system.

"What the hell are you doing?" Sunny asked.

"Running the register while you do your thing," I said, nodding at the woman holding a pudgy baby with a copious amount of drool on his chin. "What can I get you?"

"Seriously, Beck. Step away from the screen," Sunny said.

"Don't listen to her," Bethany called. "We're dying back here!"

"I can see that," I said, keying in the order.

Sunny delivered another pair of drinks to the pick-up counter. "What's so important that you had to come running over here and put yourself to work, Beck?"

"Just a second." I scanned the menu on the wall behind me and the items on display in the bakery case while fumbling through the sales screen. "Can you substitute mango juice for orange in the Rise and Shine?"

"Yessssss," Beth yelled over the roar of her juicer. "Just add it in the special instructions section."

"Okay. Got it." I blew through two more orders before saying to Sunny, "We have a serious problem."

"Oh my god," she groaned as she shook the hell out of an iced latte. "If you're here to tell me that last night was *another* mistake, I'm going to—"

"Not about that. Not for a fucking minute." I swiped a credit card and swiveled the screen for the customer. "Ranger told me the town council is voting on a motion to change the approved hours of operation for food and beverage venues to ten o'clock because some fools a few towns south had to call in the Coast Guard."

"I heard they had to turn the fire hoses on them," the customer in front of me said. She brushed some lint off her dry-fit shirt. "They should be ashamed of themselves."

"Slow down," Sunny said. "They're doing *what*? When?"

"Shaving an hour off our hours of operation, and tonight," I said.

"I haven't shaved in three years and I'm a happier person for it," the next woman in line said. She lifted her arm and motioned to the tuft of hair there. She wagged a finger at me. "It's the patriarchy, you know, telling women they have to waste time and money to conform to these unreal standards."

"Let me be the first to apologize for my brethren," I said.

"Probably the last," she scoffed.

"They can't do that," Sunny said. "It took this town four years to decide on which type of grass to put down on the soccer fields at Sheepshead Farm. They won't change something like this in one day."

I glanced over my shoulder to see Beth pull a huge cucumber from the cooler beneath the counter. It was easily the length of my forearm. With one quick motion, she snapped it in half and then halved those pieces with her bare hands. Our eyes met and she laughed at the surprise she must've read on my face.

"They say I'm sweet but a little psycho," she yelled over the jet engine roar of juicers, coffee grinders, milk frothers, and all these damn people.

"Good to know," I replied.

"Did you hear me?" Sunny asked. "They're not making any laws tonight. I really don't think so."

"While I imagine you're right about that, I don't enjoy gambling when I don't have a good sense of the odds. We need to go to this town council meeting." I grabbed two cookies from the bakery tray and bagged them for the customer still figuring out her drink order. "Is this the last of the double chocolate olive oil cookies? Are there more somewhere?"

"If I bring you a tray, can you make them look pretty in the case?" Muffy asked.

"Pretty isn't your priority right now," I replied, blinking at the line which was now longer than when I started. Agent Price was queued up just inside the door. I could never shake that shadow. "But yes, I can handle that. If I can put oysters on display and make them look good, cookies will be a breeze."

"Because everyone knows oysters look like slurpy vaginas?" Muffy asked.

I bit the inside of my cheek to swallow a smile as I met the challenge in her eyes. There were a lot of wrong answers in front of me. There wasn't much I could say without expecting to be bonked on the head with some tongs. "Because your cookies look amazing. Obviously."

She snorted out a laugh. "Good catch, bossman."

"I'm supposed to close tonight," Sunny said, seemingly immune to the casually hostile side conversation I was having with her partner.

"I can close for you, babe," Beth said.

"Thank you, honeybun. Toss me an oat milk?"

I watched as Beth threw an underhand pitch of a gallon of oat milk down the prep area and Sunny caught it one-handed. And I thought shucking required coordination.

Muffy set a fresh tray on the counter behind me. "Pretty is always my priority. The eyes eat first."

"Understood." I nodded at Ranger as he and Phil Collins stepped up to the register. "What can I get you?"

"How many hats do you wear around here?" he joked.

"As many as I can fit on my head without it exploding, but seeing as they pay me in cookies, I'll keep this gig as long as I can." I glanced back at Sunny. She didn't look at me though I did catch a smile spreading across her face.

"I'll see you at the meeting?" he asked. "If there's enough immediate backlash to this proposal, it will die tonight. On the other hand, if there's any whiff of interest from the *nothing good happens after sunset* crowd, you'll have a problem on your hands."

"We'll be there," I said. "I have a vested interest in maintaining our hours of operation and they"—I glanced at Sunny as she filled five cups with ice and espresso like she was lining up shots—"have evening events that defy the wildest of imaginations, and that shouldn't suffer because a bartender down the bay overpoured last night."

"We know all about the Naked events," Phil Collins said. It was the first time I'd heard him speak, I was sure of it. "We're really looking forward to open mic night."

I took their orders and handed them cookies fresh from the tray. "You know, Ranger," I started as I swiped his card, "it wouldn't hurt to give folks a heads-up before storming the beaches. This is a small shop. They could use some warning and—"

"Don't listen to him, Ranger!" Muffy shouted from the kitchen. "You can storm our beach any day!"

"There are only two ways I want to be slammed and this is one of them," Beth added.

"We love it when the walking club wrecks us," Sunny said. "They're our favorite."

I shook my head at Ranger. "A little notice next time," I said under my breath.

He replied with a crisp salute and they merged into the crowd. It took another fifteen minutes and the entire tray of double-chocolate cookies but the mad rush settled. The walking club returned to the trail and a blissful quiet descended on the café. Agent Price sat in the corner with a glass of basil lemonade and a paperback book, and I didn't waste my time glaring at him today because he'd dropped a twenty in the tip jar.

"I'm not sure if it's too early in our relationship to say this," Muffy said as she stepped out of the kitchen, a clipboard tucked under her arm, "but I love you very much, Beckett Loew."

"I was wondering the same thing," Beth said while washing yellow smoothie off the wall from where she'd removed the blender lid a second too early.

Sunny laughed as she wiped down the counter but didn't comment.

I wanted to hear what she had to say most of all, but at the same time I didn't know how to handle appreciation. It wasn't something I had much experience with, and that was why I said, "You have too many fucking items on your menu."

"We don't, but it's nice to know you care," Beth said. "It's just different from your menu. Much more custom."

"You are uniquely talented when it comes to pinch-hitting," Muffy said. "Is there any position you can't play?"

I chuckled. "Actually, that's Decker's skill."

"Well, you have it too," Muffy replied. "You're allowed to wander behind the counter anytime if you're going to bust your ass like you did just now. You've got some hustle."

"I'm going to take the coffee grounds to the composter," Sunny said, shooting a quick glance at me.

When she hefted two five-gallon buckets, I glared at her. "For fuck's sake, Sunny, give me those."

She marched past me, saying, "I empty these buckets multiple times a day. I've got this."

I followed her to the back door where she'd have to set one bucket down to open the door. I stepped up behind her and wrapped an arm around her waist. It was good to touch her again even if touching her made my head feel like the inside of a beehive. I curled my hand over hers, prying her fingers away from the handle until the weight shifted to me.

"You didn't text me when you got home," I whispered into her ear.

She glanced to the side but didn't meet my eye. "I did. Just not when you wanted me to text you." Pushing the door open, she said, "This town council thing could really fuck you over."

Ah. So that was how it was going to be. "Trust me, I know."

We walked to the far side of the building, the one I couldn't see from my office. A series of tumblers and canisters lined the wall. She unlocked the top and reached for one of the buckets though I beat her to it.

"I'm not saying you can't do this. Believe me, I know you can." I slapped the side of the bucket to loosen a few remaining clumps of coffee. "But I'm here so I'm going to do this for you. Be mad about it if you want." I emptied the second bucket while she stared at me. "I don't mind. You're hot as fuck when you're mad."

She had her hair twisted up with a knitting needle or something and today's skirt was bright orange with a busy blue and black flower pattern. Little tassels lined the hem. I couldn't explain why but I wanted to run my finger over them for hours.

"Obviously, we could survive with a ten o'clock close," she started, elbowing aside everything I'd said, "but it would be annoying and I don't want to deal with that."

"Right, because the moon worship crowd really prefers the dark of night vibe."

Sunny snatched the empty buckets away from me. "We have events other than moon ceremonies."

"Yeah, I heard about the open mic night from Phil Collins. Do we know if he'll be taking the stage?"

"I don't know, Beck. He doesn't talk much," she said, sounding exasperated. "So, we're doing this thing. We're going to the meeting. Is there something we're supposed to prepare? Are we even allowed to talk or is this just watching while these people make decisions about us?"

"Ranger gave me some pointers before I jumped behind the counter." I followed her inside, though instead of returning to the heart of the café, she led me into a storage room packed with paper goods and the glass bottles they used for juices. "He said they'll set aside time for public comment and the bottom line is economic impact. If people are spending money after ten o'clock—and doing it without needing the Coast Guard to restore order—it's good for the town."

She tore into a box and started shelving paper cups. "Okay. I don't mind speaking but I have"—she counted on her fingers—"like six weeks of experience running a business in this town. Not the same as you and your, what are you up to now? A century of shucking?"

I went to the other side of the box and helped with the cups. "About eighty years."

"Yeah. They'll care what you have to say. Me? Not as much."

"Don't make that assumption." She slapped my hand away from the cups so I decided to bring some order to the carryout boxes on a shelf beyond Sunny's reach. "Old business can speak from experience but new business can speak of progress. People are coming to Friendship specifically for the things you're offering. Don't downplay that."

We worked in comfortable silence for a minute before Sunny asked, "How's Parker today?"

"Parker is sipping a hydration drink by the teaspoon in a dark room without any sheets on the bed, and he's sworn multiple times he'll never touch tequila again."

"Sounds about right."

She laughed and I wanted to live inside that sound.

"I'm not sure if I thanked you for everything last night but I appreciate you bringing him home." I peered at her and forgot what I was saying when I spotted the studs climbing up her earlobe. I had to shake that thought away. "How did you get him in the car? I had to drag his sack-of-stones ass down the hall and into his bedroom, and I think I tweaked my knee in the process."

She held up an arm and flexed her bicep. God, I loved sleeveless shirts. "I'm stronger than I look."

"I've noticed." *I haven't stopped noticing since you told me to stay on my side of the street.* "So, about last night and—"

"We don't have to do that." She ripped the empty box in half. "We don't have to talk about it. Define it. Analyze it."

I took the cardboard from her hands and dropped it to the floor. "I wasn't going to do that."

She gave me a skeptical grin and that was completely valid seeing as I wanted to do all of those things. I needed to know what was happening to me. "Okay. Sure, Beck."

There was a perfectly good door with a deadbolt right behind me. I could show her how much it wasn't a mistake right now. We could finish what we'd started last night—or start all over and do it right this time. As right as anything could be in a storage room, of course. But we were long overdue to stop pretending that we weren't going to start at all.

Then my phone buzzed and the screen flashed with Adrian's name. *Fuck.* I needed to take this call. I also needed to turn off my phone and never turn it back on. "It's the defense attorney," I said, hoping that was enough of an explanation. I leaned over and kissed her cheek. "I'll see you at the meeting tonight."

I WASN'T current on Friendship's population stats but it seemed to me like the entire town had shown up for this event. The meeting room at town hall was packed with irritated residents and business owners when I arrived and the crowd had only increased since then. Ranger circulated the room with a gnarled wood walking stick in hand and Phil Collins at his side, and it was clear they knew everyone and everything about them.

I found a spot along the back wall near the corner and plowed through my emails between watching the door for Sunny. She arrived a minute or two before the scheduled start time, her hair cascading over the denim jacket draped across her shoulders and that damn basket on her elbow. She scanned the room for a moment, smiling and waving at people she knew, and it was a good thing I had the wall to hold me up because she was like the blinding bright of dawn.

I basically swallowed my tongue when she glanced in my direction.

She came over, a slight smile pulling at her lips. "Look at all these people," she said. "If this meeting runs one second past ten o'clock, I think they have to forfeit this vote on the grounds of ridiculousness."

I nodded and went back to my phone as she set her basket down a few feet away and studied the agenda. She wasn't close enough to reach, and I had to imagine that was intentional, but the meeting got under way and I had to split my time between obsessing over this distance and listening to the council members.

There were terminally long speeches about safety and preserving Friendship's small-town values, which could not possibly include late-night liquor sales because *good people* lived in this town. Sunny and I shared an eye roll at that one. Some members questioned the haste of this whole thing and, from the noise generated by this audience, everyone in attendance had the same question.

As the discussion went on, more people filled the room, pressing in along the aisles and cramming into the back until all distance between me and Sunny dissolved. It was a warm night, and with all these people packed in here the room grew stifling hot. Sunny shimmied off the jacket, effectively drowning me in that herby, organic scent of hers.

I knew the taste of that scent now.

Another group pushed into the room when the council moved to hear public comment, forcing Sunny even closer until she was tucked up against me, her back no more than a breath from my chest. I had to pocket my phone to keep from nudging her with it.

The heat was oppressive and the ceiling fan whirring overhead did little to improve the situation. When I couldn't take it any longer, I shrugged out of my suit coat and tapped Sunny's arm. She glanced over her shoulder at me with a raised brow.

"Hold this," I whispered, handing her the coat.

That eyebrow arched all the way up and her expression asked *are you serious right now?*

Instead of responding, I proceeded to unbutton my cuffs and roll my sleeves to the elbow. She watched, her gaze darkening as I moved to the other sleeve. She gulped when I loosened the tie at my throat. That was fun.

I reclaimed the coat from her and settled a hand on the side of her hip that wasn't visible to the crowd. "Thank you," I whispered.

Sunny responded by shaking off my hand and gathering her hair into a bun on the top of her head. Fine, curling tendrils lingered at the nape of her neck and not a minute went by that I didn't think about pressing my mouth to that exact spot.

Most of the people offering comments echoed the same handful of points: the incident last night was the exception, not the norm; limiting hours of service would needlessly harm local businesses; the people didn't want anything to change. While these points were solid, the council members were not visibly swayed by anything said.

Not until a big guy in a sleek suit approached the podium.

"Noah Barden, Little Star Farm," he announced in a tone that said they should know who the fuck he was. I remembered a few Bardens from high school but I didn't know Little Star Farm. That was new to me. "I'll keep my remarks brief since we all know what happens when Gennie's left with a babysitter for longer than an hour."

A ripple of laughter moved through the crowd. As with most things in this town, I didn't get the reference.

"As many of my neighbors have already articulated, implementing measures based on last evening's incident is reactive and shortsighted— not to mention in direct violation of many of the town's own regulations. More than that, I see this move as the beginning of the end for this town's pride and joy: festivals. This town boasts *seventeen* festivals each year, most of them multiday events, and the majority are scheduled right up to eleven o'clock. These festivals are a considerable source of income not only for the businesses who participate but also for the schools, the library, and the ecological preserves that utilize these events to fundraise. Now, you can find trouble up and down the bay any night of the week, and it doesn't wait until ten or eleven to start." He shot a pointed glance over his shoulder at someone. "That's not how it is here in Friendship, but you already know this, and you have more than enough data on crime levels and economic impact to verify it."

He held out his hand, and after a pause, a woman with pink hair joined him at the podium.

"My wife, Shay Zucconi-Barden, the owner of Twin Tulip, and I have been preparing to open our wedding venue for the past six months. We have more work ahead of us but today's news had us asking whether we should stop what we're doing. If we're unable to host receptions past ten o'clock, we'll book far fewer weddings. An hour might not seem like much in your seats but it's the difference between allowing Friendship to shine as the hidden gem of this bay, and cutting small business off at the knees." He stared at the council members for a long moment. "Thank you for your time."

With that, he turned and ushered his wife out of the room.

"Shit." Sunny pulled at the front of her shirt to circulate some air. "That was effective."

I brought my hand to her hip once more. "I'd say so."

The town manager leaned forward to adjust her microphone. "While I am aware that there are"—she shuffled several pages in front of her—"many more residents and business owners registered for public comment, I recommend this council move to table the matter of amending approved service hours until a more extensive study can be conducted."

Sunny sagged back against me. "Please let it be that easy."

And it was. The council voted four to one and the crowd broke out in thunderous applause.

We tried to make our way to the door but everyone else had the same idea. We ended up diverging around a row of chairs, and from there, the current of the crowd carried Sunny away. Friends and business owners I'd noticed at her housewarming party folded her into their slow-moving circles while others called for her attention or promised to text her later. She really was magnetic. Everyone wanted to be near her, to know her. To keep her.

I certainly did—and it scared the hell out of me.

chapter fourteen

Sunny

Today's Special:
Clams, Indecently

BECKETT WASN'T hard to find in the dissipating crowd and that
was mostly a result of his gaze burning my skirt off for the past thirty
minutes. That, and he was roughly the size of a fortress.

I hadn't intended to get caught up in so many conversations on the
way out of the meeting room and down the stairs but *everybody* was
there and we were all partially delirious from standing in that Victorian-
era sweat lodge Friendship called a town hall. In that sense, it wasn't
difficult to rant about the whimsy of local government and the ever-
rising price of everything, or make plans to get together soon and plan a
fun collaboration between our businesses.

And it wasn't difficult to feel Beckett watching me the whole time.
He could've headed straight for the parking lot and driven that spiffy
status symbol of his right home while I promised the head of the local
youth soccer organization that we could figure something out for team
parties at the end of the fall season.

But he didn't. He stayed while I talked to everyone and their auntie, and he did it while keeping a respectful distance. He didn't come close enough to eavesdrop and never once did he show any impatience at my extrovert running wild.

He didn't have to wait for me. Really, when I gave it even a second of thought, I knew he shouldn't wait for me. It was a touch too familiar for me. Too involved, too fast. Sure, we'd been yelling at each other for nearly two months now, but last night happened *last night*. We weren't even twenty-four hours out from that first kiss—and all the ones that followed—and I didn't know if I was ready for Beckett to suddenly respect my time and space while also waiting to get me alone.

At the very same time, I *loved* the way he watched me. I loved the heat of his gaze as it skimmed the lines of my body and the dark intention I caught in his eyes. I had no problem admitting that I enjoyed the attention. And I wanted to kiss him again. I wanted to find out whether last night's chemistry was the product of bizarre cosmic energy or the surprisingly satisfying way it would always be between us.

When I was finished chatting, I turned around to find Beckett leaning against his SUV, phone in hand, gaze trained on me. My ride was in the opposite direction but I went to him.

"Crisis averted." My sandals smacked the asphalt as I crossed the parking lot. "For now, at least."

"They'll forget about it. Then they'll invent another crisis in a few months." He glanced over my shoulder to the wide walkway in front of the building. "Is there anyone you don't know?"

"Yeah. Probably. But they weren't here tonight." I stopped a few feet away from him, saying, "You didn't have to wait for me. I'm sure you had better things to do than watch Janie from the cheese shop catalog her issues with vegan cheeses."

He straightened, slipped his phone into his pocket. "I'm quite adept at managing my time but thank you for your concern."

I stared at him for a moment, taking in the rolled-up cuffs and thick, wavy hair. He was as polished as always but I saw something raw and untamed in him tonight. Maybe it was the upheaval of this whole day or maybe it was the oppressive humidity. And maybe it was all of that and everything else I couldn't pinpoint but I knew I wanted to find all the wildness in him.

I dropped my bag, grabbed hold of his tie, and yanked him hard against my chest. I had to push up on my tiptoes to seal my lips to his but I got there with a hand on the back of his neck to help close the distance and—

—and nothing.

Beckett didn't kiss me back. Didn't move, didn't even breathe.

What the hell? Had I misinterpreted the many signals he'd sent me tonight? How about the time when he asked me to watch him roll up his sleeves, which we all knew to be the official mating dance of the modern male. Or when he grabbed my hip and chased the line of my underwear around the curve of my ass for twenty minutes. Or the part where he stared at me like I was his next meal and I side-eyed right back to let him know he'd have to work for it.

Was it even possible to misread *all* those signals? No. I didn't think so. This was simply a matter of this moody man changing his mind once again and updating me with that information while my mouth was on his. *Lovely. Charming. What a gentleman.*

It was official. This was the most awkward moment of my life, and that was a real feat considering my brain had a pesky habit of misfiring and leaving me flailing on the floor.

Since this was a lost and very embarrassing cause, I pulled back. "Oh. I'm sorry. I didn't realize you'd—"

"Shut up, Sunny." He spun me around and pushed me up against his car. "I haven't stopped thinking about this since last night."

He stared down at my mouth and frowned, shaking his head a little before he leaned in and brushed his lips over mine. It was slow at first, as if he wanted to get reacquainted and do it while tasting each rise and corner of my lips. It was like he was experimenting with being anything other than an absolute bear.

Then he forgot all about that and kissed me like he meant every one of those words and he intended to prove it too. But he wasn't the only one who knew how to play this game. He nipped at me and I nipped back. He palmed my breast and I curled my fingers around his hair. He grabbed my knee and yanked it up to his thigh and I boosted myself up to wrap the other leg around his waist.

"I haven't stopped thinking about it either," I said between long, lazy kisses that seemed to reach inside me and excavate all the tension I'd built up today. I felt infinitely soft even while heat coiled low in my belly. I understood at a fundamental level what it meant to be turned on. It was like the doors had blown open, every switch had been flipped, all the lights were burning bright. "But you drive me crazy."

"*You* drive *me* crazy." He grabbed a fistful of my skirt as if it proved something and I saw the exact moment when he realized how a wrap skirt worked. "*Ohhhh.* I approve of this." He parted the skirt and slipped his hands under the fabric to grip my backside. "Also drives me crazy."

"Why?"

He gave a single shake of his head as he traced the line of my boy shorts and I vibrated against him. "Because it's you," he said, the words little more than a growl against my neck.

I didn't understand what that meant but this was not one of those moments where it made sense to stop and ask clarifying questions. Other things were happening with our mouths and my mind was busy working through several important questions such as *What are we actually doing here? Is the fine greater when the indecency takes place on government property? Am I willing to risk bug bites in inconvenient places?*

"Why do you feel so good?" He palmed my breast and swiped his thumb over my nipple like it was all rather miraculous. "Why do you feel like—fuck, Sunny, *why*?"

But he didn't sound like he'd stumbled onto a miracle. He sounded strained, a little tortured. As if the way I felt and the mutually inspired craziness and the electricity crackling between us was a problem he'd never be able to solve. And when he kissed me, I could taste that torture.

Headlights cut across the parking lot and several horn blasts startled us apart. The car slowed as it approached and the second Beckett identified the driver, he muttered, "This fuckin' guy."

"Good evening," Ranger Dickerson boomed from behind the wheel of an electric two-seater. Phil Collins waved, seemingly unfussed by the fact Beck had me pancaked against his car and my legs were locked around his waist. "Nice turnout in there. I don't know what it is about that Noah Barden but he speaks the words people need to hear."

Beckett cleared his throat. "Right."

With a nod, Ranger said, "Well. It's past our bedtime. I'm sure we'll be seeing you around real soon."

Another series of honks echoed behind them as they cruised down the slight hill town hall sat on toward the main road.

I turned back toward Beckett. I wanted to know what was happening behind those eyes before Ranger had interrupted. I wanted to talk to him and know him because I was grudgingly becoming aware that he wasn't the same person I'd attached to my iceberg. I also wanted to rip his clothes off and do filthy, unspeakable things to him until I lost the power of speech and required intravenous fluids to recover.

However.

Rushing into things, given all of our entanglements, would only make it more difficult in the end. And, even if I tried, there was no forgetting how much of a disaster I was with intimacy and sex and relationships of the non-platonic variety.

"I need to get home. The dogs, they've been alone most of the day. I stopped in to feed them before coming here but they're trained to work and they'll give themselves jobs like moving furniture around or gnawing a table leg if they get bored. I need to take them on a walk and throw the ball around the backyard for a bit."

He gave my ass one last squeeze and set me on my feet. "I can throw the ball for them."

"I'm sure you can," I said. "Isn't that another one of your gifts? A ridiculously reliable arm?"

His lips quirked up. His eyes crinkled. If I didn't know better, I'd think he was tickled pink. But Beckett Loew did not tickle to the point of pink. If anything, he tickled to the point of a stern growl—and now that I thought it over, I couldn't find any issue with that.

"Who told you that?" he asked.

"You know, around." I gave an impatient flap of my arms. He'd understand what I meant. That it was better for everyone if we didn't mention Lance when we were still breathing heavily from almost ripping off each other's clothes. And also from getting caught by Friendship's militant mother hen.

"So, what are my other gifts?"

"Oh, would you shut up?"

"I'm just wondering about all these gifts," he said, his grin as wide as a whole mountain range. "You brought it up."

"You're not coming over to play catch with my dogs."

"But your dogs like me."

"That's debatable." I reached for my bag. "They're required to be agreeable. I can't go out in the world with mercurial dogs."

"Sure, but they like me." He crossed his arms over his chest and stared down at my skirt, a scowl pulling at his lips. "You walk them at night? In the dark?"

"Yeah, I have a flashlight. A headlamp too but it's pretty dorky."

He rocked back on his heels. "And you walk alone?"

"No," I said slowly. "I walk with two highly intelligent, highly protective dogs."

"I'm going on this walk with you." He said this in the same imperialistic tone he used when telling me that my flowerpots were on his property. Unfortunately for everyone, I didn't hate that tone nearly as much as I used to. It was amusing now, like a crusty old quirk I'd grown to love and tolerate. "Even with a flashlight and dogs, I don't like the idea of you out on the streets at this hour."

"No, you're not coming with me," I said with a smile. "But it's nice of you to try." I ran my hand down his arm before backing away. "I'll see you tomorrow, Beck. Be good."

A minute passed before he called, "Where the hell are you going?"

Over my shoulder, I shouted, "Bike rack."

Behind me, I heard a growl-sigh and "For fuck's sake, Sunny."

I had my helmet clipped on and my bag stowed when he pulled up to the curb in his SUV.

"Dare I ask why the fuck you're riding a bike? At night?"

I backed the bike out of its slot and climbed on. "Because I don't like driving at night. Headlights can be a lot for me."

"You drove last night," he said, like that would crack my argument right down the middle.

"Sometimes I do drive at night. I don't have far to go. It's usually fine," I explained. "But I knew there'd be traffic here, and traffic means lots of headlights. And my place is barely ten minutes away."

He stared at me a moment before pushing the car door open and coming around the front of the vehicle. "I'm driving you home." He pressed a button and the rear gate opened. "Get in the car. I'll stow your bike."

If I let him give me a ride home, I'd let him come inside. And if I let him come inside, I'd let him pick up where we left off. Hell, *I'd* pick up where we left off. But he'd sounded miserable earlier, when he'd said I felt good, and we had too much on the line for that.

"No, thanks." I pedaled off the sidewalk and down the parking lot. "See you tomorrow."

"If you think I won't tail you home, you're wrong," he called.

I was late to the game, due primarily to my decades-old iceberg, but I was certain that everyone else already understood this about Beckett Loew: the man meant what he said. He held his tongue until he had something to say, and when he did speak, those words were iron. He didn't stumble over his thoughts, he didn't misspeak. He didn't fuck around. All of this was admirable, especially in an era when people like Beckett spoke for the pleasure of hearing their voice, it seemed.

And that was why I was not surprised when I noticed him following me a few minutes later. He kept a safe distance and drove well below the speed limit, and, much to his credit, didn't roll down the window to holler at me.

When I arrived at home, he pulled up at the curb and watched while I stowed my bike. I climbed the front steps and waved, but he didn't exit the car. Perhaps he was making sense of his misery and he knew he wouldn't do that if he came inside.

I opened the door. "Good night," I called.

He didn't reply.

I closed the door behind me and sat down on the living room floor to greet the dogs. The sound of his car idling at the curb seemed to pulse through the walls, through my skin.

I untied my hair and played with the dogs and tried to do anything other than think about the man parked at my curb and how much I wanted to close the distance between us.

Ten minutes later, my phone buzzed with a series of texts.

> Beckett: Do not ride your bike at night anymore.
> Please.

> Beckett: It isn't safe.

> Beckett: There were a total of two streetlights on the ride over here. That's completely inadequate.

> Beckett: Most streets in this town do not have bike lanes, marked or otherwise.

> **Beckett:** If you need to go somewhere, I will drive you.

> **Beckett:** If I am busy, Parker owes you many favors and he'll be delighted to help.

I beamed down at those messages. I couldn't help it.

> **Sunny:** I usually ride on the bike path.

> **Sunny:** It's pretty safe. All bike lane, all day. It's just a few turns off the path to our corner of Small Point.

> **Beckett:** When are you walking these dogs?

> **Sunny:** Please tell me you're not waiting for me to go out with the dogs!

> **Beckett:** ...then I won't tell you that.

I sprawled out on the rug while the dogs snuggled up on either side of me. Here I was, thinking I had Beckett Loew all figured out. That I knew what I was doing.

I had no idea.

chapter fifteen

Beckett

Today's Special:
An Emotional Festival of Chickpeas

"YOU RUIN IT THAT WAY," Chef grumbled as I poured two shots of espresso over ice.

I spared him a glance before adding some cream and stirring the drink with a butter knife. "I don't need it to be good. I just need it to be effective."

He pointed in the direction of Naked Provisions. "Go. There," he said. "It is *magnifique*."

Of course Bartholomew knew the quality of the coffee across the way.

"While that is most likely true," I said between sips, "I'm more or less an insomniac. I need to wake up right now but I can't go over there yet. This will have to do."

He shook his head in disgust and returned to scribbling ideas in a notebook and sipping his sherry from a chowder cup. It was early in the afternoon but never too early for sherry.

"He's right about the coffee," Agent Price said from the bar, nose in a book, and a paper cup from Naked in reach.

I scowled at him, not that he noticed. "What the fuck are you reading, Price?"

He flipped the book to glance at the woman on the cover. "It's *Before I Let Go* by Kennedy Ryan. I picked it up for the Read Naked book club." When I continued staring at him, he added, "There's nothing wrong with men reading romance, Loew."

"I didn't say there was anything wrong with it." I shrugged, adding, "By all means, read whatever you want."

"You should try it. You might learn something."

"I don't doubt it," I said.

I had a ton of work to do back in the office but I leaned against the counter with my coffee. There was a rainbow of reasons why I wasn't sleeping, and it started and ended with Sunny. Parker, my parents, and all of my other problems were in there too but it was Sunny in my conscious thoughts, Sunny when I closed my eyes, and Sunny when I woke up hard and aching and mindless for her. As if sitting outside her house in a parked car for thirty minutes at night wasn't enough of an indication that I was well and thoroughly fucked.

I lingered in the kitchen, watching through glazed-over eyes as the chefs chopped and diced, steamed and sautéed, chorusing back responses when Bartholomew called out. I didn't really want any of this. I didn't want to be here, I didn't want to dig my family out of another one of their homemade disasters, and I didn't want this woman to consume every corner and crevice of my mind.

And of all the women to consume me, it had to be Lance's little sister.

By my math, all I could do here was fuck things up. There was no going back now. We could've gotten away with a few kisses. Those kisses had fundamentally altered my DNA and triggered a highly inconvenient need to be near her at all times, but if push came to shove, I could lie to Lance and tell him it was nothing. He'd malfunction for a while but he'd get over it.

But there was no getting away with last night. I knew what it felt like for her nipple to harden under my thumb. I knew the heat between her legs and the impatient sighs that stuttered out of her when she wasn't getting what she wanted. And I knew the relationship I'd had with Lance for the last twenty years would never be the same if I allowed this to continue.

Which meant cutting things off with Sunny, and if I was being honest, I was more likely to grab one of Bartholomew's cleavers and cut off my hand than go through with that. That left me to fuck up one of the only healthy, sustained relationships in my life. And for what? A woman who lived in Rhode Island and mildly despised me? It didn't matter whether she'd climbed me like a koala last night, there was no doubt in my mind that she still hated me. At least a little bit. So, I was bound to fuck this up too. If not now, it would happen when I sorted out my family shit and went back to Singapore.

Yet none of this mattered when I saw the aqua streak of her bicycle as she rode in from the path. I pushed off from the counter, set my glass in the wash bin, and walked out of the restaurant. I wasn't even going to pretend I hadn't been waiting for her.

I glanced up at the gray layer of clouds blocking out the afternoon sun and noticed the roof on the café. I'd always clocked it as gently weathered but now it looked worn out, in need of replacing before hurricane season kicked up. Definitely before the winter.

And this was why I needed to speak with Sunny immediately. The state of her roof.

I wasn't even halfway across the crushed shell driveway before hearing, "Hello there."

The timing of this guy was truly impeccable. Doing my best to swallow a snarl, I turned to see Ranger and Phil Collins emerge from the path. I wasn't in the mood for a postmortem on the town council meeting or another lesson on the inner workings of this town. "Hey. How's it going?"

"Glad we caught you out here. If it's not too much trouble, we'd like a moment of your time," Ranger said, last night's knobby walking stick in hand. I was positive he could kill me with that stick and make it look like I'd died of natural causes. "It won't take too long. We know you're a busy man."

There was ice in his tone, unlike anything I'd heard on his usual walk-and-talk visits. I slipped my hands into my trouser pockets. "Sure. What's on your mind?"

Phil Collins adjusted the wide brim of his straw hat while Ranger eyed me for a long moment. Goddamn, I should've eaten something with that coffee because there was a headache gathering steam at the base of my skull and my heart felt like a rusty trombone. I was not equipped for whatever lecture this guy wanted to hand out today.

"What are your intentions with Miss Du Jardin?" he asked.

I peered at him as if that would make any of this make sense. "My —*what*?"

"Intentions," he repeated with a great deal of impatience. "As you may know, we are very fond of Sunny." He gestured to himself and Phil Collins. "And it's not just the two of us. Everyone who meets Sunny loves her. You're a fine fella but we all know your sights are set beyond this town. Sunny, she's ours. She's Friendship. We won't let any harm come to her."

As if I needed him to explain that to me. "And you're telling me this because…?"

"Don't play cock and bull games with me, son," he said.

This comment required me to gulp down a laugh because A) no one called me son, not even my father, and B) I didn't know what the hell a cock and bull game was but Ranger was the last person I wanted explaining it.

"We know what we saw last night and we're here to tell you that we won't tolerate you treating Sunny with anything less than complete respect."

That was funny considering I was beginning to get the impression Sunny might want nothing more than to be thoroughly disrespected in bed.

"And we're not the only ones," he continued. "The entire town is of the same mind. If you hurt Sunny, we'll be at your door."

Great. That was just great. So good. Not a thinly veiled threat. We didn't do threats in Friendship. We gently suggested that we'd engage in some collaborative ass-kicking. Small-town charm, folks. There you had it. Coming for you with the walking stick of death. "Well. Thanks for letting me know."

Ranger tapped his stick on the ground, gave me a stern nod, and marched away with Phil Collins beside him. Stunned, I watched them until they turned onto Market Street and fell from view.

"Hey. What was that about?"

I dragged my gaze to Sunny. She wore another one of those *GET NAKED* shirts and a marigold yellow skirt that knotted at the waist. Nothing else in the world mattered. "You don't want to know."

She crossed her arms over her chest and glanced in the direction they'd gone. "It looked kind of serious."

I waved toward Market Street. "No, not really," I said unconvincingly. "Just…Ranger's deep thoughts of the day."

"Then why do you look like you swallowed a cactus?"

I rubbed the back of my neck. "Probably has something to do with the two espresso shots I downed before getting an earful from Ranger. Those things don't mix." I pointed to her building. "You need a new roof."

"Wait a second," she said, holding up a hand. "Did Beth make that espresso? She didn't say anything about you coming in."

I shook my head. "No, we have a small machine behind the bar. For espresso martinis. That sort of thing."

Sunny laughed and I didn't fucking care what happened with Lance or the pitchfork-wielding villagers or anything else. I wanted this more than I could care about any of that, and a small part of me knew that I was clinging to the one good, beautiful, sexy thing I had right now and borrowing trouble for the future but I didn't care. I knew the risks. I knew what I'd lose.

"I'm sure your setup is fine but we can do better than that," she said. "And don't forget: we have cookies too."

I'd forgotten about the cookies. "That's not a bad point." I motioned to the building again. "About this roof—"

"I know, I know," she said, staring up at it. "I know it's in rough shape but I was hoping to make it through the year before taking on that project. Best-case scenario, we'd do the roof and solar panels together and make it a one-shot renovation but we can't pull that off right now."

"It would be cheaper than dealing with a busted roof and water damage. Especially if you have to shut down for a week while it's all fixed."

"I don't require your advice on the matter but thank you for sharing it nonetheless."

"It's not advice when it's a fact," I said. "Have you called around? Received any quotes? Because I'm sure there's an option for—"

"Just the people I wanted to see today!"

At once, Sunny and I turned our heads in the direction of that voice. A white man with a remarkable salt-and-pepper mustache lumbered toward us in a lime green madras plaid suit that seemed excessive even for summertime on the coast. Sunny's shoulders sagged just enough for me to notice.

"Mr. Campbell," she said, holding a hand up in greeting as he approached. "What brings you to Friendship today?"

"After yesterday's excitement, I knew I had to pay some calls to my favorite small business owners," he said. "Don't think I didn't see you at the meeting last night, and since I know you're both engaged in local affairs—"

"I'm sorry, who are you?" I asked.

He laughed and patted his chest like this happened all the time. "Where are my manners? I'm Gaines Campbell, president of the regional chamber of commerce. Your dad and I go way back," he said.

I stifled a groan. God only knew what Rabbit had agreed to or told this guy.

"After last night, I got to thinking about the power of this community. We have festivals and farmers markets that bring out the best and brightest this region has to offer. Over the past twenty years, we've created an entire economy around these events and made this bay a destination. But as I was driving home last night, I said to myself, I said 'Gaines, we can do more.' And you know what I thought of? I'll tell you what I thought. I thought it's time to do more." He held out his hands. "And you're the people I want at the forefront. Let me tell you what I see. I see a local restaurant week. Maybe a food truck festival. You folks have food trucks, right?"

Together, we replied, "No."

Gaines brushed this negligible issue aside. "But restaurant week? That's exciting! We could have themes. All the best seafood spots on the coast. All the vegan establishments. We can do it all." He glanced at me and I knew he was coming in for the hard sell. "And it's about time we bring an oyster festival to Friendship. That's your ball game."

Before I assembled the words to send this idea back to the hellfires from which it was forged, Sunny said, "You know how much we love festivals and farmers markets. Bethany's company Roots and Shoots started out at farmers markets years ago when she and her partner were first brewing kombucha. And we're signed up to attend most of the town festivals. We *are* doing it all, Gaines."

The smile she gave him could've convinced me to play catch with a grenade.

"Restaurant weeks sound like a lot of fun and you'll have to loop back here with an update once you have a coalition of businesses signed on for that."

"Well, I was thinking, my thought was—"

"If you have a specific plan in mind for a festival and a team in place to launch it," she continued, not giving an inch, "I'm sure Beckett and the rest of the Small Point Oyster team would be willing to hear it after the summer rush is finished. Until then, Beckett and I have a meeting to dash off to so you'll have to excuse us."

She glanced at me, bobbing her head and giving me *go along with it* eyes, and I managed, "Yeah. We are late for that meeting."

"Fabulous," he boomed. "This is just fabulous. Thank you! I'll be seeing you two real soon, then."

"Not too soon," I muttered.

I followed Sunny inside the café once Gaines was on his way to blindside some other small business owner. She poured two drinks behind the counter and ducked into the kitchen to grab a few items despite Muffy's pointed glare.

"I'll be in the office for a bit," she called to her partners. "Grab me when your parents get here, Beth. I need a Linda-and-Lyle hug."

"Only if you put in that order," Beth replied. "I need celery!"

I wanted to touch her the moment the door closed behind us but Sunny pushed a glass filled with something green into my hand and motioned to one of the chairs. "The trick to getting through conversations with Gaines Campbell is to suck out all the oxygen."

"So, strangle him?"

She laughed and set a plate in front of me. "Cut him off before he

can ramble you into whichever new half-baked plan he's cooked up."
She plucked some grapes from the plate, saying, "I love a festival as
much as anyone but we don't need to add more to the calendar."

"I don't love festivals," I said, picking up half a sandwich. It looked
like chicken salad but that didn't make sense. The other half looked like
a BLT, but again, that could not be right.

She blinked at me. "You don't? Why not?"

"Because they're all bullshit folksy welcoming nonsense." I took a
sip of basil lemonade. It was so good, it was nearly arousing. See? This
was what Sunny did to me. I was in deep trouble. "Who the hell needs a
corn festival in their life?"

"The Sweet Corn Cobble is one of the best weekends of the year."
Her tone made it clear that she believed something was very wrong with
me. "The cornhole tournament alone makes the whole thing worth it,
and let's not forget the part where everyone is drunk off their asses on
bootleg corn whiskey."

I took a bite of the not-chicken salad and groaned. It was incredible.
I didn't even care how it was possible. "First, this is fucking amazing,
and second, these festivals try to make this town seem like it's one big
happy family when everyone knows that's not the case. It's putting on
the appearance of quirky traditions and wide-open, welcoming arms,
and that's bullshit."

Sunny shook her head and her hair slipped over her shoulder. It was
loose and wavy today. "But it's not bullshit."

"I remember what it was like to be the new kid in this town and I
can tell you that the only person who gave a fuck about welcoming me
was your brother. The First Fruits Festival had nothing to do with it."

She tucked her legs beneath her and leaned back in the chair, quiet
for a moment while I demolished this half of the sandwich. Then, "I like
the really obscure ones. Like the Arts and Hearts Festival in February.
Everything is love themed but there's also a strong angsty undercurrent
too. Last year, a few of the vendors teamed up to sell a box designed as

a Valentine's Day for one. Nothing heart shaped, no mention of love, and a hand-blown glass dildo thick enough to make anyone forget their ex."

I choked on the not-chicken salad. "Are you speaking generally or do you—I mean, is that something you have in your possession—"

"Close your mouth, Beck." Sunny grinned. "And there's the Craft Beer and Corgis event in September. It's basically a night at the dog park with a load of food trucks and local beer vendors. I don't think any town has ever conceived of something so simple and so perfect as dogs and beer."

That did sound like a good time. Not that I was willing to admit it.

"I love that we lean into the weirdness," she continued. "I love that people dress up like non-creepy woodland creatures for the Fox Run 5K in November, and I love the cutthroat competitiveness that everyone brings to the Jack-o-Lantern Jubilee." She grabbed the last of the grapes. "I don't think anyone is faking the appearance of a charming town. As we saw last night, this place is as complicated as anywhere else. But we have a lot of opportunities for the community to come together, if they so choose."

I pointed to the empty spot where the not-chicken salad had sat. "What was that?"

"You'll have to take that up with Muffy but you should know the answer will confuse you." She shrugged. "I've been to a lot of places. Some that were welcoming and some not so much, and I have to tell you, that difference had nothing to do with festivals or small-town charm. It was the people, the energy of the community, the sense of belonging offered to anyone who arrived."

"Where did you go after leaving Friendship?"

She jerked a shoulder up which served to remind me that her shirt screamed *GET NAKED*. "I visited everywhere but only stayed in a few spots. New York City and Boston, mostly."

It wasn't difficult to imagine Sunny as a wanderer. I was sure she adored every minute of it. "But you came back here."

"Yeah." She nodded, sipped her iced red tea. "Every time I landed in a new city, it wasn't even six months before I called my parents to help me move home. Either I was lonely or I didn't belong, or I realized being away wasn't as fun as I wanted it to be."

"There is nowhere in the world that you don't belong."

She held up her hands, let them drop. "I was never lonely in New York but I never felt like I belonged there. Even when I met Muffy and we couldn't get enough of each other, I never found my way in the city. There were a bunch of times when I was lonely in Boston but I also felt like I was constantly meeting new friends I'd keep forever. Like Meara. I was lonely but I never felt alone, if that makes any sense."

"It does," I said. I understood that. More than I cared to admit. More than I wanted anyone else to know.

"There always came a time when I convinced myself I could live in Boston or New York or somewhere else for the rest of my life. That I wanted to stay and I wanted to be part of that place, and I had the best friends in the world by my side. But when that time came, I couldn't fight off the feeling that, save for those few friends, no one would notice if I disappeared. Maybe after a few days, a week. But they wouldn't notice right away, and that was like a phone that wouldn't stop ringing in my head." She set the tea down and then picked it back up. "If I disappeared in Friendship, I know someone would notice."

I'd notice. I'd notice right away. But I didn't tell her that. I wasn't ready to say it. I could stare at her house in the dark like a fucking creep but I couldn't form those words and force them into the undefined space between us yet. "Before coming here, before the oyster company, my dad was a roadie and my mom was basically the road crew den mother. Formally, she was some kind of traveling coordinator but that was the gig. Organize schedules, lodging, meals. Look after the roadies, basically, make sure they were on time and out of trouble. She spent a lot of time looking at injuries and telling people whether or not they needed stitches."

"You lived on the road?" She tapped at her laptop, adding, "I'm listening, I just need to get Beth's produce order placed. You've seen her crack cukes in half. We don't want to awaken that beast."

"About half the year on the road, yeah. More some years, less others. We stayed in a lot of small towns when we weren't traveling. A lot of places that considered themselves just as cozy and quirky as Friendship."

"Let me guess: you hated all of them," she said.

"I didn't hate them," I replied, reaching for the faux BLT. I just knew this thing was going to blow my mind and I wasn't prepared for it. If I was being honest, I kind of resented how good the food was. Not because I prayed at a carnivorous altar but because everything that came out of this place was *so good* that it made me a little mad. It wasn't a rational response or one I could justify in any form. One bite and I was left asking myself where garbanzo beans got the audacity. "But they were difficult places to love and most were openly hostile to newcomers. The worst thing in the world is being the new kid in a class—in the middle of the year, no less—when everyone else has known each other since birth. There's no chance of competing with that. Not a fucking chance."

"I'm not going to disagree with you because that is objectively terrible. How'd you survive?"

"I didn't give a shit. Didn't care about anything or anyone. It made it much easier to tune out the whole fucking world." I bit into the sandwich and yes, it did alter my entire outlook on bacon and not-bacon and everything I believed to be true about food. Pissed me the fuck off. "It worked for me then and it works for me now."

"Beckett. Please." She glanced at me between clicks. "You care about *so much*."

"It's cute that you think so but I don't. I do whatever the fuck I want and it doesn't matter what anyone thinks of that."

"And yet you are here," she said as she scrolled down the page, "thousands of miles from where you live and work. You're rebuilding docks and showing up at town meetings, fixing my whole patio for the sake of *appearances* and hosing off your brother after he comes home wasted." She arched a brow at the screen. "Looks an awful lot like caring to me."

"That's different."

"You think so?"

I pressed a fingertip to the plate to capture a few crumbs but didn't respond.

"Maybe you're right," she went on as she scanned the screen before submitting her order. "Maybe it doesn't matter to you what anyone thinks but that doesn't mean you don't care. I think you care so much and so deeply that you are unaware you're doing it but you definitely do it. I mean, like I said, you're *here*, aren't you? Eh, no, don't interrupt me." She held up one hand while she clicked with the other before I could do anything more than open my mouth. "What you don't do is let yourself be vulnerable. God forbid you open up to anyone."

"Does this abuse come standard with all sandwiches or am I paying extra for it?"

"On the house," she replied. "I also think you project a very strong *don't fuck with me* vibe that can be felt from fifty feet away. Even the most loving, welcoming people will practice some amount of self-preservation when you're in perpetual scowl mode. Which is most of the time."

"Then what's your excuse?"

She closed the lid of the laptop and swiveled to face me. "I'm sure I don't know what you mean."

"Where's your self-preservation? If my perpetual scowl is as severe as you suggest, why didn't you run screaming that day I told you to get your flowerpots off my property?"

She leaned back in the chair and gathered her hair in her hands, laughing hard. I wanted to burn that image into my brain. I wanted to see it in my dreams and hear that laugh every time I felt like the world was a series of spinning plates never more than a second from crashing down around me.

"Because I've already burned through a lifetime's-worth of self-preservation," she said, "and you don't scare me. Not now and not when I was a kid. You do stoke rage, however, and that's quite entertaining for me."

Before I could respond, Muffy poked her head into the office. "Linda and Lyle have arrived," she squealed. "I'm in line right behind Beth for my hug and don't you even think about cutting."

"I wouldn't dare," Sunny said to her, pushing to her feet and turning toward the door. "I don't like people touching me but I wouldn't miss a hug from Beth's parents."

"Hey. Hold on." I grabbed her hand and pulled her toward me. With a tug, she dropped into my lap. "You don't like to be touched?"

"Not really, no. Aside from people I trust like Beth and everyone, I am happier when I have boundaries and personal space."

I motioned to where she sat but she gave me a slow, confused shake of her head in response. I said, "You've never had a problem with me touching you."

"Yeah, well, I mean, that's different because"—she paused, dropped her gaze to the floor. "I don't know. It doesn't matter."

"I touched you the day I came back. When you almost face-planted on the patio," I said.

"When you intentionally misread the situation so you could destroy one of my flowerpots."

"Yeah." I'd have to figure this out another time. "I wanted to talk to you. Before Ranger and Gaines and digging up all these old traumas of ours. I wanted to talk about last night."

"Can we talk about it after we say hi to Beth's parents? Because I think you'll be in a better mood after you get a hug from them."

"I don't know Beth's parents. There's no reason for them to hug me."

"That does not change the fact that they will hug you," she said, an adorable grin taking over her face. "They have the energy of a *my child was student of the month* bumper sticker. It somehow manages to be both precious and infectious. Trust me, you want in on this."

That was how I found myself outside Naked Provisions with an older white couple sandwiched on either side of me. To be fair, it was one of the top five hugs I'd received in my whole life and I did step away feeling as though I'd been dunked in warm, heady nostalgia. It was fucking weird.

"I'm Linda," Beth's mom said, patting my back. "It's so wonderful to finally meet you. Beth has told us everything about you."

I glanced to Beth, hoping that wasn't accurate. They didn't need to know *everything*.

"And I'm Lyle," her dad said, clasping my hand in both of his. "I just have to say, I read a little about the conservation work you folks have done in this cove and I'm so impressed. Not everyone would invest the time and money to look after their community that way. I'm proud of you."

When I stepped back, a little dizzy from the strangeness of it all, I shot a quick glance between Beth and her parents. In no world would I ever ask how they came to be a family given that they didn't appear to be genetically related, but I must've let confusion flicker across my eyes because Beth said, "I was adopted from the Philippines when I was eighteen months old."

"And every single day since has been a gift," Linda said as she and Lyle enveloped Beth in a hug. "Now we want to see this café. Tell us everything. Oh, look at these beautiful flowers! Sunny, did you do this? They have your flair written all over them."

Sunny gazed up at me with a viciously smug grin. I wanted to bite it off those lips.

"Yes, I did, Linda," she said. "I'm so happy you like them."

Once Beth led her parents inside, I said, "We're going to talk about last night now."

Sunny's eyes sparkled with the sadistic joy I knew, loved, feared. It was like she was cracking her knuckles in preparation to slam a sledge-hammer down on my buttons. "Allow me to make a deal with you."

"I am going to get slaughtered in this deal, aren't I?"

"Probably not, but we won't know until we go through with it," she said. "What is suffering if not a journey?"

"Sure. That sounds like my life." I rubbed my brow. "What are your terms?"

"We can talk about last night and define anything you want on the condition that you let me take you to a festival—and you actually make an effort at enjoying yourself while we're there."

"For fuck's sake, Sunny." I groaned. "Are you serious?"

"Very," she said, nudging my arm with her shoulder. "I'll pick a good one. I promise."

I ran a hand down her back and let it settle on her hip. I could go to a festival. I could muddle my way through a good time there too. Especially with Sunny as my guide. But I needed some direction from her and I needed it now. "Fine, though you have to tell me what you want."

With a nod, she melted into me and I could've been content with that as an explanation. It could be enough. Then, she glanced up at me, her lips parted and her eyes softer than ever before, as if she'd stepped out from behind a dark cloud.

"Don't overthink," she said, "even though I know it's your super-power. Whatever this is, we just have to let it happen. It's better that way, okay? We don't have to know what comes next. We don't have to control it. We can't actually control anything so there's no reason to waste our energy on it when we could"—she brought a hand to my neck and pulled me in for a gentle kiss in broad daylight, right here on the driveway between our businesses with everyone in our world watching —"do this instead."

"Okay."

I nodded. Was there any other response? If there was, I didn't know it and I wasn't interested in going to find it. I'd take anything I could get, as long as I could get it.

chapter sixteen
Sunny

Today's Special:
Toasted Pumpkin Seeds over Hand-Rolled Jealousy

"SO, THIS IS THE SHITHOLE."

I peered up at the café, trying to see it through Leary Murtagh's eyes. "It's no Soggy Dog but it will do," I said, grinning at him.

He grumbled out a few inaudible words and I knew from years of working for him that it meant, in the kindest possible terms, I was welcome to fuck off.

I loved this guy.

"Are we gonna stand out here all day like morons or do you plan on showing me around?" he asked, stamping his cane on the ground for emphasis. "And don't think I'm about to eat any of that tree bark soup or nut weed salad you're cooking up. I want my coffee and I want it black. Don't hide any of your crazy vegan things in there either. I'll know. I'll know and I'll raise hell about it, don't you try me."

"It wouldn't kill you to calm down."

Grinning, I glanced over at the man who'd accompanied Leary.

Anyone who could give it right back to Leary was a gem in my book. "Hi. I'm Sunny."

"I can't believe it took that long for someone to notice you, you big moose," Leary muttered. "That one? He's my nephew's kid. They call him Marbury. Apparently that's a name we're giving people now. Don't ask me why. But he likes to be called *Mars*." He gripped my wrist and leaned into me with exasperation in his cloudy eyes that said *can you believe this shit?* "As if that's any better."

"I'm standing right here," Mars said.

I shared a quick smile with him over Leary's head. He was tall and exceptionally broad with head-turning blue eyes and a lot of thick, dark hair. If I had to guess, I'd say he was in his early thirties.

"How could I miss him? I've seen smaller barges than this boy," Leary replied. He gave my wrist a squeeze and caught my eye. "He rides my ass like I'm one of the ponies at Belmont. Doesn't give me a single minute of peace. He took my car keys away, Sunny. Can you believe that? The kids today have some balls, let me tell you."

"Because you have glaucoma," Mars said. "You're not allowed to drive."

"It's a scam," Leary said to me. "It's big pharma and the car ride apps conspiring to suck every last penny out of us. And the old folks' homes too! Those bastards will pump you dry and then stew your bones for soup. Just like the English."

"Don't start with that again," Mars said with a sigh. "We can't be screaming about the British Empire all day."

"Just you try me, boy," Leary shouted.

The thing about Leary was that he was the definition of a curmudgeon. He was permanently irritable and impatient. Ornery, crusty, obstinate. On the surface, he hated everything and everyone. *All the time*. The only thing he didn't hate was dogs, and though he'd deny it to the death, he had the biggest, softest heart in the world. It was wrapped in barbed wire and chain mail, and he hardly ever let anyone see a sliver of it, but it was in there.

And that was why he was here today, visiting a bright, airy café with turmeric lattes and celery juice shooters on the menu and exactly zero paintings of hounds mid-fox-hunt on the walls. It was why he bought Christmas gifts for my dogs and acted as though I was doing him a favor by taking a portion of the windfall from the sale of his tavern, The Soggy Dog.

"Less for the government," he'd said.

I led them inside with Leary grumping and growling at Mars every time he tried to help my old boss. The guy was sweet and remarkably tolerant of Leary's abuse. It was fun to watch. I motioned to the high ceiling as we settled at a table by the window. "We blew out the second floor since it was going to cost more to fix the sinking joists than get rid of the whole thing, and we painted everything—"

"White," Leary said, his hands clasped on top of his cane as he surveyed the café. "It's all white."

"The floors are gray," Mars said.

"You're here for the wheels, young man," he replied. "Not another word out of you while I visit with Sunny and her dogs." He swept a pointed glance around the café. "I don't see Jem or Scout anywhere."

"They're in the office," I said with a laugh. "I'll get them and grab some food and drinks. Anything you're in the mood for?"

"Like I said, coffee. Black. I won't be eating any seaweed. Had enough of that during the war."

Mars shook his head. "You didn't fight in any wars."

Leary huffed. "There was a war going on when I ate that seaweed, I'll tell you that much."

With a sigh, Mars glanced up at me. "I'm open to anything. Really. Whatever you recommend."

"Famous last words," Leary muttered as I walked away.

When I returned to the table a few minutes later, I had a sampling of our most popular items, several beverages (including one mug of black coffee, hold the seaweed), and both dogs. "This is a little bit of every-thing," I said as I unloaded the tray. "Here you have our mixed berry corn muffin, that's the spicy cinnamon roll, this is pumpkin loaf, and—"

"Who's a good boy? Who's the *best* boy?" Leary cooed. "Oh, I didn't forget about my little sweetheart Scout. Come over here, come to Granddad."

Mars and I watched as Leary mooned over the dogs for a minute. They had their heads in his lap while he scratched behind their ears, their tails beating a steady rhythm against the concrete floors.

Mars ran a hand over his mouth to hide a smile and shifted his atten-tion to the dishes. "What's your favorite?"

I set the mug in front of Leary. "Probably the pumpkin loaf."

"Then I'll try that," Mars said.

"Would you stop with that sweet talk? Can't you see she's a smart girl with a business to run? She doesn't need a lazy bum like you in her life." Leary moved the pumpkin loaf away from Mars and looked at me. "No one can afford to feed this boy. That's why he's living with me now. Ate the doors right off his mother's cupboards."

Mars shook his hands at Leary. "None of that is true."

Leary took a long, thoughtful sip of his coffee, decided it was adequate, and returned to the dogs, saying, "You did move in with me."

"*You* moved in with *me*," Mars replied.

"Ay, what does it matter?" Leary tore the muffin in half and took a bite. "This doesn't taste like a wood chip."

"I'll pass your compliments along to the chef," I said.

He devoured the muffin and let the dogs lick the crumbs from his fingers while Mars pulled apart the spicy cinnamon roll. "This could've been worse," Leary said, scraping a sour look over the people waiting at the counter. "You've made the best of a shithole situation, I suppose."

"Thank you," I said. This was as close as Leary would ever come to paying a compliment directly to someone's face. "We couldn't have done this without you."

He leaned down to nuzzle Scout, saying, "I would've come to this microphone thing you're doing even if I don't have much care for poetry and such. You know I'm a night owl but this dirty lout won't let me out after dark."

"It's just good to see you," I said, and I meant it. I'd invited him to the open mic night because I wanted to give him a chance to visit the café but I knew he didn't roll out of bed until noon on most days and only went outside when the sun set. Such was life for a barkeep. "How's retirement treating you?"

Leary stared at Mars while his grand-nephew gulped down the last of a green smoothie and then polished off the rest of the cinnamon roll. "What did I tell you?" he muttered. He leaned back in the chair, still petting both dogs. "Retirement is boring the piss out of me. You need a dishwasher? I'll work for free. Anything to get some good kitchen noise in my life. I don't want to be alone with my thoughts." He tapped his temple. "I'm not like you kids. I don't need to know what I'm feeling."

Mars only rolled his eyes as he sampled the yellow smoothie.

"How's the family?" I asked. "How'd your nephew's knee surgery go? Is he back on his feet?"

"I told that old nugget to stop with the pickleball," Leary grumbled. "You see? That's what retirement gets you—busted knees and daytime television and fuckin' feelings. Who needs it?"

"I don't know, man," I said. "But if you want to hang around here a few days a week and wash some dishes or just sit on the patio and yell at seagulls, we'd be happy to have you." I pointed at the empty mug. "All the coffee and muffins you could ever want."

He dropped a hand to my shoulder and gave me a squeeze. "You're not useless, sunshine. I like that about you."

Leary would never admit it—and I'd never ask him to—but tears filled his eyes as he said this.

He cleared his throat and sampled a chunk of pumpkin loaf. He nodded as if it wasn't the worst thing in the world, flicking pumpkin seeds off the top before taking another bite. "My niece is having a rough go of it," he said. "First the husband died in a ditch and then that son of hers won't get his head out of his ass."

"He didn't *die in a ditch*," Mars said. He set the glass aside, another smoothie down. "He moved to Florida last winter with his second wife. The one he married ages ago."

"Shoulda died in a ditch for all he was worth," Leary said under his breath. "But that son of hers, he's a real problem. If I had a two-by-four handy, I'd knock some sense into him with it."

Muffy approached with a loaded tray, saying, "Who let my favorite cantankerous old cooter in here?"

Leary grinned up at her. "It's good to see you, love," he said, clasping her hand. "Keeping this crew in line, are you?"

"Doing my best, but you know how this one is." She patted my head. "And the Barbie doll behind the counter? God help us. Thankfully Meara doesn't mind cracking the whip so I have that on my side."

"Leary's looking for some part-time work on the wash station," I said. "Think you can keep him busy?"

"Baby, I'll do you one better," she said. "I bet you peel a mean potato."

"He *is* a mean potato," Mars said.

"You'll have to forgive my grand-nephew." Leary gave an exasperated shrug and motioned to the dishes Mars had all but licked clean. "He has three stomachs and doesn't allow me a minute of peace. He thinks I'll leave him something when I croak if he hangs around enough." He shot Muffy a glance that said *he's getting a dime, if that.*

"Well," Muffy said with a laugh. "Anytime you want to prep the veg station, there's a stool in my kitchen with your name on it." She cleared the empty dishes and set down some fresh ones. "Are you circling back tonight for open mic? It's going to be rockin'."

"Wish I could," he said, jerking a thumb toward Mars. "But the warden keeps a tight curfew."

Muffy laughed, saying, "We'll miss you, then. I have to get back to my poblanos but I wanted to leave a few new things for you to sample."

"It doesn't taste like health food," Leary said.

"I sure as hell hope not," she replied with a wave as she headed back to the kitchen.

I stood, collecting Leary's mug. "I'll grab some refills. Anything you'd like to try, Mars?"

While Mars studied the menu board, Leary said, "He doesn't need anything special. Just back the trough up."

When I returned with fresh coffee for Leary, tea for me, and three of Beth's favorite pressed juices for Mars, the men were deep in a heated conversation.

"You can't say you want to hit him with a two-by-four," Mars said. "I know he's screwed up a lot recently but he's going through a hard time."

"And that's a reason for him to start fights? Damage property? Drag his mother down to the police station to post his bail?" Leary folded his arms over his chest and shook his head. "No. He's not a child and there's no sense coddling him."

Mars glanced up at me with a strained smile as I set the beverages down. To Leary, he said, "Maybe that was the wake-up call he needed."

"I doubt it," Leary said into his coffee. "He needs to bottom out and then dig a little deeper before he'll even think about changing."

In all the years I'd managed The Soggy Dog, I'd met Leary's nephew and niece a few times and heard everything about them as well as his grand-niece and -nephews. Despite all of Leary's bluster, Mars was the big achiever of the family. Always did well with school and sports, quick to succeed in business, good person all around. His sister was very similar. The other grand-nephew, Joey, had none of that.

I didn't know the family dynamics well enough to figure out

whether there was competition between Mars and Joey but it was safe to say there was tension.

"He better not come crying to me for money," Leary said. "It's his problem to solve."

"He won't make that mistake again," Mars replied. "Trust me." He grinned at the juices in front of him and it felt like a period at the end of the family conversation. "These look good."

"Bethany's best," I said with a glance toward my squeeze queen. "So, Mars. What do you do? Other than taking this guy's abuse?"

Some clouds parted and the sun streamed in at a blinding angle. When I shifted my chair to dodge most of the rays, I noticed Beckett walking the perimeter of SPOC with a gorgeous, business-y blonde at his side. Their heads were bent together as if they were deep in conversation and their elbows bumped every few steps. A flash of a smile even crossed his face while I watched.

That was rare. A true, honest smile from Beckett was like a solar eclipse.

Not that I'd spotted many of his smiles lately. Or even his scowls. The past week had been a busy one for both of us. I worked a bunch of mornings; he always closed the restaurant. While Meara and I were busy prepping for tonight's event, he had marathon meetings with his dad's attorney several days in a row.

So I didn't get to see much of that absurdly beautiful face. He still scowled at my bike and found reasons to march himself across the driveway to argue with me about nothing. And he texted late at night to ask if I was walking the dogs alone.

The answer to that was always no, of course not, I had two dogs with me.

He hated that. I loved it very much and would never stop.

"…and that's why I'm freelancing for the next year or two," Mars said. The blenders started whirring at the same time as the coffee bean grinder, and he had to drop his arm to the back of my chair and lean in close to my ear to continue. "Given the enterprise-level demands, it makes more sense for me to have the flexibility to take on clients rather than coming onboard full-time."

"Yes," I drawled as I realized Mars had been talking about computerish things while I stared at Beckett. "That sounds—"

"Boring as hell but the fact of the matter is he's too expensive for anyone to keep on staff," Leary cut in. "I'm trying to convince him to move down here since I miss the water and he doesn't go to work in an office anymore. It's all talking at the computer screen and nonsense like that, which he can do from anywhere." He sipped his coffee. "Besides, living with him in Boston has been hell on my social life. Do you really think I can bring a lady friend home when this guy's yelling at his machines and knocking on the door every few minutes, asking if I've taken my blood pressure pills? Or telling me it's time to eat supper if I don't want to be up with indigestion all night?"

I murmured in agreement as I watched Beckett lean down and kiss the business-y blonde on the cheek.

Huh. That was strange.

I mean, I knew Beckett wasn't playing games with me, and even if he did, he wouldn't do it in plain sight of my café where my girls—and everyone else in town—were sure to see him. Beckett was a smart guy and he wasn't a trash bucket. Between his parents, his brothers, his job back in Singapore and an entire oyster company, he didn't have a spare minute in his life to juggle someone on the side.

I knew all of these things. I believed them. I really did. And yet I was still a simmering kettle of jealousy as Mars and Leary sniped at each other about which one was ruining the other's bedtime prospects. I wanted to know who she was and why Beckett felt it necessary to stand so close to her and what they needed to talk about for all this time.

"Enough about that," Leary said, knocking the head of his cane against the table. "I want to hear how the business is doing. Let's see some figures, some receipts. I'll tell you what you're doing wrong."

With an eye still trained on Beckett and the blonde as he led her to a sedan parked nearby, I handed Leary the sheaf of papers I knew he'd want to see. "Things are going well," I said. "We're sold out of the prepared items most days."

"Good, good," he murmured as he paged through the books. "And the overhead? Keeping it low?"

"As low as we can, considering—" I didn't want to tell him about the fire hydrant flood. Or any of the other oddities that had occurred since we opened. Everyone else chalked these little incidents up to unrelated accidents, but when I gathered them all together, they added up to something that wasn't quite right.

Sure, we could explain away the fire hydrant, but we'd replaced the dumpster lock three times and the back door handle twice. That just didn't make sense. Despite all my teasing, I knew Beckett wasn't to blame. And I knew it wasn't anyone from the oyster company, especially now with Mel and Beth "ignoring" each other so hard the rest of us were getting high off the sexual tension and taking bets on when it would explode.

As much as Beckett loved pointing the finger at raccoons, I couldn't see trash pandas going so hard, so often. And could they really throw rocks hard enough to bust a doorknob? I did not think so. I didn't think they'd systematically skip out on attacking the compost either. If I was a raccoon, I'd be all about that compost. Fuck the knobs.

Maybe it was teenagers who'd designated Naked as their new target for late-night entertainment and angst relief. Or something—someone— else that I wasn't prepared to contemplate.

"Considering what?" Leary asked, his eyes crinkled as he leaned in to peer at the documents.

I glanced outside and saw Beckett jogging up the stairs and into the oyster company, phone pressed to his ear like always. Everything would work out. It had to, even if it was a mess along the way. "Considering everything that can go wrong with a new venture."

"Aye. I know how that goes."

"The last time you did anything new was before the War of 1812," Mars said.

Leary scoffed but the ghost of a smile bracketed his lips. "Didn't I tell you to wait in the truck? Get outta here. Run through the broadside of a barn if you have to but I'm busy with Sunny. I'll whistle for you when I'm ready." To me, he said, "This is why I never had children."

chapter seventeen

Beckett

Today's Special:
Surf and Turf—A Duet of Jealousy

"WHERE THE HELL IS MY BROTHER?"

"Which one?" Zeus asked, busy scrolling through the reservation system on his tablet.

"Parker, but I'd take a location on Dex if you have it." I swept another gaze over the dining room. "I know Park's on the schedule tonight."

"Switched with Everleigh." Zeus glanced away, frowning. "Maybe it was Eva. I don't know. But he's not here tonight. I think he's going over to the open mic event at Naked."

I checked my phone, expecting to find a text from my brother with that info. Nothing. It seemed communicating with me was too high a bar for him. He must've learned that trick from Dex. At least I could corner Parker around the house and at the restaurant when I needed answers from him. I had to keep an eye on sports news just to know where Dex was and if he was well enough to play that day.

I knew he'd taken the field through several injuries during the last few playoff seasons. I knew this because Dex dropped off the radar when something wasn't working. He'd go from daily texts and regular calls when he was playing well and feeling healthy to radio silence when he was in pain. He never wanted to talk about what was wrong, especially when he felt like it was his job to fix it.

It was obvious to me that he was hurting now because I could count the times I'd heard from my brother in the past six months on one hand and I couldn't do a damn thing about it. There were all these people in his orbit—agents, managers, coaches, trainers—and I was stuck on the sidelines. Same place I was with Parker.

And, if this morning was any indication, Sunny.

Technically, I didn't know where the fuck I was with Sunny. I was *letting it happen* and *not overthinking*. Yeah. Sure. As if I was remotely capable of functioning that way.

But she'd seemed cozy with a guy who looked like a defensive tackle turned corporate titan. Really cozy. I wasn't running a stopwatch or anything but she'd hung out with him for at least an hour this morning. If I hadn't been pulled in fourteen different directions since the second I woke up, I would've invited myself over there for some of that infamous coffee and scoped out the situation for myself.

I would've done that and I would've died a little when confronted with the reality that Sunny was a twenty-eight year-old woman with a whole fuckton of options. It wasn't like I didn't already know that, but seeing it in living color was different from quietly reckoning with the fact there was a chunk of her life I knew nothing about and that chunk probably involved a lot of relationships. Maybe she was in relationships now.

It wasn't as though I'd asked whether she was yelling at anyone else on the regular and I hadn't made any request that she limit all that hollering to me. I didn't even know how I'd go about that.

Hey, Sunny. What do you say we pick fights only with each other?

And the semi-violent make-out sessions where I think about fucking you
through a door? Let's not do that with anyone else.

I glanced toward Naked for the hundredth time today. The lights
were low and the place was packed. Even the patio was filled despite
the drizzle and low rumble of thunder off in the distance.

I wanted to see her. I wanted to talk to her and touch her, and I
didn't care about the guy from earlier as long as he was gone and never,
ever coming back. I wanted—god, I wanted so much. More than I
deserved, more than I had any right asking for. Not simply because I
had a long history of being horrible to her though that never stopped
nagging at me. No, I couldn't ask her for a damn thing when I was over
here hanging on by threads. This disaster that was my current existence
wasn't fit for sharing with anyone.

So, that settled it. I wasn't going over there. Wasn't going to
demand any answers when they didn't belong to me. Wasn't going to
ask what she had planned after this event wrapped up. Wasn't doing any
of that.

Except—

"I need to talk to Parker for a minute," I said to Zeus. "I'll be back
in"—I glanced at my watch—"in a bit."

Zeus shrugged. "Whatever. We'll be winding down starting in the
next hour. You can leave if you want." He motioned to the dining room.
Good crowd but nowhere near capacity, and the deck was empty on
account of the drizzle. Slow for a summer evening. "You know you
don't have to be here all day, every day, right?"

"You're funny, Zeus," I said as I moved toward the door. "You
almost make me forget that we were raided by the FBI in May and that
I'm plugging the holes in this place with the corks from Chef's wine
habit while Sandy's on the run and Rabbit's facing twenty years in
federal prison."

He scratched his chin. "Oh yeah. That."

I cast one more glance around the restaurant. "Make good choices,"

I said, pointing at him. "Text me if—if anything at all seems unusual to you."

I didn't wait for his response because I knew it would stress me the fuck out. This would be a quick visit to Naked. In, out, done. Just checking on Parker. Reminding him to communicate with his guardian slash brother slash roommate. Maybe I'd get a look at Sunny while I was there but I wasn't going to hunt her down. I could live with that.

Much in the way I was living with the *letting it happen* and *not overthinking* thing. This was me, letting it happen.

The main door was propped open and the sounds of acoustic guitar spilled out. Once inside, I realized the entire café had been transformed to make room for a short stage dressed with a black backdrop and layered rugs under a stool. The overhead lights were dimmed and a spotlight shone on the stage. Every chair was occupied and many more people filled the sides and back of the café to watch the performance.

I wasn't sure what I'd expected but this was so much more. It was transformative in a way that felt unfamiliar to me. Almost magical. I didn't know why I admired this but I knew I did.

I glanced around to find my brother but found myself staring at Sunny. She leaned against the wall right beside the door, her arms crossed over her chest and that evil little smile curled around the corners of her lips. Just like she'd been there all along, waiting for me. Evilly.

She tipped her head to the corner. Mel was there, and she had Bethany backed up against a wall, kissing her like she was determined to swallow the girl's tongue whole. I glanced to Sunny with wide eyes that said *I didn't need to see that*.

On a silent laugh, she tapped my arm and subtly pointed toward a cluster of tables. Parker was huddled around one of them with a few teenagers. Hale sat at another with Nyomi on his lap. Ranger and Phil Collins were nearby, and Agent Price too. He'd made himself right at home in this town. Meara's husbands stood on either side of her behind the counter, watching the performance with their arms folded over their chests.

Everyone seemed…content. They were content to melt into the darkness and absorb the music with the people they chose.

I wanted to be content. I wanted to stop fixing things for five fucking minutes and stay anywhere long enough to let myself be content. Right now, it was the only thing in the world that mattered to me.

So I threw out everything and pulled Sunny in front of me, wrapping my arms around her waist, pulling her back to my chest, and tucking her head under my chin. Tonight she wore a skirt that resembled a funky old tablecloth and a Naked t-shirt gathered into a tight knot at the center of her back, leaving a wide strip of gorgeous midriff exposed.

As the performance wrapped up, I leaned down to whisper into her ear, "Why must you knot your clothes and hair at all times? How is this your approach to living? It doesn't seem practical."

"Why do you even like me?" she asked over her shoulder.

I loved it when her words had teeth. I didn't have to be soft for her and that made me want to do exactly that all the more. "If I said it was your propensity for tying everything in knots, you wouldn't believe me. But there is some truth to that."

"No, seriously. Why are you here? Why are you bitching about my clothes and acting like you want to be near me when you obviously don't. Or did you dislike me so hard that you've come all the way around from the other side and don't know what to do with yourself now?"

I couldn't stay away from her. That was obvious to me and probably everyone else. But I didn't say that. "Why do *you* even like *me*?" I asked.

The guitarist finished the tune and the crowd lavished him with applause, cheers, and snaps until Meara took the stage. "Next up, let's give a very Naked welcome to Paloma Wu and her spoken word poetry."

Proving that she wasn't afraid to stab me straight in the heart, Sunny said, "I'm not going to put you out of your misery and say I've always liked you because that's not the truth. I didn't like you when you were an asshole teenager and I didn't like you when you broke my flowerpot in the name of saving me from tripping." She hit me with a fiery grin and I felt that heat like I was being roasted over an open flame. "I still contend I would've been fine without your interference."

"But the three times you walked in front of the speeding forklift? You had that under control too. Right?"

"You have a very active imagination," she said.

I dragged my thumb along her belly. The restraint it took to keep from sliding my hand under her shirt was significant. "I'm sticking with my story."

"You do that." She nodded. "It would be a lot easier to not like you. It would make my day so much better to just write you off as an arrogant, bossy jerk who likes to throw money at problems. And I've tried to do that. You know I've tried just like you know you're not my type."

"I'm going to need you to explain that because what I saw this morning makes me believe I'm one hundred percent your type."

"But here I am now, in a place where I am forced to accept I do like you," she continued, ignoring me completely. "I like your scowls and your moods, mostly because I've found all your buttons and it's a lot of fun to push them. I like that you're not always an arrogant, bossy asshole though you do throw money at a lot of problems."

"Because money solves a lot of problems." *And it's all the ammunition I have sometimes.*

"And I find you attractive," she went on. "*Distractingly* so. It's actually a problem for me and I don't know what to do about that, especially considering that you don't like me."

She was so fucking brave. A million times braver than I'd ever be.

I'd never put my cards on the table like that, not without knowing the hands everyone else held.

I flattened my palm on her belly and pressed her back into me. She rocked against my hard shaft and a small breath stuttered out of her. "There's no hiding how much I like you, storm cloud. It's actually a problem for me too."

After blowing out a long breath, she said, "*That* is not about me. It's about rubbing up against someone in the dark."

"Believe me," I rasped, "it's you. It's *always* you."

"Yes, right, and if my flowerpots hadn't dared to exist an inch too close to your precious property lines, you never would've noticed me."

"I can't decide if you actually believe that or you're just fucking with me because it entertains you, but either way, you're wrong."

"If there's anything you should know by now it's that I have a pesky habit of not being wrong."

"Then it's my goddamn honor to break that habit," I said, my lips on her neck and the tips of my fingers climbing up her ribs and edging just under her shirt. "Because there has never been a moment when I didn't notice you. I can't *stop* noticing you—and I should. You know I should stop and yet you make it impossible. Fuck, I've tried. Every single day since I found you on your knees and ignoring the shit out of me, I've tried. But not a minute goes by that I am not painfully aware of *everything* you do, right down to the way you knot your skirts like you're just waiting for me to come over here and unravel you. Not one fucking day, Sunny."

At first, she didn't say anything. Didn't hardly move. It gave me plenty of time to get drunk off the scent of her hair and debate whether I'd stepped too far in the creepy-obsessive direction. But then she glanced over her shoulder, her brows bent like she expected another declaration of my complete insanity for her. Like she knew I heard her laughter when she wasn't around and wanted to know if I'd succeeded in chasing her out of my dreams yet. Like she understood

I'd catch hell from Lance for this and needed to know I could take the hit.

"It's always you," I said, "and you know that."

We stayed there through some rap-poem-chants that sounded like a fine way to open the gates to the underworld, a couple of songs, and two older women who killed it with dueling fiddles. I kept my arms around Sunny's waist and she closed her hands around my forearms.

Then, when a few kids around Parker's age took the stage for an a cappella performance, she glanced at me over her shoulder. "What's the deal with your blonde?"

"My what?"

"Your blonde," she repeated. "The one from earlier today. With the spanky little trousers and the matching blazer. Very corporate."

I stared at her, not knowing what the hell she was talking about. A slow rush of warmth moved through me as I saw the lines connecting these dots. "Are you...are you talking about Ayla? My *cousin* Ayla?"

"My god. I cannot pretend to be quiet with you anymore." Sunny grabbed my wrist and towed me outside into the light rain. "The business-y blonde is your cousin? The one you kissed on the cheek? And walked to her car? Your cousin?"

"As far as blood relations go, no, she's not, but she's de facto family. Our parents were roadies together and they always called us cousins. I've known her longer than I've known Dex." A shocked laugh cracked out of me as Sunny's brow crinkled and her lips folded into a doubtful line. "Wait a second—are you jealous? Is that what this is? You're *jealous*?"

Instead of answering that question, Sunny asked, "So, she just came to visit?"

"She visited because I invited her." Sunny's gaze darkened. I was barely containing my amusement here. You couldn't sandblast the smile off my face. I stepped toward her, locking my arms around her waist. "She's managed hotels and resorts all around the world."

"How very nice for Ayla." She rolled her eyes and I thought seriously about throwing her over my shoulder and taking her home with me right now. I wanted to know the way jealousy tasted on her.

"But she wants to be closer to family now," I went on. "Since her husband's parents live here on the bay and their surrogate is expecting twins this winter."

Sunny sucked in a breath. "Oh. That's—well, that's exciting for them."

"Very exciting." I thumbed a bit of rain off her cheeks. "So, I showed my cousin around the restaurant this morning in a weak attempt at wooing her for the general manager job since I definitely don't want it and cannot keep doing it."

Sunny nodded slowly. "How did that go?"

"She's going to think it over." I tucked a wisp of hair behind her ears. "Still jealous?"

"I am not *jealous*, Beckett."

"Salty, then."

She glanced back toward the open door, her lips pinched in a pout that I wanted to kiss more than anything else. No, I wanted to bite it more than anything else. "I'm not salty. I just had some questions."

"Yeah, I have some questions too." I felt the mist on the back of my neck, my forearms. I didn't care. "Why don't you tell me about the defensive lineman I saw you snuggling for an entire fucking hour this morning."

"An hour?" She gave me a wide, face-splitting grin and I let myself drown in it. "Are you keeping track of how much time I spend with other men now? That seems a little obsessive, even for you."

I traced the line of her skirt, my thumb sliding under the t-shirt as I went. "Tell me about the guy, Sunny."

"You should know it was two guys."

My hand stilled. I blinked. "Excuse me?"

"Yeah, two guys. One is my former boss Leary who might be

grumpier than you, if that's even possible. But he loves dogs. Which is very important to me." She studied me carefully, like she was waiting until I was halfway to cracking a molar before finishing the story. "And the other is his great-nephew Mars. Leary moved in with Mars after selling the tavern. Leary can't drive anymore with the glaucoma, so Mars, who I met for the first time today, played chauffeur."

I closed my arms around her shoulders, pulled her tight to my chest. We were wet now, both of us, just enough to be slippery, and it didn't matter. Everything else faded away until the world was nothing more than a low hum of electricity. I wasn't sure but I was beginning to think this was the first foreign prickle of contentedness. Which was hilarious, of course, because my life was in shambles and the stakes couldn't be higher. But I had this beautiful blast from the past in my arms, and right here, right now, I believed in my marrow that everything would be all right if I could just hold on a little longer.

"What's the story with this Mars guy?"

"The jealousy is cute," she said into my shirt. "I'm beginning to see why you had so much fun with it."

"Answer the fucking question, Sunny."

"Impatient we are this evening," she said under her breath. "Lives in Boston. Harasses Leary into taking his medication. Eats like he's training to climb Everest. Does something where he's too expensive to keep on staff."

I scoffed. "Yeah, I know the *too expensive to keep on staff* type because I'm the *too expensive to keep on staff* type. They're all terrible. Egotistical assholes, every last one of them, and it would do you well to ban the guy from your café."

She stretched up on her toes and pressed a kiss to my lips. "By that logic, I'd have to ban you."

I shook my head but I couldn't help smiling at her. "I'd just try to buy the building again. Eventually, I'd succeed."

chapter eighteen

Sunny

Today's Special:
A Pickled Power Struggle

I LOVED and hated special event nights at the café in equal parts because no one wanted to leave. It was a gift, an incredible, dream-come-true gift to have customers who wanted to sit in my shop and drink tea all night long—and I'd personally bludgeon everyone if they didn't go home within the next five minutes. I was beginning to forget what the outside world looked like and whether I'd existed before locking myself inside this nine-hundred-square-foot universe.

Ah, that outside world. The place Beck had slipped off to more than an hour ago after making some noise about checking on Chef Bartholomew's sherry supply. I'd figured, perhaps foolishly, that he'd come back and bait me with some comments about whether I was out past curfew or why I shouldn't ride my bike at this hour. But he hadn't come back and now the chance that I'd slip up and accidentally toss some limes directly at the people lingering around their empty mugs increased by the minute.

Really though, I was happy to have the patrons. Even if my dogs had probably rearranged the entire house and chewed the legs right off the kitchen chairs. I'd brought them home after Leary's visit, knowing they'd tolerate open mic night but be much happier alternating between bursts of sleeping, backyard zoomies, and some light redecorating. At this point, I envied them.

"This is what we get for not immediately directing everyone to the door after the last act," Meara said as we watched the group erupt into laughter.

I twisted a dish towel around my palm. "Lesson learned."

Her husbands ambled outside, a sure sign that they were ready to wrap this up, and she leaned in against my shoulder. "I'll take care of this, and don't worry, I'll make it painless. They'll think it was their idea and they'll come back again soon."

One of the many reasons I loved this woman. She was as cutthroat as they came yet managed to do that without anyone noticing the knives.

Sure enough, she moved that group of stragglers along and together we finished the last of our closing chores in record time.

"I won't see you tomorrow, right?" she called from inside the office. "Or do I have the schedule mixed up again?"

"Nope, I'm off," I said as I wiped the front counter one last time. "Muffy will be in early to bake since she didn't do it tonight."

Meara emerged, bag on the crook of her elbow and a blazer draped over her shoulders. "Then I won't see you until we meet on Tuesday morning," she said. "I'm headed to the Hamptons on Sunday for some corporate fuckery thing with the husbands and we're not back until late Monday. Whatever it is, I'm supposed to wear white, which is complete bullshit if you ask me."

As long as I'd known her, Meara always wore black. There was the occasional gray or a navy blue. Rumors existed of a deep purple moment but I couldn't confirm it. "Do you own anything white?"

"I do not." She gestured to her milk-pale face. "I would disappear in white clothes. I'd vanish."

We made our way to the door, switching off lights and pushing in chairs as we went. "The husbands wouldn't let that happen."

"I'd hope not but one wrong move and I'm swept out to sea. So long, farewell, et cetera."

"Please don't let yourself get swept out to—" I pushed open the door and found Beck waiting outside, leaning against his SUV. His tie was long gone, the top buttons of his shirt wide open like a challenge, and he capped it all off with those inexcusably sexy glasses. I really needed to dig into why that look did it for me. "What are you doing?"

"Waiting for you to finish," he said. "I didn't realize vegan cafés pushed the limits of last call so hard."

"Aaaaaand why were you waiting for me?"

He folded his arms across his chest with a laugh. "Because there's no way in hell you're riding your bike home at this hour."

"You could follow me," I said. "You didn't have any trouble doing that last week."

Meara wrapped an arm around my shoulder and pressed her cheek to mine. "See you next Tuesday."

I met her gaze and gave her a tart grin. "Unnecessary," I whispered.

"Be terrible," she said as she crossed toward her husbands, waiting in their car. "Make unapologetically bad choices."

Beck and I stared at each other as those words took shape between us, growing and expanding until they seemed to force us closer. Until we made eye contact with the truth that we *were* making bad choices, had been making them for weeks—maybe even months. Since the start, since that very first morning. And that we had yet to stop ourselves. The reasons were there. We knew them backward and forward, recited them to each other when it seemed like the appropriate thing to do. But we climbed over those reasons like hidden rocks revealed by low tide, one after the other as we chased our way down the shore. Unapologetically.

Once Meara and her husbands pulled out onto Market Street, I asked Beck, "So, if you're taking me home—"

"It's not a question. I'm taking you home. I've already loaded your bike into the trunk."

I tapped a finger to my chin as I processed this. "So, if you're taking me home," I repeated, thrilled at the way his jaw ticked with annoyance, "do you plan on parking yourself at the curb for an hour or two again or will you be going in there with me?"

He shot a thoughtful frown at the ground. "Is that an invitation?"

"If it is, how are you going to respond?"

He pushed away from the SUV and moved toward me. "Don't you think you've asked enough questions for the evening? It's late. I'm driving you home. We're going to use that time to see if you can stop being a brat for five consecutive minutes, and if you can, then I'll make some decisions about how we spend the rest of the night."

"Oh, *you'll* make the decisions," I said. "That's adorable. So precious. Did you come up with that all on your own?"

On a sigh, he yanked open the passenger door, saying, "Get in the fucking car, Sunny."

I dragged my gaze between him, all long limbs and finger-raked hair, and the mellow glow of the dome light shining over the front seats. Since my feet were killing me and I'd had it in my mind to ask Meara for a ride, I stepped under the arm he'd extended over the doorframe.

As I fastened my seat belt, I peeked up at him. "As long as you don't mind."

I heard Beck muttering to himself as he closed the door. He shook his head at me through the windshield as he rounded the hood and went on muttering about "impossible" and "like I need a hole in the head" and "good time to start a drinking problem" as he settled beside me and started the car.

"What was that?" I leaned toward him, tapped my earlobe. He stared down at me like he'd caught me sneaking cookies before dinner.

He wasn't mad but he was disappointed. Toying with this man really was one of life's great pleasures. Enunciating more clearly than anyone could ever require, I said, "I didn't hear what you were saying."

Beck pulled out of the driveway and up Succotash Lane without comment but he grabbed my hand and pulled my knuckles to his lips, and he didn't let go. Not when he turned onto Market Street, not when he stopped at both of the lights in the center of town, and not even when he glanced over at me with a gaze that seemed to fall somewhere between pissed off and penitent.

Perhaps it was unapologetic.

Since I was overtired and hopped up on the gambler's high of bothering him, I said, "I will need to walk the dogs when I get home."

That did it. He heaved out a breath against the back of my hand and lowered it to his chest, which was no less intimate than his lips.

"At this fucking hour of the night?" he asked. *"Alone?"*

"We've been over this so many times." I shook my head. I could feel his heartbeat against my fingers. "I have *two* large dogs, Beck."

Another rib-rattling sigh. "Then I'll walk the dogs with you."

"I should also start some laundry. I'm at least a week behind and I'm going to run out of underwear any day now. Probably tomorrow, actually."

"Hmm. No. Not a problem."

"Maybe not for you and your endless supply of three-piece suits and such," I said, "but I have a limited number of Naked t-shirts and you already know the underwear situation."

"I can make that problem go away."

"Is this where you suggest I go without underwear? Because that seems forward even for you."

"Even for me," he repeated, laughing. "No, that wasn't what I had in mind."

"And I need to check on some orders," I went on. I did not have the wits about me to ask for clarification on what he did have in mind, not when I was exceptionally committed to being impossible and the source of his future fictitious drinking problem. "The shipment was already delayed and we're running dangerously low on glass juice bottles. Beth is going to start demanding people chug their drink in front of her and hand the bottle right back."

He shifted our hands, flattening mine to the unbelievably fine weave of his shirt and layering his on top. It was like we were holding his heart down which was, of course, ridiculous because no hearts were involved with anything in this vehicle. We were just two people who liked to harass each other and sometimes paw at each other like savages. Nothing out of the ordinary.

"You've been working since first thing this morning," he said. "Probably sixteen hours."

I watched as he turned toward my neighborhood, his eyes on the road and his smartwatch glowing in the darkness. Cuffs rolled up to his elbows, jaw sharp and rigid as always. He had that solid, stately confidence that seemed to come so naturally to some men and project out of them like radio waves. "Just about sixteen hours," I said. "Same as you, right?"

"Yeah. Sure. Except I've spent at least half of that time sitting in my office while you haven't sat down since that hour with your friend *Mars* this morning."

"Ah, we're back on that."

I felt a growl move through his chest. "Okay, so, five consecutive minutes *is* too much to ask. Noted."

He came to a stop at the curb outside my house. Or, my parents' house. It was mine now. I'd lived in it long enough to dismantle three decades' worth of intense coastal cottage décor, right down to the sand-dollar-stenciled toilet lid. So, it was my place. Where I lived with my dogs.

Where I had yet to bring a single romantic partner.

It wasn't that I'd chosen to drop out of the dating scene so much as

I'd diverted my energy to things that didn't suck my soul out by the spoonful. It wasn't *that* bad but it was shabby, and that was worse than bad. Shabby to the point that I missed nothing about the whole song and dance, and it didn't bother me at all when I just…stopped doing it.

For two years.

Intimacy had always been tricky for me, especially so with new partners, and when everything happened with winning the bait shop and then The Soggy Dog closing and the birth of Naked Provisions, I didn't have a good reason to go looking for love. Or whatever it was I got out of dating.

Yet here I was, sitting outside my house with my hand pressed to Beckett Loew's chest at eleven-thirty at night, wondering if this was the end to my accidental vow of chastity. Wondering if this was the moment when decisions went from bad to irreversibly, unapologetically bad.

I motioned to where Jem and Scout's faces filled the front window. "They are not going to put up with us sitting here for long. Jem will howl."

Beck studied me for a moment. "And we don't want that?"

I shrugged. "The neighbors don't love it. Especially at this hour."

"Right. Fair enough." He nodded, saying, "Then we better get in there."

I didn't move. Not when my hand was in his possession and I had an idea what was coming next but also no ideas at all because what would really happen when we got in there? What would I say and what would he do and how would everything change? It *would* change, there was no arguing that. He would change and I would change, and the things that orbited us would change.

A grim smile stretched across Beck's mouth because he knew it too. The only question was how much we were going to let that bother us.

"We don't want to wake the neighbors," he said. Unapologetically.

chapter nineteen

Sunny

Today's Special:
A Flight of Locally-Raised Rules

I SHOULD'VE ANTICIPATED the first thing that happened when we stepped inside the house because I knew my dogs. Most specifically, I knew Jem and the way he riled Scout up, and it should not have been a surprise that they bullied Beck the Bridge Troll to the floor within thirty seconds of the door closing behind us. He ended up flattened to the living room rug, paws on his chest and tongues lapping like he'd bathed in bacon, which led to the second thing I should've anticipated because I knew Beck.

He was kind to my dogs. More than kind. He was *good* to them.

He treated them with the same interest and concern he had for my friends, his brother, Mel, and Hale. But the difference here was that he wasn't stoic about it. He didn't pretend to be cool or emotionless. He played with them, rolling around on the floor and not once attempting to dodge their slobbering inspection. He scratched behind their ears and clapped their flanks, laughing as they yipped and howled, and he talked to them like he'd known them for years. Like they were his.

My heart felt spiky and leaden in my chest as I watched my dogs give this one their stamp of approval. As much as it frustrated me to admit, I approved of this one too.

After a few more minutes of play, I sat down on the floor beside Beck and said to the dogs, "Gentle."

They clamored away from their new friend and stalked into the kitchen where they sloshed water from their bowls. Beck started brushing the dog hair from his clothes.

"Eh, fuck it," he muttered. "That's what dry cleaning is for." Then he shifted, dropping his head to my lap and roping one arm around my waist while sliding a hand under my skirt. "Can they wait ten or fifteen minutes before hitting the streets?"

He gazed up at me as he traced my knee and, not for the first time, I wondered what his life was like back in Singapore. He'd wear suits, always with the vests and the rolled-up cuffs and the ties he wouldn't stop tugging, but who did he see every day? What were his routines? How did he spend his nights? Who did he date? Who did he fuck?

I knew without asking that they were nothing like me. No, he went for the corporate type. Like the cousin who wasn't a cousin. He liked that whole vibe. Ice-pick heels and coordinating pantsuits, sleek, obedient hairstyles and the kind of flawless makeup that could trick someone into believing it wasn't makeup at all.

And somehow, for some reason, he was here. With me. *Painfully aware* of everything I did. Nestled in my lap. Asking for ten or fifteen minutes for—for what, exactly? For sex? To step outside and shake the dog hair off his clothes? To unload my bike and leave?

"What is it you think will take ten or fifteen minutes?"

He smoothed his broad palm up my thigh, stopping right in the middle. Too high for there to be any confusion, too low to get off to the races. "I could talk a big game and make a lot of promises, but the truth is, I want ten uninterrupted minutes to kiss you the way I've wanted for —for a really long fucking time, Sunny."

I wasn't sure who moved first. Maybe we moved at the same time, both shifting and fumbling to fit ourselves together on the floor, and then we were there, wrapped together like vines that had sprouted from nowhere and grew back every time they were uprooted. No hedge trimmer could keep us apart.

He moved over me, his tree-trunk thigh heavy between my legs and one hand cupping my breast while the other cradled my head. His shaft was hard against my belly and he kissed me like he wanted to know if I could handle it.

I wanted him to know that I could handle anything—maybe, possibly—but I didn't have his focus, his precision. My kisses were quick, biting, sloppy affairs that revealed more about what I needed than I was prepared to admit. More than I even understood before this moment.

My hands were everywhere at once, pulling at his clothes, his hair. Stroking his biceps because who the fuck gave him the right to have muscles like that? Grabbing for his belt and his trousers despite knowing I couldn't reach. Not when his torso was approximately seven feet long.

To be clear, his torso was not actually seven feet long but to someone who required a stepladder to reach the back of the freezer, it certainly seemed that way and I was content to exaggerate without restriction. And right now, I wanted my exaggeration with a side of thick, hot friction between my thighs.

"What are you doing?" He laughed against my lips as I made another futile attempt at getting him where I wanted him. He smiled down at me, his gaze warm and hazy as he swept a thumb over my nipple. It was enough to rip an appalling whimper-whine from my throat that turned his smile into a smug grin. "More of that, I take it?"

"Do you have to be so pleased with yourself?"

"Pleased that I got that sound out of you? Fuck, yes. I'll take anything I can get." He kissed my lips, my jaw, my throat. Scraped his teeth over my skin, nipping just enough to send a shiver through my body but then soothing it with tiny, gentle brushes of his lips. "You have no idea how many times I've thought about this, all the ways I've thought about you. How you'd feel, how you'd sound." He groaned. "How you'd taste."

He pressed his face to the crook of my shoulder and stayed there a moment, just breathing while his thumb moved in slow, steady circles around my nipple. If he knew he controlled every muscle in my body from that single point of contact, he didn't show it.

"Tell me," I whispered.

"This is better," he said, his lips on my temple. "God, it's so much better."

I wanted to push on his chest and force him to look around and realize that we were making out on the floor, fully clothed. He wasn't allowed to have so much reverence for this. But he was right. It was so much better than anything else we'd shared up to this point. I didn't know if that was due to gaining some privacy or not caring about the lines we were crossing but I wanted to keep going and never, ever look back because it was so much better than anything I'd ever experienced with *anyone*. I didn't know my body could feel this way, like an avalanche and the sunrise and a cannonball dive into cold water all at once.

"I know." I tilted my head back to catch his lips in a kiss. "I *know*."

Then he ruined everything by saying, "We should stop."

I pushed against his chest *hard*. I knew my nails had no impact on the granite slab of his pecs but I dug in regardless. Pinched, even if he didn't feel it. "What?"

He blew out an enormous breath and cut his gaze to the side. "The dogs, Sunny. We should walk them now because if we stay here another minute, I won't let you go the rest of the night."

"Oh." I pinched a little harder. "They're fine. They don't need a walk."

"Hey. Ow." He batted my fingers away and blinked like he was having trouble translating my words into a language he understood. "But—you said—"

"Yes, I did." I shimmy-shuffled out from underneath him and settled on my knees, a little breathless, a lot flushed. From being pinned under the granite slab but also from the otherworldly things he'd done with *one* thumb on *one* nipple. "I said that and it's true that I often walk them in the evenings. But something I didn't mention is that they have a dog door to come and go as they wish, and the backyard is fully fenced, and while they'd love to go on a stroll-and-sniff, they can do without tonight."

He sat back on his heels and ran a hand over his mouth. He was no more than two feet away but this sudden burst of distance came at me like gulps of water, too much, too fast. He was breathing hard and flexing his hands by his sides, and his hair was just like his eyes, wild and everywhere at once. His trousers stretched across his massive thighs, across that impossibly thick shaft—and all at once I was dizzy, *dizzy* and hot, and we weren't even touching each other.

"My god, you are such a little brat."

The rough laugh in his words was enough to get me moving. I pushed to my feet and ran a finger around the waist of my wrap skirt, over the knot that gave him so much trouble. Gathered up all the audacity I could fit in my hands. "The bedroom is this way."

For a big guy, he was quick on his feet. I was barely across the hall when his hands closed on my hips and his heat came around me like a cloak. "You don't get to say things like that," he growled into my neck.

I pushed open the door to my bedroom, a space that barely fit a queen-sized bed and a slim dresser but in the morning, drowned in gorgeous, gentle slants of sunlight. "And why is that?"

"Because I am already clinging to the edge here and I don't think I'll survive if you turn out to be as mouthy as I'd dreamed."

He gathered my hair in one hand and dragged his lips over the back of my neck. He was unhurried about it yet frantic at the same time, kissing and tasting but also tightening that grip on my hair and rattling out low growls as he went.

But then he peeled away from me, let my hair fall. He was silent for longer than I could handle in moments made entirely of heartbeats and I shifted to face him. "What?" I asked, a touch of acid in my tone.

Beck took a few steps away from me but paused, his eyes narrowed as he glanced around my room. He dragged a hand over the blanket folded on the foot of my bed. He looked away, tipping his head as if he was trying to hear something. Then, "It smells like you. In here, it smells like you."

He sounded like he'd finally figured out a puzzle that had plagued him for years, a little dreamy, a little relieved. But it was such a strange thing to say. I didn't wear perfume. Most of my products were unscented. No one had ever said anything like that to me before and I had to ask, "Is that a good thing?"

He cut his gaze back to me with a deep nod as he tugged the curtains together. Though it made no sense, he moved around my room as if he'd always been here, closing my curtains at night and scooting between the wall and the bed as if he knew this two-step backward and forward. He kicked off his shoes in the corner like he did it every night. Like it was his spot. "Very much."

"Okay," I started, crossing my arms over my chest, "so, what do I smell like?"

"Remember that flowerpot?" He scooped up the stack of books on my bedside table and glanced at each cover, stopping to frown and arch his brows more than once. His interest in the celebrity tell-all memoirs would fit on the head of a pin but he paused to read the back cover of all my romances. Gave several appreciative nods. Held a few up with sharp stares that seemed to say *We'll talk about this later.* I could hardly wait for those conversations. "The one I dropped to prevent you from cracking your skull open?"

"All of this is debatable but yes, I remember the flowerpot. Fondly."

"You smell like that." He put the books down and shoved his fingers through his hair. "The only thing I can say is that every time I'm near you, all I can think about is gardens and herbs, and"—he shot a resigned glance at the floor—"it does something to my head. Sometimes I notice it when you're not around and I drive myself crazy trying to figure out where it's coming from but I never can. I'm just—I don't know. I'm kind of obsessed with it. With..." His gaze settled on me. "Well."

"Oh." The word gusted out of me.

"Yeah." He laced his fingers around the back of his neck but quickly abandoned that position and shoved his hands in his pockets. "Why are you all the way over there?"

"I'm not all the way anywhere," I said. "This room, it's quite small."

He shook his head like those details were irrelevant to him, and held out a hand. "Still too far away."

Instead of shuffling around the bed and meeting him on the other side, I hiked up my skirt and climbed onto the mattress. I knee-shuffled toward him and he reached for me with both hands like I might tumble right over the edge.

"There will be rules," I said, pressing my palms to his chest.

He fussed with the hair tie I'd used to cinch my t-shirt until it came loose. "Rules," he echoed. "Such as?"

A breath skittered out of me as he ran his hands up my sides, his thumbs sliding just beneath my breasts. I had to focus. I had to put words into a logical order and speak sentences. "We don't talk about Lance."

He made a harsh, impatient noise. "Please explain to me why, for any reason at all, we would talk about Lance."

"Because he's like"—I fluttered my hands around—"everywhere. Between us."

Beck locked his hands on my waist and pulled me toward him until there was no space, no air, only heat. He was hard against my thigh, unbelievably so. Just like everything else about him, it was too big, too much.

"Sunny, sweetheart, I don't know what you think this is, but it's not Lance."

"*That* is not what I meant and you know it." One corner of his mouth crooked up in a smile. "We don't talk about Lance anymore. What he's going to say, how long his tantrum will go on, none of it."

"It will go on for six or seven months and he'll sink into the core of the earth in order to have peace while resenting us for disrupting the order of his universe."

He gripped my backside, rocked against me at an angle that brought my eyelids down and forced my lips apart. Light flashed behind my eyes, and for a second or fifty I wondered how any of this was possible. How did it feel this good but also this easy? Like my body knew what it wanted, knew what to do, and I just had to let it.

"One more rule," I managed.

"I think we have enough already."

"We promise that, no matter what happens with us, nothing has to change. I don't want you to lose your best friend because of"—I drummed my fingers on his chest—"you know. This."

He reached between us, adjusted himself in his trousers. Groaned like he wanted me to know I was killing him. "I don't know if either of us can promise that but if it's what you need, I will try." When I nodded, he asked, "Can we institute the not-talking-about-Lance rule now? The things I want to do to you can't exist in my mind while Lance is there."

"What do you want to do to me?"

He swallowed up my question with his kisses, shoved his hands into my hair, growled like he was a wolf and a bridge troll and a bossy, broody man all smoothed down and folded away into one complicated creature. I loved his sounds, the way his hands seemed to flex against his will, how he'd exhale into my skin like this was torture, true, endless torture.

I hadn't known it could be like this. Not for me. Everyone else, sure, but nothing about my body was like everyone else. I'd always had to work a little harder, focus on getting comfortable, getting into it. But here I was, a landscape of goose bumps and a throb between my legs that ached like nothing I'd known before and I *wanted* him. I wanted him in a panicked, humiliating way that had me hooking my fingers into his belt loops and between the buttons on his shirt, holding on like it would be all too easy for this to disintegrate in my hands.

"I want to put my head under this skirt and eat you for fucking *hours*."

"*That's* what you want?"

"Only every time I see you in a skirt." He looped a finger around the neck of my t-shirt, tugged it down to kiss his way across my collarbones. "I'd die under that skirt if you let me."

"I don't think I will, no," I said, a hysterical giggle slipping out of me.

"That's disappointing." He was a rush of kisses and scraped teeth, sighs and raspy hums. His hands were everywhere. "I would've thought you'd take an opportunity to get rid of me."

"Yeah, but I don't have time to hide a body. If I kill you, it's going to need to be somewhere that I can wipe my hands and walk away."

"Why am I not surprised that you want me to fuck you in the woods, at night, like the little witch you are?"

"You said it," I whispered. "Not me."

"I want to bend you over this bed and watch that perfect mouth of yours pop open every time I thrust into you," he said, smiling against my neck. "I don't think your feet will touch the floor."

"We don't need any short girl slander here." I needed to tell him. I needed to be clear about my…issues. I closed my fingers around his shirt and buried my head in his chest, a small, defensive position that would save me from nothing. "This might not be the best time to tell you that I don't usually like a lot of penis."

He froze like we were playing a game of statues. "I'm sorry, *what* did you just say?"

I heaved out a breath and glanced up at him. He stood beside my bed, his stance wide and solid like he'd grown out of the floorboards. "I don't like—the penis part of this whole thing doesn't always work out well for me."

"Okay." He nodded like *oh, yeah, I hear that all the time* and *maybe I should check under the hood to see for myself.* "Because it's painful? Or is there something else?"

"I just—" I stared around his shoulder, dying a little at putting all of this into words. I didn't embarrass too easily, not after everything I'd gone through as a kid, but I was still learning how to talk about the things I wanted when it came to sex. Because I didn't have a lot of it. Hardly any. "It just doesn't do anything for me."

"Then"—he leaned in close, his words barely more than breaths on my neck—"what do you like?"

"There are a few things," I admitted. My knees were sinking into the mattress and I had to weeble-wobble to keep my balance. "But I haven't done a lot of"—I wiggled my shoulders, hoping he understood the multitudes contained inside that gesture. Though also still wobbling. "I haven't done a lot. With a lot of other people."

He reared back, his eyes flashing wide. "Tell me you are not a virgin. Please, Sunny, I am begging you—"

"I'm not a virgin," I said. "I've been with people." When his brow crinkled, I added, "But not a lot with penises. Just two, actually."

"Oh. Okay." This time his nod was like *there's no winning a land war in Russia but that's not about to stop me from rallying the troops.* "And it wasn't good for you?"

"The first time was—well, I'll save you the story and say it didn't end positively for anyone involved." I glanced up at him, my bottom lip snared between my teeth. "Another time, with another guy, we didn't get all the way. In, that is."

His gaze darkened. "You're practically a virgin."

"No, I am not," I cried. "And you know what? Sex isn't just about where you put a penis, and virginity is a very strange made-up thing that doesn't really matter."

"Oh my god. Sunny." He closed his eyes and pressed his fingers to his forehead, grimacing as if I'd told him my vagina was sealed up like a soup can and he'd need to provide his own tools. "At the risk of you throwing me out on my ass, I have to ask: Do you want to slow down? Stop?"

"*Don't you dare.*"

He dropped his hands and blinked at me as if these things didn't compute, and perhaps they didn't. Perhaps sex was a straight arrow for Beck. Perhaps he'd woken up one teenage morning and known without question that he'd find satisfaction from the standard slate of hetero-sexual experiences, and he'd pursued that with clear-minded vigor every day since. Perhaps most people who didn't have decades of bodily autonomy issues lived that way. Perhaps anyone who hadn't won the bonus prize of a seizure *in the middle of their first time* lived that way.

I didn't. I had a handful of experiences with men and women ranging from unbelievably bad (see: the one with the seizure) to luke-warm to actually kind of okay, and all that got me was a cringey conver-sation when the only thing in the world I wanted was to pull him down on top of me and turn off my mind.

"I really don't want you to stop. I want to try it again," I said, searching his eyes for some sign that he believed me. His answering groan reverberated into the chambers of my heart. "If you'll go slow with me."

"Oh my god. Sunny." He drew his hands down my hips, held me close, his fingers pulsing into my skin as shaky breaths passed between us. "I will do *anything* you want but I need you to be very clear about what that is." His words were tight, like bolts turned too far, but his face was calm, steady. Even. "Tell me what you do like. We'll start there and figure it out as we go. Okay?"

"Okay." I moved his hand to my inner thigh. I covered his fingers with mine, pressing hard, navigating as best I could in the comfy new darkness of not knowing what came next. For once, I kind of loved that confusion. "I like it when you touch me."

"I can do that."

He ran his knuckles up my leg and I had to look down and watch him do it because I didn't understand how these hot, bubbling sensations could be real. How they could come from nothing more than skin on skin. How my entire body could light up from *this*.

His thumb swept over my underwear, careful and methodical, like he was counting in his head, and I appreciated that he made not a single comment about the soggy condition of the fabric. He brought his other hand to the back of my neck and brushed his lips to mine, and I was certain I'd dissolved into liquid.

Minutes passed and my internal temperature spiked to somewhere around the surface of the sun while he made no move to pull off my shirt or slip that thumb into my underwear. I wanted those things. I wanted everything—and I had to be the one to take it. In the absence of any other readily available solution, I flopped back on the mattress to wriggle out of my skirt.

Beck watched from beside the bed, one arm folded over his chest while he held the other toward me, as if prepared to intervene if needed. And that made sense seeing as this was the most complicated possible way to get out of a skirt made of multiple miles of fabric.

"It's in the way," I said, red-faced and slightly breathless as I kicked it off.

Beck caught the skirt and folded it in half, then in half again. He set it on the dresser and gave me a *that was really something* glance. "I could've helped you with that."

"I had it under control."

"And what an amusing show of control it was."

The t-shirt had settled past my waist, around my hips, though it was rucked up on one side. I felt the weight of his gaze there. I reached down, wanting to know how that weight would feel with a lot less underwear in this equation, when a raw, growly noise rasped out of Beck.

He brushed my hands away and flattened his over the front of my boy shorts, his thumb pressed into the line of my cleft. The pressure of his palm *required* me to do something, anything to find some relief and, without thinking about what it meant, I rocked against him. A shrill, shameful whimper broke out of me and our eyes met, locked.

"Please."

"You have to tell me what that means, sweetheart." He gave a slight shake of his head as he stared at me. "What makes you feel good?"

And I was supposed to answer that with words? That I spoke out loud? While he looked at me? "This is good for me," I managed. "But, more."

He leaned down, braced one arm beside me while he rested his forehead near my belly button. He held himself steady for a moment, his shoulders a mountain range over me. "Can I take these off?" He tapped his thumb near my clit and that bolt of indirect pressure hit me so hard, I choked on air. "Or not, that's fine too."

"No, yes, please, off." I tried squirming out of the shorts myself but he pressed a forearm across my hips, holding me in place. With that, the few fully formed thoughts in my head turned to sand. "Off," I said again, since I was doing a bang-up job at being coherent. "Please."

"Off, then." With one annoyingly efficient flick of his wrist, the shorts skimmed down my legs and dropped somewhere over his shoulder. "And you want me to touch you again?"

"I think I'm going to implode if you don't."

"I won't let that happen." He said this like I wasn't dissolving into a loose collection of pieces right in front of him. Like I wasn't flailing and helpless, barely capable of stringing together words. Like he wasn't the cause of it all. "Can I tell you what I'm thinking or is that too much?"

He ran a hand between my legs in patient, soothing passes as if there was a billboard over my vagina reading *Proceed with caution.*

"It's not too much," I said, pulling him to the bed. I didn't want to be naked and splayed open for study. I wanted him close. "I'm used to you saying ridiculous things. I'd be concerned if you stopped."

He nudged the t-shirt up, leaving it bunched under my breasts, and kissed his way down the center of my belly. He tapped above my clit again though this time it felt like he was drumming his fingers on a tabletop. The vibrations thrummed over my nerves and I shifted, hoping to find a little more pressure, a little more direct contact.

"This?" he asked, sliding a finger between my folds and circling right where I wanted him. "That's what you need?"

"Mmmyes" slurred out of me as I rocked against his hand.

"That's my girl," he rumbled, his mouth on my hip. "Show me. Don't stop." He murmured in approval as I worked my way into a jerky rhythm that tightened every string in my body. "You are so fucking soft, Sunny. I'm losing my mind here."

He shifted and I felt the thick ridge of him on my thigh and everything inside me clenched in response. All I could think about was *more*. I needed so much more. I reached for his hand, guiding him lower. Deeper. "Could you—"

"Anything." He edged closer, bowing his head to meet my lips as he pushed into me. "I feel as though I've been thinking about this forever. Like I've wanted you so long, I can't remember a time when I didn't."

At first, I couldn't speak. I couldn't produce coherent words with those fingers moving inside me and the heel of his palm grinding against my clit. And the worst part was that Beck *knew*. He didn't even try to hide that smug smile of his when he met my fogged-over gaze. I glared at him but that only cranked his smile up even more.

I didn't have words but there were sounds. Deep, sweary, guttural ones that required me to break away from Beck's kisses in order to let them tremble out of me. Gasps and cries as I pulsed around him. Breathy shrieks as I arched into his hand.

The words came back to me gradually. It was like my body had decided that we wanted this and we were doing this, and that single-minded focus came with a specific vocabulary. *Please* and *yes* and *there*. *More*.

"That's it," he whispered against my lips. "There you are. There's my perfect girl."

I didn't think I'd come this way. I knew I could, based on a fair amount of independent study, but it didn't happen often with a partner. It *never* happened this fast. But here I was, barreling into the best, most destructive orgasm I'd ever had with the help of another person, my hand in his hair and my pussy clamped around his fingers so hard that I had a real concern about breaking them.

"You're fucking miraculous," he said, tipping his forehead against my temple. "Tell me I can keep touching you. Tell me we're not done, Sunny. I can't be done with you yet."

I shook my head. Everything inside my chest quaked. "Not done," I whispered.

"Do you need me to stop?" His hand was steady between my legs, a solid weight that only made the aftershocks more intense.

I closed my hand around his wrist. "Not yet."

He kissed my cheeks, my jaw, my lips. He drew in a deep breath when he tucked himself into the crook of my neck and he sighed while I tossed my working knowledge of sex and intimacy in the shredder.

If I could come like *this* from only *that*—well, things were different tonight.

"I remember a time when you didn't want me," I said, unreasonably proud of myself for finally stringing together a complete sentence and not once dissolving into a quivering puddle. "Like the time you tried to buy my building."

"Do you know what I'm going to do now?" he asked, his breath warm on my cheek. "I'm going to see if your clit feels just as soft on my tongue as it does on my fingers. I'm going to lick you until I've memorized the way you taste. I'm going to learn what you like and do that over and over until you pass out." He swatted the outside of my leg, cracking a startled laugh out of me. "And I'm going to use these perfect thighs of yours as earmuffs so I don't have to hear any more of your heckling."

He pushed up on an elbow and caught my eyes, his searching stare asking *Is that okay? Are you comfortable? Do you want this? Can I be rude to you while we're naked?*

I think so. Yes. So much, yes. I don't know what to do with you when you're not rude.

I nodded and ran a hand down his back, pulling his shirt from his trousers as I said, "You could probably take this off."

His lips quirked but he said nothing as he sat up and started unbuttoning his shirt. Then, he glanced over his shoulder at me, his gaze traveling over my bare skin, my parted legs. I shifted, pulled the t-shirt down. He looked away, knowing I needed to regain a touch of control.

"I wanted you then," he said.

I rolled my eyes but he was busy with his buttons. "No, you didn't."

"I did," he said, shrugging out of the shirt. He placed it on the dresser with my skirt, leaving me to stare at the broad expanse of his back. He was strong, all carved muscles and sun-kissed skin. "I wanted you right from the start."

Since I wasn't going to let him pander to me while I was half stripped and orgasm-drunk, I scooted up to the pillows and tucked my knees all the way under the t-shirt. "You had quite an odd way of showing it, Beck."

He turned, his hand resting on his belt buckle. I swallowed hard. I really wanted him to take those trousers off.

"It wasn't my best day," he said, holding my gaze as he unlatched his belt.

I held my breath for no reason other than wanting to hear every clank of metal, every catch of the zipper. Those sounds crawled along the back of my neck and over my shoulders, leaving behind goose bumps and a shiver that arrowed through my limbs.

With his trousers gaping open, he studied my new position on the bed. "Getting comfortable?" he asked. "Good call. What do you think about losing the shirt? I'd give anything in the world to watch you play with your nipples while I'm sucking your clit."

"That depends," I said with a glimpse to his trousers. "I don't like being the only one undressed."

Not once breaking eye contact, he set his glasses, phone, and wallet on top of my book stack and stepped out of the trousers, adding them to the pile on my dresser. Wearing only black boxer briefs that left nothing to the imagination, he motioned to himself. "More? Or should we wait a little longer to cross this bridge?"

I curled my hands around the hem of my t-shirt. I didn't know how much longer I could wait. "Get over here."

He dropped a knee to the mattress, watching while I pulled the shirt over my head. He glanced to the ceiling and ran a hand over his mouth before saying, "Talk to me, okay? Tell me what you want, what you like. What you don't like. Stop me at any point."

I leaned back against the pillows, my knees locked and my legs folded up in front of me. "I know."

He nodded like he'd settled some internal debate and then he launched himself onto the bed and between my legs, one arm banded low on my waist as if he knew he'd have to hold me steady.

The first swipe of his tongue brought me all the way back to the edge. It was unreasonable. Unfair, really. He had no business being so good at everything. I hated him for it. I also loved it. The many mysteries of my life. "Oh my god," I whisper-cried.

His response came in the form of sliding two fingers inside me and returning his tongue to my clit. I bucked against him and I could *feel* him laugh into my flesh. Because he knew. He knew I was past the point of caring who won this round of our power struggle. Past the point of caring whether I was spread out and pinned down, vulnerable in the most stressful ways.

Again, "Oh my *god*."

Then he ran his lips along the inside of my thigh, saying, "You're calling out to the heavens, but I'm the one in need of deliverance."

I stared down the length of my body at him, bleary-eyed and disoriented like I was in a dream that kept turning upside down and starting over in strange new places. Like nothing I knew would be of any use to me in this world.

I ran my fingers through his hair, letting the wavy strands coil around my knuckles. "I want you inside me. I want you to fuck me."

"No." He nipped a soft, fleshy part of my leg, right near the curve of my bottom. "Not yet."

And then the discussion was over because he went back to dragging his tongue around my clit in a way that left my mind chanting *This. This is what we've been waiting for.* Part of me—the part that had believed I wasn't good at being intimate with other people—was throwing a grand parade because even the best toys in the world couldn't actually simulate *this*. The other part was flat-out perturbed that Beck was better at this than any of the people I'd ever been with. Didn't he have enough already? Wasn't he blessed forty different ways to forever? Why did his tongue have to be a literal weapon too?

"When?" I asked, back to my weeble-wobbling in a desperate attempt to get more. I didn't know what *more* really was, but I knew I'd die if I didn't get it. "I mean, you said you wanted to bend me over the bed and—"

"*Fuck.* Stop it, Sunny."

He groaned into my leg and I was one giant goose bump, every inch of me overly sensitive and electrified. It was almost painful, this gathered swell of want. I pressed my palms to my breasts because my nipples were so tight, they ached. That was when I realized he was slowly, subtly rocking his hips against the mattress.

I grabbed at his shoulders to drag him toward me but it was like dragging a boulder out of the ocean. "I want you here," I said, and I could hear myself pouting. "With me."

"Not yet," he said again. He twisted the fingers inside me, hit an angle that made me feel like I was sitting in the bottom of an hourglass, sand spilling over me. Burying me.

"When?" I whined.

He leaned on an elbow, watching as his fingers shuttled in and out of me. The brackets at the corners of his lips popped. "When you're ready."

"You alone make those decisions? I thought I was supposed to talk to you and tell you what I wanted."

He swung a tense glance toward me. "And I'm happy that you did, but you're not ready."

"I feel ready." As I said this, he shifted his fingers a little more and I knew I'd combust and drown and float away like a feather on the breeze if he so much as breathed on my clit.

I wanted to hate him for this. I really did. All these years I'd stumbled through awkward and disappointing experiences, eventually settling into the only available explanation which was that I didn't find much satisfaction through sex. Enter Beckett Loew, of all the damn people, and here I was, blinking at his head between my legs through upside-down eyes.

"I'm ready," I repeated, grasping at every stitch of strength I could gather. I refused to whine. Or beg. Again. "I want it."

"I know you do," he said, "but if you think for a second that I'm not going to do every damn thing in my power to prevent this from being another one of your bad experiences, you're confused." He dropped a series of kisses on my thigh, my belly. I pinched harder at my nipples though it only made the current spiraling inside me stronger, more restless. "Now, tell me what you need."

"Lick me," I said on a gasp.

"Good girl." His words rumbled like thunder against my skin and then he was there, his tongue circling me in long, lazy passes.

"Beckett, I need—*please*—"

Again, the words broke apart, leaving me with strained moans that seemed to start in my toes and gather speed like a dark, lusty tornado until it blazed through everything in its path. Perhaps it was better this way. Safer. A little less vulnerable. If I didn't tell him that the only thing in the whole world that I wanted was to feel him push inside me and for it to finally, *finally* be good in the soft, shattering way that everything with him was good, then I wouldn't be disappointed. I wouldn't have to reckon with the reality, once again, that my mind and my body didn't always play on the same team. I wouldn't have to accept that these kinds of relationships probably weren't for me.

"You are the most beautiful thing I've ever tasted," he said. "I'm going to lose my entire mind when I get inside you. You're going to fucking ruin me, aren't you, Sunny?"

I felt the tingle in the far edge of my eyes first and then it was lower, across my chest and down the line of my belly. It was strange, almost like the buildup before a sneeze. Suddenly, it was everywhere, that peculiar twinge spiraling and shooting out in a race of bone-melting release that was so surprising, all I could do was watch as my body shook from the force of it.

He growled into my flesh. "Mmm. Now you're ready."

It required real effort to open my eyes and watch while Beckett stripped out of his boxer briefs. His shaft was long and thick, jutting out from his body in a way that had me pressing my knees together. Nothing about him came off as rushed or impatient, but there was a second when his hands shook as he ripped open the condom packet.

When he climbed over me, he settled between my legs and rested his head between my breasts. "We can stop at any time," he said, pressing a light kiss to my nipple.

The entirety of my body tensed, desperate to clench around something, anything. "Even if we stop, we're not done. Okay?"

He exhaled on my breast and another riot of goose bumps spread across my chest. "I don't think I'll ever be done."

He slipped a hand under my backside and edged my legs open with his knees. I usually hated this part, hated those eternal seconds when I willed my body to cooperate, to accommodate. When I braced for the first signs that it wouldn't work.

But then Beck said, "Breathe, baby, it's just me," and all of that faded away.

I stared up at him as he pushed into me, focused only on cataloging the quirk of his brows, the pleats at the corners of his eyes, the twisted fault line of his mouth. I watched the way his throat bobbed and his jaw flexed as he sank deeper. When he dropped his forehead to mine and a soundless *fuck* passed over his lips, I didn't even blink.

A breath rushed out of him and he rolled his hips, and I had to close my eyes against the immense, glorious weight of him moving inside me. I couldn't believe this was happening. I couldn't believe I was here, full—*so full*—and desperate for more.

"Say something, storm cloud. Tell me you're good. Tell me you're with me."

"Good," I managed. He was bigger than anyone I'd been with—all two of them—and he was bigger than any of my toys. But it didn't hurt, probably because I was such a sloppy, slippery mess of wet. The life-altering orgasms he'd served up had also helped out. But even still, I needed him to move. To do something with all of this pressure. "It's—it's good. Don't stop. Please."

So much for doing away with the whining. And begging.

I dug my fingertips into his flanks, urging him on as he offered one tentative thrust, then another, and another. With each one, he dragged a hot, piercing stare from between my legs and up to my eyes, always waiting for some sign that I wanted to continue.

"I thought you were going to lose your mind," I said in response to his arched brow.

"Trust me, it's long gone," he said on a gusting exhale.

"I was real with you." Everything inside me tightened as he tapped two fingers against my clit. Much more of that and I'd misplace my words again. "Now it's your turn. What do you want?"

"This is what I want," he ground out, his eyes pinched shut and his jaw locked like he had the entire world on his shoulders.

"I don't think so." I shifted beneath him as I tried to find the move that would bring back all those filthy ideas, those words and promises that made me feel like I could do anything with him, *be* anything. Be everything. "You want to be a little wild."

"I want it to be good for you," he said against my jaw. "Let me do that."

He picked up the pace then, rocking into me with steady thrusts that pulled apart nearly every stitch of coherent thought in my mind. There was never a moment when it wasn't blindingly, frighteningly *good*. If anything, it just kept getting better. "What if I want you to be wild? What if that's what makes it good for me?"

"Not yet. Not now. The next time—all the times after can be wild."

He kissed me, presumably to shut me up, and I let him. I drowned in those kisses, opening and melting even more, and I let him continue with his careful, measured pace. I was unbelievably full, stretched in the best, most addictive ways. It had never been like this before and a sliver of me wondered if this would always be the way of it for us. Could it? No. No, this was a collision of crossed lines and tension. This was a single moment in time, a flash of lightning, a shooting star, a blue moon.

This was already better than all my previous experiences, independent study included, and if I quieted down for a second, I could sense the catastrophe of an orgasm pulling together behind my belly button.

Perhaps that was why I ran my hand up the back of Beckett's neck, my fingers tangled in his hair when I lifted my lips to his ear and whispered, "Can I tell you what I need right now?"

"Anything," he rasped, his steady rhythm faltering for one perfect, unrestrained moment. "Anything, it's yours."

"I need you to fuck me like this is your one and only chance," I said, deadly calm. I needed him to believe me, even if I wasn't sure I believed it myself. "If you don't, I'm going to throw you off this bed and finish the job by myself. Is that what you want?"

"Not tonight, no, but *definitely* soon."

The tension in his shoulders gathered like he was shifting into another gear and he hooked one arm under my knee, tucking it up against his ribs. I could barely swallow around the overwhelming pressure of him. I loved it. I wanted to pick up the fragments of this moment and rub them into my skin so I could remember it everywhere, always.

With a one-sided smile that sent a shiver through my chest, he said, "I'm well the fuck aware that this is my one and only chance, storm cloud."

He thrust into me hard, sending the headboard hammering against the wall. I ran my hands up his arms, over his shoulders. Holding on anywhere I could. "Show me."

"I think you like to see how far you can push me," he said, trailing his fingers down the side of my neck, between my breasts, over my belly. Stopped a few inches away from my clit.

It was torture. I loved this too.

My eyes rolled back as he fell into an unrelenting rhythm and my heartbeat lined up with the bang of the headboard against the wall. "Of course I do."

"I think you like this too." He settled more of his weight between my legs and slipped two fingers between my folds, finding my clit like he knew it better than his own name. "Even though you said you didn't."

That catastrophe, it was coming for me. "I didn't think I would. Like it," I added. "I haven't before."

He ducked his head to the crook of my neck while his cock split me in half and his fingers drew patient circles around me. "What changed?"

"You know what changed." I tipped my face back to kiss him, but we were lost in this moment, breathless and frantic and somehow shocked that we were there, out of control and careening toward that cliff. I settled for a hand on the back of his neck and my parted lips on his jaw, his throat. "You know exactly what changed."

It was then that Beck lost his grip on the promise to make it good for me—and by extension, hide away all his wild and his reckless. And it wasn't good anymore, it was otherworldly. He looped my legs around his waist and shoved his arms underneath me, and buried himself inside me like he wanted to hide all of his secrets there. He dropped his head to my chest and worshipped my nipples, sucking and teasing.

"I want to watch you ride me for *hours*," he said through a groan. "I want to taste you everywhere. Roll over in the middle of the night and slide into you. Wake up in the morning and do it all over again. I want to fuck you forever and then another forever and then even longer. I want every fucking inch of you, Sunny."

"Okay." There was no other answer. I was almost drowsy from the rush of pleasure building inside me and though it hadn't crossed my mind until this precise moment, I wanted all these things too.

"I think," he started, his hips pumping in erratic thrusts, "you just needed to find the right cock."

"What do I do now that I have?"

The arms banded around me tightened and Beck stilled for a second, pressing his teeth to my breast. He growled, saying, "Anything you want. Anything, Sunny. You could rip my heart out of my chest and make me stare at it while I die, and I wouldn't fault you for it."

I arched up, wanting to feel that fine nip of pressure from his teeth. "I won't do that."

"You might," he said. "You might not even know when you do it."

He surged into me, his teeth biting into my skin and his arms crushing me to his chest and a raw, primal noise rattling out of his throat. I wanted to say something, wanted to claw at his skin, squeeze my knees to his hips, taste that roar as it ripped through him. I wanted to grab these seconds out of the air and cling to them, gulp them down, carve them into my skin—anything at all to remember this as long as I lived.

But then everything went blank—in the best way.

It was like a small coma, one with white fireworks behind my eyelids and waves rippling through my body, contracting until all my muscles quit the game and collapsed. There were sounds, but only the ones inside me—blood pounding, lungs filling and emptying. Everything else was static. I wasn't sure but it seemed like I might've dipped out for a minute or an entire day, but when I forced my lids open, Beck was staring down at me with wide, troubled eyes like something was Very Wrong.

"I asked if you were okay *twice* and you didn't answer," he said.

I managed to lift an arm and motioned to the utter devastation of my overcooked noodle body. "Sorry. You fucked me into a quick coma." His eyes flared wider like things were Very, Very Wrong, and I rushed

—as much as I could rush right now—to say, "A good coma. Great coma, actually. Can we do that again? In a minute. After I learn to exist again. I want to see if it will always end in a coma. I might need to start a coma journal."

Beck sat back on his knees and massaged his temples. I didn't even care that my legs were splayed open and I was wet in a way that made me think I'd need to chug some water very soon. I didn't care that I was thoroughly exposed and vulnerable because I'd experienced more intimacy tonight than the sum of my adult life. Because I knew I *could* experience it.

And I really liked it.

"Sunny, you're—for fuck's sake, you're not allowed to say that."

I watched as he reached to the bedside table for some tissues. He handled the condom as I asked, "Why not?"

"Because it stresses me the fuck out," he said, glancing around for a wastebasket. "There are several things I'd rather do right now than worry about fucking comas."

"Like what?"

He shot the ball of condom-y tissues to the basket beside the dresser. It went in, of course. "I'd wanted to pass out with you on top of me." He said this like it was an accusation.

I giggled. He scowled. It was perfect.

"I had some ideas about waking up in a few hours and feeding you breakfast," he continued. "And then rolling you over onto some of these pillows and fucking you from behind so I don't have to think about baseball to keep from blowing it all while you play with your tits."

I patted the mattress beside me. "We can still do that."

He slapped a hand to his chest. "I'm going to need a minute to recover. I'm still mentally running wind sprints here, okay?"

"It's almost like you're unaware that you caused my little coma."

"You presented me with a problem." He ran a hand from my ankle to my knee and back down again. "I merely did what was necessary to solve it."

I grabbed hold of his wrist and tugged him toward me. This time, the boulder rolled right out of the ocean and into my arms. We shifted to our sides, my bottom tucked against his hardening shaft. I didn't see how that was remotely possible but I wasn't going to ask questions. He slipped one arm under my pillow and wrapped the other around my waist, his hand flat on my belly. I could still feel the quivers and pings of that last orgasm. I wondered if he could feel them too.

"Do you think that one time was enough to solve the problem?" I asked. "Or should we spend some more time testing it out?"

Beck kissed his way down my neck to my shoulder, and once again I was a single, giant goose bump. "One time wasn't enough," he said. "I don't think I'll ever have enough."

chapter twenty

Beckett

Today's Special:
Wild Deer

SUNNY FELT PERFECT RIGHT THERE. Like I'd existed for thirty-six years thinking I was a full, complete human being, but the truth was I'd been waiting all my life to hold her like this. We just stayed there, locked together and touching each other like we were starved. Like there would never, ever be enough.

And yet I could not stop myself from burying a laugh in the crook of her shoulder.

"You know, I've had a lot of strange experiences when it comes to sexytimes, but I don't think anyone has ever laughed at me while we were still in bed," Sunny said.

"Fuck, I'm sorry. I'm not laughing *at* you. I swear," I choked out. "But this is all catching up to me now. You tell me that dick doesn't do anything for you. You're *shy*. You need me to go slow—"

"Right, so hilarious," she muttered.

"—and then you basically grab me by the throat and order me to fuck you into the mattress. And you end it all by blacking out for a minute. I don't really know what happened here tonight but it changed my entire life."

"This isn't the time to tell me that I did it wrong," she said with a yawn. "If that was wrong, I don't want to talk about right."

I grabbed a handful of her ass and gave it a rough, shaking squeeze. "You were a fucking dream, Sunny."

She ran a finger down the arm draped over her waist, her touch burning a tiny path across my skin. "So," she said, dropping her gaze, "does that mean it was good for you?"

I blinked at her for a second because I was certain this was a joke. She was joking. I'd laughed at her for manifesting kinks I'd never thought I'd have and now she was teasing me. This was what we did. We sniped and snarled at each other. Yet I needed her to know the truth. I couldn't leave any doubt between us. Not after *that*. "You've ruined me. Rewritten my rule book on sex. Altered my DNA. Something. I don't know, but you're not getting rid of me."

"You're not one of those guys with a one-night policy?"

I shook my head, saying, "No, I'm not, but even if I was, you shredded the policy tonight."

"Does that mean," she started, running that finger down the center of my chest, "we can try other things?"

"We can try anything you want." I was more than half way hard and, until right now, neither of us had been concerned with doing anything about it. "You're not too sore?"

She wiggled against me, her brows knitting in concentration, and a groan rolled out of me. "I don't think so."

I slipped a hand between us, between her thighs. Stroked her until the wiggling settled into a steady rock against my palm. "You're sure?"

"It's annoying that you're so good at this," she said, her fingers flexing on my chest.

I shifted my hand to her hip. She whined and rubbed her legs together as if that would give her what she needed. "Answer the question, Sunny."

"Do you think it would feel different if I—" She flipped onto her belly and blinked at me over her shoulder, her lip trapped between her teeth as if she didn't know how to finish the sentence. "Like this?"

Because I was fully incapable of doing anything but exactly what she wanted, I climbed between her legs and skimmed a hand over her bare backside. "Yes."

"Will you show me how?"

I grabbed her hips, dragged her to my lap. Rocked my shaft against her. I was helpless here. Just fucking helpless. "Yes."

"Is this something you like? Will it be good for you too?"

If only she knew the half of it. If only she could crawl inside my mind and see how little I needed for it to be good. "*Yes.* Sunny, of course."

"Can we try it? Now?"

She shimmied against me and I didn't even have to think before reaching for a condom. "If you're sore, we're going to stop." My hands shook as I tore open the package. I fumbled *twice* before rolling it down properly. Thank god she was too busy being devious to notice. "Understood?" She went right on shaking that ass at me and I had to clamp both hands on her hips to hold her still. "*Sunny.* Sweetheart. Do you want me to come all over you right now? Before I even get inside you? Because that's what's going to happen if you don't stop."

She swung a glance over her shoulder, all wide eyes and round, rosy cheeks, and though it took a second to form, that evil grin of hers swallowed me whole. "Maybe I want to see how that works too."

I ran a hand down my face, truly wondering whether I was capable of handling this woman. "Let's save that for another day," I said, sliding between her folds. "I swear, there will be plenty of time for you to learn every filthy thing you can imagine."

I pressed inside her and the moan we shared seemed to bounce off the walls, echoing and vibrating back into us. She felt incredible at this angle, even more incredible than the first time. Hot, hot muscles clamping down like a fist. Tiny, humming flutters that made it impossible to think *and* keep my eyes open. Warm, luscious skin rocking against mine. That ever-present scent of gardens mingling with sex and sweat.

I knew without question that I could stay here forever.

"Just so you know," she said, her words stuttering with each thrust, "I already know lots of filthy things."

"If this is where you reveal that you've been screwing with me this whole time and you were not a quasi-virgin until I fucked you the right way, then this is where I tell you that I have no problem denying orgasms."

I would deny her nothing. Ever. Not even for a second.

"If you reference virginity again, I'll deny *you* an orgasm."

I squeezed her hips, angling her to take me deeper. I hit some perfect, precious spot and we couldn't bicker anymore. Not when our souls were busy sliding out of our bodies and surrendering themselves to whichever deity invented this position.

"I read a lot of romance," she said, both hands fisted in the pillows. "I know things. Filthy things."

Since I was clinging to the last, fraying threads of control over here, I couldn't believe myself when I asked, "What kind of filthy things?"

Her back arched as she moaned into the mattress. "All of it." She made a loose gesture to the books stacked beside the bed. "I've done some research."

Those books. I'd noticed them earlier. Lots of candy-colored covers and cute, punny titles. Several of them had little sticky notes and tabs feathering out from the pages. I grabbed the first paperback I could reach and set it in front of Sunny. "Tell me about it, then."

"What does that mean?" she asked.

I ran a hand over the generous curve of her ass and asked myself the same question. What the fuck was I thinking here? The truth was, I wasn't thinking. I couldn't think. Not while buried so deep inside her that I expected her to gag any minute.

"Read me your favorite part," I said.

"Out...loud?"

"What's the point of research if you don't share it?"

She was still and quiet long enough that it seemed like she wasn't up for this kind of thing. But then she said, "Promise you won't make fun of me?"

I skimmed a hand up her spine, over her shoulder. "I wouldn't dare."

She struggled to flip through the book as I moved in her, frequently stopping to press her face to the pages and cry out. I wasn't prepared when she said, "'I brought a hand to my erection, squeezing it through my trousers.'"

I lost the rhythm for a second and had to steady myself. "Keep going," I ordered.

"'I pushed her legs apart. Even in the darkness I could see'"—she breathed out a low cry that seemed to grab me by the balls—"'the shine of her arousal. I dragged two fingers through her'—oh, *fuck*, Beckett— 'her slit. I breathed her in as I circled the pearl at her apex, tracing around and around while her hips rolled and her stance widened.'"

I realized right then that I'd made a serious miscalculation. I couldn't listen to this *and* last for more than a minute or two, and if the glorious rush of wet was any indication, Sunny was feeling the same way.

But I didn't stop her.

Instead I leaned down to nip at her shoulder and reached a hand around to circle her clit the same way the guy in this story did. I knew an instruction when I heard one.

"'I leaned forward,'" she continued, "'dropping light kisses up and down her'—oh, god, yes, I'm right there, don't stop, Beckett, *please don't stop*—'her cleft. I ran the tip of my tongue around her clit and pumped my fingers into her cunt and—'"

Sunny went off like a goddamn rocket and there was nothing left for me to do but follow. I couldn't see her face but I knew she was lost in the outright rush of pleasure. I knew she was melting like she had all the other times tonight and I knew she'd disappear into another dimension for a minute. But then I'd get to gather her to me and get back to the sense that I was finally, finally all the things that I'd ever wanted to be.

We groaned together as I slipped out of her and we groaned again when I ran my fingers over her slick folds.

"I think you're trying to kill me," she said, her face in the book.

"Would you like me to stop?"

She paused. I did the same. Then, "No."

With a hand on her ass holding her in place, I leaned down, sucked her clit for two relentless minutes while she shook and screamed and finally broke apart all over me once more. "Sex tastes good on you," I said, shifting to clean up the condom.

She murmured something incoherent while I straightened the blankets and sheets. I climbed in beside her, turning her body to tuck into mine and kissing every inch of skin I could find.

"Are you going to finish?" I asked.

"Finish what?" She sounded like a drunk sleepwalker. I *loved* it. I wanted to fall asleep to that sound for the rest of my nights.

"I'm invested, Sunny. I need to know what happens after he pumps his fingers into her cunt." She glared at me over her shoulder, bleary-eyed and too deeply sated to generate any of her usual sadism and giggles. I gave her ass a light slap. She tried to glower but it was more of an adorable pout. "Does it end well for them?"

With a huff, she flipped back to her page, cleared her throat, and read, "'—and there was nothing more perfect than this moment.'"

Neither of us said anything for a minute. We couldn't. Not when it ended with *that*. Not when everything inside this room seemed to press in tight, like the air had thinned out and we had to work that much harder to breathe now.

Eventually, I took the book from her and set it on the table. "That's a relief."

"You might think that," Sunny said, "but he doesn't get his cock out until much later."

"A relief for her, then?" She bobbed her head. "Sometimes, that's all that matters."

She hummed to herself for a moment. "Really? Is that actually true or just a nice thing to say?"

I held her tight, as tight as I could without hurting her. "There are times when it's true for me. If you'd decided that you didn't want me inside you, I would've been content to give you what you needed and be done."

"I saw the way you were grinding on the mattress. You would've come in your boxers at some point."

"That's probably true," I admitted. I ran my hand over her hair, down her back. "Close your eyes, storm cloud. It's been a long damn day and I'm not nearly done with you yet."

A few minutes passed while we figured out how to keep our bodies as close as possible while also finding comfortable positions that didn't leave either of us with numb limbs or neck cricks. Once we got there, we started to drift off. Sunny's breathing evened out. My head succumbed to the mental softness that followed two massive orgasms. Everything was great.

And then—

"What was that?" She lifted her head from my chest, glanced around. "Am I hearing things? Did something snap inside my head?"

I stared at the ceiling, not sure I could hear anything over the thump of my heart. But then a muffled buzz sounded from somewhere in this shoebox room, and I said, "It's my phone."

She shuffled away from me and to the other side of the bed, nestling into her pillow. "Do you need to get it?"

I didn't want to leave this bed. Not for anything. But the things I wanted had a way of clashing with my reality. Even now, in the middle of the night with my body still buzzing from the feel of her in my arms, I didn't know how to turn off the incessant toe-tapping of my responsibilities.

"Let me check," I said. "It will just take a minute."

Sunny pushed to her feet and snagged my shirt off the floor, saying, "Don't worry about it. I need to use the bathroom anyway."

I almost swallowed my tongue as I watched her shrug into my shirt. I'd never found anything sexy or even interesting about a woman wearing my clothes before but I stared after Sunny for a solid minute.

Accepting that I couldn't do anything about this confusing new kink until she returned, I dug my phone out from under a pile of pillows and clothes. The notification was an alert from one of the motion-activated security cameras at the oyster company. When I tapped on the video, I barked out a laugh at what I saw.

"We're back to inappropriate laughing?" Sunny called from somewhere down the hall.

"Get in here," I replied. "You need to see this."

A few minutes later, Sunny returned with a glass of water and her hair braided over one shoulder. She curled up beside me, her chin on my shoulder and her hands everywhere as I reloaded the video.

"You can tell me I was right at any time," I said.

"One, two, three, four. Hmm." She tipped her head to the side. "Five. Six? Six. Okay."

"Right, that's *six* deer on the Naked Provisions patio," I said. "Do you see them eating your flowers? And knocking over your pots? Look, look—that one kicked over a chair."

She pointed at the screen. "Why are they running away?"

"Fuck if I know," I said. "The point, storm cloud, is that you now have proof that wild creatures living around the cove can and will ransack your patio." I locked the phone and set it on the bedside table. "Not me. Not anyone else. Just wildlife. Like I said."

"This time," she replied. "You can't prove anything about the time before."

"Yeah, well." I grabbed her around the waist and rolled with her across the mattress. "Let's see what I can prove with my cock in your mouth."

"WHAT ARE YOU DOING TODAY?" Sunny asked as she twined her fingers around mine.

I squinted at the narrow beam of sunlight crossing her room. "I'm pretty flexible though I need to check in at the oyster company at some point."

"Then you have time to take the dogs on that walk with me? Maybe grab some breakfast?"

"Breakfast is good," I said, kissing my way across her collarbone. "But I want to take you out some night. Whenever you're free."

She laughed. "What would that involve?"

"Hanging out with you while dressed and not at work," I said. "Isn't that the structure of most dates these days?"

Her eyes popped wide. "A *date*?"

"Yeah. What's wrong with that?" Because there was clearly something wrong with that.

She sat up and folded her legs in front of her, not bothering to hug the sheets to her bare chest. Which was fantastic as far as I was concerned. "I'm not so fond of dates," she said, her expression pinched.

"You weren't so fond of dick until last night."

She rolled her eyes at me. "That's different."

"In what way?"

"It's just"—she slapped her hands to the mattress—"it's different. Okay?"

I pushed up to sit beside her. "So, I can't take you on a date?"

"I'm bad at relationships," she said. "I'm a lot to deal with. There's the seizure disorder, the dogs, the parents who used to call every single day to check on me but have recently dropped down to weekly since they know my partners and have the entire town of Friendship watching over me."

"So far, you've not mentioned anything I don't already know."

"Okay, sure," she continued, "but there's my whole thing of changing my mind about what to do with my life every couple of months and moving to a new city to try new things. Or wanting to travel all over the place while also being happy living in a small town. Not everyone can keep up with my contradictions, Beck."

"Yeah, it's a tall order," I drawled, fully unimpressed.

"Is that another short joke?"

"No," I said. "Listen, Sunny, you're saying lots of things that probably sound really good in your head, but they're complete bullshit."

Her gaze darkened. "Some people just can't take on all the things I bring with me. Either they have their own things to deal with or they aren't equipped for more or it's just how their brain works, but they take one look at me and say, *No thanks*."

"You just haven't been in the right relationship," I said.

She gave a hesitant shrug. "Maybe that's true. Maybe it's hard to find someone with the mental operating budget that my particular collection of goodies requires. Both can be true."

I leaned back against the pillows and studied her. "You know my parents, my brothers. You know I've spent my entire life looking after everyone's issues, and I still found the time to take on a huge job that sent me to multiple foreign countries. My operating budget for you— and your dogs—is substantial." I brushed some hair over her ear. "Let me take you out."

She pressed her lips together, holding back a smile. "Let's start with breakfast and walking the dogs."

A win was a win, even if it wasn't the win I wanted.

I climbed out of bed and searched for my boxers, asking, "What are your favorite breakfast spots?"

I distinctly recalled leaving my clothes in a tidy pile on her dresser, but it looked like this entire room had been fucked sideways last night. I didn't remember there being four hundred pillows on Sunny's bed though that was roughly the amount on the floor. The laundry basket was overturned. Books were everywhere. Even the curtains were askew. I spotted my shirt and trousers in front of the door, my boxers nearby.

"There's a place in Bristol with a few good vegan and vegetarian dishes that I—"

"Hello! Good morning! I'm here! If you're still in bed, please ignore me, but I wanted to drop off these scones that I made last night. They're a little unusual but I feel like our customers are really digging some of my wilder flavors—OH MY GOD, *there's a naked man in your house*!"

Perhaps it was the limited amount of sleep Sunny and I allowed each other last night. Perhaps it was the oxygen deprivation I experienced due to my constant arousal. Or perhaps it was the fact I hadn't expected to find Muffy McTeague in Sunny's house at this hour. While I was stark naked.

For her part, Muffy marched right into the kitchen without another glance in my direction and set down the scones.

"She has a key," Sunny said, shrugging. "She comes over a lot. I don't usually—" She motioned to the bed. "It's never been a problem before."

I stepped into my boxers. "Good to know."

"I'm leaving now," Muffy yelled. "I am shuffling sideways toward the door. I cannot see anything. I'm also shielding my eyes in case there is anything dangling in the periphery."

"Sorry," Sunny called to Muffy.

"Can't talk now," she replied. "Very happy for you, but I must bleach my eyes. Don't forget to use protection. Bye!"

The door slammed behind her. I turned to face Sunny. "How long until everyone in town knows?"

"Were you hoping to keep this a secret?"

"Not at all, but I've already been on the receiving end of a stern warning from Ranger and Phil Collins about my intentions with you," I said. "I have to assume more of that will be coming my way."

She glanced at her watch. "We've got time. Muffy isn't a chatterbox and she's probably very busy being mortified about getting an eyeful of your ass. She'll keep this in her back pocket for a bit and wait to drop it until it can have the maximum impact."

"Great, great," I murmured. "So, breakfast?"

She grinned. It was evil and wonderful, and there was a fizzy little burst in the back of my mind that felt something like contentment.

"Breakfast," she said. "But first we need to get you into something less formal. It's summertime on the seacoast, Beck, and being outside is like walking through Vaseline."

"Come on, then." I beckoned to her and that burst seemed to expand, pushing at the base of my skull, behind my eyes, down my throat. It could be everywhere, if I let it. "We'll go back to my place. You can pick something out for me."

———

Beckett: Where are you?

Parker: Don't you already know?

Beckett: I know you're supposed to be at the oyster company and your shift started 10 minutes ago.

Parker: I know you didn't sleep at home last night.

Beckett: Is there a point to this?

Parker: Will you be home tonight?

Beckett: Will you be coming to work today?

Parker: I don't know. I feel like I'd be happier doing other things.

Parker: Did you sneak in at 6 in the morning for a reason?

Beckett: WTF are you talking about?

Parker: I watched you sneak into the house this morning.

Beckett: So then why are you asking?

Beckett: And why were you awake then?

Parker: Because I was sneaking in too, you turnip.

Beckett: You were asleep in your bed when I left last night.

Parker: Yeah. Then I woke up and did stuff.

Beckett: You're not allowed to do stuff in the middle of the goddamn night!

Parker: But you are?

Beckett: I am 36 years old.

Parker: I see you're really invested in age as a barometer of knowledge and maturity.

Beckett: Please stop sneaking out in the middle of the night. It's not safe.

Parker: I'm probably going to do what I want. I have a high rate of success with that.

Beckett: Please remember that you have an appointment with your guidance counselor at 10 tomorrow morning.

Parker: Tomorrow being...?

Beckett: Monday.

Parker: Oh right.

Beckett: Do you want me to go with you?

Parker: ...why

Beckett: To participate in the discussion regarding your academic future.

Parker: Yeah, I'll pass on that.

Beckett: What about paying your athletic fees to run track this fall and play baseball in the spring?

Parker: I'll find the cash.

Beckett: I'll meet you there at 10.

Beckett: You're on the schedule tonight until closing.

Parker: That sounds interesting.

Beckett: Will you be there?

Parker: Probably. I need the money for gas.

Beckett: Will you be going home after closing?

Parker: That's at least 9 hours from now so anything could happen.

Beckett: Okay. Let's try this a different way. I'm driving Sunny home tonight and I'd like to have a reasonable certainty that you are not out wandering the streets while I'm doing it.

Beckett: There's a gas card in it for you.

Parker: Since you're being such a peach by helping Sunny, I guess I could go home after my shift.

Beckett: Excellent. Thank you.

chapter twenty-one

Sunny

Today's Special:
Butter-Glazed Panties

MY HAIR still wet from the quick early morning shower we'd just shared, I watched from my perch on the bed as Beckett fastened his belt and zipped his fly. I'd never admit it but I loved watching while men did this. Maybe not *all* men. Maybe just the one in front of me right now.

I liked a lot about the one in front of me right now.

"I want to take you on a date."

"I have a meeting this morning," I said with an outrageously long sigh. "And you haven't stopped talking about dates since Saturday. Please explain to me why this is so important to you."

"I want us to go somewhere neither of us have seen the inside of the walk-in or begged the point-of-sale to work," he continued, turning to knot his tie in the mirror. "Bonus points if the entire population of Friendship isn't there to listen in on our conversation."

"What is it with your generation and dates?"

He rounded on me, either end of his tie in his hands. He'd brought a change of clothes with him this time. "Don't ever say that again. I don't want to hear it. Not a damn word about generations or the year you graduated high school or how you're barely old enough to drive. Please, no."

I shrugged out of my robe. "Hmm. Okay." I wasn't wearing anything underneath.

"For fuck's sake, Sunny." He all but snarled the words as he fisted his hands around the tie.

"What?" I twirled some hair around my finger while Beckett stared at my breasts, his jaw flexing. "I'm not saying anything about it. Just like you asked."

He dragged his gaze to my face with a low growl. "You know what I'm talking about."

"Something about dates." I leaned back on the pillows. He dropped a knee to the mattress. "For reasons I still do not understand, you want me to put on clothes and go places with you."

"Yeah, I'm an idiot," he rasped. "Complete fool."

"I wouldn't go that far. Just a minor misstep. I'm sure you won't do it again."

He ran his hand over my leg, his gaze fixed on me. "You're saying you don't want to be seen in public with me?"

I frowned. How had he lost the thread of this conversation? We were clearly giving each other a hard time here. Like always. "That's not what I'm saying. It's more like why should we go out"—I patted the bed—"when we could stay in?"

"Are you thinking about your partners?" he asked. "Especially given that Muffy walked right in here."

"I really am sorry about that." I cringed. "But they've been on your side since the start."

"Are you worried about what the villagers will say?"

"The villagers," I said with a laugh. "That's funny but no. Shocking as it may be, I'm only concerned with whether the villagers prefer the basil lemonade to the lavender limeade."

"Are you worried what Lance will say?"

Oof. That one landed hard. Nothing like an older brother to ruin the mood real fast. "I guess that depends on what you want him to know."

"What do you want me to tell him?"

"What I want is for us to stop talking in a maze." I pulled my robe shut only for Beck to make a wounded noise. "I'll go on a date with you. Okay? It's fine. If that's what you want, I don't mind."

He dropped to the mattress and traced the line of my robe from my neck to my breasts. "No," he said softly. "It's not fine."

I raked my teeth over my bottom lip and studied the wall to the side of my bed. I hadn't finished decorating this room. Several frames leaned against the wall, waiting for me to make decisions about where they'd live. "And why not? Or is this your new way of being impossible? I can't tell if we're fake-arguing or not. It's a lot more confusing when I'm not getting the *don't fuck with me* stare."

Beck sighed, giving a quick shake of his head. "I want to take you out. I want to look forward to it. I want to obsess a little bit about where we'll go and whether you'll like it. Maybe I want to obsess a lot. But I still want to pick you up, bring you flowers, lose my fucking mind because you're unbelievably gorgeous but we can't be late so I'll have to fuck you up against the door later—which you'll love, I promise. I want to choose a special place to eat that has things you'll like and I want to talk to you for hours. I want to hear about everywhere you've been and everything you've done, and all the places you want to go and things you want to do. I want to sit across from you knowing that everyone else in the world wants to be near you, wants your attention, and I was the one who got it for these short hours. And I want to bring you home and walk the dogs with you and take you to bed. And I don't want it to be something you tolerate. I want to do better than that."

I didn't respond for a long time. Honestly, I didn't know how to respond. I didn't have the words to react to him describing an evening that resembled the opposite of a casual summer fling.

Eventually, I managed, "That sounds really nice."

"But you don't want it."

"I didn't say that." I stilled his hand on my chest, let my fingers tuck in between his. "I'm just surprised that you want it so much."

He jerked a shoulder up and cut a glance to the side. To my frames leaning against the wall. "It surprised me too."

I wrapped my free hand around the ends of his tie and tugged until he was sprawled on top of me. "I want to look forward to it too," I whispered.

"I KNEW the bakery items would be a hit but I didn't expect them to blow up like this," I said, paging through the newest sales report. "We're generating enough profit on cookies alone to hire some part-time kitchen help. I think we should start meeting some candidates."

Meara ran a highlighter across her copy of the report. "We need to sell them in half-dozen bags too. Maybe special occasion cookie trays. Like cheese trays but more fun."

"While that is fabulous news for my general sanity," Muffy said, "I'd really love to talk about the naked man I saw the other day."

I knew she'd wait for a moment like this one. I had to hand it to her. It was a smart move.

Beth glanced around. "Where? Here? There was a naked fella here?"

Muffy patted her shoulder. "No, and thank god for that." She glanced at me, an expectant arch in her brow. "At Sunny's house."

Beth turned to face me. "Ohhh. So it was your naked fella."

"Do we happen to know the naked fella?" Meara grinned at me and it was obvious she knew the answer to that. "Perhaps someone from the neighborhood?"

"You know," I started, tapping my pen on the table, "I'm thinking we should probably bring in the painters to deal with the pheromone stain Beth and Mel left on the wall over there."

"Mel, you said?" Beth made a sour face and glanced at the sales reports. "Sorry, I don't know anyone by that name."

"I can't go through this again," Muffy said under her breath. "Why can't you girls have a conversation and decide whether you want to bang each other at regular intervals? Just sit down and talk it out."

Meara leaned toward Muffy, saying, "Just a guess here but I'm thinking they'll need a few more rounds of this before they get to that stage."

Muffy ran a hand down her face. "Who has the time?"

"Can we get back to the issue of Sunny's naked fella, please?" Beth asked. "I, for one, am very interested in this topic and have many questions. First of which, is Beck's ass as biteable as I imagine it to be?"

"I can't answer that because I don't know what you're imagining," Muffy said. "But I'm comfortable saying it has strong onion qualities."

"Onion," Meara repeated slowly.

Muffy nodded. "It would make you cry."

"That was what I was imagining." Beth hummed in appreciation. "My next question: How did this happen?"

"I was testing out some new recipes and—"

"Not you, Muffs," Beth cried. "I'm sure it's a fascinating story and I'd love to hear it just as soon as Sunny tells us how she got the broody bossman out of those trousers."

All eyes turned toward me. I made a point of taking a long sip of my tea before saying, "The usual way. One leg at a time."

"I'm more than a little bit amazed you didn't set the house on fire," Muffy said. "The two of you together must be actual fireworks."

"It is *not* that bad," I said.

Meara leaned back, crossed her legs, and folded her arms over her chest. "Hmm."

"Don't lie to my face like that. You've fantasized about strangling him," Muffy teased. "We all know it. We've seen you choking the dish towels."

"Well." I returned to my tea for a moment. This was the price I paid for being loud about all the ways in which Beck aggravated me and quiet about all the ways I was slowly, stunningly obsessed with this man. Perhaps not *everything,* but things were a world apart from where they had been when he told me to get my flowers off his property. "We're going out together tomorrow night."

"That sounds like a fancy way for you two to scream at each other before getting naked, but okay," Muffy said. "I like it for you."

"Hate sex is the best," Beth said, a sigh ringing in her words. "It's so much fun to just tear someone apart. I'm officially jealous."

I stared into my tea, my usual hibiscus. The familiarity was a fine alternative to admitting to my friends—and myself—that this thing with Beck was a tiny bit more than hate sex. And there really wasn't any hate involved. But I wasn't prepared to explain that today. It was too early and I was too tired after another night of talking and touching and laughing. And sex. Lots of sex. More in the past few days than I'd ever had.

I mean, Friday night alone was more than I'd ever had.

Every day since then had been a new lesson in the ways my body could experience sexual pleasure. If you'd asked me last week if I'd want to learn anything with my cheek flat on the kitchen table and my feet nowhere near the floor, I would've said *hell no.*

It was a good thing I embraced change with open arms.

And legs.

It didn't bother me that my friends thought Beck and I were just working out some frustrations on each other. There were moments when that was exactly how it felt. Like in the shower this morning. And

Beck's bedroom on Saturday before breakfast when he'd had enough of my commentary about his vampire-red ties. Like last night, when we'd started watching a movie and peeled our clothes off piece by piece, completely unhurried until I climbed on top of him and learned how good it could be that way. How I'd rocked against him with confidence so new it tasted bitter and under-ripe on my tongue.

What was a little stress relief between people who couldn't stop arguing with each other over nothing? No problems there. Perfectly healthy. A happy accident of mismatched parts that fit together in strange yet very nice ways.

But there were moments when it felt like something very different. Like we were staring out into a big blue ocean of possibility and we were all by ourselves, just waiting for the waves to pull us under.

"Hmm." I glanced up from my tea to find Meara staring at me. "You like him."

"Well, of course I *like* him." I set the mug down. "Liking people is one of the many boxes that must be checked off before I get anyone naked. You know that."

"I do know that, and I also know you like him more than your standard sex threshold." She tipped her head to the side, peering at me. "You like him quite a bit more."

I gathered the papers in front of me and tapped them on the table. I wrote a note about nothing on one of the pages but it gave me a moment to think while looking busy. I shared many, many things with these women, but not everything. They didn't know about my struggles with intimacy. They didn't know that my sex life had been cobwebbed over until a few days ago. And they didn't know that I was hoarding the moments I had with Beck and examining them while we were apart, trying to understand what was happening to me. What was happening to us.

"Maybe," I said, "but we're just having fun. Just blowing off steam."

Meara gave a slow nod as she watched me. "Is that all?"

I wrote a few more notes of nothing and flipped through the pages. "I don't know, but it's okay. I don't have to know. I'm sure something will happen that forces us to figure out what comes next, but until then I'm going to enjoy—" I stopped myself, not sure how to fit the relationship I had with Beck into something as insignificant as hooking up or hate sex. Because it wasn't insignificant. And I didn't like calling it hate sex. I didn't hate him. Not now. Not for a long time. "I just want to have fun with—"

"Onions," Muffy cut in. "You want to have fun with the onions."

———————

"THERE'S A DELIVERY FOR YOU." Muffy poked her head inside the office later that morning. "You should come check it out."

"Is it the bottle order? I've been waiting on that."

She glanced toward the front of the café. "I don't think it's bottles."

Something about her tone had me pushing to my feet and following her to the counter. Meara and Beth stood on either side of a sleek black gift box tied with silky silver ribbon, sharing glances that spoke volumes.

"It's for you," Beth said.

"And we want you to open it right now," Meara added.

"Yeah, I need to know what all this fuss is about," Muffy said. "I tipped the delivery guy with cookies. I hope that's okay."

I peered at her. "Why wouldn't it be?"

She shrugged. "I don't know how it is with rich boyfriends and their delivery guys."

I pulled at the ribbon. "I don't have a rich boyfriend."

"No, not at all," Meara said. "Now open the box that was sent by your rich boyfriend and delivered straight from an ultra-exclusive boutique in Manhattan." She motioned to the logo embossed on the box. "Have you heard of this place?"

"No," I replied suspiciously. "Should I have?"

"Everything is handmade and it's outrageously expensive," she said.

I passed the lid to Beth and pushed through layers of tissue paper to find— "What did he do?"

"We don't know, sugar. You have to tell us," Beth said.

I held up a pair of butter-soft panties. People liked to call things butter-soft all the time, but this was literal, cream-based butter. In fabric form. "I cannot believe he did this."

"He did it," Meara said. "And he got them to deliver."

I skimmed my fingers over each neatly folded pair. At least thirty of them, if I'd counted correctly.

"Is he replacing something he destroyed?" Muffy asked. "I hear that's customary among his type."

"He's not," I said, still too stunned to assemble complete thoughts. "Laundry. I told him I needed to do laundry. Or I'd be out. Of undies."

"Awww," Beth sighed. "Beck is too sweet."

"Wait a second," Meara said, plucking one pair after another out of the box. "*All* of these are boy shorts? That's a choice."

"That's what I wear," I said to her.

She blinked. "Seriously?"

"Yes, seriously." We stared at each other for a second, both of us with fists full of underwear. "Why? What's wrong with boy shorts?"

"It's just—" She waved at my skirt. "There are better options."

"Such as?" I asked.

"Thongs, to start."

"Oh, hell no." I shook my head. "Absolutely not. I will not invite that kind of discomfort into my life."

"They're not uncomfortable," she said.

"I can't do a thong either," Beth said, swirling her hands over her tiny denim shorts. "I need more containment. Hold me in, please."

"And that's what I like about boy shorts," I said.

"But what about sweat?" Meara asked. "Bikinis and boy shorts are not going to help you when it's ninety degrees and four hundred percent humidity."

Beth shifted to face Meara. "Are you trying to tell me that you think a *thong* is the answer to your below-decks sweat?"

Meara tossed one of her braids over her shoulder. "Yes, I am, and bikinis only make the matter worse."

Beth threw her hands up. "What is this devilry?"

"I mean, I'd go without altogether," Meara started, "but I run hot and things can get a little balmy."

"Go without?" Beth cried. "How is that even an option?"

"I really don't know how I got mixed in with you girls," Muffy said, mostly to herself. "You're like alley cats."

"But the thong doesn't solve that," Beth insisted.

"Not that you asked, and I'm sure this is going to sound super weird coming from a stranger, but I'm team bikini."

We all turned toward the rose-gold-haired woman waiting on the other side of the counter. Obviously, she'd heard enough of this debate to weigh in and that was fine. Naked Provisions was all about community. Even below decks.

"Hi," she said with a quick wave. "I'm Shay. I don't think we've met. I live on the other end of the cove at—"

"Oh, right," I said, cutting her off like I hadn't been house-trained. "Little Star Farm. I'm Sunny, that's Meara, Beth, and Muffy. I remember seeing you at that town council meeting."

She bobbed her head as if she was a little embarrassed by this. "My husband had a whole lot of big feelings that night."

Meara collected the undies and tucked them back into the box, each pair folded carefully but with a lot of contempt.

"He put an end to that conversation real quick so you won't find me complaining," I said with a laugh. "So, you agree that thongs make no sense."

Meara chuckled. "Okay, okay, you've convinced me to look at other options. Maybe," she added.

Muffy headed back to the kitchen, saying, "I need to tend to my lentils and reevaluate my life choices."

"Thongs have their place on the panty spectrum," Shay said diplomatically. "I wouldn't choose one for a day of hazy, hot, and humid, but that's just me."

"Thank you," Beth said. "Now, what can we get you, doll? You've been waiting an age and I won't have you wasting away."

"I'll have a large cold brew and one of these chocolate cookies," she said, pointing at the bakery case.

"You get two cookies for not running away from us and our sweaty underwear conversation," I said. "I'd like to say we're not usually like this—"

"You'd be lying," Muffy called.

"—but we're always like this," Beth finished.

Smiling, Shay motioned toward the handful of empty tables along the wall. "Is it cool if I sit here for a little while and pretend to work on lesson plans but actually read a book on my phone? I don't want to overstay my welcome."

"Sit your buns down," Beth said as she dug a scoop of ice from the freezer.

I set the cookies on a plate and pushed them toward her. "What are you reading?"

Her smile was wide but shy. "It's a love story about dragon riders at a war college," she said with a self-deprecating laugh, pink rising in her cheeks. "I'm completely obsessed. It's so good. I just know I won't be able to do anything else until I find out how it ends. At which point I'll probably read it all over again to find everything I missed the first time."

"You should come to our book club." I pointed to the pile of cards announcing the Read Naked meeting dates. "We're all about the love stories."

Shay picked up a card and skimmed the details, nodding. "This sounds great. We have a book club at the elementary school, but it's always books about teaching reading or social-emotional learning— which is important, obviously, but I'd much prefer this kind of book club."

"We'd love to have you," I said.

"Here you go, babe," Beth said, sliding the cold brew across the counter.

"Thanks," Shay said. To me, she added, "Not to continue being obscenely weird or anything but whoever sent you all those undies from *that* boutique?" Her brows lifted. "Not a single concern for price tags and excellent taste. Exceptional."

I nodded. "Like you wouldn't believe."

"Well, of course. He chose you," she said.

"He picked a fight and neither of us wants to be the first to back down," I said, rolling my eyes at myself.

"I'm married because neither of us was willing to back down," she said with a laugh.

"How's that working out?"

She smiled at me with heart eyes. "No complaints."

"I'm happy you came in today, Shay. It's good to meet you."

"You too, Sunny." She grabbed a pen out of her bag and scribbled something on the back of a book club card. "Here's my number. In case you ever want to commiserate over life with a strong-willed man. Or books about dragon riders, or whatever." Collecting the cookies and coffee, she added, "Good luck with that boy of yours. You're going to need it."

More than I even knew.

chapter twenty-two

Beckett

Today's Special:
Salt-Rubbed Anonymity with Wine Many Ways

I WASN'T WORRIED.

Not in any significant way.

Not about my date with Sunny tonight.

I mean, no more than anyone worried about a first date—which was to say that I had some worries. Normal, reasonable worries.

But then I had the rest of my world to contend with, and there were many more worries there.

Parker had been two hours late in returning from the beach this afternoon. I'd used that time to research whether those electric shock collars people used to keep their dogs in the yard would work for teenage pains in the ass. Inconclusive.

My attorney found it necessary to call me once an hour with the kind of updates that gave me acid reflux because my mother had gotten her hands on another burner phone and she remembered not only my number but also Parker's and a few of her girlfriends too. It seemed she had a day off from babysitting.

My firm wanted to know if I could give them an update on when I'd be returning to work. I'd laughed and closed my email before I could respond with *Fuck if I know.*

Add to all of that the fact that everyone in Friendship knew about this date. *Everyone.* They'd all dropped by to offer advice and more than a few words of warning. It was painfully clear that everyone loved Sunny to death and they'd take up arms if she didn't enjoy every single second of this evening.

Even better: Mel was running the restaurant tonight and that would've been great if Bethany hadn't parked herself at the bar with a book and proceeded to ignore the shit out of Mel. Now I had Mel pacing like a caged lion and biting off every head that crossed her path.

When Parker had noticed me glaring at today's episode of The Mel and Beth Situation, he pulled me into the office, saying, "I see what you're doing and it's stupid."

"What am I doing?" I asked.

"You're inventing reasons why you shouldn't go out with Sunny tonight. It's classic self-sabotage."

I rubbed my brow. "And why would I do that?"

"Any number of reasons." He ticked off on his fingers, saying, "You subconsciously question whether you're good enough for her, you'd rather end things early and by your own hand than lose control and risk getting hurt, and there's always the Freudian issues of—"

"Okay, that's enough," I said. "I am concerned about the oyster company. That's it. This place is never more than one strong sneeze away from disaster and Mel's head isn't in the game."

"Go on the date," Parker said. "This place will be fine. Worst-case scenario, I run the restaurant. I've done it before. It didn't burn down."

There was a headache forming behind my right eye. "When did *you* run the restaurant?"

He shook his head and steered me toward the stairs. "All that matters is I lived to tell about it. Now, get outta here and don't let me see your face until morning."

I glanced back at him. "Aren't I supposed to be parenting you? Not the other way around?"

"This isn't parenting," he replied. "It's the trauma-informed psychology I learned from Instagram and TikTok."

"Oh." I continued down the stairs. "Is that...a good thing? Is that something you should be learning on the internet?"

"Count your blessings. I could be getting far worse from the internet."

WHEN SUNNY OPENED the front door, the sight of her in a red sundress with her hair spilling over her shoulders had me bracing myself on the doorframe. I scowled at that dress while mentally debating whether I could throw out this whole date night plan and lock her in the bedroom until sunrise. Or longer.

"What's that face all about? What's wrong with you?" she asked.

I shook my head and flailed to grasp at words. "I'm just—I guess I'm wondering whether you're ready to go." I reached out, skimmed my knuckles down the front of her dress. I tugged it down far enough to catch sight of the mark I'd sucked into the side of her breast yesterday. "You look good enough to eat."

"Oh, is that what you have planned for tonight?"

She smiled and it was like seeing the sun for the very first time. Like everything I thought I knew about warmth and brightness was a half-truth, a delusional fragment of the radiance in front of me. I gripped the doorframe harder. "Yes, but not until later," I said.

"Hmm." She eyed my jeans and untucked button-down shirt. Her gaze lingered on the button-fly. "This is cute. I approve."

"One less thing to worry about." I leaned in closer. "Do you have a sweater or a jacket?"

She blinked at me. "It's still in the high eighties. I don't think I'll need a jacket."

"You will where we're going," I said.

She laughed. "Which is where?"

I took a step back and then another. Distance would prevent me from doing something ridiculous. "Get that jacket and you'll find out."

SUNNY LEANED FORWARD in the passenger seat, peered out the windshield, and then swiveled to face me. "I thought we weren't going to a place where either of us knows what the inside of the walk-in looks like."

"We're not going to SPOC," I said, tracing a finger over the thin strap of her dress. Too damn tempting.

"Then why are we here?"

I nodded toward the dock. "We're taking one of the boats."

Her cheeks rounded as she grinned. "Where are we going?"

"A little place down the bay. It's small and very under the radar, but I called today and they have vegan and vegetarian items on the menu for you. If you don't like any of that, they've promised they can make something to order," I said. "If we leave now, we'll catch the sunset on our way there."

She pressed her fingers to her lips and leaned back in the seat. A high, giggly squeal sounded in her throat. "This date involves sailing? At sunset? To a restaurant that's confirmed its plant-based options? My goodness, Beckett Loew. What the hell does a second date with you look like?"

It was as though she'd reached in and closed her fingers around my heart, squeezing along with each beat. It was as terrifying as it was exhilarating because I knew then that she really could rip that heart right out. She could end me and she wouldn't even have to try that hard.

I exhaled against the pressure in my chest. "You'll just have to wait and find out."

We sailed out of the cove and down the bay as the sky turned a bright, endless orange. I tucked Sunny in front of me at the controls and I swallowed a groan every time she leaned into me. Though she'd tied her hair into a bun before casting off, the wind blew some fine tendrils loose and they teased at my jaw and lips. I told her it was like having a jellyfish in my face but we both knew I didn't mind at all.

When we pulled up to the dock beside this no-name café with only four or five tables and questionable legality, Sunny asked, "Is this a real place or just someone's backyard?"

Rather than answering that, I said, "I think you're going to love it."

"I think I already do," she said, laughing.

We sat at a wrought iron table that was small enough that I could lean in and count the tiny cinnamon dust freckles on the bridge of her nose. She reached over and straightened my collar. I patted my thigh and motioned for her to rest her feet there. Her smile came gradually, and a little lopsided. The hand around my heart gave a ruthless twist.

I closed one hand around her crossed ankles and gestured to the deskjet-printed menu with the other. "See something you like?"

Nodding, she said, "I think so, yeah." She took in the courtyard with its hedge of beach rose and sea grasses, the string lights overhead and hand-painted directional sign listing the distances to Block Island, Nantucket, Prince Edward Island, Key West. "How did you find this place?"

"We supply their oysters," I said. "When my family first moved here and took over the oyster company from my great-uncle Buckthorne, he taught me to sail so I could do the delivery runs. He wanted my dad to do it, but he kept falling off the boat or getting seasick. And my mom loves being on a boat though refuses to learn anything about operating one."

"Would it be rubbing salt in the wound to ask how things are going with them?"

I reached for the wine list, which was scrawled on a yellow index card. No prices. "Same old shitshow," I grumbled. "Do you like wine? I don't think I've asked you that."

She plucked the card out of my hand. "Only a few sips. Not enough to justify ordering a whole bottle."

"Red or white?"

She waved this off, saying, "Neither. I'll have a sip of whatever you get."

I snatched the card back. "Either you tell me what you want or I'll order every single bottle."

"Why are you so ridiculous?"

"Because you won't tell me what you want." I slid my palm up her calf. "If anyone's being ridiculous, it's you."

"That is a fanciful way of saying you're not getting what you want."

"Funny how my only objective here is making sure you get what *you* want." With a flippant shrug, I added, "Ordering all the wine this hole-in-the-wall has to offer is nothing. Five, six bottles? Please. If it made you happy, I'd buy an entire winery."

"Okay, yes, speaking of your outrageous spending." She clasped her hands under her chin and shot me a prim frown. "The underwear."

She whispered *underwear* and I had to bite the inside of my cheek to keep from laughing. "Yes, Sunny? What about them?"

"You didn't have to do that."

"You're right. I didn't." I leaned in, brushed my fingers over her forearm. "I wanted to."

"So I could spend more time having sex with you and not doing laundry?"

That she didn't lower her voice to say this ripped a full-throated laugh out of me. This girl. Goddamn. "That wasn't even part of the mental calculus," I admitted. "I just wanted to have detailed, specific knowledge of what was underneath those skirts of yours."

She pursed her lips together, looked down at the table. "They're very nice. Thank you."

"Then I'm happy." I swept my thumb over a bruise near her elbow. "What happened here?"

"Oh, it's nothing. I was moving some tables and banged into something."

"You are one accident after another, storm cloud," I said. "I don't know how you haven't tripped over one of your dogs yet."

"They're trained to never let that happen." She said this as if she'd clarified it to me a million times already. Maybe she had. I still wasn't convinced. "Even if I did trip or lose my balance because of them, they know how to react so that I don't get hurt. I used to explain that on the first day of school so everyone in my class would understand the dogs' behaviors and responses, and the appropriate ways to interact with them."

The server approached then with a carafe of water and a discussion of the day's specials. Before we could get into any of that, I said, "We'd like one of each of your wines."

"No, we don't. Seriously, Beck, stop it." She swatted my hand, adding, "The cabernet, please."

I grinned at her. "Good choice."

She glared at me. "Shut up."

"Have you made any other decisions or should I come back in a few minutes?" the server asked.

Sunny ordered ravioli. I went with scallops. When the wine and a bread board arrived, she clinked her glass to mine, saying, "To first dates."

"To many more," I replied. "Can I ask about your business partners or are you going to break that glass over my head?"

"I wouldn't do that. This is a nice glass," she said, pointing to what must've been an olive jar in a previous life. "What do you want to know?"

"They aren't all from around here, are they?" She shook her head. "How did you meet them? *Where* did you meet them?"

"I met Muffy when I lived in New York. I wasn't there too long, but we stayed close after I left because she hated Manhattan and fine dining, but she'd also invested so much time and energy into being a chef in the fine dining world of Manhattan and couldn't convince herself to walk away."

"And yet here she is."

Sunny took a small sip of wine and set the glass on the table. "Yeah, some unpleasant things went down at her restaurant and that was it. She was done." She grabbed a piece of bread and ripped it in half. "I met Meara in Boston. Her roommate was doing a semester abroad and I picked up the sublet. We did not love each other at first. It was a little tense, a little awkward. It took us a few weeks to figure out the vibe, and after that it was like we'd been friends forever. Like twins separated at birth. We were going to move into a different apartment after the lease ended, but then she got an amazing job offer in LA and I realized I didn't want to stay in Boston without her."

"I take it she didn't have the two husbands at that point."

"No, she didn't meet them until after she moved to California. They came back out this way when some things changed with the husbands' consulting firm." She paused to sample the bread. "Bethany is a local, she's from Rhode Island, and we had a few classes together at the community college while I was there. She started a juice business with her best friend, and when they got it up and running, I helped them with their farmers markets."

"What happened to the best friend?"

"She sold everything and moved to a farm co-op in New Mexico last year," Sunny replied easily, as if this was very common.

"Tell me about college," I said. "I haven't heard about that."

She gave me a knowing grin, one that said *Lance can't be trusted to update anyone about anything.* "Well, it was a compromise," she said carefully. "I'd wanted to travel. Just go anywhere at all. I wanted to be somewhere other than this tiny town where everyone knew all about me, and live without anyone hovering around me." She smiled down at the table, shook her head. "I don't know if you know this but I was supposed to grow out of the childhood epilepsy. The doctors were convinced that the episodes would taper off—if not completely end—when I was seventeen or eighteen. My parents were skeptical and they said they'd support my travel plans if I could go one full year without a seizure. So, I took business classes at the community college, waited tables, read a lot of books that ended more happily than anything I'd ever experienced." She leaned back, exhaling in a deep, exhausted way. "And I had a seizure two weeks before that one-year point."

I took her hand but I wanted to scoop her up and hold her close to me. "I'm so sorry."

She shrugged like it didn't matter but it obviously did. "I spent another year at home. Took more classes. Read more books. Started bartending. Had another episode." She ran her tongue over her teeth and I could see her fighting back the emotion rising inside her. "At that point, I didn't care about compromises anymore. I had to go find some freedom for myself and I couldn't let my parents keep me in that safe, protected box any longer. I knew they meant no harm but I was suffocating."

"I understand that," I said. And I did. I knew about being suffocated by people who wanted only the best. "Where did you go?"

She rolled her eyes, laughing. "Everywhere? Nowhere? Somewhere in between? I spent two years traveling compulsively. Small trips at first because, really, I'd never even been to a sleepover at that point. I went anywhere that sounded good, even if it was just a quick road trip. New York, of course. Hopped on the train and spent entire days just walking the island of Manhattan, top to bottom. I went all around New England. I worked on Nantucket for a summer, Bar Harbor another summer. Tons of wandering in the off-season. But after that, when I'd moved to Boston and was trying to figure out what to do when Meara left, was when I realized I was not a nomad."

"That must've been the most upsetting realization after everything you'd been through."

"I was so mad," she cried, tossing up her hands. "I didn't really accept it until moving to New York and living there for a few months, and realizing I had a small-town heart. Even though it was super frustrating to find myself back at the start of that loop, I know I needed the time to rebel after all those years of limitations, and my parents needed to see me living on my own and being healthy. I mean, they've never recovered from the years when I was very sick. Things got better as I grew up, but they were always waiting for it to get bad again. They're still waiting."

"It must've been hard on you, as a kid," I said.

She swept her gaze around the courtyard before answering. "I had a good, loving family that did everything they possibly could to keep me safe. When the epilepsy was at its most unmanageable, my world never stopped getting smaller and smaller. There were only a few safe spaces for me. Everything was dangerous and my freedom was nonexistent. Like, I could read about horses and watch horse movies and I could even go to the Castros' stables to visit horses but I could never ride a horse because I'd already had too many falls, too many injuries, and everything was too risky for me. And all I could do was build up these angry, silent icebergs because everyone was trying so hard to help me and I just wanted to run away from all that *help*."

At some point while she was speaking, I realized a few things about Sunny. First, she wasn't as young as I'd convinced myself she was. This woman was smart and sophisticated and mature in ways that far exceeded her age. The years between us didn't matter. Not in any way that was worth caring about.

"Enough about me," she said, brushing some crumbs from her dress. "What's really going on with your parents?"

I swallowed half the wine in my glass. "The situation is bananas in pajamas."

"Is that the expression? Not bananapants?"

"Both seem appropriately outrageous to me," I said. "You know my parents. Right?"

"A bit," she said with a shrug. "Enough to wave in the grocery store but not so much that we'd stop to chat."

"Okay, well, you know they're very kind, very generous. Everyone loves them. Much more than they like me and—"

"We will not be self-deprecating tonight," she sang.

Another thing I noticed—and had probably known all along—was that Sunny was so much stronger than me. More than most people I knew. But it was the kind of quiet strength that didn't show itself in any loud, aggressive way. It was steady and unwavering, and though I hadn't realized it then, I'd heard it every time I pushed her away saying we couldn't do this, and every time she pushed right back saying we could. Plus the many, many times she refused to let me get away with any shit whatsoever. I loved that about her. I wanted to breathe it like oxygen.

"No one likes me in this town. It's the truth," I argued. "Regardless, my parents aren't the right people to run an oyster company. Great for hostessing, terrible for managing anything. Since I cannot run a restaurant in Rhode Island while living on the other side of the world and having a job of my own, I've always hired the most qualified people I could find to run the place for me. The best general manager, the best chef, the best front of house and bar managers, the best oyster farmer. I put all the right pieces in place. And the pieces cracked. I didn't even see it coming."

"You are not allowed to blame yourself for this," she said.

"I should've known," I said. "I should've had some clue that things were falling apart. That a goddamn criminal enterprise was being run out of my family's business."

"Like you said, you live on the other side of the world and you've been working at what I have to assume is a big, demanding job where you're required to scowl and brood *all day long*. You cannot blame yourself for anything that happened at SPOC. You did the best you could and shit still happened, which means it was bound to happen regardless of whether you chained yourself to the raw bar and refused to blink."

I drained the rest of my wine. "My father could spend twenty years in prison and my mother might live the rest of her life on the run. All because I didn't watch the books closely enough. I should've caught this when it started. It was right there in front of me."

"You cannot shoulder that blame," she said, closing my hand between both of hers. "I won't let you. You're here now and you're doing everything you can to make it work. It's actually really amazing that you still find the time to come over to Naked and harass me every day."

"It's all a matter of prioritizing," I said.

"Do you miss it?" she asked. "Living on the other side of the world?"

Yes. No. Sometimes. Ask me when I'm not touching you. "There's a lot to love about Singapore. Between Zurich, London, and Singapore, those would be my top three. And I do miss the consistency and predictability of my life there. I spent zero minutes a day trying to understand the mind of a seventeen-year-old and it was glorious."

"Do you hate it?" she asked, her eyes soft and sparkling like she already knew the answer. "Being here again? Shucking oysters and chasing teenagers?"

Yes. No. Sometimes. Ask me when I'm not touching you.

Before I could respond, she added, "Or is it that you're so focused on solving all the problems that you don't stop to ask yourself what you feel, other than the byproduct feelings of exhaustion and frustration?"

Our meals arrived then, buying me a minute to think through a question that felt like she'd trailed her fingers over every shelf and corner in my mind to come up with the one thing that was both devastatingly true and impossible to put into words. But she did. She found the words. Packed them into one neat, clean sentence. Delivered them like they were as easy and simple as drinking wine from an olive jar on a summer night.

Then, because she was a sadist and an assassin and possibly the most perfect woman in the world for me, she asked, "Have you ever stopped to ask yourself how you feel?"

I stroked my hand over her calf. I didn't need both hands to eat. Not when her skin was the only thing anchoring me to the earth at this moment. "I know how I feel right now," I said.

"And how's that?"

"Content," I said, though I wasn't sure how that word had pushed to the front of my mind.

Another thing I realized was that Sunny made me honest. Not that I'd been *dis*honest, though I'd never put as much time and energy into saying exactly what I meant as I did when I was with her. The words mattered tonight the same way they'd mattered last week when we stepped into her bedroom and all those weeks ago when I'd almost kissed her in the café. When I'd been a fool and said it was a mistake. These words between us existed on the iridescent surface of a bubble and they had to be the truest, rightest ones.

"Content is good." She smiled at me. "What would you do if you just happened to be back here in Friendship but didn't have all these crazy legal problems to worry about? What would you do if you were content every day?"

"Is harassing you all day not an option?"

"Let's pretend you find time to do other things," she said, snorting out a laugh.

"I don't know," I said, watching as she sampled the ravioli. She seemed to like it so I could breathe again. "Maybe build a shellfish hatchery."

"Build a what now?"

"Oysters are hatched from seeds, essentially, but the conditions necessary for that are precise. It requires careful feeding of the seeds and manipulation of water temperatures, and a ton of observation. We already do this to some degree because the ecosystem of the cove can be unpredictable and weather patterns only add to that."

"Building a hatchery would mean more oysters for you?"

"Yes, but more than that, there's also an opportunity to research the impact of climate change on aquaculture in real time. Would we be able to expand our distribution network beyond trucking out four or five hundred dozen oysters to local restaurants and markets each day? Yes, definitely, but if we want to continue farming oysters for another seventy years, we need to know how the ecosystem is evolving before the species is wiped out."

"Then why don't you do that?"

"Because it's a project that would take years to even get off the ground and I do have to worry about crazy legal problems and teenagers. Aside from all that, I like my job. I'm good at it and I want to keep doing it. I don't have the bandwidth for a shellfish hatchery. Not right now."

"But someday?"

I chuckled. "Yeah. Someday. When things calm down."

"Have things ever calmed down for you?"

I reached for the wine bottle and poured a small amount into my glass. I didn't want it, but I needed something to do. "There have been times," I said.

With a nod that said she knew I was full of shit, Sunny said, "Are you aware that not everyone else can keep so many balls in the air and make it look easy?"

"I take my balls very seriously," I replied. "But don't forget the part where I also harass impressionable young women."

She tossed her hair over her shoulders and gazed off at the bay. "Impressionable, am I?"

The last thing I realized tonight—and by far the most important—was that I was almost completely certain I'd fallen in love with Sunny somewhere between yelling at her about flowerpots and being happy that she liked the ravioli, and there wasn't a damn thing I could do about it.

"MMM. THIS IS GOOD." Sunny gave a tentative rock of her hips and I died a little at the unbelievable pressure that came with being fully seated inside her. "I like this position."

I loosened my hold on her waist as she shifted, swiveling into a steady rhythm over me. I leaned forward, swiped my tongue over a nipple. Died some more at the answering clench around my cock. "Do you want to read another chapter?"

She dropped her hands to my chest as she found the angle she liked. "Later. I'd lose my balance if I tried to hold a book."

"I'll keep you steady."

She nodded as her eyes closed and her lips parted. "I don't think we need to hear how hard she's getting pounded right now or how he is quietly trying to tell her with his cock that he loves her." She dug her nails into my skin as she sped up, her legs tensing and a breathy sigh passing over her lips every time she hit the sweet spot. "I want to save that for—"

I'd say my favorite part of sex with Sunny was when she lost her words and turned into a feral creature capable only of gasping out syllables and chasing orgasms like her life depended on it, but it was all my favorite part. Even the uncertain moments at the beginning when she had to remind herself that she was safe with me, that we'd stop if it was ever too much. All of these moments were my favorites.

"I'm," she panted, "going—to—"

"I know," I whispered, stroking deep into her and telling her I loved her the only way I could right now.

chapter twenty-three

Beckett

Today's Special:
Confit of Calamity

AS I JOGGED down the back stairs from my office, I couldn't stop myself from smiling. I was having a damn good day. Hell, a good week. I'd spent every one of the past seven nights with Sunny. Parker was speaking to me on a regular basis. Ayla officially gave notice with the hotel she was running at Lake Louise and she had committed to taking over management of the oyster company in September. SPOC was finally back to pre-FBI-raid staffing levels and I didn't feel an overwhelming urge to throw any of the new servers over the deck and into the cove.

My life, it wasn't in complete shambles today.

"What's wrong with your face?" Mel shouted from behind the bar. "Did you get stung by a bee or something?"

"I just got off the phone with my lawyer," I said.

"And you're going into anaphylactic shock as a result?"

"No," I said with a laugh. "There's been some progress on Rabbit's case. They got a few of the charges tossed out."

"We'll take it. Every inch we can get, we'll take." Mel tapped the touchscreen in front of her, adding, "Any update on Sandy?"

I drummed my fingers on the bar top. "Adrian thinks the charges against her could be dropped if she returns to the US and immediately surrenders to the Marshals."

Mel glanced at me, her eyes bright. "Really? Sandy's coming home?"

It wasn't until this moment that I realized other people missed my parents. My tendency was to assume everyone else loved my parents to pieces and still breathed a sigh of relief when they weren't around. The way my brothers did. The way *I* did.

"Bringing her home requires her getting in contact with us," I said carefully. I didn't know where my mother was and I had to make sure no one caught an impression to the contrary. Agent Price was sure to be around here somewhere and I knew it would make that dude's day to slap cuffs on me. "We'll just have to wait until the next time she finds a burner phone to pass that message along. And this stuff moves at a glacial pace. Even if she hops on a plane tomorrow, Adrian says she'll spend some time in federal custody."

Mel bobbed her head but kept her gaze down. "I just miss her, you know? I miss sitting here with her after service and talking about everything. She gives the best advice, even if it's kooky as hell and requires five non sequitur stories about being on the road with a bunch of gnarly rocker dudes to get to the point."

"Yeah. She does."

"You have to brace yourself for the stories though," Mel said with a watery laugh. "If you don't know what you're in for, it seems like she's just talking out of her ass about something too ridiculous to be believable."

"I hope it doesn't come as a surprise to you but all that ridiculousness is rooted in reality."

"And that's what makes it even more ridiculous."

"Trust me, I know all about it." I glanced at my watch. I could've sworn Sunny said she was due at the café early today but neither her Jeep nor her bike were parked outside, and I didn't have any messages from her. It was possible I mixed up her schedule in my head. Our dawn conversations before I returned home were barely coherent on the best days. I'd have to bother her partners for an update. "I'm going to grab some coffee. Is there anything you'd like me to pass along to Bethany?"

"If you valued your life, you wouldn't ask me questions like that," she grumbled.

It was a hot, hazy late July day but the humidity didn't bother me as I crossed the driveway toward Naked. The café was quiet when I stepped inside, with only a few tables occupied. Agent Price sat in his usual spot, a glass of iced tea beside his open hardcover book. I was in such a good mood, I called out, "How's it going, Price?"

"Can't complain, Loew," he replied without looking up.

I rounded the counter, setting my hands on the butcher block. Beth and Meara stood beside the espresso machine, their heads bowed together. "Hey. Nice to see you two. Any idea where your cult leader is today? I thought she was opening this morning but I think I mixed up my days."

Meara glanced up at me and I realized her eyes were red. "You didn't hear?"

Cold spilled down my spine. "Hear what?"

"There was an accident early this morning," she said. "She's in the hospital and—"

"She's fucking *what*?"

"We don't know all the details," Meara said with a sniff. "All she told me was that she wanted me to cover for her this morning and not let anyone freak out."

"And you decided to allow that?" I cried.

"I thought she'd already called you," she replied.

I couldn't listen to this. I turned away from the counter. I had to leave. Right now. I had to go. I patted my pockets for my keys. When I found them, I blinked down at my hand for a moment, trying to remember how to get to the hospital.

"Give me those." I looked up to find Agent Price glaring at me. "You're not driving anywhere with that crazy look in your eyes. Give me the keys. I'll get you there in no time."

And that was how I ended up sitting in the passenger seat of my car, nearly paralyzed with panic while Price drove like a bat out of hell to the regional hospital. He talked the whole time, going on about FBI training and knowing everything in the book about defensive driving. He cracked a few jokes, it seemed, but I couldn't focus on any of them.

"When you get in there, you tell them you're her husband," Price said as he pulled up to the emergency room entrance. "They won't let you in if you say you're just the guy who gives her grief."

"I don't give her—oh, shut up," I muttered, my hand on the door handle as I waited for him to come to a stop. "Thanks for the ride. I owe you one."

"I'll chill in the waiting room until they kick you out."

I pushed open the door. "I don't plan on getting kicked out."

"Then mind your manners in there. Nurses will fuck you up."

I jogged into the emergency room and dropped the husband line on the first person in scrubs I could find. It worked like a charm and we might as well start a tab for everything I owed Agent Price. A nurse led me through a maze of hallways until passing me off to someone with a physician's badge who finally pulled back a long curtain to reveal a very small, very broken Sunny sitting up on a gurney, her legs folded in front of her and her hair tangled around her shoulders. One side of her face was bruised, the line of her jaw scraped raw. Her arm was enclosed in a hard plastic brace from her bicep to her fingers, and wires snaked out from under the hospital gown.

"Hey, Beck." She offered a wobbly smile and my heart cracked right down the center. "Don't worry. It wasn't a forklift."

"For fuck's sake, Sunny," I breathed. "Who did this to you?"

"Your wife was struck by a motor vehicle while riding her bicycle," the doctor said.

Your wife? Sunny mouthed.

Yes, I mouthed back. To the doctor, I said, "My wife is present and conscious, and I'll thank you to not speak of her as if she's an object."

The doctor glanced between us and gave a slow nod. "Right. Well. Sunny. As you know, you fractured both your humerus and radius, and you have a concussion."

"I've had worse," Sunny said, wiggling her fingers near her temple.

"That doesn't make me any happier," I replied.

"We're going to monitor you for signs of seizure activity for another few hours given your history and the symptoms we noted when you came in," the doctor continued. "Assuming nothing else happens, I expect we'll be sending you home."

"Nothing else happens?" I repeated, staring at Sunny.

She lifted a shoulder, winced. "My brain got a little spicy after all this went down, but I held it all together."

"Sunny," I breathed, brushing my fingers over her forehead. "Tell me who did this to you so I can find them and drown them in the cove."

"You wouldn't do that." She reached up and closed her fingers around my wrist. "It would mess up your ecosystem."

"Let me worry about those details."

The doctor cleared his throat and made some noises about coming back to check on Sunny later, then dragged the curtain shut behind him.

I pressed a kiss to her forehead and took a moment to inventory the injuries I could see. Cuts, bruises, scrapes. Broken arm. Loopy look in her eyes that said she'd had her bell rung hard. I didn't even know where I could touch her. *If* I could touch her. I was powerless in the most enraging ways. I wanted to fix something—anything—and I wanted to scream at the world for harming this one perfect thing of mine.

"Sit down." She pointed to the chair behind me, adding, "Breathe. I hear it's very important if you want to continue existing."

I sat, closing her hand in both of mine. "Please tell me what happened."

"There's a spot where Old County Road cuts through the bike path. It's just two lanes and the speed limit is low in that area because it's near the elementary school. There was a car stopped on the side of the road. I waited at the intersection for a minute but the car didn't move. But then they sped up and—" She rocked her head from side to side, let out a heavy breath. "I don't know how it happened. One minute I was in the crosswalk, the next they were speeding away."

I blinked at her. Now I was really going to drown someone. "They left the scene?"

"Yeah," she said, her brows pitching up. "But there was a runner on the path. He was a few yards behind me and saw the whole thing. He stayed with me after it happened."

That guy had a lifetime of oysters coming his way. "There's a shred of hope for humanity."

She squeezed my hand, saying, "I know I'm a little fuzzy right now but I don't remember you getting down on one knee and begging me to marry you."

"You will," I murmured. When she gave me a puzzled frown, I added, "Agent Price said they wouldn't let me back here unless I told them I was your husband."

"Agent Price?"

"Yeah. He drove me here." I lifted her hand to my lips, kissed her knuckles. "I went over to Naked to see you, and Meara told me there'd been an accident. You could've called me. I don't like that you were here all alone."

"I have a lot of experience with being alone in ERs."

"Not anymore," I said.

"And my phone died in the accident," she said. "Totally destroyed. Same with my bike."

I nodded. "Yeah, about that." I kissed her knuckles again. "I promise I'll buy you a bike just like the one you lost today as long as you promise to never, ever ride it."

A smile curled at the corners of her lips. "I don't think I'll take that deal but I am wondering if you're finished with the murderous freak-out yet because I need to ask you a really huge favor."

"You were involved in a hit-and-run and you have two broken bones *and* a concussion. I don't think I'll be finished with this freak-out until next year. At the earliest." I gave her a manic smile that made her laugh. "What do you need? There's very little in this world that I can't give you."

She raked her teeth over her lower lip and ducked her gaze. Silence stretched out between us.

"Sweetheart, if you don't tell me right now, I'm going to—"

"My parents are going to be here any minute," she said, reaching for my tie and yanking me in close, "and I know I shouldn't ask this of you but I really need you to step in front of that runaway train for me. They're going to turn this place upside down. They're going to panic and they're going to move in with me for at least two months and they will become a pair of planets orbiting me until I burn out and explode. I need your help holding them off."

"Sunny. Sweetheart. Storm cloud. You were *hit by a car*. A runaway train of panic is appropriate." I tapped my chest. "I'm living it right now."

"Beck," she whispered, her eyes soft and pleading. "*Please.*"

As if I could say no to her. As if I could do anything but exactly what she wanted. As if I had a single bargaining chip in hand.

"I'll take care of your parents," I said, "but don't think *I* won't be the one orbiting you. Understood?"

chapter twenty-four

Sunny

Today's Special:
Vanilla-Scented Stew of Shuffles and Stumbles

I HEARD them before I saw them, which was not unusual. My dad was a little deaf and a lot loud and my mother, permanently exasperated from decades of him misunderstanding everything she said, yelled as a means of self-preservation. They loved each other very much though you could only see it up close.

"My daughter was brought here," she said as if she was ordering a half pound of ham at a busy deli. "Someone, please, where can I find my daughter? Sunny Du Jardin?"

I pulled Beck closer. "Things are about to get very real in here."

He brushed some hair off my forehead, his lips firming into a hard line. The fine serif brackets at the corner of his mouth appeared as he gave a single, small shake of his head. "Let me worry about that. Please. It will give me something to do."

The curtain flew open and my parents gusted toward the gurney, yell-talking over each other.

"My god, Sunny. What have you done now?" My mother threw her tote bag down and rushed toward me, hands held open. "How did this happen?"

"Have you seen the neurology attending?" Dad drummed his fingers against his belt, ready for action. "What's their name? I'll have them paged. We need an update right now."

Mom flattened a hand to her chest. "What did ortho say about your arm? Will you need surgery?"

"Have they run an EEG?" Dad asked.

"If they didn't, they're going to very soon," Mom said.

My parents had a habit of approaching my epilepsy with a frustrated kind of concern that leaned toward indignance. It was like they'd received a broken teapot in the mail one day and had never stopped asking for an explanation about this teapot, all while trying to boil water and pour tea from it. They'd gesture to the places where the tea leaked down the sides as if someone would know why it was like that and give them the secret to making the pieces fit back together. Even after all these years, they hadn't accepted that the teapot didn't function the way most teapots did, but that it could do so many other things if only they allowed themselves to see past the cracks. I knew they just wanted answers about their strange, shattered package.

"Where is the damn doctor?" Dad stepped outside, swung a gaze up and down the hall.

"You didn't have them paged, Edouard," Mom shouted.

"Are they treating the pain?" Dad asked.

A pinched frown pulled at Mom's face. "We're going to need fresh aloe for all those cuts and scrapes. Your poor cheeks."

The throb in my head forced me to slow-blink my way through this reunion. They hadn't even noticed Beckett standing beside me, and that was quite remarkable seeing as he was the size of a wind turbine and had his hand on my shoulder.

"Obviously, we'll be here to nurse you back to health," Mom said. "We're not going anywhere for a *very* long time."

Fighting words, those were.

"Okay, well, let's not rush into any plans," I said, the words coming in wobbles and slurs. "All the doctors and nurses have been here, and they're feelin' good about putting Humpty Dumpty back together again. So, we're good. All good."

Beck snorted out a quick laugh saying, "Oh, storm cloud," under his breath. He gave my shoulder a light squeeze. "You just missed one of the doctors," he said to my parents. "They've diagnosed a concussion—"

"Not another concussion," Mom panted, her hand clutched to her chest.

"—and they're monitoring Sunny for a bit but expect to discharge her later today. I'll be taking her home and keeping a close watch on her."

As if they'd just realized he was in this sliver of a room, my parents fully shifted their attention to Beck.

"Who's this guy?" Dad asked. "When did he get here?"

"Beckett Loew," he said, completely unfazed by the riot in my father's tone.

"Oh, goodness, Beckett Loew?" My mother went to him, scraping a glance from head to toe and grabbing him by the biceps. "Honey, I haven't seen you in years! Look at you, all grown up!" She paused, held him away from her. "What on earth are you doing here? Last I heard from Lance, you were living overseas somewhere."

Beck glanced at me, the fragment of a smile warming his eyes. I returned that smile though I was relatively certain it was more of a droopy-faced grimace. Thank you, narcotics.

And that was all it took for my parents to glance between us a few times and whisper-yell, "Ohhhh."

If I'd put any planning into this introduction rather than arriving here after an ambulance ride, I would've carefully considered how I framed all of this for them. Especially since they'd never met anyone I was dating. That was mostly the result of my romantic life being something of a tumbleweed bumbling around Death Valley but also a fair amount of my family being a noisy, boundary-less lot.

Also, I would've spent some time on how I'd present the evolution of Beckett from Lance's best friend to my—well, to mine.

"Lance's friend Beckett?" Dad asked, his bushy dad-brows furrowed while he did the math in his head. I saw it the second he arrived at eight, the number of years between me and my brother. The years between me and Beck. I watched as he grappled with that number, turning it over and around in his mind until he came to some conclusion that left him looking like he was trying to swallow a peach pit.

"The same one," Beck replied, still calm as could be. He wasn't choking down stone fruit today. No need. Where anyone else would've been panic-sweating and swearing under their breath, Beck had the balls to look like he was having fun. "It's good to see you again, Edouard."

"And you're—" Dad wagged a finger between us. Stared at the hand on my shoulder.

"We are," Beck said easily. "I promise to take very good care of her as she recovers. I won't leave her side." He glanced down at me. "Not for a minute."

There was some kind of threat in there, and probably a sexy one, but I was too fluffed up to do anything but toss an unsteady thumbs-up and say, "Yep."

My mother's lips quirked into a bewildered smile. "Oh. Well. I had no idea. That this was going on. You didn't mention anything, Sunny."

Before I could say something about requiring some personal space in my life and the need to respect my privacy and boundaries, Beck said, "That's probably my fault. I've been a little greedy with Sunny's free time." He met my gaze with one of those smug grins that made me a little murderous. "And she has been busy this summer. The café has really taken off." He reached over and lowered my hand, which I'd left suspended in the thumbs-up position. Like a dork. "You should head over there now. Sunny's partners will want to know how she's doing and I bet they'd love to show you around."

"Oh." My mother cleared her throat. Her turn with the peach pit. "Well. I thought we'd stay and—"

"You've had a long trip, Darcie." The gentle way he cut her off at the turn was art. It could've been an internet meme. "You came all the way from Vermont. The Green Mountains, right?"

"We're there for the summer, yes," she said. She looked around like she wanted to drag the first person in scrubs she could find in here and regain control of the conversation. "But we live only about forty-five minutes away. It's no problem at all. We know what Sunny needs. We've been down this road plenty of times."

If I could've rolled my eyes, I would've. And I would've hated myself for it because my greatest grievance was that my parents wanted to swaddle me in safety and never allow me to wander more than an arm's length from them. So terrible, my parents caring about me.

"I'll take Sunny home," Beck said. His words were warm, friendly even, but the finality in them was like hitting a stone wall. "Her phone didn't survive so you'll have to call me until I'm able to get a replacement for her. I'll be the one to keep you updated."

He palmed his phone and sent a message to my parents after they rattled off their numbers. I stared up at him with hearts in my eyes. When I'd asked him to jump in front of the train for me, I figured he'd diffuse a bit of the chaos. Maybe turn down the panic. I never thought he'd turn off the panic altogether. Even if I'd had a crystal ball and the most intuitive tarot cards in the world, I never would've guessed he'd volunteer to be inundated with their check-ins and questions.

"I still want to hear from the neuro attending," Dad said, his hands back on his hips as he ducked his head into the hall.

"I'll update you after they come back around," Beck said. "We're going to let Sunny rest now. I'll walk you out."

I nodded my way through a long round of goodbyes and watched as Beck guided my parents out of the emergency room as if he'd been training his whole life for this moment. If I asked him, he'd probably brush it off and say something absurd about frying bigger fish before breakfast, but I'd been waiting years—decades!—for someone to know exactly what I needed and give it to me. To *know* me.

Yeah, I'd asked. Begged, if we wanted to be extremely technical. But the real magic was that he answered. I'd asked and he answered all the way, and I felt that in my chest like a spilled cup of coffee, hot and inevitably messy and just a damn catastrophe as I raced and failed to contain it.

AFTER A WHOLE SQUAD of orthopedic interns learned how to apply a cast to my extra special fracture—and they gave me a gorgeous rainbow swirl because I'd decided long ago that if doctors were going to learn on me, I was going to have fun while they did it—the neurologist performed the whole concussion protocol song and dance as if I hadn't memorized that number years ago. Every time I said *Yeah, I get it*, Beck cut me off with *Quiet down* and *I am going to hear every word of this*.

The hospital offered up a pair of scrubs since my clothes were a pile of scraps and Beck had to help me into them like I was a toddler. He crouched at my feet and rolled up the pant legs, muttering to himself the entire time. I didn't know what he was saying and I was too tired to care.

I asked him to take me home, to my house, and Beck agreed when I'd mumbled without context, "My dogs."

He insisted on carrying me from the car to the front door, and then to the couch in the living room. A small portion of me wanted to argue about that simply because I didn't need Beck thinking he could get his way all the time. The larger and more heavily medicated portion of me didn't give a fuck.

"You don't have to stay here." I watched as Beck took stock of my kitchen, opening the fridge and cabinets, examining apples and plums, lifting the lid on a takeout container. "I'm sure you want to get back to the oyster company for dinner service."

"I don't think so," he said.

"The dogs will be here," I went on. "And Meara can come over when she's finished at the café."

He laughed, saying, "I'm not going anywhere."

"I don't want you to be stressed about SPOC." I settled my hand on Scout's head. She huffed out a sigh as if to say none of this would've happened if she'd been there. I should've named her Darcie Junior. "And I'm just going to sleep."

"I will be stressed if I'm not here." He moved toward me, his hands in his pockets and his collar open at the throat. I didn't remember him ditching the tie. "Stop trying to get rid of me. I promised your parents I'd stay and even if I hadn't, you'd have to physically throw me through the door to get me to leave. Would you care to try?"

Jem gave a low howl like he supported these kinds of sweeping statements.

"Do you want to sleep here?" he asked, motioning to the couch. "Or would you prefer the bedroom?"

A dry, painful laugh shook out of me. "I always prefer the bedroom, Beckett."

He glanced up at the ceiling as he blew out a breath. "Don't do that."

Everything was gray and blurry yet I still knew he was as aggravated with me as always, and I loved it. "Do what?"

"Tell me where you want to sleep and don't be a brat about it."

"Take me to bed."

He rubbed his brows. Sighed, again. Pointed to me like I was a puppy learning to sit. "Stay there," he said. "I'm going to get your room ready and then I'll come back for you. And be quiet. No more comments." He knelt down to look at the dogs. "Bark if she tries anything."

I DIDN'T KNOW what day or time it was when I woke up but I definitely felt like I'd been hit by a car. Everything hurt, even my fingernails. My belly churned like I'd eaten gravel and my mouth tasted like metal from all the activity in my brain and I didn't enjoy anything about this useless arm of mine. Even the rainbow cast was a bright, blaring reminder that I was in a bad spot. I wanted to scream, just for the pleasure of getting that noise out of my system.

But then I caught a glimpse of Beck sitting beside me, working on his laptop, phone, and tablet all at once. Three devices, two hands, and somehow it all worked. Businessman magic. Very powerful stuff.

His sleeves were rolled up to the elbow and he'd lost the vest at some point, and he wore those glasses I loved beyond reason. If not for the overall shambles of my body, I would've crawled into his lap and stayed there until he put me into a little coma.

"There she is," he said, piling the devices on the bedside table. "What do you need?"

"I feel"—I waved a hand down my body—"filthy."

He blinked at me. "Okay."

Another floppy gesture at myself. "Do I have to be filthy? Or can I wash any of this? Can I take a shower?"

He ran a hand over his mouth but that didn't hide his laugh. "Not by yourself, you can't." Climbing off the bed, he added, "I'll help you."

"That seems"—I shook my head, struggling to get the words that I wanted and then force them out of my mouth—"advanced. For our relationship."

He opened the closet, grabbed my robe. "Not really." He came around to my side of the bed and peeled back the blankets. "I think it's exactly right."

Since the hallways in this house were too narrow for anyone to carry a large baguette without breaking it in half, we had to execute a sluggish two-step shuffle to the bathroom. The air was warm and humid in here, and the rush of running water into the bathtub seemed to match the constant thrum in my head.

He backed me up against the sink and stilled me with a hand on my hip, saying, "Let's take these scrubs off."

Back on my sexy bullshit, I said, "I thought you'd never ask."

"Stop being so weird. You're going to make me fall in love with you and your injured brain." He said this mostly to himself as he drew the pants down my legs and I knew he was being quippy and smart-assed. He was teasing me. I knew that. But I patted his shoulder and funneled my affection for him into a loopy grin all the same. The ultra-fancy boy shorts followed and he dropped down to the floor, a hand closing around my ankle as he said, "Give me a tiny step. That's it. And another. Very good."

"My hair feels gross." I tried to run my fingers through a tangle but it was hopeless. Worst of all, my hand came away covered in dried blood and dirt. "Do you know how to wash long hair?"

"You can tell me what to do," he said, standing. "I'll learn."

I peered at him. "I have a lot of hair."

"I have a lot of time." He turned his attention to my oversized top, running his finger along the inside of the sleeve where it draped over the cast. "We're going to take this slow, all right?" He cupped my good elbow, lifting it gently. "One arm up, baby. Okay, good."

I was on my way to naked and it wasn't even fun. This was the definition of being in a bad spot. "When will the 'I told you so' parade be starting?"

He glanced at me as he slipped the top over my head and down my injured arm. "No parade," he said. "Not tonight. Come on, let's get you into the bath."

The water was perfect, even if there was a glaring lack of bubbles. Too slippery, according to Beck. He propped my arm on the lip of the tub with half the towels I owned and that made the whole waterproof sleeve-slash-elephant condom situation a little less bizarre.

He passed a soapy washcloth over my legs, tending to each set of scrapes and bruises he encountered. "What do I need to know about washing long hair?"

"You're going to need a big cup or a pitcher to get everything wet," I said, watching as he aimed a scowl at a bruise near my hip. "Although you don't usually have much trouble with that."

"Sunny. I swear to god."

"What? You swear what?"

He exhaled like he had a real problem with oxygen. After a moment, he said, "I don't know. I'm just—you're being cute and I'm still trying to convince myself that you're okay."

"I am very cute." I pouted as if he needed more proof. "And I'm okay. You don't have to worry about me."

"You're"—he motioned to my arm, to the bruises that shouted from my skin like an angry mob—"you're going to be okay. But I am going to worry. Let me, please. I promise I won't suffocate you."

He went in search of a pitcher and returned with a large salad bowl, the heavy cast-iron kettle off my stove, and an empty almond milk jug that he must've found in my recycling bin. It hurt too much to laugh so I pressed the back of my hand to my mouth, saying, "Choices were made, I see."

Beck knelt beside the tub and reached for the salad bowl, a determined glint in his eyes. "Let's start with this one."

I tipped my head back and closed my eyes as the water spilled over me. Even if we achieved nothing else, rinsing away today's unhappy accident made me feel better. Beck smoothed his palm over my hair after each bowl of water and I sighed into his touch.

"How much of this?" He held the shampoo bottle over his palm.

I nudged him to pour, saying, "More. More. A little more. That's good."

He worked the shampoo into my hair, his fingers massaging in controlled circles over my scalp. I was half convinced he'd watched a video on how to wash hair while not finding a pitcher because every move was precise, meticulous. *Heavenly.* "How am I doing?"

"This is good," I said, still sounding like I was six margaritas deep.

He took extra care to rinse out all the shampoo and then started on the conditioner which was, of course, a semi-complicated masque that had to be combed through and left on for five minutes unless I wanted to be a frizzy, dull mess, but none of this seemed to deter Beck. He refused to go with my conditioner of last resort, the product that worked just fine for ponytails and buns, which would be my life for the next six to eight weeks.

I leaned toward him as he raked his fingers through my hair after completing the process. We'd shared a lot of things and he knew more of my body than anyone else, and somehow, *this* felt so much deeper than sex. It was like a level of intimacy that dismantled everything I'd believed about myself and my ability to connect with other people, and all the ways that I could be open and unafraid.

"You're good at this," I said as he wrung the last of the water from my hair. "Thank you."

He dried his hands on a towel and leaned back against the wall, his long legs stretched out in front of him. "Don't mention it, storm cloud."

We stared at each other for a moment, a spiral of heat and awareness passing between us that spoke nothing of sex but everything of that startling new level of—what? What was it when you allowed another person to care for you so tenderly, so completely that they became *the* person, the only one you could ever imagine knowing you in such a raw, thorough way?

I didn't know. I didn't have the words for it. I hadn't learned them yet. From the looks of it, neither had Beck. But we had time. We'd figure it out.

"Why do you always smell like vanilla?" I asked.

He dipped his head, laughing. "Oysters."

"Oysters don't smell like vanilla."

"They don't," he agreed. "We keep vanilla extract around the raw bar for that reason. Soap and water doesn't always cut it."

"I like it."

"Then I guess it's a good thing I spend so much time shucking."

"You are quite good at it," I teased.

His phone buzzed across the tile floor and though I couldn't see the screen, his answering glower told me everything I needed to know. He declined the call though another came through almost instantly. He growled like he was prepared to gnaw on that phone.

"Just take it," I said. "I don't care."

He held up his phone to show me an old photo of Lance passed out in a ball pit on the contact screen. "Oh," I said. "Might as well answer. He'll just keep calling."

"He will." Beck offered the screen another resigned glare before accepting the call. He tapped the speakerphone icon. "Hey, Lance."

"Would you care to explain to me what the fuck is going on there? Because I just got off the phone with my parents—who reamed me out for not telling them that *you* and *my sister* are *together*. And she was in a car accident today? For real, Beck, what the fuck have you done?"

Beck scowled at the phone and I could almost see him formulating a response that would balance us and everything *we* had together against his best friend and all the things *they* had together. And I realized I didn't want him to balance anything. There was no reason for him to be stuck in the middle.

"Slow yourself down, Lance," I said.

"Sunny? What is going on? Are you all right?" he cried. "Mom said you broke your arm?"

"Yeah, but I have another," I said. "I'll be fine."

"What happened?"

"I was hit by a car," I said.

Beck rubbed his temples.

"What? Why?"

"I don't know," I said. "The guy didn't stop to explain his thought process. But, look, you can't call Beck and go off like this. You're not allowed to do that."

"Sunny, I am just trying to figure out what the hell is going on there," he said. "Can someone explain to me why Beck was with you at the hospital? And why you're with him now?"

"I don't actually think you need an explanation," I said. "You want an explanation but that doesn't mean you're entitled to one."

"Sure, I get that, but you're my sister," he said. "And he's—he's—"

"Go ahead," Beck drawled. "Finish that sentence."

"You're almost a decade older than her," he snapped. "And you damn well know it."

"Just like you know you're leaning into some extra patriarchal bullshit right now," I said. "You can fuck right off with that, by the way."

My brother was a horrible poker player. He bet too high, went in too fast, and his cards were as good as written all over his face. All of which was to say I wasn't surprised when he declared, "I deserve to know what's going on and when it started, Sunny, and don't you dare lie to me."

"Hey," Beck snapped. "Do not speak to her like that."

I held up my hand to settle him, saying, "I get that you were blindsided by this just as I was blindsided by a car today." I didn't shoot for sympathy points often, but when I did, I scored. "But that doesn't mean you're allowed to stomp around and make demands."

"I'm sorry," he said, and it sounded like he meant it. "Mom just dumped all of this on me and she was so mad that I hadn't told her and—"

"Yeah. I know," I said, exhaustion sliding over me. "So, Beck and I are together. I'm going to need you to cope with that."

Everyone was silent for a moment before Beck said, "This isn't how I wanted you to find out. I wanted to talk to you first."

"Well, you fucking didn't," my brother replied.

"No, I didn't," Beck said. "Probably because I knew you'd be a complete dickhead about it."

"I'm not the one being the dickhead," he snapped. "You're the one who did this to me."

"No one did anything to you, you big baby," I said. "Go sit in a corner and be mad about it. Goodbye."

I could almost feel Lance frowning through the line. Eventually, he said, "Feel better, Sunny."

The call ended. Beckett and I stared at each other again. He set the phone down and dipped his hand into the water, trailing his fingers along my shin and over my knee. I leaned back and shifted, parting my legs a bit.

"I'm sorry about that," he said, his gaze unfocused.

"If there's one thing we can rely on Lance for, it's his maturity and perspective."

Beck tipped his head back against the wall. "He's such a little bitch sometimes."

"Why do you even like him? I'm required, but for you, it's a choice."

"I have my reasons."

I opened my legs as much as the tub would allow. I wanted to feel his hands on me, to feel good and alive. And I wanted the safety I found in his touch. The knowledge that he knew me, he understood me. And he'd care for me.

He skimmed his fingers along the inside of my thigh as I soaked, that gorgeous face of his settling into an old familiar scowl while his gaze moved between my face and my body. I loved seeing him like this, just sitting on the floor in his outrageously expensive shirt and trousers as he watched me in the bath. I loved the way the water clung to his arm, beads traveling down his forearm with the lines of his veins. I loved that I could find enough comfort and power in being exposed this way that I spread my legs and asked for more. I loved that nothing had really changed for us today, even with all the drama and upheaval. I loved *this*. I was beginning to think I might love *us*.

I arched my hips up, asking for more. He shook his head, grumbling out, "Sunny, I can't."

But he swept his fingers between my legs and I sighed out a raspy, "Yes."

He stroked me with the backs of his fingers and the pad of his thumb, and wispy curlicues of pleasure, of lightness twisted through my body.

"I can't have you blacking out on me," Beck said, and I felt the apology in his words. "I can't risk that."

I reached for his wrist, trapping his hand on my pussy. "Just a little more."

"I swear to god," he murmured. "If I have to take you back to the ER tonight—"

"I'm not going to come," I said. "I don't even think I can, but I just want—" I didn't know how to explain that I needed this. I needed him. "Please, Beck."

Minutes passed as he drew his fingers over me, circling near my clit but never giving it the kind of attention that would get us anywhere. My nipples were hard. An ache settled behind my belly button and it pulsed whenever he lingered near my opening, caressing my flesh with so much restraint that I could hear his jaw click.

Eventually, he said, "You're going to be a raisin. And the water's getting cold."

"But—"

"You can spend the next month riding my face if you get out of this tub right now," he said. "I'll fuck you twice a day and suck your clit until it throbs at the sight of me. I'll make you a punch-card and give you a freebie after every ten fucks, but I can't do this with you tonight. Or for at least a week."

"A punch-card," I repeated.

"If that's what it takes."

"How would I ride your face with this?" I motioned to my busted arm.

"I won't let you fall," he said.

"And if I do?"

"I'll catch you," he said.

Beck helped me out of the bath and took great care to towel off every inch of me. There was a line between small, helpless child I'd been so many times and pampered adult, and I didn't know which side of it I was on.

"I lied to your mother," he said, studying the products in my cabinet. "I told her you have fresh aloe and—"

"Jesus, not the aloe again."

"—I don't think you do." He held up a bottle of thick body lotion and the prescription-strength antibiotic ointment from the hospital. "This will have to do for tonight."

He started with the antibiotic, dabbing at the worst of my scrapes. He dropped light kisses on the few spots that were neither bruised nor broken and I broke out in goose bumps everywhere he touched.

"If you'd asked me yesterday, I would've said there's nothing sexy about ointment." I ran my fingers through his hair. "But your work here is flawless."

He moved on to the body lotion, warming it between his palms before spreading it over my legs. "You make it easy on me."

"I don't see how that's even close to the truth. I look like the unlikely survivor in a dystopian movie."

"Stop it," he chided, leaving a kiss on my waist. "You're a very likely survivor. You can summon Satan, after all."

"Oh, that's right. It's how I got you." I leaned into him as he rubbed the lotion over my back and shoulders. "You're welcome to bring this bottle into the bedroom with you. I'm open to all forms of massage. I'm open to a lot of things, actually. Help me get to my bookshelf and I'll provide examples."

"Read all you want, but the only thing you're going to get from me for the next few days is a fond pat on the ass," he said, laughing.

I rested my head on his chest. I was naked, my hair wet and dripping all over his fancy shirt. My arm was still in the condom. The faint scent of vanilla lingered between us and I exhaled like I'd just remembered how. "Will you stay? Will you read with me?"

"I'm not going anywhere, storm cloud," he said.

chapter twenty-five

Beckett

Today's Special:
Soufflé of Native Cherry Sympathy

Lance: Are we going to talk about this?

Beckett: Should I give you a call?

Lance: No, because I'll say things I'm going to regret
if I don't have a chance to delete them before
sending.

Beckett: Awesome. Glad we're playing on that level
today.

Lance: Well? Go ahead. Explain.

Beckett: What do you want me to explain?

Lance: Are you FUCKING kidding me right now?

Beckett: ...I don't think so, no.

Lance: I thought you were my friend.

Beckett: I am. That hasn't changed.

Lance: You're my friend. That means you don't go after my sister.

Beckett: Okay, but I think you're wrong about that. You have to take a minute to remember that I'm not some misogynistic prick. Then you have to ask yourself why I'm good enough to be your friend but not good enough for your sister.

Lance: Because she's a kid!

Beckett: Dude, she's 28. She wins commercial real estate in poker games. She owns her own business. She's very much an adult. Arguably more than you.

Lance: I'm sorry but I can't process this. It really messes with my head to think about you and my sister together.

Beckett: Listen, I know you prefer things in clean, black and white boxes. I know this isn't that. But nothing has to change between us.

Lance: You should've told me then.

Beckett: Should've told you what?

Lance: When it started. When you decided you wanted to get involved with her. Anything at all. The fact that my mother blindsided me with this is such a dick move.

Beckett: But I didn't decide to get involved with her. I didn't want that to happen. I worked my ass off at avoiding it.

Lance: Apparently not enough of your ass.

Beckett: What is your endgame here? You want me to drop your sister so you, all the way out in California doing whatever the fuck you do, can keep things tidy in your head? Does Sunny have any say in this? Do I?

Lance: I'll deal with Sunny on my own.

Beckett: The fuck you will.

Lance: You want to try that again?

Beckett: Under no circumstance will you bother her with this bullshit. She doesn't need any stress right now. The only thing you're going to do is tell her that you love and support her, and you are only concerned with her happiness. If you so much as imply anything to the contrary, you and I will have some real problems.

Lance: Wait, so you care about her?

Beckett: What the actual fuck do you think I've been saying to you?

Lance: How the fuck should I know? No one tells me anything!

Beckett: You moved in with Chantal and didn't tell anyone about that.

Lance: Chantal isn't your sister.

Beckett: Look. I'm sorry you heard about this the way you did. I'd like to say I had something better planned but I'm juggling a lot of balls right now and I thought I had a little more time before breaking this to you. But you not liking that I'm with Sunny isn't going to change that fact. It will make her sad which will piss me off, and that's on top of the shock of realizing my oldest friend is willing to blow up our friendship.

Lance: I'm not blowing anything up.

Beckett: Are you sure about that?

Lance: Yes. I just need some time. Okay?

Beckett: Okay, but don't you dare bother Sunny.

Lance: Can you calm down for a fucking second? My god.

Beckett: If it's all the same to you, I'm going to be annoyed as hell until you pull your head out of your ass.

Lance: You're not the one allowed to be annoyed here.

Beckett: I am allowed to wonder what the hell is wrong with you.

Lance: Are we good?

Beckett: Based on this conversation? No fucking clue.

Lance: I'll call you when I'm a little less traumatized.

I WISH I was exaggerating when I said the entire town of Friendship was concerned about Sunny but it was the truth. There was a nonstop stream of visitors at her door. Everyone wanted to check on her or offer to help with anything she needed.

With that came an outpouring of flowers and gifts. I'd called Parker to come over here with some of his friends and make a dent in the food that people kept dropping off for Sunny. If there was anyone who knew how to make casseroles disappear, it was seventeen-year-old boys.

I woke up a few days ago to find someone's grampa in Sunny's front yard on a riding mower, cutting her grass. He bagged it up and took it with him too. Just waved when I stepped outside, and asked me to send his best to Sunny.

Somewhere along the way, rumors about me raising hell at the hospital spread and took on a life of their own. According to some, I barged in there with a roll of hundred-dollar bills and demanded the doctors and nurses move Sunny to a private room. A few others claimed I called the president of the hospital and insisted she personally oversee Sunny's treatment. Others maintained that I helicoptered in a neurologist from New York City and I had Dex send his orthopedic surgeon.

That one was amusing, especially given that Dex wasn't even reading my texts and, if the sports news stations could be trusted, he was out for the season with an injury of his own. Not surprisingly, he wasn't returning anyone's calls or texts. I had the sense that something was very wrong, maybe something unrelated to major league ball or the injuries that had dogged him since high school, but I didn't even know where to start looking for him.

The funny thing was, I knew what Dex would say. I didn't know any of the details as to why he was reportedly out for the season but I knew he'd hunch forward, his hands clasped between his legs, and tell me the situation was well and fully shucked. He'd say it and I'd laugh because I always laughed when he determined a situation was shucked.

Aside from this tsunami of love for Sunny and the grudging admiration for me, the town was fired the fuck up. The walking club had taken it upon themselves to lobby for the installation of speed bumps near the intersection of the bike path, and they'd already collected enough signatures and letters of support on the issue to land a spot on the next town council agenda.

Ranger and Phil Collins dropped by over the weekend with a peace lily the size of a St. Bernard and a promise to put pressure on the local police to make moves on the hit-and-run case. Ranger was certain someone on Old County Road had a doorbell camera that caught sight of the car either before or after the accident, and he had no problem knocking on doors to find out.

Everyone wanted to know what they could do to help. Since lawn mowing and peace lilies couldn't mend bones or heal a brain—and I was quite exhausted from being cordial to all the people banging on her door—I redirected that concern by sending them to Naked. The best thing they could do to help Sunny was to make sure the café didn't struggle without her.

Unfortunately, Naked did struggle. Whether it was a coincidence or a result of this crazy town's collective power, Naked rocketed to local fame overnight. Two regional news stations showed up on the same day to profile the shop—seemingly unaware that Sunny had been involved in a hit-and-run accident—and several high-profile foodie influencers visited throughout the week, all posting on their social sites and flooding the café with their hungry followers. One of them even posted a wacky shot of a giant chocolate cookie sticking out of the back pocket of her jeans.

That drew *a lot* of attention.

Yesterday, Muffy texted me to arrange a parking lot meeting. She marched outside with her braids tied up in a pair of buns and her apron splattered with red and purple.

I motioned to the apron. "Double homicide?"

"Close enough. Cherry season." She folded her arms over her chest. "Now listen, Loew. I know what you're doing and I love you for it but if you don't ease up, we're going to have a real problem."

I eyed the people queued up to get inside Naked and those crowding the back patio. "Why? What's wrong?"

"We cannot keep up," she said, her voice pitching higher with each word. "We're selling out of everything before noon. We ran out of tea yesterday. *Tea.* And the phones don't stop ringing. We're getting calls about catering parties and weddings. *Weddings,* Beck! We don't have the production capacity to meet this level of demand and we don't have the staff to serve this many people. Beth and Meara have been working all day, every day since the accident." She pointed to the café. "They're probably dying in there because I've been gone for five minutes. And all because you said Sunny wanted everyone to visit Naked."

"I did say that." I dipped my hands into my pockets. "And I can help with those issues."

She barked out a laugh. "You're cute but that doesn't mean you know how to knead my dough."

"I certainly do not," I said, "but I can lend you some people who do."

And that was how I ended up working the counter at Naked while Muffy put two of the oyster company's line cooks to work.

chapter twenty-six

Sunny

Today's Special:
Mini Meltdowns with a Dusting of Organic Panic

Beth: Hi! I was wondering if you'd like a visitor today. I have a care package with your name on it but I can leave it at the door if you're not up to seeing anyone.

Sunny: Yes, I want to see you! Always!

Beth: How about two-ish?

Sunny: Wait. Did Beck put you up to this?

Beth: I don't need Beck to put me up to visiting one of my best friends!

Sunny: So, he strongly encouraged it?

Beth: Don't insult me, Sunny.

Sunny: Don't bullshit me, Bethany.

Beth: He said he had to go to an important meeting with his lawyer and your parents were there, and it would be a good day for any of us to swing by if we wanted BUT I was planning on texting you anyway because of the care package.

Sunny: How do you feel about me using you to nudge my parents out the door?

Beth: We'll nudge together. Team effort.

Sunny: See you around two!

"YOU DID NOT HAVE to do this." I held up the cutest damn PJ set in the world. It was soft like a baby blanket and printed with dogs in various states of snooze. "And there's a matching eye mask! Awww, Bethy. You're the best."

"Actually," she said, wiggling her shoulders, "it's from me and Mel."

"Ohhh really." I folded the pajamas and set them back in the gift bag. "Tell me more."

She shifted on the sofa, tucking her legs beneath her. "We've had some ups and downs, but we're going to give this a try."

I clapped my hands together. "When did it happen?"

"We had a feisty little moment last week," she said, rolling her eyes. "She picked up a whole mood and I told her I liked the game, but I was tired of playing it all the time."

"How did that go over?"

She glanced away, smiling. "She stuck with the mood for a minute, but then we had a really good conversation." She giggled. "And then she broke my vagina. I'm still a little woozy."

"I am so happy for you."

"Thank you, babydoll." She rubbed her palm over my forearm, her pretty smile sliding into a pout. "And I miss you. When are we going to get you back?"

"Soon," I said. "I should be able to come in for shorter shifts starting on Monday, which is great because I've been driving myself crazy here."

The truth was, I was going to snap if I didn't get back to my life soon. Being cooped up here, in my childhood home, in the middle of the summer, was straight out of my own personal horror movie.

"Then you should really try to not get hit by cars," Beth said. "This seems like a super preventable problem."

"Is that what I'm supposed to be doing? Huh. No one told me."

"Well, now you know," she said. "So, tell the gross, gnarly truth. How are you really doing?"

I took a breath before I responded and that gave me a second to figure out whether I'd tell Beth everything or *everything*. She could handle either version, that I knew, but I wasn't sure I wanted to put one of them into words yet. If I held it close, it would exist only in my mind, which wasn't real. But holding it close was costing me. It was draining my energy like a crockpot left on for days and days.

I laced the tips of my fingers, pressing my middle knuckles together hard for ten seconds and releasing for five before repeating the process several times. It was one of many mechanisms I used to claw my way out of the prodrome and aura phases before they manifested into a seizure. It was always the strangest things that worked for me. Sitting in a dark spot and focusing on every inhale and exhale. Thinking about the scent of lavender, the taste of basil. Imagining the feel of the ocean rushing over me as my feet sank into the sand. Singing. Closing my eyes and counting to ten while forcing the image of each number into my mind.

Most of the time, these things—plus meds and my entire way of life —functioned well enough for me. But I was working really hard at convincing everyone that I was doing just fine since the accident and my body kept tossing out little flares and asking, *Are you really?*

So, I steepled my fingertips and visualized numbers because the epilepsy I lived with was a hoarder, always hunting around for enough stress and fluctuating hormones, skipped meals and the neighbor's flickering twinkle lights to spark some irregular electrical activity.

Since I didn't have time for this shit, I thought about pesto and low tide.

"Physically, I'm feeling better," I said, nodding to my cast. "My head is back in the game, mostly. I get tired pretty fast and I get a lot of seizure symptoms but they fizzle out before they get going."

"All good things," she murmured.

"Emotionally, I'm a little fucked over," I said. "It's not even the accident itself bothering me, but the feeling that I am trapped and powerless all over again. I know it's irrational though I feel like the only answer is to plan my escape."

"Then do that. Make those plans. Decide where you'd go if you could go anywhere, do anything. Write up the itinerary. Research the flights. Whatever. Just feed that need inside you to know that you are *not* trapped."

"We *just* opened a café together. We have contracts and shit," I said. "This doesn't freak you out?"

"No, because I look at houses for sale in Laguna Beach, California every night before I fall asleep. These places are millions of dollars for houses that are so spectacular, they don't even make sense to me. I zoom in, I look at all the angles. Imagine how I'd change the floorplan or redecorate. I don't have ten million dollars for a house and I'm not moving to California, but sometimes I need to pretend that I am. And you need to pretend that you're leaving on your next great adventure."

"Okay." I shrugged. "I can try that."

She rolled her hand for me to continue. "Give me the rest of your problems. I want to rub my hands around in them and make a pretty picture."

"I don't love being here in the house and—essentially—not being able to leave. I know it's temporary. I know it will get better. But I am fraying. Beck keeps suggesting we go to his place, and that's great, but the dogs know this house and this yard, and—"

"And his little brother is there," Beth said with a laugh. "He's a sweetheart, don't get me wrong, but that feels like a complication you don't need."

"And also," I said, leaning in close, "Beck's bedroom has *bunkbeds*. From when he was a child. So, that's not something that interests me."

"Understandable." She rested her head on the sofa cushions. "How's Beck doing?"

"Beck is fried," I said. "I mean, he's been incredible and I owe him the world for putting some space between me and my parents, but he's going to snap any minute now. I try not to pry because talking about it stresses him out, but the legal issues with his parents are still messy. He'd never admit it, but the whole thing has been emotionally exhausting for him."

"Do you think he knows what it means to be emotionally exhausted?"

"That is a great question. Thank you for asking. No, I don't think he has a clue. The boy lives in two modes: all hell has broken loose and only some of hell has broken loose."

"And somehow he manages to hire angels to tailor his pants. Amazing, really."

"That is true," I said. "Also, Lance won't talk to him, which is supremely shitty, even for my brother. There's a bunch of not-great stuff happening with his brother Decker too. I've watched Beck leave a voicemail or text him, and then compulsively check his phone for the next hour, just waiting for the guy to acknowledge anything."

"Now I'm offended on Beck's behalf," she said.

"Me too. He doesn't deserve to be on the receiving end of all this. Like I said, he's been the absolute best, but everything with the accident has hit him like a boulder. I know he's not sleeping enough. He's trying to balance managing the oyster company with keeping my parents off my back. He worries every time I blink a little too long. I swear, he's in the fast lane to a meltdown. I can see it coming. He's going to trip over some tiny, stupid thing and he's going to crack right in half."

"Oh, honey." She laced her fingers under her chin. "Is there anything I can do to help?"

No. She couldn't. And neither could I. We just had to let it happen. "If he comes into the café," I started, "half-caf him. He does not need to be running around with a full dose of caffeine."

"We're fighting dirty, then?"

"We're fighting the only way we know how."

And that would have to be good enough to get us through.

chapter twenty-seven

Beckett

Today's Special:
An Assortment of Artisanal Tensions, Seasonal Anxiety, and
Clusterfucks

THE FIREFLIES and Fried Dough Festival was held at a large park that doubled as the town's soccer and lacrosse fields, and was home to very few, if any, fireflies. This fact did not seem to trouble anyone at the festival, certainly not Sunny, who'd insisted we come to this illogical event despite her doctor's orders for light activity only.

According to Sunny, two weeks of light activity was more than enough for her and she didn't see how strolling around a soccer field while eating fried dough could be strenuous.

So, here we were, wandering through a maze of pop-up tents and folding tables with every bit of firefly kitsch imaginable while kids— and Agent Price—screamed their way through an obstacle course and the scents of cinnamon and sugar wafted into the air.

If I looked at it from a certain angle, I could see how this could be entertaining, especially for parents needing to burn some energy out of their kids. I could understand the local charm of it too. Vendors, food trucks, all of that stuff. It was great. I couldn't even argue that.

There were many strange things about this—the lack of actual fireflies, for one—but the part that confused the hell out of me was how everyone stopped to say hello and they seemed authentically happy to see us. At first, I'd assumed it was all about Sunny and the dogs. Everyone loved Sunny and her accident was still the top story in town, so of course they wanted to visit with her. And they adored the dogs. But then they started talking to me too, asking about the oyster company and fretting over my parents and their present situations.

I didn't understand it. More than that, I didn't trust it. The people in this town liked my parents because they didn't have to live with them, they liked Decker because he was famous and always donated valuable baseball items for fundraising auctions, and they liked Parker because he was a cartoon character. I was the one who didn't stay in one foreign city long enough for it to be memorable, and with the job no one under-stood. They didn't invite me to their barbeques, they didn't send me Christmas cards, and they didn't ask me to sign baseballs. I was the Loew they didn't know.

After another uncomfortable pit stop with someone I didn't recog-nize but who seemed to know everything about my family, Sunny bumped her shoulder into mine, saying, "Just think about all the Friend-ship festivals we can go to now that you've broken through your festival phobia."

Without any finesse or forethought, I let slip the first—and worst—thing that came to my mind. "Yeah, but I'm not staying in Friendship much longer."

What the fuck was wrong with me? Aside from everything that was always wrong with me, why did I say that?

Well, there were a few reasons.

My firm had not stopped calling for the past two weeks. They wanted updates and timelines. Some indication of when I'd be back to work. I couldn't give them one.

The lease on my condo was due to renew soon. For reasons I could not explain, I hadn't been able to sign the papers.

My attorney was finally doing something right and making progress on deals for my parents, and I was relieved about that. But I couldn't bring myself to believe any of it would come to fruition.

I had a new general manager lined up for SPOC though I kept thinking about how Ayla would need several months off for maternity leave this winter. What was I going to do then?

So, I said this to Sunny because it was front-and-center in my mind. Because I didn't know what to do about it. Because I was tired and stressed and just worn the fuck down from holding everything together for so long that I couldn't keep those words to myself.

Sunny glanced over at me, her brows raised. "Is that so?"

Instead of walking back that statement, I embraced the tension corded between my shoulders and barreled ahead. "Yeah, well, with Ayla taking over the general manager job and the charges against my mom possibly being dropped, I should be heading back to Singapore soon enough."

"So, this is how it goes." Sunny gave me a thoughtful nod and kept walking. "Okay."

"Okay?" I repeated. If she was troubled by this news, she didn't show it. And that troubled me. Maybe she hadn't heard me. There was a lot of screaming at this festival. Or maybe she didn't understand. "What does that mean?"

"It means it's okay, Beck. We don't need to know what comes next," she said. "All we need to know is that we have right now. We're just having fun. Right?"

"We're just having fun," I repeated, since that was the only thing I could do tonight.

"Yeah," she said, staring up at me like I'd lost my mind. Maybe I had. "We're having fun together. You don't have to stress about what happens when things change for you."

"Right," I said, the word cracking out of me with such force that my jaw hurt. "Fun. Okay. Good to know."

Sunny leaned away, skimmed a glance over me. "What's happening here?"

"Nothing," I said, nowhere near in control of the velocity of my words. "Just having *fun*."

She frowned and my heart gave a trombone-y thump that couldn't be healthy. "Do you want to talk about it?"

"Is there something to talk about?" I asked. "Since we don't need to know what comes next?"

"I can only promise this moment," she said. "That's all I can ever give because nothing else is certain." When all I could do was stare at her like she'd just peeled back the surface of the earth to reveal an ocean of apple cores, she went on. "I don't make forever plans, Beck. I have today and probably tomorrow and a bit beyond that but I refuse to pin down the future because I don't know what it will be until I get there."

"Sunny, sweetheart, I love that for you but what the fuck? Did you not just open a business?"

"I did, and that means I'm going to put my energy into building something special *right now*. It doesn't mean the rest of my life will be Naked Provisions."

I didn't understand this. Not a single word of it.

"We should get you home." I stared at my watch much longer than necessary because I was afraid Sunny would see the swirling hurricanes in my eyes. "You've had seventy-one minutes of walking around, one questionably vegan slab of fried dough, and zero living fireflies. Let's call it a night."

I didn't know what to say on the drive back to Sunny's house. I didn't trust myself to keep a lid on all the snarly noise that pressed up at my edges and blurred my vision. And I didn't trust myself to stop before I said something I'd never be able to take back.

Sunny's parents called to check on her as they had several times a day since the accident and that distraction gave me a minute to breathe. I didn't figure anything out but I didn't feel like I was going to crack my jaw from all the clenching.

Once Sunny closed the front door behind us, she said, "I'm not doing this, Beck. Either you tell me what's wrong or you take yourself home and glare at your own walls."

Again, I said the first—and worst—thing. "When were you going to tell me that you were *just having fun*?"

She dropped onto the sofa and folded her legs in front of her, her hands clasped in her lap. "To be clear, you're upset that I didn't dissolve into a fit of screaming and crying because you told me that you won't be living here forever and ever, as I always knew? That's the problem?"

"The problem is that I don't know what the fuck *fun* means to you because I thought we had a real relationship but I guess I was wrong about that."

She pressed her lips into a sad, stiff line and gave a *that'll do it* nod. "Okay, Beck. You need to spend the night figuring yourself out. You can come back after you've made sense of all those big feels inside you."

"Sunny, stop it. I'm not going anywhere."

"Actually, you are." She tipped her head toward the door. "You don't get to say things like this to me and then sleep in my bed."

"I'm not leaving you alone," I said. How I managed to speak through that gut punch was a mystery to me. "Come on. You know you still need help." When she only stared at me, I added, "I promised your parents I'd stay with you. I'll sleep on the couch."

"Not tonight, no." The finality in her voice raised the hairs on the back of my neck. "I want you to go, Beck."

I went to her, crouching in front of the sofa. "Sunny. Sweetheart.

I'm sorry. I don't know what the fuck is wrong with me tonight. I just—"

"Beck." Her tone was solid ice. "Listen to me carefully. I'm not mad. I'm not giving you the silent treatment. I'm not ending anything. I'm just sending you home to give you the time to think about why you're feeling this way."

I peered up at her, certain that I was being ripped in half. "I'll stay on the couch. Just in case you need me."

"I've had a lot of people hovering over me recently and I would like to be alone tonight."

Since there was nothing left for me to say and I'd ruined enough things by opening my mouth tonight, I pushed to my feet and marched into the kitchen to feed the dogs. Their dishes needed to be washed so I did that too, along with the teacups and plates in the sink. I filled a glass of water and set it on the bedside table and then plugged her phone into the charger there. I checked the lock on the back door and picked up the dogs' toys so Sunny didn't trip over any of them.

"I'll be back in the morning to take you to your doctor's appointment," I said. "Call me if anything happens. Even if you're not-not mad at me, I want you to let me help you." I wanted to throw myself at her mercy. I'd beg. I'd plead. I'd promise impossible, ridiculous things. Instead of doing any of that, I walked to the door. "Lock this after I leave."

She nodded but said nothing else.

Things didn't get better for me when I arrived at home. I opened the front door and heard a softly gasped *Fuck* from the staircase. Glancing up, I found Parker on the landing with a girl about his age. From the disheveled look of them and the deer-in-headlights expressions on their faces, I had a pretty good idea what they'd been doing up there.

"Hi," I said to them. "Park, I'll be waiting in the kitchen."

I sat down and stared at the table, running my thumb over the scratches and grooves. A few minutes passed before I heard the front door close. Parker appeared in the doorway, lingering there until settling whichever internal debate he had going. He dropped into the seat across from me and leaned back, crossing his arms over his chest as if he had nothing to explain.

I almost laughed. On a different night, I would've laughed.

"Do I need to have a sex talk with you?" I asked.

He slumped forward and shoved his fingers through his hair. "Absolutely fucking not, no."

"It's important that you're smart," I said. "Are you taking precautions? To prevent babies and infections? Do you *know* the right precautions?"

Blowing out a long breath, Parker pushed to his feet and went to the refrigerator. He returned with two bottles of beer and passed one to me. "Yeah. I know."

I stared at the beer bottle. "Are we adding underage drinking to the list of lectures for the night? Again?"

Parker tipped back the bottle and drank deeply. He studied the label for a minute, tracing the edges with his fingernail. Eventually, he hunched forward, the bottle loosely clasped between his hands on the table. "How old were you when you sat in this kitchen and had your first beer? Because I'm willing to bet it was a lot earlier than twenty-one. If I had to guess, I'd say it was right around sixteen or seventeen." He glanced at me, a crooked grin on his lips. "I hadn't been born yet but Decker was still a kid, like ten or eleven. Old enough to be really annoying, right? And Mom and Dad were flaky as always, weren't they?" He took another sip. "You didn't sneak beers out of the fridge. You didn't get wasted in forests or on the beach with your friends. No, you sat here with a drink because you were really fucking tired from having to grow up so damn early. And you want to know how I know this?" He slapped a hand to his chest. "I know this because after you and Dex left home, I had to grow up too. It didn't matter how much money you threw at the oyster company or at Mom and Dad because it didn't change anything about this place. It didn't change them. They were still max-level, full-blast ADHD at all times, and that left a guy to drink alone in the kitchen and wonder how the hell he'd wake up the next day and deal with another stupid new crisis."

I reached for my bottle, took a sip. I nodded. He was right about everything, but he didn't need me to say that. He already knew.

"And the really horrible thing about it," he went on, "the most unpleasant, unbearable part is, was that I really love them. They are impossible and exhausting and constantly disappointing, but they're my people. And *good* people too."

"It would be so much easier if they were assholes," I said.

"Fuck yes," Parker replied. "Dad emails me every day. From jail. He wants to talk about the community softball league and his big plans for an October tournament this year. Because he's under the impression he'll be home in October."

"Something to look forward to, I guess."

"I feel like I can breathe for the first time in my life now that they aren't around, and that makes me feel like hot trash." He picked up his beer but immediately put it back down, saying, "There will be years of therapy in my future. So much to unpack. Like a hoarder's storage unit."

"Then you understand why Dex and I left."

"And without one glance in the rearview," he quipped. "Yeah, I get it—and you get that it sucked for me that you left and never fucking came back. That's why there are days when I drink a beer at the kitchen table. Usually after turning off the stove that had somehow been on all day long. It's only a matter of time until this house blows up, Beck."

I couldn't argue with any of this so I sipped my beer in silence. When Parker tossed his empty bottle in the recycling and poured himself a glass of water, I said, "I'm sorry. For staying away."

Parker flopped back into his seat. "I can't even blame you for it. I would've done the same thing. I probably will, after graduation." He held up a hand. "Before you say anything, no, this is not an opening to talk about colleges."

I shook my head. "Wasn't planning on it."

He pressed his hands together and turned his gaze to the ceiling. "Thank you, god."

"About protection," I said, because we could not add a surprise baby to this situation.

"Condoms," he said tersely. "And just because you think you know what you saw tonight doesn't mean you know shit."

"Please don't explain any of that to me. Just—just use the condoms. Every time. Always."

"Hey, why are you here?" he asked.

"Is this another one of your philosophical questions? Like, what is consciousness?"

He rolled his eyes like I was unbearable. "No, I mean, why are you here tonight? I thought you were with Sunny."

"Do you always invite girls over here when I'm with Sunny? Because condoms or not, that isn't—"

"Dude, no," he cried, drilling a finger on the table. "If you're determined to parent me, you're going to have to be a lot less obvious about it."

I blinked at him. This fucking kid. "I'll do my best."

"Now, why aren't you with Sunny?"

"I don't spend every night with her," I said.

He bobbed his head. "Wow, so, you really fucked up?"

"No," I said with more vehemence than necessary. "I did not fuck anything up."

"It was a matter of time," he said, sage as always. "It sure as hell wasn't going to be Sunny to fuck it up." He leaned back, folded his arms once again. "What did you do?"

I drained the beer and mirrored his stance. "I'm not really sure what I did," I said. "And I don't know if I can undo it."

chapter twenty-eight

Sunny

Today's Special:
Hand-Crushed Hope

"SO, you said it was okay that he's leaving town because y'all are just hanging out? And that's when the malfunction occurred?" Muffy asked.

"Pretty much," I yelled over the shower.

She murmured something I couldn't make out as she scrubbed my scalp. True friends were the ones who offered to engage in bent-over-the-bathtub acrobatics and wash your hair when you only had one functional hand. She'd probably say it was payback for all the times I'd sat in emergency rooms with her after anaphylactic incidents or when I tended to her hair after a slipup with knives required twenty-five stitches across four fingers, but she would've done this without any of that history, and we both knew it.

"I think he expected me to take his news a little harder," I said. "He definitely wasn't expecting me to say 'Yeah, dude, I figured as much.'"

"I'm going to bet he didn't expect you to toss out the *just having fun* bit either," she said.

"Um, no, he did not." I paused while she rinsed out the shampoo. She even shielded my ears from the spray. Muff was the whole damn best. "I think it hurt his feelings."

"No shit." She cackled. "The boy has been overboard for you since the first time you told him to go fuck himself."

"I never said anything like that!"

"You didn't *not* say it." Another cackle as she worked conditioner into my hair. "He is whole-ass overboard though."

"He likes getting his way," I said rather than addressing any element of Beck falling over anything for me. After last night, I knew that was not the case. "It's part of his whole bossy bossman bridge troll thing."

She hummed. "I might be hypothesizing a little too hard but I get the sense that if you'd told him y'all were just hanging out and it was temporary, separate from any discussion of his plans, he'd probably upend the entire world to make it permanent with you."

"I don't know. I think he's just trying to figure out his feelings. It's been a roller coaster, you know? Everything with his parents and the oyster company and the accident—well, it's a lot. It's catching up with him and this just got more complicated than he expected. Or less complicated. I don't know. That's why I need you to agree with me about everything."

"Another hypothesis: it must be hard for him to expand past his usual grimace," she said. "He's so focused and task-oriented, and experiences what—three? Four emotions in a given day? All of which could be described with a blue frowny face. And then you show up and—bam! Big feelings bonanza. Feels of all colors."

"Yeah. I can see that."

"If you think about the way his grumpy little brain works, he probably needed you to give him a huge reaction to the incredibly obvious news that he wouldn't be staying here forever."

I laughed. "And why would he need that?"

"Because, subconsciously, he wanted to know how much you value this relationship, and by extension, him. In that sense, telling him that you knew and weren't worried because it's just casual must've landed like a kick in the shins. I know he didn't see it coming because he loves you too much to consciously blow shit up like that. That boy willfully works our counter just for a chance to talk to you."

I groaned as she squeezed water from my hair.

"He is in love with you." Her tone made it clear she wasn't about to repeat herself and I wasn't allowed to misunderstand. "Everyone can see it. We all know. The two of you are the only ones in the dark about it."

"Yes, well, please allow me to keep on living in my ignorant bliss," I said. "At least until I've finished requiring you to be on my side about last night."

"If I'm anywhere, it's on your side."

"Thanks," I said, the pout thick in my voice. "You know, you are astoundingly good at breaking down other people's relationship problems."

"Yes, it is one of my better qualities. I'm an expert on everyone else's love lives while having no desire whatsoever to have a love life of my own," she mused, helping me up from the bathroom floor. "Maybe he was fucking it up because he's the type who doesn't trust a good thing. It's not the best sign of secure attachment or healthy adjustment but who even is secure or adjusted these days? In this economy?"

"There is no such thing as healthy adjustment anymore. We're all carrying around reusable grocery bags of trauma simply as a product of being alive in this world and pretending everything is fine." Muffy motioned to the closed toilet lid with a comb. I went obediently. "And that's just the basics of existing. It doesn't even figure in the junk we pick up all on our own."

"That must be a personal problem because I don't have any junk," she replied. "I'm the model of mental health. I'm pristine."

"Of course. My bad. I must've mistaken you for my other best friend, the one with a wardrobe composed entirely of overalls, and a giant, burned-out hole where her life as a rising star chef in New York City used to be."

"What a shame. She sounds fascinating."

"Oh, she's the tits. You'd love her."

"Now, about that Beck. What are you going to do there now that you've possibly-accidentally shattered his tender ego and bruised his beastly little heart? Or are we going to let him marinate in his moody, broody funk because you did zero-point-zero things wrong in that situation and you don't have to fix his feelings for him."

"I'm not sure," I admitted. "I know he's a big softie under the scowl-and-growl but sometimes I think there's more. Like maybe he needs to have someone on *his* side for once."

"What do you mean?" She tapped the crown of my head with the comb. "Before you answer that, what are we doing with all this hair, Rapunzel? Are you good with a top knot?"

"A top knot would be perfect," I said. "I mean he's the one always showing up for everyone else. You wouldn't believe the amount of time and money he's dropped into helping his parents. And he's looking after Parker and taking care of the oyster bar—he's put his entire life on hold. But who shows up for him?" I shrugged. "I don't know. I don't know if that's the answer to anything."

Muffy started gathering my hair in a loose tail. "You're a big softie too and you invest a lot of emotional energy in people. It's why everyone loves you. But I don't want you investing everything in him if he has one foot out the door and can't make heads or tails of his feelings."

When Beck arrived, it was obvious to everyone that he was surprised to find Muffy here but he slipped into easy conversation about the café without missing a beat and she went right along with it.

Once again, I appreciated the hell out of Muffy.

I hugged Beck when it was the two of us and I allowed him to fuss over me before leaving to go to my doctor's appointment. I reached for his hand when he started the car and I let him kiss my knuckles and hold my hand to his chest while he drove. Everything fell into place and I could breathe again.

"The police department called this morning," I said. "They wanted me to know they're still working on the case but didn't have any updates yet. Apparently they're going door-to-door on that street, you know, the one that crosses the bike path? They're asking people if they have any home surveillance that might've caught something."

Beck nodded as if he already knew this and I realized he probably did. I wouldn't put it past him to insist on regular reports from the chief of police. Highly on-brand for Beck.

"Ranger inserted himself into the matter," he said. "I believe he was behind the doorbell camera inquiry or at least he's claiming some credit for it. What his involvement actually means, I don't know, though I can imagine we'll see a lot more of him."

"I don't mind. I'll take him and his eagle-eye watch on everything in town. He tips like he has a swimming pool filled with gold."

Beck was silent for several minutes before asking, "Have you heard from Lance?"

I let my eyes close as he kissed the inside of my palm. "Nope. You?"

He shook his head. "Not since the accident."

"I'm sorry."

"You have nothing to apologize for, storm cloud. Nothing at all."

At the appointment, Beck was on his best behavior, never once pretending to be my husband or requiring second, third, or ninth opinions when the doctor announced I wouldn't need surgery if everything continued to heal normally.

There was plenty of the good old scowl game but beyond that, I couldn't get a read on his mood—which was an increasingly dense problem because I didn't know what was going on with us.

Most of the time, I didn't need to know what was happening in Beck's head. If I had to guess, it was probably a running list of issues to handle, reasons to roll his eyes, and a hyperfixation on the mechanics of wrap skirts. But right now, after everything that went down last night, I needed some information. I couldn't fill in the blanks by myself. I mean, I *could* but that wasn't a great idea. Not without Muffy's supervision.

"I'm taking you home," he said once we were back on the road to Friendship. "Right?"

I'd planned to go to Naked this afternoon. Even if I only covered the counter for a few hours, getting out of the house and doing something felt essential to my survival. "Yeah," I said. "That works."

Later on, I'd get a ride from Meara or Beth. Or I'd walk. It wasn't that far and the exercise would do me good. I just didn't want to go to this place Beck and I shared—the rough, weathered edge of Friendship Cove—and go to our separate shops as if everything was normal. This wasn't normal.

"Can we—" He stopped, reached for my hand. I let him have it. "Can we talk about everything that happened last night?"

"Of course. What would you like to talk about?"

"I can't stay here," he started, the words rushing out like a popped balloon, "but I thought what we had was a little more serious than some summer fling. Maybe it started out that way but it feels like more than that now." He shrugged, tapping his thumb on the steering wheel. "Maybe it has something to do with your accident or—I'm not sure. It's probably a misplaced sense of—of something. But we can't—I can't— this isn't"—he flattened my palm against his chest— "I can't stay, Sunny."

I stifled a sigh. "Beck, who are you trying to convince? Because I know you aren't staying forever and I don't need you to explain the dynamics of that to me. It would help if you could tell me what you do want because I'm definitely stumbling around in the dark on that one."

He stared ahead, silent, his jaw tight.

I watched a minute pass on the clock without a response from Beck. He slipped his fingers between mine and squeezed my hand as he drove. After another minute, he said, "I don't have an answer to that."

"Then you should take some time to find one and come back to me when you've sorted it out."

"What? No. No, Sunny, I'm not going anywhere. That's ridiculous."

"It really isn't," I said. "As you've stated a few times, you can't stay here and I'm not about to ask you to change your entire life for me—"

"You could." He rubbed my knuckles over his lips once, twice. Did he understand what he was saying? Did he realize this had started with him insisting his time here was short and he had other places to be? Or was it just as Muffy had suggested, a foil for an issue that had nothing to do with this town? "You could do just that."

"And yet I am not going to," I replied with a broad, salty smile that he didn't notice. "We all know how you feel about Friendship and there's no doubt in my mind that if I—or anyone else in your life— asked you to stay here, you'd grow a moss of hostility on your north side before the end of a year. If you *choose* to change your whole life, it has to be for reasons that have nothing to do with me." I peered at him for a moment. "And I don't think that's possible, Beck. You're not going to wake up tomorrow morning and fall in love with Friendship."

He pulled up in front of my house and stopped, his steely gaze focused on a spot down the street and his hand still warm around mine.

"Take some time," I repeated. "Think it all over, even if that means getting cool with the idea that the future is out of our control and the best we can do is choose the paths that feel good while they're open to us."

A laugh creaked out of him as if he hadn't laughed in months, maybe years. Then, "Are you breaking up with me?"

It was my turn to laugh, even if Beck seemed to take grave offense to it.

"No, I'm not breaking up with you," I said, "though I do find it precious that you're this ultra-buttoned-up guy who juggles millions and billions of dollars, and you're fixated on the precise condition of our relationship when you're hardly the type I could ever imagine wanting to be called anyone's *boyfriend*."

He drew a gaze up from my skirt and over my chest to settle on the almost-healed bruises and scabs on my chin. "As you've always said, I'm not your type."

"And what a helpful reminder that is." I gave him a tart smile and tried to pull my hand back but he held tight. "Beck."

"I appreciate that you're not breaking up with me," he said, still focused on my chin, "though I have to admit I don't have the foggiest fucking clue what *is* happening."

This was like ripping off someone else's bandage. I hated it. "I know there are a load of big, messy things happening in your life right now and everything is up in the air but I can't define your feelings for you, Beck. I think you should spend a few nights in your own bed. Just sort out what you want so we can have fair expectations for each other."

He pushed a hand through his hair. "Can't I just tell you right now that I don't want this to end?"

"Yeah, no problem. Except for the part where you told me a literal minute ago that you couldn't stay here." I gave him a *please cut the bullshit* face. "It sounds to me like you need to get a handle on all that."

"And when I do?" His words were crisp, cool. That tone ran contrary to the utterly adorable fact that he was zipping between complete shambles and the unshakeable belief that he'd find true north and serve it up on a platter before noon.

"And when you do, I'll welcome you back into my bed. At the very minimum, I'll let you watch me take a bath." I leaned toward him because I couldn't tolerate all this brood and gloom. "Even better, I'll let you help me take a bath. That was fun, wasn't it? Really, I need you to tell me because the memories are all upside-down."

"For fuck's sake, Sunny." He pinched his brow like I was very tiring.

I grinned.

"This is how well-adjusted adults work through things," I said, happy to sink back into the groove of incessantly bothering him.

He didn't let up on the brow. "I didn't realize either of us were well-adjusted adults."

"We can still dream big."

"Can I stay on your sofa while I'm doing all this emotional juice-cleansing? It's not your bed and I did promise your parents I'd keep an eye on you."

"Invoking parents isn't the way to go with me," I said. "You can do better than that."

I was aiming for levity but it didn't land that way and I could see Beck visibly closing in on himself. The temperature between us dropped to freezing and I wondered if this was what my iceberg had felt like to him. If this was his iceberg, what was it made of? Who—or what —did he resent so hard that it froze over?

He tipped his chin toward the house and dropped my hand. "I'll walk you inside."

He held the car door open for me and gripped my elbow as I found my balance on the uneven sidewalk but he didn't say anything as he followed me into the house. Instead of coming inside and inventing reasons to linger, he sat on the floor in the entryway with my dogs.

He talked in low, hushed tones, saying, "I won't see you for a few days. Sooner if I can swing it but I'll need you to be on your best behavior until then. You know what I'm talking about, Jem. Scout, you're in charge. Take good care of your mom. Remind her to eat and drink water, and put her to bed when she needs it. Bark extra loud if she tries to get on a bike—anything with wheels, really. Howl if you have to. I promise, I'll hear you and I'll bring the juiciest meat my chef can find as a reward. Protect your mom for me, okay?"

I turned toward the kitchen under the pretense of making a cup of tea, but the truth was, I felt like I was being pulled apart from the inside out. I didn't know if I could do this. Distance seemed like the answer in this moment but there had to be a better way than sending away someone who cared so damn much he didn't even recognize it as caring.

From behind, arms wrapped around my waist. He dropped his forehead to my shoulder. "Just tell me, Sunny. Tell me what you want and I'll give it to you. Please."

I let him hold me for a long, painful moment. I closed my hand around his wrist, felt his pulse thrumming under my fingertips. I didn't want him to leave. I didn't want to take a break or force distance between us when everything was so good—save for the tiny issue of him having no idea what he wanted from me, from himself. From right now and from the rest of his life.

"Go to work, Beck," I said. "Focus on money and oysters for a little while. Go shuck something. It'll do you good."

chapter twenty-nine
Sunny

Today's Special:
A Whole Loew Reign of Terror, Served Chilled

WE THOUGHT we knew all about Beck's bridge troll tendencies. We were so naïve.

On the day he'd left me at my doorstep, Beck went to the oyster company and did exactly as I'd suggested: he shucked oysters all night. He didn't speak a word to anyone and that was the truly terrifying part of it all. He barely even looked up long enough to see the orders coming in.

Bethany reported this to me from her seat at the Small Point bar, where she sat all night, reading spicy books and flirting with Mel. Being the incredible friend she was, Bethany made sure to tell me on several occasions that Beck looked "distraught and also delicious" and watching him shove a knife into a rock-hard shell and work it open over and over again qualified as some kind of fishy porn. Apparently the rolled-up shirtsleeves and flexing forearms combo was a thing of miracles, and while she supported me wholeheartedly, Beth had some questions as to whether I was serious about dying on this hill.

On the second day, he arrived at the oyster company before Hale and took it upon himself to drive Chef Bartholomew to the brink of insanity by reorganizing the walk-in fridge *and* the entire shelving system for linens, glasses, and dishes.

I knew without question that Beck believed in his soul that he was taking care of the things that needed taking care. He didn't wake up—if he'd even slept—with the intention of upending his chef's entire belief system or creating massive headaches for his kitchen staff.

He also tried to take over Hale's hose-down process for freshly harvested oysters and started changing the layout of the dining room for "efficiency purposes" until Mel kicked him out. At least, that was how she told it when she came to Naked in search of coffee and some attention from Bethany.

I didn't need the salacious details. Not when I'd already watched him shuffle out of the restaurant, climb into his car, and sit there with his head tipped back against the headrest, his eyes closed and his breathing jagged enough to spot from all the way across the parking lot.

Not when he caught me staring and when his lips curled into a tragic sort of smile, like he'd known I was there all along and he appreciated me watching over him but he was very busy experiencing big, foreign feelings the way a garbage disposal experienced chicken bones.

An entire silent conversation passed between us while I stood on the patio, watering can tipped over a pot of sprawling, gangly oregano.

Why are we doing this? he asked.

Reasons. Good ones.

Are you sure about that?

I think so. I shrugged. *Just do this for me. This one thing. Okay?*

He closed his eyes and started the car, and I accepted that as agreement even though I knew it wasn't.

When the third day rolled around, I woke up in a terrible mood. My cast was itchy and annoying, and I felt like an overworked muscle, stretched too far, too hard to function properly. And I wasn't functioning properly. I wasn't sleeping well and my body was off in every possible way. Everything still ached from the accident and concussions were no joke but this was more than that. It was like I hurt in a place that had nothing to do with nerve endings and bones and tissue.

I hurt in a place that missed Beck.

I was lonely and sad, and I couldn't remember how to sleep by myself, and there was nothing I could do to make it better. I had to give him the space I insisted he have, even though I wanted to gather him up and invent some nonsense for us to argue about.

Since nothing felt right and my body was a swirling vortex of dysregulation that would take any opportunity to have a seizure, I decided to stay home from work today. It was the healthy, grown-up thing to do. Even if I could push through, I'd end up paying for it later and I didn't want that.

Also, I didn't think I could see Beck without going to him and trashing all the well-adjusted, mature groundwork I'd laid. If we were going to be in a relationship, it was going to be a functional one, dammit. We were not going to suffer for a few days and throw it all away simply because no one was getting any sleep and following through was hard.

So, I did the well-adjusted, mature things. I threw laundry in the washer, watered my plants, fed myself day-old muffins from the café. I stripped off the bedsheets, the ones that still smelled like Beck, and I dumped all the junk mail I'd accumulated in the kitchen.

I let the dogs nudge me toward the sofa, a sign that my body was even more dysregulated than I thought. With their heads resting on my thighs, I put on noise-canceling headphones and picked up the embroidery project I used whenever I needed to get in control of the energy inside of me.

With the quiet from the headphones and the steadfast weight of the dogs on my legs, it was almost meditative. If one could meditate while rhythmically stabbing something.

The truth was, the stabbing gave me a place for all the heavy emotions gathered behind my breastbone and at the base of my skull. It gave me somewhere to put the pain of pushing Beck away and having a front-row seat to his run through the obstacle course of figuring out what he wanted. And it gave me hope that he'd find a way through all of it and come back to me.

I needed him to come back. I needed him to catch me when I fell— because that was what was happening here. I was falling for him.

And I didn't know what would happen if he wasn't there to catch me.

chapter thirty

Today's Special:
Friendship Cove Oysters Steamed in Insomnia and Raked through the
Garden

PARKER KICKED me out of the house this morning. All because I ran the vacuum within fifty feet of his bedroom door.

Maybe five o'clock was too early for him but it wasn't like I'd vacuumed under his bed.

It didn't seem early to me. Not when I'd been awake on and off all night. I'd tried to sleep but I couldn't turn off my mind long enough to get there. Couldn't sit still for more than a few minutes at a time or even zone out watching sports. I'd tried reviewing SPOC's operating costs for the past couple of months, but I couldn't focus on the numbers long enough to make sense of them. And I sure as hell wasn't welcome at the oyster bar, not after Mel, Bartholomew, and Hale all ordered me to leave and not come back until I'd unfucked myself.

Or, as Parker had screamed at me this morning, "Fix what you broke with Sunny or go back to Singapore because I won't put up with you violating my civil rights."

The problem was that I couldn't fix what was broken because it wasn't possible. I couldn't put these pieces back together and go forward when forward placed us on two different continents. There was no way I could stay here. I couldn't see how that would work. And there was no way I could ask Sunny to give up her whole life here to come with me. She'd *just* opened a business here in Friendship. The last thing she was going to do was pick up and leave just because I liked the life I'd built for myself overseas.

Sure, I didn't have any real roots outside of this town and my career wasn't everything, but I *liked* my lifestyle. It worked for me—and Sunny would hate it. She'd find a community and people and make a home for herself in Singapore, and then I'd be sent to UAE or Monaco or back to London and she'd have to do that all over again. And then again six months, a year later.

And what had she said about being a small-town girl at heart? She didn't want to live in any of the places I'd end up. She didn't want an executive penthouse at the top of the newest high-rise and she didn't want to hang around with a bunch of private wealth managers who entertained themselves by ordering the most expensive bottles of everything and playing credit card roulette at the end of the night. She wanted *this* place and *this* community, and her café and her friends. She wanted festivals dedicated to *corn* and *asparagus*. She wanted Friendship, and she wanted it more than she wanted me.

That realization hit me like a punch that plowed through my gut and grabbed my spine, and then yanked it out my belly button. I couldn't think past it. I couldn't function. Couldn't bring myself to care about anything else.

So, there I was, flat on my childhood bed, heart pounding in a way that didn't seem healthy, staring down the fact that I was going to lose the one person who'd come to matter more than anyone, anything else in this whole fucking world—and all because I didn't know how to get over my issues with this strange little square of earth.

That was it.

That was my bottom line. I had issues with this place and they were standing in the way of everything I'd ever wanted and never believed I could have.

It wasn't just that she mattered. A lot of people mattered to me. But Sunny...Sunny was *mine*.

But only for now.

That was when I'd decided to start some laundry, but on the way up from the basement I noticed the backyard grass was nearly knee-high so I mowed the lawn. But mowing the lawn required me to climb over some very old, very rusty paint cans, and rather than get myself into a situation that would necessitate a tetanus shot in the middle of the night, I loaded them into my car to take to the local recycling center.

When it opened.

Once I had the lawn clippings bagged, I went room to room with a trash bag, gathering all of Parker's forgotten iced coffee cups and protein bar wrappers, and all of this eventually led me to cleaning out the fridge. When I found two dozen eggs, I did the only reasonable thing and made some scrambled eggs. I couldn't remember the last time I'd eaten and it seemed like a fine solution but then I noticed a trail of dried grass and dirt tracking from the kitchen door all the way through the first floor and leading up the stairs to Parker's room, which was why I needed to ruin his life by vacuuming.

Since I wasn't allowed in the house and neither Singapore nor Sunny were in the cards today, I nodded my way through a call with Adrian that should've had me praising the heavens and then I went to the gym. I hadn't been intentional about exercising since returning to Friendship, not nearly as religious as I was when my life wasn't a runaway train, so it shouldn't have been a surprise that I overworked every muscle group and left with hands shaking too hard to hold my phone steady.

From that pain came the clear-as-dawn realization that I needed to speak to Sunny. I didn't know what I'd say or how it would be any different from all the other things I'd already said but I knew I couldn't go on this way. I couldn't live in the murky limbo of *this can't continue* and *what if it does?* I needed Sunny and the rest of it—well, I was damn good at solving problems. I could solve this one too, even if I didn't know how I'd do it yet.

Once I was washed and dressed, I drove straight to Naked. I knew Sunny was on the schedule this morning and I was fairly confident she'd talk to me. If she didn't, I'd park myself at a table and wait until she was ready.

Except this plan went down harder than the *Edmund Fitzgerald* when Meara shook her head, saying, "Sunny isn't in today."

"But—why?" I ran my hands over the butcher block counter. "She's supposed to be here."

Meara gave me a sympathetic nod. Did she know about all of this? Did she know Sunny had sent me on a suicide mission? "Yeah, she was supposed to be in today but she's not feeling great and—"

"What's wrong?" I patted all of my pockets in search of my keys. I found them in my hand. "Is it her arm? The concussion? Aura symptoms?"

"I'm not sure, sweet pea, but it sounds like she just needs a low-key day."

"She shouldn't be alone," I said, more to myself than Meara. "I'm going—"

"Wait!" She pinched my shirt between her fingers, drew me across the counter. "You look like you've been through the spin cycle, sir, and I'm not letting you go anywhere until you pull yourself together."

"I don't want her to be alone." My gaze bored into hers, begging her to recognize that, while I respected her and her position, I wasn't backing down on this one. "Meara. I'm going."

"Not right now you're not," she said, her gaze just as solid as mine. "The last thing our girl needs is you running over there, raggedy as all hell and strung out on more stress than a boy with your bank account should be allowed to experience. You're going to sit your ass down, put some food in your belly, and hydrate until you stop looking like dried seaweed. Do you understand me?"

My jaw clicked as I stared her down. I'd accomplished more in my life with this stare than any collection of words. I knew what I was doing here.

"Oh, you think you can intimidate me?" Her laugh had a lot in common with fairy-tale villains. "Sweet pea, I have *two* of you at home." She released my shirt and pushed me backward with one finger. "How do you take your coffee?"

"I've got it," Beth called from somewhere behind the counter.

"Good," Meara said, crossing her arms over her chest. "Go sit down."

My quads *screamed* at me as I dropped into a seat and it must've been all over my face because Beth asked, "Have you been stabbed? Are we missing some key points from this story?" She set the coffee down and motioned to the scrapes on my forearms, which were an unexpected product of mowing behind the garage. I didn't know what the fuck was growing back there but it had teeth. "Who did this to you? Want me to beat them up?"

"All me," I grumbled. "It's nothing. I'm fine."

She sat across from me. "Yeah. Sure. I can tell."

A small dish with a pastry landed in front of me. "You're not allowed to speak until this plate is clean," Meara said.

A significant part of me wanted to sprint to my car and break every traffic law on the books to get to Sunny's house right now, though a much smaller, much less compelling part knew her friends wouldn't let anything happen to her. They wouldn't leave her alone if she was unwell.

With this knowledge clutched in my fist, I inhaled the scone. It was more like the idea of a scone formed entirely by chocolate chips. Then I demolished a plate of vegan scrambled eggs, which seemed extremely contradictory but tasted better than the mess I'd left on the stove this morning.

Two cups of cold brew coffee later, Meara set a bag on the table, saying, "Much better."

"Thanks," I said, more than a little humbled by my whole fucking life right now.

She flicked the bag with a black fingernail. "These are for Sunny and the pups. Tell her we miss her but we don't want her back until she feels better." She shook her braids off her shoulders. "Believe me when I say I don't want to see you stumble into this café looking like something the cat dragged in ever again."

"Check your facts. Stumbling did not occur."

"I don't know what you did to yourself but you have the grace of Frankenstein's monster," she replied. "It goes beautifully with the dead eyes and misbuttoned shirt."

"I'll add it to the list of things I need to fix today." I reached for my wallet. "What do I owe you?"

She scoffed. "Do not insult me with questions like that. Go. Out. On your way."

Still holding her gaze, I dropped several twenties in the tip jar. "Do you abuse everyone who comes into Sunny's life this much?"

She lifted one delicate shoulder and tipped her chin up. "Yes."

I nodded. "Good."

I didn't break that many laws on the drive to Sunny's house although that was only because there was no traffic in the heart of Friendship this morning and both of the stop lights turned green as I approached. But the smooth sailing ended there because she didn't answer the door.

My initial reaction was that Meara must've tipped her off and she didn't want to see me. To which I responded with a flurry of text messages that went unread after twelve full minutes while I paced on the sidewalk. Enough time to allow for most anything. Then I realized something had to be wrong. Sunny wasn't mean, she wasn't vindictive. She wouldn't ignore me—unless something had happened and she couldn't come to the door.

I hit up the doorbell again and fired off a few more texts but my tolerance for the unknown was inch-deep right now. I tried the door but it was locked—excellent—but that led me to the discovery that I didn't have a key. *Why* didn't I have a key? I needed a key. Specifically for situations like this one. We'd remedy that very soon. Right after confirming she was alive and well and bizarrely incapable of hearing the doorbell *and* seeing texts. And after we remedied all the other things.

Since I wasn't getting anywhere with the door, I jogged around the side of the house, thinking I'd be able to let myself into the backyard. Maybe I'd find her in the yard with the dogs or the back door would be open, and then my heart would be able to reacquaint itself with a normal rhythm for the first time today. Like all my other plans, this was practically foolproof—save for the singular issue of the backyard fence.

Now, I'd known the yard was fenced and I knew it was a tall fence because Jem was a jumper but I'd never considered whether I'd be able to climb it. To be fair, I didn't evaluate whether I could climb much of anything and it had been a very long time since such a thing had crossed my mind but here the fuck I was now, wearing a suit and tie, bumbling around with exhausted muscles, and panicking my ass off.

My first attempt at vaulting myself over ended with a mouthful of grass and a serious dent in my pride. It didn't matter whether anyone was watching because *I* saw this and that was more than enough. The second attempt got me over but I ate grass again, I looked like I'd woodchucked my way through a garden, and I lost my glasses and phone for a minute. All that and I knew I'd have some weird bruises on my ass tomorrow.

I dragged myself to the back door. Also locked.

There was a minute where I debated prying off the screen over the bathroom window and climbing in from there but then I noticed the dog door.

It was the only option I had left, short of breaking down a door or falling headfirst into the bathroom. If this went south and I got stuck in there for—what? hours until Sunny came home?—she'd die laughing. She would laugh so hard she'd drop dead and I'd be the one to blame for it. With any luck, I'd go right along with her because I had no use for this world if she wasn't in it too.

I knew then, and probably long before then, that finding a way to keep Sunny was the only problem I had to solve here. Nothing else mattered. Not Singapore, not my firm, not the mental health benefits of living far away from home.

Armed to the teeth with this knowledge, I learned that I could fit through a dog door but only if I went in at an angle, didn't breathe, and lightly dislocated both shoulders. My shirt was ripped in several spots, my trousers too, and I was pretty sure my wallet fell out in the process, but I ended up sprawled on Sunny's kitchen floor, heaving out breaths like I'd just lifted a car over my head, and wondering whether my bones were in the right places.

And that was when I noticed Sunny and her dogs staring at me like I'd materialized in her kitchen from another universe. She sat on her sofa with the dogs on either side of her, some kind of needle and thread in her hand. She pulled off a pair of big-ass headphones and blinked at me.

"You didn't hear," I panted, "when I knocked on the door. Or rang the doorbell. Many times. And I thought"—I rolled onto my back and pressed a hand to my heart—"I thought something was wrong. So I climbed the fence. Well, I fell over the fence. Then the door was locked. And the bathroom window was too high. And I saw the dog door."

"You climbed the fence," she said. "And decided to crawl through the dog door. These were thoughts that crossed your mind and then you decided to make them reality. These things seemed like a good idea to you."

It took me a minute but I got to my feet and crossed the kitchen into the living room, and dropped down in front of Sunny. "Yes, because I needed to see you and make sure none of the worst-case scenarios in my head were coming true." I set her sewing project on the floor and gathered her hands in mine. "I like you. A lot. It's very uncomfortable for me. But it's more uncomfortable when you're not around or when you're around but I'm not allowed to be near you. Let's not do that ever again."

She wrenched her hands free and scooted forward on the sofa, tucking me between her knees. "Then you won't hiccup too hard next week and change your mind about everything for no reason?"

"I won't as long as you don't tell me we're just *hanging out* and *having fun*."

"You upped the ante," she said. "I just raised the bet."

"Let's not do any more of that either."

"Sure." She watched me with cool, steady eyes. "Tell me what else you have on your mind." She tapped a finger to my forehead. "I can see the gears turning in there."

"You know what you want. You've been out in the world and you've figured out what you want from this life." I ran my hands up her legs, to her waist. It was so good to touch her again. Like being plugged in. "I've been out in the world and I never thought to ask what I wanted until you forced me to do it."

"I don't think that's entirely accurate." She pushed a hand through my hair. "I think you're being a little tough on yourself. And you might be bleeding internally."

"Maybe, but the only answer I ever came up with was that my life wasn't in this town."

She dropped her gaze, brought her hands to her lap. I felt her exhale.

"My attorney says there's a plea deal coming for my dad any day," I said. Jem licked the side of my face and then blew a hot, disgusting puff of dog breath at me. "He'll have to serve a short sentence, but that's a lot better than twenty years. Probably a deal for my mom too. It's a little hairy since she's technically a fugitive but they're arranging for her to turn herself in some time in the next few days. She could be home in—I don't know—a month or two?"

"Really? Beck, that's incredible!"

I lifted a shoulder. It hurt like hell. Strong possibility that it was actually dislocated. "Yeah. Yeah, it's great. I had a hard time believing it when Adrian called this morning. I'm still not sure I believe it. I don't think I will until it all happens and we're safely on the other side of this shitshow."

"Don't do that to yourself," she said. "Don't plan to be disappointed."

"I'm not. I'm being realistic."

We stared at each other for a moment. "When will you leave?"

I shook my head. "I'm not."

She tipped her chin. "You're not—what?"

"I told you I don't like the idea of leaving you."

"You also told me your life isn't in this town. Like, just a second ago."

"I said my life *wasn't* in this town," I replied. "I don't really know where my life is right now or where it will be in six months or a year. Anything could happen and it kills me to not know what comes next but I know I want you."

She held my gaze like she was looking for proof of this concept in there. "And you're sure about that?"

I motioned to the tear along the side of my trousers. "Enough to cause my own internal bleeding by climbing through a *dog door* to see you. Pretty fuckin' sure, Sunny."

A smile tugged at her lips, unfurling from each corner until it met in the middle. "I like you too."

"That's a fucking relief because I had some real questions about that and I didn't enjoy any of the answers I came up with on my own."

The corners of her lips curled up. "Now that I think about it, I might like you a lot, Beckett Loew. I think I'm going to like you for a long time, if you'll let me."

"I'd let you throw your moon rocks at me every day for the rest of your life for the honor of draining your bath water."

"If you're talking about crystals, then you should know I'd be more likely to hide them in your pockets than throw them at you."

"That, yes." I dropped my head to her lap and felt my body unclench for the first time in days. "What do we do now?"

"We'll take it one day at a time." She dug her thumbs into my shoulder blades, and the noise I made, well, it wasn't entirely human. "Unless we're talking about the Craft Beer and Corgis Festival in September, in which case we should definitely commit to that."

"Fucking festivals," I muttered. "I'm profoundly traumatized from the last one. I'm not sure I have the stomach for much more."

"We'll pet dogs and drink beer," she said. "Nothing traumatizing about that."

"Let us pray." I shifted up on an elbow to meet Sunny's eyes. "Tell me how you're feeling."

"I'm fine. Just tired."

I arched a brow. "Not sleeping well?"

Her answering smile was slightly evil. "Why? Do you have some experience with that?"

I glanced to the side. "I might've mowed the lawn at two in the morning."

She nudged Scout and Jem off the sofa and patted the cushion beside her. "Get up here. Come on. Shoes off. Lose the vest. No one relaxes in a vest. No one should jump fences in a vest either. We'll discuss that some other time. Yes, very good, leave the phone in the kitchen. No one is allowed to need you for a few hours. They will survive." She pulled a small pillow to her lap and drew me toward her. "There you go. I'm going to stab my little project and you're going to rest. Close your eyes."

When I settled on the pillow, she brought her hand to the back of my neck and slipped her fingers into my hair. I died a little. "Wait," I managed. "What are you stabbing?"

"Oh, this." She held up a piece of fabric in a wooden hoop. Lots of tiny flowers were sewn around the words *Peace, Love, and a Little Go Fuck Yourself.* "It's embroidery. Sometimes when my brain gets spicy, it helps to get away from screens and lights and just focus on this one thing."

"I love it. I love—"

Whoa. *Whoa.* That was not happening today. For several reasons but most importantly because I was going to pass out any second now and I had no business dropping that kind of statement and not sticking around for the response. Whatever it was.

"I love the whole thing. It's very you."

"This, and the whole twisted tale leading up to it"—she ran her finger along the rip high on the shoulder of my shirt—"is very you. Also, I think you should know that I plan to tell the story of you birthing yourself into my kitchen for many, many years to come."

"Only if I can be there to die of mortification while you tell it."

I heard the smile in her words as she said, "I wouldn't want it any other way."

chapter thirty-one

Beckett

Today's Special:
Heirloom Gnome with a Black and Blue Salad

LIVING with a mother on the run, a father in federal custody, and a teenage brother under my care meant I answered my phone at all hours. No rest for the boundaryless.

After grunting out some form of greeting, Hale's voice came across the line. "How are you sleeping through this, man?"

I nuzzled my face against Sunny's back and debated hanging up on him. The guy kept obscene hours. Up with the bleeding dawn, every damn day. It was inhuman, truly. And even after a few nights back in Sunny's bed, I barely felt like I'd gotten my fill of her. I needed every second I could steal. "Get to the damn point or I'm hanging up."

"Right, well, an epic thunderstorm blew through here last night. Trees are down all over town and the power is out up and down the cove. They say it's going to be out until the afternoon. Maybe later."

"We have a backup generator that runs on wired-in gas *and* backup-backup solar reserves," I mumbled.

"We sure do," he said, altogether too chipper for this hour. "But Naked doesn't."

I dropped my forehead to her spine with a groan. "Shit."

"Yeah, and they lost a chunk of their roof too. I can't tell if there's any damage inside but y'all should get over here."

"Fuck." I sat up, rubbed my eyes. "You can rig up a portable generator without getting inside?"

"What's wrong?" Sunny asked, yawning.

"Give me a real challenge," Hale scoffed.

Phone wedged between my shoulder and ear, I jumped into yesterday's clothes. "Since you asked, find me ladders, tarps, and people who know something about fixing a roof. And wake up Mel too."

"All over it," he replied.

"We'll be there soon." I ended the call and shoved the phone in my back pocket. I watched as Sunny sat up, the sheets pooling around her waist and her hair spilling over her shoulders. She was naked and perfect, and leaving this room was the last thing I wanted to do. But we had to go. "Apparently there was a storm last night."

She glanced to the window, frowning. Bright, intense sunlight knifed through the curtains. "I wonder how we missed that."

We'd torn into another of Sunny's favorite books, one featuring people who shared an enormous amount of hostility and were forced to spend time together at work. Strangely enough, the hostility never stopped them from fucking the stuffing out of each other.

We'd started out innocently—if sucking her clit while I had several fingers buried in her pussy could be innocent. But then, well, things got a little adventurous. She came on my tongue and I spurted all over her luscious ass, exactly as she'd requested. The shower was next and it was there was we discovered—after taking all the precautions necessary to keeping her cast dry—that Sunny was an incredible cocksucker. I'd known something of this from our first night together, but that was a blur like the middle of a marathon.

Later, we ate leftovers from the café and talked about all the places we'd been over the years. The places we wanted to go next. Somewhere in our debate of Vietnam's best destinations, we fell into each other— and her book—all over again. I'd propped her up on a mound of pillows and slow-fucked her as she read. The people in her book liked to incorporate toys, which led me to do the only reasonable thing and learn how she liked to play with her vibrator.

That lasted through half a chapter and a long, rolling orgasm from Sunny that made me a believer in all the gods, all the higher powers. Then, that sweet, shy girl who'd told me she "didn't like a lot of penis" climbed on top of me and sank down on my cock. She put the vibe in my hand and ordered me to make good use of it, and then she rode me like she'd never want anything else.

I let myself believe she'd never want anyone but me.

"Yeah, a real mystery." I shook my head. I felt the lingering stretch in my abs, heard the filthy things she'd whispered in my ear. The frankly shocking things I'd whispered back. "The power's out at Naked and—"

"Muffy is going to implode if she loses everything in the walk-in." She sprang into action, yanking a t-shirt over her head, finger-combing her hair into a bun. She'd gotten good at doing all these things one-handed. Not that she'd accept any help. She stepped into a small pair of gauzy shorts and my heart tripped into the kind of rhythm I only felt when running uphill in a Singaporean heat wave. "How long has it been out?"

"I don't know but Hale is working on hooking up a generator." I ran a hand down my face because those shorts were a catastrophe. I didn't know how I was supposed to function. I didn't know if I could *function*. Had I exhaled since she pulled them on? I didn't think so. It was one endless gasp, drawing more and more air in and leaving me stretched impossibly tight.

Sunny snapped her fingers, calling, "Scout. Jem."

The dogs clamored into the room, all lolling tongues and wagging tails as they circled Sunny. She spoke to them in commands that skated between firm and gentle, and she had no idea I was breaking down into fractional parts over the sight of her legs. As if I hadn't camped between them for an hour last night. As if I didn't know every inch from her ankle on up.

"And the roof," I said, still staring at those shorts. I had to start producing complete sentences. I had to *breathe*. This was what happened when someone religiously wore repurposed tablecloth skirts and then, out of the blue, switched it up with a scrap of fabric that could only be described as a modern-day loincloth.

"Eyes up here. What about the roof?" She grabbed my wrist and towed me out of the bedroom, the dogs following close behind.

I shoved a hand through my hair. "Uh, yeah."

"Button your shirt, Beck." She flipped open her pill dispenser and dumped the morning's meds into her palm. She held a glass under the faucet, still staring at me. "Are we starting the day with riddles? Is that how it's going to be? I have to guess what's wrong with the roof? Will it end with you saying you told me so?"

She downed the pills with a gulp of water and chased it all with two heaping spoonfuls of almond butter. In the deep recesses of my mind I knew we had to go, but in a very specific sense, we needed to stay here forever. With those shorts. Or without them.

"Yeah, I'm definitely getting a lecture about responsible roofing today," she muttered. "So exciting. Can we save it for after I secure the perishables?"

"You can't be a brat while wearing"—I motioned to the thick expanse of thigh on display—"*that*. There's a real possibility my heart's going to stop."

She dropped a hand to her hip, a small smile pulling at her lips while she stared at me. "Resuscitating you sounds really time-consuming and we have places to be this morning so why don't you get your mind off my clothes by thinking about something spicy like profit and loss statements or parking lots, hmm?"

"I do not need to think about parking lots," I snapped. "I'm just— I'm not used to seeing you in anything but long skirts."

Sunny put my keys in my palm and led the dogs out the door. "I believe you've seen me in a lot less without complaint." She looped that basket of hers around her good arm as I closed the door behind us. "And I wouldn't suggest you experiment with telling me what to wear."

"That is the *last* thing I'm going to do, storm cloud." I dragged my gaze over that soft, pale skin before opening the passenger door for Sunny. "I just need a minute to adjust to the idea of you walking around half naked outside the bedroom and get some blood moving to all of my extremities."

She peered up at me, her lips pink and swollen from last night, a faint wash of red on her neck from my beard. A lock of golden hair spilled out of her bun. I twisted it around my finger as she said, "Your penis is not my problem right now. I need you to work through this without me. Adjust while you drive. We can't afford to lose everything in that walk-in."

Fuck, I loved this girl.

One of these days, I'd find a way to tell her.

"OKAY," I said, dropping my phone into the cupholder. "They're sending a few guys now and the rest of the crew will be here within the hour. They'll patch everything up."

Sunny gave up on texting one-handed, saying, "You know, I'd keep you around without the magic minions."

A brittle laugh gasped out of me. "I know that."

"You don't have to save the day for me to like you."

"Sunny, please." I took the turn onto Market Street a little faster than necessary and the dogs stumbled around in the back.

"It doesn't matter to me that you have an on-demand maintenance crew ready to clean up the random disasters that tend to occur at my café each week."

"Shall I call back and tell them not to come?" I snapped. I didn't know why I was doing this. I had no reason to be snappy. Aside from the facts that I required another hour or two of sleep and those shorts had evolved into something akin to bikini bottoms Sunny was while seated.

"No, because that would bother *you*," she replied. "I'm just saying, I don't like you for your willingness to do things for me or your insistence on paying for those things. I keep you around because I—"

She stopped herself when we turned down Succotash Lane and I muttered, "What the hell?" at the sight of the seventeen-year-old shroomster Parker, of all people, lugging a ladder across the driveway toward Naked. At six forty-five in the morning.

"Do you think he's here because he slept on the dock?" she asked.

"No, but only because I'm tracking his location on my phone now and I know he was at a friend's house all night. And I checked with the parents too."

I pulled into my usual parking spot and paused a moment to survey the storm damage. And to steal a second before we had to leave the quiet of this little world we'd created.

"What were you saying?" I asked. One of the dogs panted over my shoulder. It was Jem. I could feel his muggy breath on my neck. Scout had better manners than that. "You keep me around because—why, exactly?"

She abandoned her texts once again. "I like you. That's all. I like you and I care about you, and I know you care about me, and that's why I keep you around. Not for any other reason." She dipped her head to catch my eyes, shot me a *listen up because I'm not saying this twice* look. "I need you to understand that calling in the minions or jumping behind the counter to take orders when we're slammed has nothing to do with it. I don't like you because you do things for me. I'm not an acts-of-service girlie. I'd like you without any of it."

To say I handled this poorly would be a serious understatement. I would've done a better job catching a line drive watermelon than I did hearing this from Sunny.

"Half your roof blew off. Someone has to deal with that." I said this like she was a disobedient teenager trying to wish her problems away with angst and eye rolls and I was the adult who knew better, *as always*. I regretted it immediately. No, I regretted it as the words spilled out of my stupid mouth but that still didn't slow me down. "I'm not going to stop fixing things for you just because you tell me you don't need it."

"That's not what I said."

"I solve problems, Sunny. It's what I do. It's what I'm good at." I jerked my chin toward the oyster company. "They *need* me to fix things for them."

Agent Price pulled up behind me and, without so much as a hairy eyeball in my direction, he joined Parker and Hale around the back side of the café. A few members of the oyster company crew emerged from the dock wearing waders and wide-brimmed hats. They brought tarps, a sump pump, and a gas tank, presumably for the generator.

"I don't need you to fix anything." She sat there with her fingers locked in her lap and her shorts moonlighting as underwear and her gaze as steady as the sun. "You might not want to hear this but I think you're good at a lot more than solving everyone's problems. Anyone who knows you—the real you, not the broody troll—knows there's a lot more to you than the things you fix."

I didn't know what to say. I wasn't sure I knew how to speak. There was a rumble in my gut, a ribbit, like I'd swallowed a frog whole in the past minute and now we had to coexist. Eventually, I said, "I'm not sure what you're expecting me to say." I shook my head as the silence stretched out, proof that I wasn't equipped for these kinds of conversations. Hand me a crisis and I was solid gold but ask me to talk about feelings and other intangibles? No, I was better off alone with the frog alive against all stomach acid odds. "What do you want, Sunny?"

"I don't want you to say anything." She watched me for a steady moment before adding, "I just want you to know that this"—she motioned to the maintenance vehicles rapidly filling the lot and the workers spilling out—"isn't what I like about you."

"Then what the fuck do you like?" I yelled. "I don't know the first thing about showing affection—"

"Not true." She shook her head like *not this again*.

"—and I'm not great with gifts unless they're the functional, need-addressing type. I'm not a lot of fun—"

"Also inaccurate."

"—and I don't stay in one place long enough to make real connections with anyone. But I can fix just about anything. I can make issues disappear and put safety nets in place so they don't come back. That's what I do for the people I—" I stopped, swallowed hard. This wasn't the right time. For so many reasons. "That's what I do for the people I care about."

A smile lighting up her face, Sunny gave me a meaningful nod that said my life was about to be twist-turned upside down. "Do you know what I do for the people I care about?"

I rubbed my forehead. "I'm going to assume it has something to do with flowerpots."

"When the situation calls for it, yes, there might be a flowerpot," she said, laughing. "But more than that, I care about people by making sure they know they don't have to do anything at all to be with me. It's enough that you came here with me today. It's enough for you to hold my hand while I figure out today's iteration of the truth behind the saying 'anything that can go wrong, will go wrong.' It's enough for you to listen while I vent or help put the café back together." She pointed toward the maintenance trucks. "That isn't required. It's not expected. And it's not why I want you here with me."

I watched as the people from Rainey's crew jogged a wheelbarrow around the building. That could not be a good sign. A second later, Mel arrived—with Beth on the back of her motorcycle.

I nodded toward them. "Is this happening for real or are they going to go back to hating each other tomorrow?"

Sunny laughed though it didn't sound like it was meant for me. "Is that what you want to talk about?"

I shoved a hand through my hair, tugged at the roots. Sunny wasn't even looking at me but it felt like she was peeling away everything that separated me from the world and staring straight at all my dried-out, undernourished pieces. It was ugly in there, a pile of sun-bleached oyster shells and insomnia, frequent flier miles and jarring adrenaline spikes. And I knew she saw it all.

"If I can't solve your problems, I don't know what else I have to give you," I said, hating the desperate exasperation in my words. Hating the *truth* in those words. "I don't know who I am if I'm not the one who takes care of things."

She shrugged like these answers were all very obvious. "Has it crossed your mind that you don't have to take care of anything?" She glanced over, a little smile pinning the corners of her mouth. "That you should just...care *about* me?"

"How would that be enough?"

Sunny dragged her gaze over me, from the shirt I'd barely buttoned correctly to yesterday's wrinkled trousers, and back up to the fucked-beyond-belief hair. She reached for me, grabbed my hand. "Of course it's enough." Before I could insist she was getting the raw end of this deal, she said, "We should get out there. We're supposed to host a yoga thing tonight. Plus, we have to determine how big Muffy's freak-out is going to be and how much of a skylight we have for ourselves now. Also, I'd really enjoy it if we could get Parker off that ladder. Love the kid but it's hard enough keeping him upright when he's on solid ground."

I shifted in the seat to catch a glimpse of my brother ascending the ladder while Hale held it steady. It was like a slapstick comedy duo in action. An anvil was bound to fall on them at any moment. "We're not having another emergency room visit," I said, killing the power. "Let's go."

We found Agent Price inside the café with Mel, Beth, and several folks from Rainey's crew. I did not scowl directly at Agent Price because he was shoveling debris in a suit and tie, but I did feel as though I deserved some form of recognition for that. The damage wasn't too bad, mostly isolated to a dirty puddle of rainwater in the middle of the seating area and some water stains where the roof suffered the most damage. The walk-in fridge had stayed *just* cold enough that nothing was lost and Muffy's freak-out had been averted on that front, but there was no saving the dough she'd left proofing overnight on the sheet rack. Apparently that stuff didn't handle changes in heat and humidity too well, and the post-storm conditions were like trying to breathe with your head in a bowl of clam chowder.

As soon as I sent Parker and Hale out into the cove to recover the buoys and lobster traps kicked up by the storm, and away from roofs and ladders of all sorts, Ranger Dickerson and Phil Collins rolled up in a three-wheel vehicle that looked like something out of a superhero-and-sidekick movie, complete with driving goggles and matching helmets.

"These fuckin' guys," I said to Sunny over the thunder of the generator. "I still think I'm living in a skit."

"That's Friendship for you."

"How is that thing street legal?"

She laughed. "You're asking me?"

I glanced down at her. She really was pint-sized, even more so in those shorts. The skirts always settled past her ankles and swirled around her in a way that tricked me into thinking there was more to her but the shorts shot that out of the sky. "If anyone would know, it would be you."

"Quite the storm," Ranger called as he climbed out of their version of the Batmobile. "How's the damage?"

Sunny beat me to it, saying, "Not too bad. We've always known the roof was on its last legs and this storm showed us all the soft spots. But we're lucky that this crew was able to get out here and help put things back together." To me, she whispered, "*Again.*"

"Very good, very good," Ranger said, nodding up at the crew tearing off long-useless shingles. Phil Collins nodded too. "Doesn't seem like you need much assistance."

"We're lucky to have a lot of hands on deck this morning," Sunny said.

I scratched Jem's head while I waited for the next line of questioning. There was always another line of questioning when it came to Ranger. One of these days, I was going to find out which intelligence agency he worked for prior to leading the Friendship Walking Club.

"Did I hear correctly that the oyster company has a full-service generator?" Ranger asked.

I kept my attention on Jem. "You did."

"Then you won't have any trouble pouring me and Mr. Collins a cup of coffee," he said. "With the power out all over town, we're—"

"All over town?" I repeated. "I thought it was just the cove."

"It might've started that way but the whole town went down when the last cell moved through overnight," he said.

I glanced at Sunny. Had the power been out at her place? Had we missed that? She lifted a shoulder as if she had the same questions and none of the answers.

How did we sleep through that? her eyes seemed to ask.

We weren't sleeping, I replied.

She pressed her fingers to her lips to hold back a smile.

"Now, about that coffee," Ranger continued, at least somewhat oblivious to our silent conversation. "Mr. Collins turns into a real bear without his morning cuppa and we don't want that."

I glanced at Phil Collins, with his genial smile, his driving goggles nestled on his forehead, and his hands locked behind his back. I had to believe he was a bear in the way Paddington was a bear. "We can get some coffee going." I ran a hand down Sunny's back. "Sell me your muffins."

She belted out a laugh. "Excuse me?"

"All I have on hand is raw oysters which no one wants at this hour. Sell me the muffins, rolls, scones—everything Muffy prepped for the morning. We'll feed the crew and everyone here, and anyone else who comes through, and you won't post a loss for the day."

Sunny's brow crinkled. It was adorable. "We just talked about this, Beck."

"I don't know what you folks talked about but I sure would like a fresh muffin with that coffee," Ranger said. "Warmed up with a pat of butter? That would be all right."

Sunny rolled her eyes at me. "Looks like you've created a problem that I'll have to solve."

"Just remember, Sunny, I don't keep you around because you can snap your fingers and make muffins appear. I actually like you."

"I take it all back." She stomped toward the café. "I hate you."

I watched her walk away and I had the distinct sense she was taking my heart with her. "No, you don't."

THE MORNING ROLLED on with a steady stream of locals making their way to the oyster company, most at Ranger's telephone tree urging though some did come hoping to find Naked open and eyed our collaboration with many misgivings. I could understand that. Vegans and the oyster farmers were not a likely pairing.

That confusion aside, everyone who came in was happy to have a place to charge their devices and some air conditioning to do it in. Strangely enough, these people also stopped to talk with me like we were old friends. I hadn't expected that, and for so many reasons. I didn't actually know these people. Maybe in passing but not enough to hold a conversation past the basics of weather and sports. More than that, I'd never had the impression that they'd want to talk to *me*. I had a lot going for me but I wasn't the fan favorite around here and I knew that. I accepted that. Fixers were never the favorites.

Yet they thanked me for being open today and also for keeping the oyster company going while my parents dealt with the "troubles"— which was the most ridiculously polite way to bring up racketeering charges. Some of these visitors told stories about coming to SPOC for special occasions back when they were young kids. They talked about being here with their parents and grandparents who'd passed on. The ones who remembered my eccentric great-uncle Buckthorne wanted me to know he'd be so pleased with the way we'd carried on his vision. Others mentioned my parents and how proud they were of us, always talking about where I was living at the time and the unbelievable vacations I planned for them, or Decker's recent record-breaking streaks and last year's spread in *Sports Illustrated*.

Without fail, as soon as the topic of my brother came around, they leaned in, dropped their voices to a level that wandered between sympathy and skepticism, and said they hoped he was doing all right. Everyone was pulling for him.

My silent nods ended those conversations quickly but they also seemed to serve as proof that Decker was going through something. Not that anyone needed confirmation from me when every sports news station, podcast, and annoying bro with a social media account were all saying the same things.

And the little bitch still wouldn't return my calls. Neither would Lance. Maybe they could start a little bitch club and chat about how easy it was to ignore me.

The power was restored to Friendship early in the afternoon and Naked's roof was well patched to hold until the renovation started in a few weeks. Sunny and I ducked out to shower and change at home when the commotion started to die down.

A few muffin-scrounging stragglers lingered in the SPOC dining room, seemingly unbothered by the waitstaff setting tables around them. Eventually, Mel assigned Zeus the task of moving them along, which he passed off to a bartender, who made a deal with a line cook only for it to land in Parker's lap. As much as I wanted to see how he handled this group, a call came through from Adrian and I had to duck away.

"To what do I owe this billable hour?" I asked as I took the back stairs two at a time.

A stiff sigh was the only response for a second which was long enough to drop my stomach into my shoes. Then, "A new witness has come forward. Any deals previously on the table have been rescinded."

I kicked the office door shut behind me, let my head fall back against it. "What the fuck?"

"A former employee. He has detailed knowledge of the oyster company's inner workings and the management. From what I've been able to gather, he's provided the prosecution with audio and video recordings that appear to incriminate your parents, along with a lengthy statement that goes into depth about cash handling and off-the-books payments." He shuffled some papers, adding, "Guy by the name of Devon Fallon. Ring any bells?"

"That motherfucker."

"I take it you know him?"

"Know him," I croaked, the words sticking in my throat like rocks, "I fired him a few weeks ago."

"Ah, wonderful," Adrian murmured. "So, this is revenge testimony. We'll have fun with that when we go to trial. It won't do shit to discredit the video evidence but we'll make him look like a prick in the process. That's always beneficial."

I hated that we'd lost the deal but I didn't regret firing Devon for one second. If anything, I regretted not doing it from the start. And not throwing him in the cove. I really should've dunked his ass. "What about another plea deal or—"

"Not a chance in hell." His maniacal laugh had me worried. More worried than usual. "The prosecution knows this video puts us up a creek. They have no reason to bargain."

"The guy's a dickhead," I said. "Accumulating evidence and sitting on it until he felt like fucking us over isn't the first dickhead thing he's done."

"I'll see what I can find," Adrian said, though he sounded resigned. "We'll talk soon."

The call ended and I crossed to the window. It was busy at Naked. The tables were full and the patio was packed with people who didn't mind being bled to death by mosquitos and greenhead flies.

Since I was only going to drive myself crazy here, I jogged down the back stairs and let Mel know where to find me if needed. I was one step out the door when my phone lit up with Adrian's number.

"What now?" I asked, pacing to the dock.

"They pulled the deal for your mom too," he said. "She missed the window to turn herself in and—"

"She probably mixed up the time or day," I said.

"The feds don't care. They do not care."

I dragged a sigh straight out of my bones. I couldn't believe this. "So, what's next? What's the move?"

"I don't know," he admitted. "There's nothing we can do today."

"There has to be something we can do," I said. "We can't—Adrian, we cannot give up now. We can't leave my mother to a life on the run in

—in I don't even fucking know where. And my father, he can't die in prison because he just didn't know what was happening around him. We have to—"

"Believe me, I know," Adrian cut in. "But we need to take these losses today and go back to the drawing board tomorrow. That's my best and only recommendation."

I turned away from the water and stared at the *Small Point Oyster Company* sign out in front of the gray-shingled building. It was lettered in a rolling, weathered type of font that had fallen in and out of fashion over the decades yet managed to stand immune to those forces. This place had always been a headache but at least it was home, and now I wanted to burn it to the ground. I couldn't hold all these pieces together anymore, not when I was the only one doing it.

"Call me tomorrow," I said.

I stood there for a long moment, my hand crushed around my phone and all the blood in my body pounding like war drums.

"Hey, Beck?"

I heard the slap of sandals and I turned toward that sound. An aqua skirt printed with shimmery gold constellations swished around Sunny's legs and I felt the corner of my mouth kick up in some janky fragment of a smile at the sight of her.

"What's going on?" she asked, her gaze narrowed. "It looked like you were trying to set things on fire with your eyes. I left Muffy in charge of the counter because I was getting worried you'd succeed."

"Something like that, yeah." I shook the hand holding my phone. "Just the usual daily tragedy," I said. "I guess I skipped a day or two last month so they showed up to fuck me extra hard today."

She ran her palm down my arm. "Start from the beginning. What happened?"

Since rewinding today's shitshow and playing it back for her was not going to make me less incendiary, I swept her into my arms. She dropped her hands to my flanks and rested her head on my chest, and I pulled a ragged, jittery breath deep into my lungs.

"I need you to say something," she said into my vest. "You're worrying me."

"My parents," I rasped. "Just—more shit with them."

"I'm sorry." She rubbed her hands up and down my back, and I felt the tension locked in those muscles easing by inches. "Is there anything I can do?"

"Nothing anyone can do at this point." I shook my head. "Every time I think I've got a handle on these disasters, something new comes along to prove me wrong."

"It will get better," she said, still stroking my back. "I don't know how but it will."

I wanted to agree with her. I wanted to share a shred of that faith. I couldn't.

We stayed locked together until a black SUV with dark tinted windows pulled up to the oyster company's entrance. Sunny and I shifted toward the vehicle just in time to watch the driver hold open the door only for my brother Decker to spill out of the back seat and onto the ground.

"Fuck," I panted.

Neither Decker nor his bespoke suit had been clean in several days. The funk of weed lingered around him and his knuckles were bruised and bloody. He rolled onto his back and howl-laughed up at the sky. "Honey, I'm home," he cackled.

I slumped against Sunny. *"Fuck."*

The driver tipped his head toward the interior of the vehicle. Empty liquor bottles littered the floor along with several takeout containers. Agent Price chose this moment to stroll past. His raised brows and immediate reach for his phone said it all.

"I have to deal with this." I tilted Sunny's head back and dropped a kiss to her forehead. "Remind me not to kill anyone."

"Think of it this way," she said, "if you're in jail, that leaves Parker in charge. Do you really want that?"

I caught her in a quick hug. "You're absolutely right."

My plan was to drag Decker upstairs and lock him in the office until his present condition improved. If I was lucky, I'd get some answers about what the hell was going on with him, why he was here, and what kind of mess he'd left in his wake.

Decker's plan went something like this: invite me and my "big brother boss bitch routine" to fuck off, stumble-crawl into the oyster company, tuck himself behind the bar and start slinging drinks, chug whiskey straight from several bottles, break an entire rack of water goblets, shove his bare hands into all the garnishes, recount the behind-the-scenes story of last year's playoff games to anyone who'd listen (and could hang on to the meandering through-line), shit-talk most of his former teammates and loudly allude to which ones were using unde-tectable performance enhancers, and then dive face-first into the raw bar, contaminating the whole damn thing.

All I could do was watch and there were moments when that felt like too much. Parker appeared at some point, taking in Dex's reign of destruction from the far side of the bar. His forehead crinkled and he gave a small shake of his head like he didn't understand what was happening. I didn't either. I didn't know what had gone wrong or why he was digging this hole to hell now, but I didn't know how to stop it either.

Mel motioned for me to step outside with her while Zeus distracted Dex with a drink and questions about that infamous playoff series.

"We aren't doing this," she said the minute the door shut behind us. "We are not hosting Dex's Dank and Drunk Variety Hour tonight. You need to take him home. Or to an asylum. I don't know if those still exist but this would be a good time to look into it."

"You don't think I know this?"

Mel held up her hands. "I think you've passed on several opportunities to tackle his ass to the ground. Between you, me, Zeus, and Woot, we could get that boy hog-tied without breaking a sweat. He's a big brute, but he's too stoned to realize what's happening until it's over."

I folded my arms. "You really think we could do that?"

"I'll get the bungee cords." She pointed to my SUV. "You open the rear gate. We'll toss him in there."

"Some containment would be nice," I murmured.

"If anyone else destroyed that many of our homegrown oysters, you wouldn't be out here waffling around to find the right answer. You would've raised all kinds of hell, and you know it."

Before I could respond, a man in an alarmingly bold pair of electric blue and neon pink plaid trousers approached, his hand extended. I winced at the sight of his matching polo shirt. My retinas weren't equipped for the kinds of colors Gaines Campbell kept in his closet.

"My god," Mel said under her breath.

"How are we today, Beckett Loew?"

I accepted his hand, saying, "What can I do for you, Gaines?"

"I heard through the grapevine, I'll tell you what I heard around town today, what I heard was that you fine folks opened up your doors after the storm. Hot food, coffee"—he leaned in conspiratorially—"air conditioning."

I shrugged, dipping my hands into my pockets. "The food came from Naked Provisions. We just turned on the coffeepots. Not a big deal. Truly."

"That's not how I hear it," he said, wagging a ruddy finger at me like I was holding out on him. "I'll tell you what I hear. I hear the people in this town singing your praises. This town has a lot of love for the Loew family. But I bet you knew that already, didn't you?"

A crash sounded inside and a watery groan stuttered out of me.

"I'm just going to—" Mel turned around and walked back inside.

"This town has always embraced Small Point Oyster Company and we've always appreciated that. It's kind of you to remind us of that goodwill," I said as diplomatically as possible. "Can I pour you a cold drink? Show you to a table?"

"No, no, none of that," he blustered. "Here's what I want to do. I thought to myself this morning, I was thinking about your oysters and I was thinking it's time to get that oyster festival on the books. That's what I want to do."

The door banged open and Decker emerged with a pint glass filled to the brim with what I had to assume was more whiskey, and he was wearing heart-shaped sunglasses. He crip-walked across the driveway toward Naked while Zeus and Agent Price watched from the entrance. They gave me *what do we do now?* shrugs.

This day was cracking under many, many layers of catastrophe but nothing could be worse than Decker, unsupervised, in Sunny's café. Those women would barbeque his balls.

"And that got me to thinking, what I thought was, I think we need a whole oyster weekend. If we're going to do this, we should do it all the way. That's my thinking, that is."

"Yeah, sure," I said to Gaines. "You'll have to excuse me."

"I'll come by next week," he shouted as I jogged toward the café. "We can hammer out the details."

I didn't know what the fuck we were hammering but I'd figure it out some other time. Preferably when my brother wasn't seconds away from dancing on a tabletop or chopping a hand off in Muffy's kitchen.

I found him leaning over the front counter, the majority of his upper body sprawled on the butcher block and a puddle of amber liquid on the floor beside him. The pint glass was empty though not broken. He had the sunglasses on the top of his head and his chin resting on his upturned palms as he grinned at Sunny, Meara, and Muffy. Sunny had a hand over her mouth, restraining a laugh.

"What are you doing?" I asked him.

"Talking to these pretty ladies," he replied. "And what do you do for fun, Miss Pigtails?"

The subtle arch of Meara's brow cried out like a record scratch. "That depends on your definition of fun. Not everyone can"—she tapped her chin—"*handle* the same kinds of fun."

A laugh bellowed out of him. "You're a bad girl, aren't you?"

"Terrible," she deadpanned, her expression crisp and cool. "Even worse than Sunny."

"I like it, I like it." He bobbed his head like she wasn't disemboweling him with her mind. "What about you?" He tipped his chin toward Muffy. She flipped him off and returned to her kitchen. "That just makes me want you more," he called.

"Shut up," I said to him. "Come on. You've already made enough of a mess here."

"Would you just back the fuck up and let me live?" he asked over his shoulder. When I didn't reply, he turned back to Sunny and Meara. "So, tell me, Sunny, what kind of trouble do you like getting into around here? Are you naughty like your bad girl friend?"

"Shut the fuck up." I grabbed him by the back of his collar and hauled him off the counter. "Not another word out of you."

Decker swung a glance between me and Sunny, awareness crystalizing in his eyes faster than should be possible given the volume of substances in his body. "Is that how it is?" he asked, a devious smirk pulling at the corner of his mouth. "But what about the fiancée back in Singapore?"

It came out as *Slingafore* and I would've laughed if I didn't feel like I'd fallen overboard into choppy, freezing waters and was drifting toward the seafloor.

Because he hadn't done enough, my brother turned to Sunny, asking, "Did he tell you about her? About the fiancée?"

Sunny opened her mouth to respond though stopped herself, pursing her lips together. Meara glared at me like it was my turn to be disemboweled.

"I know Beck has been in plenty of relationships before me," Sunny replied, "and there's nothing wrong with that."

It was dark down here on the seafloor. Bitterly cold. Empty and alone, and painfully quiet. No comfort in watery graves.

"I don't think she knew about that," Decker said to me, helpful as ever.

"That's probably because I wasn't fucking engaged, you fucking moron," I cried.

"It's okay," Sunny said, coming around the counter. She herded us outside and away from the watchful eyes of her customers. Meara followed. She wasn't finished scooping out my entrails. "Nothing to worry about here."

"She's nothing like you," Decker went on, because of course he did. "Tall, blonde, stiff and scary in a corporate kind of way. But you're cute too. Like a little munchkin. I could eat you in one bite."

Pain flickered across Sunny's eyes and I seriously considered punching my brother in the face. All the frustration and unsnapped tension balled up inside my chest pressed forward and I didn't try to hold it in this time.

"Why the sudden concern with *anything* I do? Is it any surprise you don't know what's happening with me when you don't answer your fucking phone for months?" I snapped. "And since we're on the topic of marital status, where the hell is your wife these days, Dex?"

He stared at me for a beat, his eyes dark, endless caves. "Say another word and I will take you apart, limb by limb."

"Okay, well, we have a sunset yoga event this evening and it would cause a lot of problems if you guys tried to beat the fluff out of each other while we're setting up for that," Sunny said. "Maybe this would be a good time to go on home and you know, just not be here anymore. Okay? Thank you so much."

"What kind of setting up do you have to do?" I asked.

Sunny rolled her eyes and adjusted her skirt. I hadn't seen this one before. Or the white top that was almost thin enough for me to make out the brown of her nipples Why did she see fit to torture me that way? I wanted to ask all of these questions—and so many others, important ones like *we're good, right?* and *tell me where it hurts so I can make it better.*

"We're just moving the outdoor furniture around," Sunny said. "It's not a big deal, Beck."

Dex held up his palms, staring at them like he didn't understand their purpose. "Where is my drink?"

"On my floor," Meara replied.

"I'll send someone to help you with that," I said. "And moving the furniture."

"You will not," Sunny said, stabbing my chest with a surprisingly sharp finger. "We are fully capable and you have your hands full."

"Argue all the fuck you want," I said to Sunny, "but you have one functional arm and I'm—what the hell are you doing now?"

My brother paced away, unzipped his trousers, and pissed on the side of the café. We watched, speechless, as he shook off his dick and shoved it back into his pants. He did not bother to zip up.

"I'm sure Sunny would agree with me," Meara said, "when I say we would not object to someone who is neither of us coming out here to power wash and disinfect the exterior wall. Now that it has been so thoroughly marked with human fluids."

I unlocked my car and pointed toward it, saying to Dex, "Get your ass in there now or I'm letting Mel and Wooten tie you up with bungee cords."

"Already got them." I shifted to find Parker jogging toward us, an assortment of cords in one hand and zip ties in the other. As if sensing we needed some explanation, he added, "Woot uses this stuff on the boats."

"I'm happy to hear those aren't things your chef keeps on hand," Meara said.

"I know I'm obnoxious when I'm drunk and high, but at least I'm nice about it. All these people around here, they think you're something special, Dex. Like you're some kind of big deal. But your behavior is complete horseshit," Parker said. "Come on. You're done here."

"I'm sorry, but when did your balls drop?" Dex replied.

Parker set his hands on his hips and blew out a breath. "I'm a nonviolent guy, but I've never wanted to break someone's nose more than I do right now."

"Go ahead, I'll hold him for you," Meara said.

As if sensing he'd run out every shred of his welcome, my brother slunk off toward the car and dived headfirst into the back seat, leaving the lower half of his legs hanging out the open door.

I reached for Sunny but she didn't move any closer. As if I could blame her. "I'll pick you up later," I said.

Sunny shook her head and Meara jumped in, saying, "I'm driving you home tonight, babe."

No room for discussion there.

"I'm sorry about all of this," I said. "About everything."

"I know." Sunny nodded. She gave me a tight smile and I would've preferred a knife through the heart. "We'll talk later."

"Beck," Parker called. "I could use a hand over here."

"Go," Sunny said when I didn't move. "Everything is fine. I promise. Do what you need to do."

I backed away, not ready to take my eyes off her. I felt like I was making an irreversible choice right now, stepping over lines I wouldn't be able to revisit once I crossed them.

"Seriously, Beck," Parker called.

I rolled my eyes, muttering, "Fuck" to no one in particular.

"Don't forget about that power washing," Meara shouted. "Kind of a big deal."

When I reached the car, Parker slammed the back door shut, saying, "I've never hit anyone, but I want to beat his ass to a pulp."

"Believe me, I know."

The drive back to my parents' house was short in distance and excruciatingly long in the amount of grumbly noise spewing out of my brother's mouth. I barely survived a thirty-second call with Rainey to get him back over to Naked. Every few minutes, Parker and I would exchange a glance and shake our heads, mouthing *we should've used the zip ties* and *what the fuck?* as if an answer existed.

As I pulled up and climbed out of the car, Dex said, "If you think I'm staying here, you're out of your damn mind."

"Then why the fuck did you come here?" I roared, reaching and flying far past the end of my rope in that moment. "If you're not staying, why are you here, Decker?"

"I could ask you the same thing," he shouted, slamming his door so hard the SUV rocked.

"I'm here holding this whole place together," I yelled. "Who the fuck do you think was supposed to get the oyster company back to work? Who did you expect to find an attorney for Mom and Dad, or babysit Parker?"

"Hey," Parker cried.

"You know what I mean," I said to him. "I'm doing what I always do, Dex, and fuck you very much for noticing."

"No one ever asked you to do any of it," he said, strolling across the front lawn like we weren't verbally tearing each other to pieces. "You think you're so fucking important because you ride to the rescue, you save the day over and over again. But the truth is, it's the only time you're happy. You want everyone else to fuck up and fail, just so you can remind us that you're so much smarter than the rest of us. Because that's all you have, isn't it? That's all you fucking have."

Before I could respond, a jet of water shot out across the yard and hit Dex square in the chest. I shifted to find Parker aiming the hose at him.

"You know what Mom would say if she was here?" Parker yelled as

Dex tried and failed to dodge the spray. "She'd say it was time to wash your mouth out with soap, you asshole."

Now soaking wet, Dex yelled, "If you don't turn that off right now, I'm going to make you wish you were never born."

"Go ahead and try," Parker said, angling the water to hit the back of Dex's head.

I shoved my hands through my hair and groaned as Dex went sliding on his ass. "Park, he's going to hurt himself or—"

Just then, something whizzed right over my shoulder and crashed on the driveway behind me. I turned and found the jaunty, decapitated face of a garden gnome smiling back at me.

"What the literal fuck, Decker?"

"You want to play with me," he said, belly-crawling toward the bushes and several more gnomes, "you better be prepared to play *my* way."

I pointed at Parker. "Keep the water on him."

Agent Price's sedan came to a stop on the other side of the street. He rolled down the driver's side window, regarding us with mild curiosity. As if all families solved their problems on the front lawn, with yelling, hoses, and gnomes.

"Planning on it," Parker replied.

Another gnome sailed toward us and this one connected square on my thigh. Unfortunately, even drunk and stoned, Dex still had a killer arm.

Ducking under the laser focus of Parker's water cannon, I grabbed a few gnomes and sent them flying. If we'd ever cared about not causing harm, that time was over and our singular goal became mortally wounding each other. Given the multitude of gnomes in this yard, it wasn't difficult.

Dex started to wind up, but he lost his footing on the slippery grass and fell into a split that ended with his trousers tearing right up the ass. That only made him mad, and his aim turned brutal. I took several pointy hats to the chest and face, one very unpleasant bulbous body to the crotch, and so many more to my legs and arms.

Parker even got in on the action, pelting Dex with the small—but still very hard—gnomes Mom liked to hide in her flowerpots. He deflected most of the statues that came his way with the hose, but he had a thin, gnarly scrape across his jaw and there were chunks of gnome in his hair. Somehow, he was just as wet as Dex.

For his part, Dex had a bloody nose and was on his way to a black eye, though I'd argue he did that to himself, and his shirt was ripped and bloodied in a few spots.

When he bent at the waist, palms on his knees and his back heaving as he fought for breath, I motioned to Parker to turn off the water. "For now," I added.

Dex dropped to his knees and fisted his hands in the wet grass. "The kid's got an arm," he said with a rueful laugh. "No one mentioned that."

"Probably because you never call or return texts," Parker said.

Another laugh moved through Dex but it looked more like a shudder. "Enjoy it while it lasts," he said, still staring at the grass. "Wish someone had told me it wouldn't."

I kicked the remains of several gnomes out of my way as I crossed the yard, Parker following close behind. "What the hell are you talking about?"

He crumpled to the ground, his arms and legs splayed as he stared up at the evening sky. "My shoulder's fucked. Knees too. They say I have the hips of an eighty-year-old." He ripped out handfuls of grass and tossed it in the air only for it to fall in his face. "There's nothin' good left of me."

Parker dropped to the ground, his long legs stretching out for miles in front of him. "That's obviously bullshit."

Dex shook his head. "I've had second, third, fourth opinions. Surgeries. Cortisone shots. Ice baths. Infrared saunas. Acupuncture, massage, reiki. Physical therapy, hypnotherapy, cryotherapy. Everything. All of it. There's no hope for me."

"Dude, you are just so dense," Parker muttered. "There is more to you than the game."

Pushing up on an elbow, Dex said, "Like what? Because everything hurts all the time and I'll never play another pro game. I've pissed off everyone in the sports media establishment so much that I'd have to grovel my ass off to even be allowed to appear as a guest commentator for a spring training game. And if I got through all that, I'd fuck it up because my dyslexia hates teleprompters. And, as Beck reminded everyone, I haven't heard from my wife in *years* and I am the last person in the whole world she'd want crashing into her beautiful life right now. So, please, boy genius, enlighten me. Tell me what else I have going for me because I don't fuckin' know anymore."

"Okay, let me give this a try." Parker bobbed his head. "How about the part where you've earned many millions of dollars every year for almost a decade? Or the part where you're not special because you pissed off the media. You're just another dickhead player and if you wait five minutes, they'll be back to licking your asshole."

"*Parker*," I gasped.

"No, he's right about that," Dex said.

"And I'm sorry you're in pain," Parker went on, "but you have access to the best healthcare in the world. If there's anyone who has the resources to be well, it's you. As far as your wife goes, I don't know what to say, but there's gotta be a reason you still call her your wife after all these years apart."

"But what do I *do* with myself now?" Dex asked, bitterness ringing through his words. "This is the only thing I've ever been good at."

"How does anyone know what they're supposed to do with themselves?" he replied. "How am I supposed to know? I hate the idea of going to college right after I graduate high school but what are my options? What else can I do? I know I'll *die* if I stay in Friendship, shucking oysters and waiting tables. But college is expensive as hell and I don't want to go into debt for a degree I might not use."

"You don't need to worry about that," I said to him. "Don't let money concern you."

To that, Parker threw a handful of grass at me. "I'm not letting *you* do that."

"You should. I can easily afford it and—"

"*No*," Parker yelled. "It has to end somewhere, Beck, and I guess it's going to end with me. You've rescued us and bailed us out too many times. Just look at everything you're doing right now for Mom and Dad. It's too much and I'm not going to be another person who takes from you, who expects everything from you." He shook his head, ripped up more grass. "No, that's not how it's going to be. If I decide to go to college, I'll figure out how to pay for it."

Dex jabbed a finger toward Parker. "The kid makes a good point."

"Does he?" I asked, dropping down beside them.

Dex nodded, saying, "Yeah, but I'm going to need you to bail out my whole life. I didn't really mean what I said before. If you don't mind, I'll end the cycle when we're finished sorting out my shit."

"Well," I said with a sigh. "Mom is still a fugitive and there's a good chance Dad will spend decades in prison." I tossed a gnome carcass into the bushes. "It's not like I'm getting out of this town anytime soon."

Even as I said this, it tasted like a half-truth. But the other half wasn't a lie, it was a betrayal—though I wasn't sure who I was betraying, me or Sunny.

"You say that as if you're not nauseatingly in love with Sunny and looking for any reason in the world to stay here past the summer," Parker said. "Just work remotely, man. Everyone does it."

"Is that how it is with them?" Dex asked him.

Parker bobbed his head, saying, "You know that's Lance Du Jardin's little sister, right?"

Dex turned to me, his eyes wide and his smile consuming his entire face. "The golden boy turns cradle robber," he said. "And she's your best friend's baby sister? Shit. How are you still alive?"

"Well, he's not talking to me."

Dex glanced down at the grass stains on his shirt. "My life seems a lot less fucked up knowing that."

I glared at Parker. "Thanks."

"Hey, I'm just getting everyone up to speed on you and the child bride," he replied.

"That's it." I pushed to my feet. "I'm getting the hose."

"Settle down, settle down. No one is getting the hose," Dex said. "I guess I should apologize for hitting on your girlfriend. I probably wouldn't have done that if not for—"

"The drugs and alcohol?" Parker asked.

"Yeah." Dex seemed to consider this. "And, you know, that people only like me because I can throw a ball, but I can't do that anymore." He waved that away, asking, "So, you're gonna marry this one? Seal the deal this time?"

I rubbed at a tender spot on my jaw. There was going to be a bruise there soon. "Shut the fuck up."

"Nah, I'm not so good at that game," Dex said. "What's the deal with your munchkin?"

"I don't know where it's going. Okay? We're together right now. That's all we know." I glowered at him. "And don't call her a munchkin. She doesn't like people picking on her size."

"I'd say her size is quite right," Dex said.

"The hose," I warned.

"I am already wet," Dex yelled. "You can't make me more wet. Unless you're going to whip me with it, the hose isn't going to do you any damn good. Sit your ass down and listen to me."

I glanced over at Agent Price. He tipped his chin up in salute. Because I needed witnesses for all of this. "Sure. Fine. Whatever you want." I sank down again, grimacing at the seep of wet through my trousers and feeling every stray scrape and bruise from the war of the gnomes. "What do you need to say, Decker? I'm all ears."

He stared at me intently for a long, irritating moment. Then, "Use that big brain of yours and figure this shit out."

"That's it?" I asked. "That's the wisdom I had to sit down to receive?"

Dex threw the bottom half of a gnome at me. It pinged off my forehead. "Figure it out," he repeated, "because you don't want to end up like me, miserable and alone and obsessing over the biggest mistake of your life. You don't want to wake up some morning and realize you allowed your wife to walk out because you let your career become more important to you than that woman. And maybe your career won't grind you up and beat you into the ground, but mine did and now I'm cold and wet, and cruising to one hell of a hangover." He cast a glance over the yard. "And surrounded by creepy gnome body parts."

We were quiet for a minute and that was great because I needed that time to swallow down the solid mass of emotion lodged in my throat.

"Do you know where she is?" Parker asked. "Your wife? Maybe you could give her a call or go visit her."

"I always know where Jenn is," he said. "And I know she doesn't want anything to do with me."

"How can you be sure?" Parker asked.

"She's good," Dex said fondly. "Things are good for her. She's happy. She doesn't need"—he motioned to his grass-stained shirt and split trousers—"any of my shit."

"You never know," Parker said.

"I know Jenn," he replied. "And I know she doesn't need me anymore."

"Okay." Parker shrugged. "If Mom ever comes home, she's going to be pissed about her gnomes."

"If." I scoffed. "She does seem to be happy with her babysitting gig."

"She wants to get back here," Dex said. "And don't worry about the gnomes, kid. Now we know exactly what to get her for every birthday and holiday until the end of time." He glanced over at me. "Do you think I could find someone to make a gnome couple? Like, a big, ugly, snarly one and a pretty little child bride one? She'd love that."

I pushed to my feet, yelling, "I'm getting the hose."

chapter thirty-two

Sunny

Today's Special:
Hand-Tossed Truths Drizzled with Oven-Roasted Omissions

"THE FASCINATING THING about leaving a super niche boutique marketing firm to run publicity for a brand-new baby café in Nowheresville, Rhode Island is that there is—inexplicably—more drama on a minute-to-minute basis than anything I saw in Los Angeles."

I swung a salty glance toward Meara but she was busy edging into the intersection, waiting for an opening in the traffic to make a left turn. With a sigh, I stared down at my lap. The headlights were a lot tonight. "It's only called drama when it primarily involves women," I said. "The rest of the time it's just a messy issue with multiple viewpoints and lots of strong feelings."

"I don't know what qualifies as drama in your book but the nearly weekly upheaval of fire hydrant explosions and raccoon attacks and all the drunken Loew boys requiring your aid, and I'd say we are in the company of dramatic people and living in dramatic times." She shot me a silly pursed-lip expression that said she didn't need me to confirm that she was right because she already knew. "Anytime a professional athlete motorboats a bucket of oysters and makes a real effort at blowing up his brother's relationship, it escalates beyond a messy *issue* for me."

"He didn't try to blow up our relationship. He was just being a dick." Except that didn't feel right. With a sigh, I added, "He's obviously going through a lot of things right now and he lashed out at everyone who crossed his path. It's not about me or even Beck."

"You know, you're allowed to be pissed off," Meara said.

"And yet I am not."

"I'd really prefer it if you'd cut the Sunny sunshine bullshit and admit you hated hearing all of that from your future brother-in-law."

I was quiet while Meara drove toward my neighborhood. I'd thought this over during the yoga event and I came to the conclusion that no, I didn't love getting all that info dropped on me in that particular way. But aside from the sting, none of it really mattered.

"Come on," she prompted.

"Beck had a life before he landed here a few months ago. I can't fault him for that," I said. "Was it weird and uncomfortable to hear about it from Decker? Seriously, yes. Does it change anything for me? No."

Meara let out a snarly groan that made me want to pull one of her braids. "I need you to tap into your possessive side. I need you territorial. Primal. It's so much more fun when you stop being reasonable about everything."

"Oh, is it?"

"Like you wouldn't believe." She glanced over as she pulled into my driveway. "It makes the husbands totally wild, the territorial thing. If I'm ever possessive in public, it's only a matter of time until one of them whispers in my ear that I have five minutes to find a semiprivate location or the other throws me over his shoulder and runs for the door."

"How do you handle *two* of them?" I asked. "My hands are full with one." I gave a slight nod toward my lap. "And I don't think my body would be able to keep up with any more than that."

"Well," she started, gazing off into the distance, "it's a balancing act."

"That sounds complicated."

"Not really," she said. "Not anymore. These things take practice but that's just how relationships are." With a shake of her head, she went on. "So, what do you think is going to happen with the first meeting of the book club? What are the odds these folks actually read the book?"

"I'm guessing it's fifty-fifty. I know there are people reading the book because they mention it every time they come into the café. But some will show up tomorrow night and immediately admit they haven't even read the back cover."

"That's so funny to me because I'd never go to a book club event without having read the book," Meara said. "If I don't do the homework, I keep my ass at home."

"Right, because that's your brain and the way you experience books. You and Muff could exist in your own little book world without anyone else and be happy as peas in a pod. For other people, book clubs are as much about the social experience as they are about the literary experience. They want to hang out with folks who love stories about love and other bookish things, even if they can't always contribute to the conversation themselves." When Meara only raised a brow, I added, "We're going to have a great turnout and everyone will love it."

She shrugged. "I'm going to trust you on that."

"Do you want to come in? Beverage, snack, bathroom break? I want to make sure you're prepared since you have a very long drive home," I teased. She lived forty-five minutes away from Friendship which, by Rhode Island standards, was a hefty commute. "Perhaps you should stay the night."

"I do not miss LA traffic," she said, "but at least the people in LA knew they wouldn't fall off the edge of the earth if they ventured more than ten miles from their front door."

I laughed. "So, you're coming in for a drink?"

"No," she said, though she didn't sound convinced. "I'm good. I need to get home."

"Thanks for the ride."

As I pushed open the door, Meara grabbed my wrist. "Wait, wait, I just remembered. I figured out what's been happening with the back door and why it keeps getting banged up. I noticed tonight that it's not closing all the way, and if there's any wind at all, it blows the door open and slams it against the side of the building. I watched it happen and I saw exactly why we've had to replace that handle so many times."

"So, it's just…the wind? It's not raccoons with tools or angry deer or—hell, any of the crazy and somewhat disturbing ideas I thought up?"

"Just the wind," she said. "And we need to get that handle fixed again."

I climbed out of the car, laughing. What a damn relief. "Hopefully for the last time."

I waved as Meara drove away and let myself into the house where I was promptly swarmed by dogs. They circled me, sniffing up and down my skirt and licking my palm, huffing and whining the whole time. Before they could finish this inspection, a knock sounded at the door. Meara was back.

"I knew you'd need to pee before—"

I swung the door open to find Beck standing there, one shoulder leaned against the frame while he rubbed his eyes, his glasses dangling from his other hand. He was dressed in button-fly jeans that renewed my faith in the church of denim and a t-shirt that looked like my next sleep shirt. His hair was shower-damp and he seemed to smell like lawn clippings. There was a bruise blooming on his jaw and an ugly welt near his eyebrow.

"I wasn't about to get married," he said, his fingers still pressed to his eyes. "Or even engaged. It ended *last year*."

I nodded but he didn't see it. "Okay. That's good to know."

He dropped the hand from his face. "It is?"

"Yeah, because it's helpful context for this little downpour of information. But I wasn't worried, Beck. I know you. Even when you're a warty old bridge troll, you're honest."

"Bridge troll?"

"You have your moments." I motioned to his face. "Do I even want to know what happened here?"

"Gnomes," he said gravely. "So many fucking gnomes."

I grabbed his wrist and towed him inside, saying, "Come on. These dogs need to burn off some energy and you've made lots of noises about the quality of your pitching arm."

We settled in the backyard, me flopped down on a chaise and Beck throwing an endless stream of tennis balls for Scout and Jem as stars twinkled overhead. It was a new kind of sexual pleasure for me.

"Why is it you don't throw balls professionally?" I asked.

Beck laughed. "I'm good, but I'm not as good as Dex." Another laugh, this one without any warmth. "He's sorry for being a fucking douchebag, by the way."

"I figured as much." When he didn't continue, I said, "You're welcome to vent about everything that happened today. I'm very good at being on the receiving end of venting. I can listen or I can help you come up with solutions, or I can see if there are any movies we might want to watch to forget about all of it. I also came home with a bunch of new cookie samples from Muffy, so that can figure into tonight's equation too."

After a long pause where I watched the obscene stretch and pull of his muscles under that t-shirt, he said, "I can't stay. I wish I could trust Dex to stay home alone but there's a very solid chance he'll burn down the house or fall off the roof simply because he believes it's easier to destroy things than fix them."

I'd figured as much but I was still disappointed. "Is Dex all right?"

He blew out a breath. "No, but he will be. Eventually. It might take the better part of a decade and probably a good divorce attorney, but he'll make it."

"I didn't even know he was married."

Beck shook his head. "Most people don't. They've been separated a long time."

I needed to hear a lot more about that though this wasn't the moment. "And your parents?"

His chuckle was so painfully bitter that it almost hurt. "The plea deals are gone. Dead. And all due to completely stupid shit."

Jem trotted over with a slobbery tennis ball and dropped it in my lap. I flicked it away and pointed to Beck, hoping he understood who was playing ball tonight. "What happened now?"

"My mother didn't turn herself in at the agreed-upon time. She wasn't even on her way to the airport," he said. "Fucking ridiculous."

I murmured in agreement. Beck didn't need my comments or reactions here.

"And everyone's favorite fuckhead Devon approached the feds with a shit ton of highly incriminating evidence."

"That guy really is a fuckhead."

Beck fell silent for several minutes, focused on throwing the balls and wrenching them from my dogs' jaws when they returned. They loved him so very much and my favorite thing was how he loved them right back. I had quiet, secret moments where I wondered whether he came for me but stayed for the dogs. I didn't mind. I'd take that. I'd take anything I could get.

Then, "Remember how we talked about us both being terrible at relationships? You said I refuse to be vulnerable, I said you needed to find the right cock?"

I smothered a laugh. "Vaguely, yes."

"That was the problem with the woman in Singapore. She was actually terribly at relationships."

"Good to know it wasn't about finding the right cock."

"No, that's all yours," he said. "She wasn't actually *in* Singapore though. She's a Swede based out of Dubai and her firm sent her on quarterly trips to the island."

"Sure. That sounds like an important distinction."

"Yeah, that's not the point." He pushed a hand through his hair and glanced over at me with a tight expression that fell somewhere between a frown and a grimace. This was going to be awesome. "Though it didn't occur to me at the time, I wasn't particularly open or vulnerable with her. She didn't know much about me and I guess I didn't know much about her because I found out through a friend of a friend that she was married. I heard about it because that friend was taking over for her since she was moving to the Munich office to be closer to her husband." He fired off another ball and both dogs streaked across the yard toward it. "And the crazy thing was, I didn't really care."

"You didn't care that she was married or that she was leaving?"

He started to reply but stopped himself, shook his head, and threw another ball. "It pissed me off that she'd cheated with me, but the rest of it didn't matter. I'd forgotten about the whole thing until my fucking brother brought it up tonight. What the fuck is wrong with me?"

"Nothing. Not every relationship is revelatory," I said. "They're not all instructive." I held up my hands and let them drop to my lap. "It doesn't have to mean anything."

He shifted to face me and I could read the torment all over his face. "It will mean something to me when I can't be with you anymore. I *care* about you, Sunny. I care so fucking much that I can't even believe it most of the time." He looked out at the yard, shook his head. "I will remember everyfuckingthing about you. I'll remember every day I've spent with you, everything we did together. I'll remember your hair and the way you laugh and how you feel next to me in the morning. There is nothing that could happen to me that would make me forget."

Then stay with me because it's going to break my heart when you go. Since I couldn't ask that of him, I reached out a hand. He came over, laced his fingers with mine. "I know. Me too."

We made our way inside and the dogs sprawled out on the kitchen floor, huffing, tongues lolling, tails giving exhausted, happy wags every few minutes. Beck and I sank into the sofa, his bicep under my head and our bodies pressed close together like we were trying to chase away the distance before it came for us. I made noises about finding a movie to watch but that involved leaving the safety of his embrace so we listened to crickets and cicadas, the passing cars, and the slide of his fingers through my hair.

Eventually, Beck leaned down to brush his lips over my temple, saying, "I do want to get married someday."

That surprised me. More than I expected. I kind of thought he'd go hard for the untethered life since he seemed to embrace it with both hands. But then again, the things I wanted were contradictory as hell. I wanted to travel the entire world and live in a small town forever. I wanted to chase whimsy and swim in happy accidents, and I wanted to come home to constancy and stability. I wanted a man who lived thousands of miles away and I wanted him to love my weird, wonky side of the world as much as I did. I wanted him to love me as much as I loved him.

All I could say was, "Me too."

His lips still on my temple, he asked, "What else do you want, storm cloud?"

I hummed, wiggled a shoulder. If only it was as simple as saying it out loud and making it real. But he wasn't meant for this town the way I was. He didn't love it and I couldn't force it on him. "I don't know," I said because it was far less dangerous than the truth. "I guess I'll just take it one chaotic adventure at a time."

We stayed there on the couch until I could feel Beck's stomach rumbling and I forced him to weigh in on Muffy's cookie experiments. He didn't "understand" the rosemary shortbread but he inhaled the gingerbread.

"When did Decker get married?" I asked as he moved on to a dark chocolate variation of our chocolate chip cookie. "I'm having a hard time wrapping my mind around this."

He blinked down at the cookie, frowning. "Six? Seven years ago? I'm not sure."

"He's been married for *six years*?" I cried. "Who is this person?"

Beck shrugged like he was just as confused as I was. "I hardly know her. It happened around the time I was moving from being based in Europe to Asia, and I didn't have a minute to get involved. Not that Dex would've allowed that anyway. He's always been crazy protective of her."

"I cannot believe the town rumor mill failed me on this one."

"I don't think the town really knows her. She's not from Friendship but they met here one summer. I don't remember how that all happened. They went to the same college and then got married not long after he was drafted to the majors. Within two or three years, I think. I'm fuzzy on the timeline. Switching continents and hemispheres really fucked with me. They separated pretty quick."

"Separated but not divorced," I said.

"Right." He brushed some pine nuts off the top of a tahini cookie. "I'm not sure why they haven't finalized things."

"Because they don't want to?" I ducked to meet his eyes and give him my best *when are you going to wake up and realize this is a goddamn second-chance love story waiting to happen* stare. "Because they just need a reason to reconnect and remember how much they want to be together?"

Beck fired back with his best *you're imagining things and it's scaring me* stare. "I don't think that's the case."

"It could be." I handed him the last cookie and went into the kitchen to clean up. "You never know. This might be the push they need."

"Maybe the push he needs is out a window," he grumbled.

As I washed a week's worth of teacups, Beck came up behind me, crossed his arms over my torso and rested his chin on my head. He let out a long breath and I allowed myself to believe that a single thought pinged between us right now, that we wanted everything to be different but also the same, and *that* would be perfect. *We* would be perfect.

"Can I stay with you tonight?" he asked, his words low and sleepy, like he was already tucked into my bed.

"I thought you couldn't."

"I can't," he said, miserable. "But I'm tired of being responsible for everyone. I just want to be responsible for you." He let out a breath. "Can I stay?"

"That depends. Are you going to be stressed the whole time and sleep with your phone under your pillow?"

I felt him shrug, murmur something noncommittal. Then, "You can put my phone on your side." He kissed the crown of my head, adding, "If they can't survive one night without me, I have more problems than I thought."

"If Dex hasn't already passed out, he will soon," I said, drying my hands.

Beck turned me to face him, his hands looped at the small of my back. "I don't want to talk about him anymore. I just want to be here with you."

We turned off the lights and locked the doors, and drifted toward the bedroom like we'd done this dance for ages and knew it even with our eyes closed. He fussed over my skirt like it was the source of all his pain and I chastised him for baiting me with those button-fly jeans. I claimed his t-shirt the second it flew over his head and—despite his grumbly glaring—I pulled it on. "Mine," I said.

"Why can't I have you naked?" he asked, still glaring as I slipped between the sheets.

I wiggled out of my undies and tossed them toward him. He caught them without breaking eye contact with me, another one of his obscenely unnecessary skills. "You didn't request naked."

He spread out his hands. "Is it not implied?"

"This isn't one of your negotiations." I patted the mattress beside me. "Get in here or go home."

Beck stared at me for a beat, but then climbed in, hooking an arm around my waist and dragging me across the bed. "Mine."

He moved his palms up my legs, across my belly, over my breasts. He was hard, grinding against my backside with enough force that he had to hold me in place with a hand between my thighs. I closed my eyes and let the need rise up in me, each minute that passed made more intense by the still, steady way he held me. He left lazy, open-mouthed kisses on my neck and shoulders along with quiet whispers of *you're so soft* and *don't you ever take this shirt off* and *can I have you now, please?*

A drowsy nod was my only response and then he was there, pressing inside me. I felt him everywhere. The tips of my fingers, the jowly place behind my jaw, the unholy clench in my chest that hinted at how much it would hurt when he left. But I couldn't think about that now. Not tonight. Not when I could drown in the glory of his breathless growls or memorize the unhurried slap of his hips against my ass or the indelible dig of his fingertips into my skin.

"Do you know," he started, his teeth on my shoulder and his arm banded across my waist, "what I mean when I say I *care* about you? Do you get it, Sunny? Do you get that I don't think I'll ever stop caring about you?"

"I know," I said, though I wanted more than anything for him to spell it out. *Give me all the details. Leave nothing unsaid. Don't let me misunderstand.* "I *know*, Beck."

He stilled for a moment, his lips parted on my throat, and the air between us changed. No longer were we half asleep and sliding toward easy, indulgent orgasms. We were clinging to this kernel of truth, hoarding every last ounce we could snatch up and rubbing it between our palms to make it real, make it shine. And we were sealing that truth in stone because we weren't leaving here without proof—proof that we *cared* and proof that we'd said that word out loud, even if it wasn't the correct word. It was the one we had right now and that would have to be enough.

"Sunny," he groaned, curling himself around me even more.

I felt like a circle, a loop of skin and limbs and pleasure that came around in arcs that stole the words off my tongue. I was powerless in this position, left to do little more than take what Beck had to give—and that was how it would always be for us.

"Tell me what you need," he said, his tone sharp and insistent like he could bait me into being the one to go all in when we both knew he'd fold.

I reached for him, twining our fingers together, and I let him skim our hands between my legs. We traced my clit while he pounded into me and whispered half-formed promises to my skin. My body gathered and pulsed around him, threatening to fall apart at any moment.

"*Sunny,*" Beck said, a demand and a plea. "Do you understand? That I've never cared for anyone else? Not like this."

I squeezed my eyes shut because yes, I did know this, even without him saying it. Nodding, I shifted back against him and it was like we'd stumbled into a new, super-sensitive plane of existence. Raw, ravenous noises filled the room and I was certain I'd perish if I didn't soon find an outlet for all this unbound energy.

"Let me have it," Beck panted. "Let me have you. Let me keep you."

I clenched around him, saying, "Yes, yes, yes, yes."

chapter thirty-three

Beckett

Today's Special:
Calm Chowder Before the Stormy Salad

IT WAS the kind of slow August evening where it felt like everyone had decided they were finished with summer. The deck was empty save for a handful of regulars who enjoyed gravy-thick humidity and the dining room was moving along nicely but we weren't flat-out packed. I kicked Mel out because the only thing she could do was stare out the window and watch the book club meeting in progress at Naked.

Since I didn't have anything else to do—and I wasn't inserting myself into that book club—I posted up at the raw bar and went to work on the bivalves. This spot gave me a perfect view into Naked and the group gathered inside. Every now and then I caught a glimpse of Sunny and her rainbow cast. It made me smile and I felt like a lunatic, grinning as I shucked my way through an endless supply of oysters.

About an hour later, a lull in the service had me studying the waning crowd in the dining room. A large group of women sat on the far end, near the deck, and if the constant hoots of laughter were any indication, they were having a damn good time out there. Some of them looked familiar too. One in particular, with pinkish hair. I'd seen her before, I was positive, though I couldn't figure out when or where.

I tapped the handle of my shucking knife against my palm as I tried to place that face. More specifically, that hair. Friendship was a strange town but there wasn't a lot of pink hair and not knowing was driving me crazy.

Sunny would know. She knew everyone. Their histories, their coffee orders, the right thing to say to make them smile.

At the sound of a harsh throat-clearing, I swung my gaze away from the woman to a customer sitting a few seats away at the bar, an empty beer glass rolling between his palms. I met his expectant stare and realized after a blank beat that he was Noah Barden. From Little Star Farm. Everyone knew Noah. Hell, he owned half the farmland in this town. Maybe more than half. Everything bordering the cove.

Did that make us neighbors?

Probably, yes.

"Noah, hi." I set down the shucking knife, wiped off my hands. "What can I get you?"

He set the empty glass to the side. "Another brown ale would be a good start, and if it's not too much trouble, I'd thank you to stop staring at my wife."

Oh...shit.

"Sorry about that. Not my intention. I'm terrible with faces," I said, grabbing a fresh glass. "There are so many people that I semi-recognize from high school and I kept thinking she looked familiar but I couldn't remember her name. Between names and faces, I'm always forgetting someone." He stared at me while I poured the beer, his expression flat. "Now I realize I saw you two at the town council meeting. The one where they threw together that plan to change the hours of operation."

"Yeah." He nodded when I set the fresh beer in front of him. "It's always something around here. Either the town wants to make it more difficult for us to do business or they're hollering at us for not doing enough business. There's no winning."

"Then why do you stay?"

He laced his fingers around the pint glass and lifted his shoulders. "How long have you been back here?"

"Since May," I said. "About four months."

"And where were you before this?" He took a sip, adding, "You don't remember faces, I don't remember gossip."

I glanced over at Naked again. It was a madhouse in there. "Overseas. Singapore, most recently."

"Right, yeah," he murmured, like that sounded familiar. "And you've been gone a while?"

"More than a decade. Closer to thirteen years." This seemed like a highly indirect way of answering my original question but I had time to kill here. "Why do you ask?"

"You have to give yourself time to adjust. You can't come home to Friendship after living in any major metropolitan area for any period of time—let alone a damn decade—and expect to do anything but rebel against this town in the first couple of months." He met my eyes, nodding like he wanted to hammer home the point. "It takes time to understand this place and to accept it for what it is rather than what it is not."

I stared at him for an uncomfortable minute. It felt like he'd hammered that point right between my ribs.

He went on, saying, "I moved home after working in corporate litigation in New York City. That wasn't the plan as far as I was concerned but my dad passed suddenly and decisions had to be made and—" He blew out a long breath and stared into his beer for a second. "And this is the last place I ever thought I'd end up but I wouldn't change a single thing."

"I'm sorry about your father," I said. "I didn't know."

It was possible that I had known in a passing comment kind of way but I'd always worked hard at tunneling my vision down to the handful of things I could immediately fix and manage, and a guy several years behind me in school losing his father wasn't one of those things. Even if my parents had said something, I probably would've rattled off some standard condolence and suggested they send flowers that I'd pay for.

Coming all the way around to the other side of that tunnel vision made me feel like an asshole now. An asshole who prioritized stability and safety for his family above all else but an asshole just the same.

"Thanks," Noah replied, nodding in the way people did when talking about loss. "I'm sorry about the legal troubles your parents are having but I know Adrian and his firm. You're in good hands."

"Expensive hands," I said. "Pretty sure I've paid for all of his great-grandkids to go to college on private islands by now."

"He'll get them out of this and then you can get the hell out of here." He took a sip, shrugged. "Unless you're thinking about staying."

Without conscious thought, my gaze turned back toward the café. Sunny was behind the counter now, a radiant smile on her face as she keyed in orders. "It's crossed my mind."

"Then learn to accept Friendship while you figure out what you can change about it." He stood, dropping a credit card on the bar. "For this" —he motioned to the pint—"and my wife's group outside."

I glanced over at him as I ran the card. "What did you change about this town?"

He shifted to watch his wife and her friends, his clear, full gaze cutting right across the dining room. I recognized something in that gaze, something I understood but couldn't enunciate.

Eventually, he said, "I changed anything I could get my hands on and I did it unapologetically. I made things I was proud of, things I cared about, and I made my own place here because I had to. I wasn't the same person who left after high school and I couldn't find a reason to pretend I was." He shot me a sidelong glance. "Give it a real chance. Once you stop fighting it, everything falls into place."

Noah escorted his wife and her friends out as the first rumbles of thunder sounded overhead. A dark blanket of clouds had settled low over the water after sunset and it now seemed like the skies were about to open up. As if we needed another destructive thunderstorm. The town was still cleaning up from the last one.

I flagged down Zeus, saying, "Let's work on clearing this place out, moving these tables along. Tell the kitchen to start shutting down for the night. I want these people home before it gets bad out there. I'm going to help Sunny with—" My phone buzzed in my pocket. Adrian, speak of the devil. "I have to take this but then I'm going over to Naked."

"You got it, boss," he said.

I jogged toward the back stairs to take the call with a shred of privacy. "Were your ears burning?" I asked. "Because I was just talking about you."

"I'm going to consider that a compliment," Adrian said with a laugh. "Unless you were talking about me to my assistant while trying to poach her again, in which case my fee for this hour triples."

"I was talking to Noah Barden." I sat on the landing and stared out the porthole windows at Naked. Sunny must've had the same idea when she heard the thunder because the crowd had thinned considerably and she was busy flipping chairs onto the tabletops. "He sang your praises."

"He's not a bad client," Adrian murmured. "For an attorney."

"I have to imagine you'd be a peach of a client," I said.

"Yeah, well." He blew out a breath, saying, "I have some updates for you. Remember how I told you I had a specialist checking into that video? The report came back and they detected some slight irregularities. It's possible the video was edited at several points, specifically when Rabbit was speaking. We can't be sure it means anything substantive because we don't know what was altered but it's enough to raise doubt."

"That's great," I said, still focused on Sunny. Only a few more customers to send on their way and then I could take her home. "Right? This is good news, isn't it?"

"I am optimistic about this. We're drafting motions tonight to throw out the entire video and we're calling around to find additional experts to examine the video. We might have something to work with here but you know the road ahead of us is long. This isn't wrapping up anytime soon. Rabbit's going to be in there for a while."

I rubbed my neck and stared at the dark, shiny hardwood beneath my shoes. "Yeah. Okay. What else? Any news on my mom?"

"It would've been helpful if she hadn't missed that damn flight."

"Believe me, I know. That's pretty much the Ballad of Sandy Loew these days."

"There does not seem to be an appetite to extend her another deal. I'm going to keep working on it, though we do need her to be a tad more cooperative in the process."

"Tell me how to make that happen, Adrian. I'm all ears. Short of flying to Central America myself and searching every island down there, I don't know what to do."

He sighed like his entire skeleton was disintegrating, and then said, "I might have some ideas but it's going to take a considerable amount of time and money."

"It's funny how those are the only things you ever want from me."

"We've exhausted all the straightforward solutions available to us. We can't help her if we can't get her home, and we can't get her home unless we send someone in to get her."

It was my turn for my skeleton to disintegrate. "Are you talking about some kind of Navy SEAL-style extraction? Because that's what it sounds like."

He barked out a laugh. "No. Nothing like that. There's a firm based out of Washington, D.C., and while it is run by some former intelligence operatives, their work is all very civilized." He paused. I braced for impact. "That's why they're so expensive."

I turned my attention back toward the café while Adrian went on about minimizing exposure and Sandy-proofing these plans. I tuned him out, delighted to find the café empty and most of the chairs stacked on the tables but cold poured down my spine when I set eyes on Sunny.

She took a step backward and then another, a hand raised as if she was trying to calm someone down. Everything inside me turned to ice when I followed her hand to the person there. My organs, my blood, my muscles, everything. Frozen solid.

I could taste the panic on my tongue when I saw the ski mask pulled over his face and the long, heinous hunting knife he pressed into Sunny's chest.

chapter thirty-four

Sunny

Today's Special:
Naked Flambé

TWO PROBLEMS PRESENTED themselves at the same time: first, a strange, nearly sweet scent filled the café all at once, and when I went in search of the source I found myself face-to-face with my second problem, which happened to be a giant knife pointed directly at me.

Oh, and a guy in a ski mask.

Although I got the impression it wasn't actually a ski mask but a thick beanie pulled down over his nose with some slits cut for his eyes. He seemed really toasty in that thing, what with the sweat pouring down his jaw and neck. Perhaps it was the combination of armed robbery stress and a poor choice of disguise given the weather.

"Hi. What's up?" I wasn't versed in knife-wielding intruder protocol. It showed.

"Shut up," he yelled, jabbing with the knife.

I shuffled back several steps. The more distance between me and that gnarly blade, the better. "Okay, okay," I said, holding a hand out to steady both of us. Of all the days to leave the dogs at home. "Just tell me what's going on and I'll see what I can do to help." I took a few more steps until I had the windows on my side. Someone leaving the oyster company would notice this—this *situation* sooner or later. Sooner would be so much better. "Are you hungry? I have cookies and—"

"I don't want your fucking cookies," he roared. "You shouldn't even be here. This should've been mine, all of it, and you just swooped in and fucking took it."

This was the wrong time to realize that I hadn't asked many questions about the bait shop before accepting the title. Another protocol I didn't know was the one for winning property in poker games. "I'm sorry," I said. "I didn't know. It all happened so quickly that—"

"No, it fucking didn't!" he yelled, slashing the air with his knife. Every time the sharp, hooked end of the blade caught the light, I mentally begged Beck to look out his window. *Spy on me like you always do.* "You think I didn't notice how you weaseled your way in?"

"Really, that's not how it happened. It wasn't—"

He flipped several tables and advanced on me, yelling, "I told you to shut up."

"Right, right." I closed my fingers around the back of a chair. It would've been nice to have the use of both arms tonight. Would've been so great. "How can I help? What can I do to fix this?"

He groaned as if these questions were the height of ignorance. "I've been trying to *fix* this for months. You don't know how to get a fucking clue." He scratched his head with the butt of his knife. "How many times do I need to fuck up this place before you realize you don't fucking belong here?"

"The patio," I whispered.

"The patio," he mimicked.

"It wasn't an animal."

"Uh, duh. You have to be extra stupid to think that." He shook his head, disgusted. "I don't know how the hell someone so pathetic conned my uncle into thinking you gave a shit about him."

"I—" I peered at him for a moment. *Uncle?* "What?"

"I knew the old man was losing it but I didn't think he'd give you the whole damn bar," he went on. "How'd you do it? How'd you get him to give you everything?"

Because I truly didn't follow, I asked, "What are you talking about?"

He kicked over a chair, pushed another out of his way. It tipped back toward him and knocked him in the shins. "I had big plans for that bar," he shouted, pointing the knife at me as he hopped around to shake off the self-inflicted sting, "and then you showed up and talked Leary into signing the place over to you."

If I'd read up on the knife-wielding protocol, I probably would've encountered a tidbit about not arguing with the knife-wielder but I was behind on my worst-case scenario preparedness so I said, "That's not what happened. Not at all. I didn't ask Leary for anything."

"And yet you walked away with all the money after he sold the building!"

A roll of thunder rumbled overhead and he kicked a chair in my direction. I held on to the one in front of me but didn't move. I needed to stay in front of the window.

"That bar was supposed to be mine. Uncle Leary promised it to me, and you came along and fucking stole it."

So, this was the other grand-nephew. The one Leary referred to as "shit for brains" with a grouchy sigh and roll of his eyes. His name was Joey and his mom was a sweet lady who didn't understand why her son always managed to stumble into bad situations. I didn't know if this qualified as stumbling so much as barreling in with some big ideas and a knife that looked like it could skewer a dinosaur but I'd take that up with Leary at another time. Right now, I had to get myself out of here alive.

"Because you spent so much time at the bar," I said, and the knife-wielding protocol was flying right out the window now. As best I could manage with the cast, I clasped my hands behind my back and went to work loosening my watch. "You visited Leary all the time. You did so much for him. You played barback whenever he was short-staffed. You knew all about the tavern. You were always there, weren't you, Joey?"

Seeing as we both knew none of that was true, he responded the only way he could: by grabbing the chair in front of me and throwing it at the bakery case. The glass shattered and a weight landed in the pit of my stomach as I realized that strange smell was gasoline.

This guy was wrong about *everything* and he was out of his mind, and he was going to burn this place to the ground.

"I should've killed you that day," he snarled. "Thought I did, the way you went flying off that dumb bike. Didn't think I needed to turn around and hit you again but you're one of those bitches who just don't know how to stay down, aren't you?"

"It was you?" I sucked in a breath as lightning cracked nearby. It was loud enough to snap his attention for a split second and I threw my watch to the floor behind me as hard as I could. "At the bike path, it was you?"

"I've been watching you ever since Uncle Leary told me he gave you the money. You didn't even know it."

He reached out, shifting his sweaty grip on the hilt and nearly dropping the knife before pressing the tip of the blade to my chest. I felt the unyielding pressure through my t-shirt and I understood with terrible clarity that this guy wouldn't stop until I was dead. He'd probably kill himself in the process too but he was determined to take me down with him. I cut a quick glance to the side, hoping, *praying* that anyone from the oyster company looked this way.

"That's not what happened, Joey. We can call Leary right now and clear it all up. He'll tell you that's not what happened."

He rounded on me, grabbing me by the hair and dragging me across the café. Since I didn't have even the slightest whiff of a plan, I didn't bother fighting back. I didn't have a lot going for me with one arm and I had to save my strength until I knew I had a real chance to get away. Because I was going to get away. This was *not* how it ended for me. This was not the chaos that came for me. There was more ahead of me, more to do, more to see.

And Beck. There was so much of this life left to live and I was going to live it with Beck, regardless of how and where we made that happen. Those details didn't matter now and they never would. We'd work it out. We *had* to.

Forcing me into one of the only upright chairs, he said, "Now it's time to tie you up."

"Is there an itinerary we're following? Would you be willing to share this timetable with me?"

He slammed the butt end of the knife against my temple, muttering, "I told you to shut up." Stars swam behind my eyes and wet trickled down the side of my face. Washes of gray and red hazed my vision and I held back a groan as the taste of metal washed over my tongue. If this guy triggered a seizure, I'd kick his ass as soon as I could see straight. "Didn't think you'd talk so fucking much. Can't even think."

Thank you for that helpful information.

"These are reasonable questions." I cringed as he pulled a length of rope from under his black hoodie. I'd really hoped he was planning on improvising this part. "I'm just wondering how you plan on righting all these wrongs I've committed. I mean, how does any of this get you what you want?"

"You have no idea what I want," he yelled as he crouched behind me.

If there was ever a chance to get the hell out of here, it was now, when he was on his knees and focused on the rope. I could run for the door—which I'd already bolted but that would only hold me up for an extra second or two—and then to the oyster company. I *needed* to get over there.

But I thought a second too long and that chance dissolved before my eyes.

Joey yanked my arms behind the back of the chair and looped the rope around my wrists. He stopped, unfurled the rope, and started over. It sounded like he put the knife down for a second but then I felt the cold steel on the flat of my wrist.

"You wanted Leary's tavern and then, the money from the sale of Leary's tavern. But how does hitting me with your car or tying me to this chair get you any closer to those things?"

"Because—because you should pay for what you've done to my family," he sputtered.

"Okay. Sure." I nodded. "But wouldn't it be so much better if we talked this out and we found a solution that didn't involve—"

"Shut. Up." He pushed to his feet and kicked over the last table standing. It was enough entertainment to distract him while I worked the ropes open. "Just stop talking."

Another bolt of lightning filled the night sky and Joey fumbled the knife, grasping for it as it flipped end over end until it skittered along the length of his forearm and sliced his sweatshirt open. Blood poured down his arm, over his fingers, and all he could do was stare.

I didn't waste a minute on thinking this time, not when I didn't have a minute to spare. I jolted up to knee him in the crotch and swung the rainbow cast into his nose, and though I had a feeling I'd invented a new way to break my arm all over again, the resulting crunch of his bones was immaculately satisfying.

"Fuck me," he grumbled as blood spilled down his face.

Then, the anger avalanched and he lashed out, throwing punches with one hand while he held the other to his face. I backed away in time to dodge one hit but the second landed high on my cheek as I fought my way around overturned tables and chairs.

My head filled with static and my balance wavered but my attention shifted toward the back door, and in the tiny moments between a slow, throbbing blink, a blur of movement crossed the café. A series of crashes and grunts filled the space as I worked to process the scene unfolding in front of me but the signals were taking too long to travel from my eyes to my brain.

"Talk to me, Sunny. Tell me you're all right."

Beck.

Maybe it was a delayed reaction to being punched in the face, maybe it was hearing his voice. Either way, my eyes filled with tears and I melted back against the counter. "I'm all right," I managed.

"Okay, sweetheart, that's great. Do me a favor and slide down to the floor."

"Why?"

"For fuck's sake, Sunny. I need to hold this guy down and I don't want you hitting your head if you fall because I plan on strangling you later for throwing karate chop moves while someone had a knife to your throat."

My backside met the concrete as another round of thunder and lightning hit. I forced the memory of the scent of lavender to the front of my mind and some of the fogginess cleared. Fighting with Beck helped too. "Yeah, well, I'm going to strangle you first for yelling at me during a literal hostage situation."

"I believe the situation warrants yelling, Sunny."

"A lot of opinions from the guy who waited until the absolute last minute to get his ass over here. It's not like you've ever hesitated to stomp across the driveway and unload your mood of the day."

"Good news for you, I'm not going to be stomping across the driveway because I'll be right here, all day every day, keeping you out of trouble."

I blinked and I got a hazy look at Beck where he held Joey flat on the ground, one hand on the back of his neck and the other binding his wrists. "You're not staying here because you'll end up hating this town even more than you already do and resenting me for making you stay."

"Give me a year," he said.

I wanted to roll my eyes but my face hurt too much for that. "And then what?"

"Then you marry me," he replied, as if it was the most obvious thing in the world.

I touched a finger to my temple and found I was bleeding. Where the hell were the emergency services? I'd thrown that watch entire *minutes* ago. "Two years."

"Nine months."

"Who the hell do you think you're negotiating with? I'm not one of those people who gets an eyeful of scowl and hands over the house," I yelled back. "Eighteen months, take it or leave it."

"Fifteen and we tell people we're engaged tomorrow."

"Yeah, sure, if I was into bargaining against myself *and* making deals with the devil," I replied. "We can make this work. I believe it. But not without a whole lot of figuring it out as we go."

I blinked and realized some of this wavy gravy vision was from my cheek swelling. Another delightful development, but at least we weren't hurtling toward a seizure. "Fifteen months and we don't speak a word about making it legal until then."

Beck was quiet for a moment. Then, "Can we talk about the honeymoon?"

A blinding crack of lightning struck very close by and the entire building shook. Hell, it was possible the entire town shook.

A cackle rang out and Beck asked Joey, "What the fuck is your problem?"

"This entire place is going to be a fireball any minute," he said. "I unloaded five tanks of gas around the perimeter and doused the outside walls, and soon enough, your girlfriend and her stupid vegetable restaurant will be gone."

"That's enough bullshit out of you," Beck replied.

"No, Beck, he's telling the truth," I said. "The gasoline, I noticed it earlier."

"When this is all over, we're going to have a conversation about the correct order of items to communicate when you've been held at knifepoint," he said, his words freakishly calm as he stood, dragging Joey with him.

"Maybe you shouldn't have picked a fight about when we'll get married."

Another crack of lightning pierced the night and we all turned toward the back of the café as a great whoosh sounded. I didn't know what it was but I knew it couldn't be good.

"We'll have the next fifteen months to hash that out. Right now, we need to get the fuck out of here," Beck said. "Can you walk, sweetheart?"

"Yeah. I think so." I'd pushed to my hands and knees to find my balance when one enormous crash after another froze me on the spot. I couldn't tell if the building was on fire or it was thunder or just a noise inside my head. Or maybe the blare of sirens in the distance? "What the hell was—"

Broken glass rained into the café and then I heard, "Loew!"

"Where the fuck have you been, Price?" Beck shouted. "The one time you can be useful happens to be the one time you're not crammed all the way up my ass."

I pushed to my feet and found Agent Price stepping through one of the now-shattered windows. "The front door's barricaded with sandbags and the gable wall is on fire." He pulled a pair of handcuffs from his back pocket and slapped them on Joey. For his part, Joey started howling about being framed, which made fine sense considering the rest of his logic. "I've got him. Get your girl. Let's *go*."

I pushed my way through the wreckage of my happy accident café and let Beck help me out the window. Rain poured down as sirens drew close but none of that stopped Beck from folding me into his arms.

"Fifteen months is no bargain." He pressed his lips to my forehead. "But I'll take it. I don't care whether it's fifteen months or fifteen years. I love everything about you, even the sadistic way you drive me mad, and as long as I get you, nothing else matters."

Flashing lights filled the night sky and bounced off the buildings as the first responders arrived.

"Close your eyes, storm cloud," he said, cradling my head in his hand and tucking me under his chin. "Don't look. Stay right here."

Tears of relief, of adrenaline, of exhaustion flooded my eyes and immediately spilled over. "I love you too," I said into his shirt. "And I'll accept fifteen as long as you understand that you're not allowed to move in with me for at least nine months."

"I'll agree to those terms only because I know you'll break them before winter."

"Go ahead and antagonize me, Beck. That's worked out so well for you in the past few months."

"Go ahead and test me," he replied. "We know how well that works out for you."

chapter thirty-five

Today's Special:
Free-Range Fallout Finished with a Vinaigrette of Intentions

THE BACK SIDE of the café went up in flames but the rest of the building came out of the ordeal unscathed and no one sustained any serious injuries.

The guy with the knife, one Joey Waller, who managed to stab himself before Sunny broke his nose, was in police custody.

Sunny had a few new cuts and bruises to add to her collection, and her cast was a little worse off but that could be replaced. She couldn't.

My knuckles were in rough shape and it didn't seem like anything could scrub the memory of that guy waving a hunting knife at Sunny from my mind but I was all right.

We were all right—and the people crowded into the oyster company dining room seemed determined to remind us of that every few minutes.

Dex and Parker stood by the bar with Meara and her husbands while Bethany helped Mel mix drinks. Every so often, Mel grabbed Bethany by the ponytail and kissed her. Muffy lingered nearby, EpiPen in hand.

Hale stood by the entrance with Nyomi, an arm slung around her shoulders while he talked to Zeus. I didn't know what Chef was doing back there but he was busy barking orders at the kitchen staff and it wasn't important enough for me to find out. A bunch of the servers were still here, along with Sunny's parents who were taking this as well as could be imagined. A few stiff drinks from Mel seemed to be helping with their general helicoptering.

Naturally, Ranger and Phil Collins had rolled up shortly after the fire engines. Ranger came prepared, dressed in a waterproof poncho, muckers, and a headlamp. Always ready for action, that one.

Sunny's old boss Leary had been the last to arrive, escorted by none other than the infamous Mars. They'd heard about the events of this evening from Leary's niece, who also happened to be Joey Waller's mom. Leary hugged Sunny tight and said there was no explaining or excusing great-nephew's corrupted mind. Though I still had a profound desire to glare at the guy, Mars hadn't stopped apologizing for his homicidal cousin since walking in the door. He'd offered to help pay for the damages to Naked and I wouldn't let Sunny turn him down.

"That does it," Leary said. "We're moving to Friendship." He slapped his nephew on the back. "Make yourself useful and find us a new place to live."

"I really don't think—" Mars started.

"I don't want to hear any of your guff," Leary interrupted. "That fella over there looks like he knows a thing or two. Go on over. See if he knows of any houses for sale. If not a house, a barn will do. Lord knows you need the room." He pointed toward Ranger. "Don't come back until you have an answer."

"You don't have to do that," Sunny said to Leary.

"Maybe not, but I don't like Boston," he groused. "Too many people. And pigeons." He gave her a knowing nod. "You'll need my help, sunshine."

Leary shuffled toward Mars and Ranger, who was bubbling with the excitement of being useful.

"Why do I get the feeling this guy has semi-adopted you?" I asked Sunny.

"Because he has." She smiled. "You too."

"The doctor orders whiskey," Bartholomew said, setting two tumblers on the table beside us with a plate of elaborately shaped truffles. "And chocolate. It helps."

"Thanks." I picked up one of the glasses and downed the liquid in one go. If ever there was a night for it. "And thanks for running out there with the fire extinguisher. You probably prevented the entire building from going up."

"Most important tool in the kitchen." He held up his hands, shrugged. "Back home," he started, abandoning all pretense of a French accent, "my dad's a firefighter. I know enough of the basics to get by."

"My compliments to your dad," Sunny said.

When he stalked back into the kitchen, I adjusted the blanket around her damp shoulders and held her tight. "Can I take you home now?"

She bobbed her head against my shoulder. "Yeah. I want to see my dogs and sleep for at least twelve hours, and I want you to give me another one of those baths but without the concussion protocol this time."

"In that order?" I asked.

I felt her smile. "We'll see."

It took us half an hour to get out of there. Everyone required many hugs, many reassurances that we were all right. They all wanted to drive us home or offer a guest room at their place or any number of other things. Beth and Mel would walk the dogs. Hale and Nyomi would bring breakfast in the morning. Ranger would be over with plywood to shore up the damage at Naked. They meant well and I appreciated that we had all these people to fuss over us. It was a gift. Even if it annoyed the hell out of me sometimes and confused me the rest of the time.

When we stepped outside, the rain was still coming down in sheets and we ran to my car, laughing the whole way. Once we were inside, I reached over and kissed the rain off her lips. It was good to feel her smile against me. It was good to have her here with me.

The drive to Sunny's house was quick and I laced her fingers through mine, pressing them to my chest, but I didn't say anything. I didn't feel like I could say anything until we closed the door behind us and sealed ourselves off from this day and everything that had led up to it.

The dogs were waiting at the door and they yipped and nosed at us like they couldn't believe Sunny had gotten into more trouble and they hadn't been there to help. With a hand between Sunny's shoulder blades, I steered her toward the bedroom. "Go," I ordered. "I'll feed the pups. I want you in that bed when I come back."

"I was only taken hostage, Beck," she called as I headed into the kitchen. "I don't need to be babied."

"Can I speak to your manager?" I called back. "Because none of that makes sense."

I heard her laugh while I prepared the dogs' bowls. The sound warmed me all the way through. It was a sunbeam right to the heart and I couldn't believe I'd ever lived without it.

I took my contacts out in the bathroom and then pulled together some food and two glasses of water. I knew we were both going to crash soon, but we loved midnight snacks in bed.

When I stepped into her room, I found Sunny sitting up in bed examining her cast. Her hair was tied in a loose ponytail and she wore a baggy t-shirt with *The Soggy Dog* scrawled across the front. I set everything on the bedside table and started unbuttoning my shirt. "How's the arm?"

"Eh, you know," she said, gingerly rotating it from side to side. "It's still broken, and maybe a little more fucked-up than it was this morning, but I don't think it's going to fall off or anything."

"Well, that's a relief." I tossed my shirt and tie to the chair in the corner and went to work on my trousers. "We make a pretty good team."

"It's nice how you say that now, but from the first minute that you walked in there—"

"I believe I broke down the door, thank you for noticing."

"—all you could do was complain about how I knocked the knife out of his hand and broke his nose and nailed him in the balls—"

"All I was trying to say was that you didn't have to take those kinds of risks."

"—as if I wasn't fully aware of what I was doing. I'll remind you I managed to get my watch off and throw it hard enough to trigger a call to emergency services—"

"At no point did I suggest you were anything but capable. I simply suggested that you didn't have to take down the bloodthirsty maniac by yourself."

"—and I did it while tied to a chair, Beck! I wasn't tied especially well but the point remains and I had no reason to believe you or anyone else would notice what was going on over there—"

"All I do is notice what's going on over there. I've been staring at your café since the day you told me to stay on my side of the street." I settled beside her on the bed and pressed a finger to her lips. The evil glimmer in her eyes told me how much she liked that. "I'm just sorry I didn't get there sooner."

She nipped at the pad of my finger with a small smile. "I need you to lower the bar for yourself," she said. "You're not always going to be able to show up the minute the bloodthirsty maniac decides to set the building on fire."

"Maybe we plan on this being the only incident where a bloodthirsty maniac sets a building on fire with you inside it." I shrugged. "Just an idea."

"I'll see what I can do." She leaned in, kissed the corner of my mouth. "Just so you know, you don't have to do any of the things you said while I was a hostage. It was a crazy moment. Crazy things happening. We don't have to live by all the crazy things said."

"Sweetheart, that was a legitimate negotiation. Don't tell me you're backing out of our deal."

"It was really scary in there," she said by way of explanation. "It's possible we didn't mean all the things we said."

"And by *we* you mean me?" I tapped my chest. "Or you?"

She lifted a shoulder, let it fall as she ran the edge of the blanket between her fingers. "I don't know. Anyone who might want to rethink anything they said while I was in mortal danger."

"There is no more honest moment than the one that could be the last." I ducked to meet her eyes. "I meant everything I said and it's tough shit if you want to back out because I'm not going to be able to let you out of my sight for at least three years. Most likely four. I didn't plan on falling the fuck in love with you, Sunny, but that didn't happen tonight."

"I love you too but I don't want you to make any big decisions about—about anything."

I studied her for a heavy moment. I knew what she was doing. And I knew I couldn't let it happen. "You were right when you told me to let myself be vulnerable. To open myself up. To let myself be part of this place without constantly looking for the exit. And I've learned that—"

My fucking phone started ringing.

"Ignore it." She motioned for me to go on, but a second after the ringing stopped, it started up again. "Okay, get it and turn it off. Nothing's happening that requires our attention."

I held up the screen to Sunny.

"Oh, god."

I tapped the screen and held it between us, saying, "Hi, Lance. How's it going?"

"What the fuck is happening there?" he yelled. "My sister was *kidnapped*? And trapped in a *burning building*? And—"

Sunny winced. "It really wasn't that dramatic."

"Are you all right?" he asked her, still yelling. "I just talked to Mom and Dad, and they said you disarmed the guy who attacked you?"

"Your sister is a certified badass," I said. "She destroyed his nose and there's a very good chance his nuts will never recover."

"What the fuck, Sunny?" he breathed.

"A very exciting night for the town of Friendship. They'll mythologize this for years," she said. "But I'm fine. Beck broke down a door—"

"Beck broke down a door?" Lance repeated, back to the yelling.

"All by himself," Sunny said. "Wrestled the guy to the ground too." Smiling at me, she added, "I don't know what I would've done without him. I'm lucky to have him."

Lance blew out a long breath. "Thank you for being there, man. I'm sorry I gave you a hard time about everything. You know you're family to me and—"

"I know. It's all good," I said. "We'll give you a call tomorrow, okay? It's been a hell of a day and we're running on fumes."

"Say hi to Chantal for me," Sunny said.

"Hmm." Lance was silent for a moment. "Yeah, so, Chantal moved out months ago. That's over."

"And you didn't tell us?" Sunny cried.

At the same time, I said, "You had the balls to sit there and holler at me for not telling you the minute things started with Sunny while Chantal moved out *months* ago?"

"Once again," he started, "Chantal is not your sister."

"You have several screws loose, Lance," she replied.

"I just didn't see how it was relevant," he said. "Whatever. Okay? It's done. Beck, thank you for being there tonight. I'm still trying to wrap my mind around this but I'm happy Sunny has you to lean on. And Sunny, I don't know where you learned how to destroy someone's nose or nuts, but I'm damn proud of you for doing it. Even if you are with my best friend now."

"Does that mean you can be an adult about it?" she asked.

"That depends," he replied. "Beck, what are your intentions with my sister?"

Sunny brought a hand to her face. "No, we're not doing this."

At the same time, I said, "Well, I asked her—"

"Beck, stop," she interrupted. "Lance, learn some boundaries. You are not allowed to ask about *intentions*."

"I think I can," he replied.

"She told you to back the fuck off," I snapped. "Either you understand that or you don't."

"I understand," he grumbled. "Somewhat."

"Work harder at not being an asshole," I growled.

"I know, I know. Listen, I have to go. Things are breaking all over the place here and I can't keep my head above water. I'll call soon. Please don't get kidnapped again or hit by any more cars."

"I'll see what I can do," she said.

"Bye, Lance." I ended the call and then did the one thing I never, ever did. I turned off my phone. "I'm all yours, storm cloud."

"What were we talking about before Lance decided to have the worst timing in the universe?"

I shook my head. "It was something important but I don't remember the specifics. All you need to know is I'm not going anywhere. I can work from wherever I want, and I want to be here with you. Just so long as you let me take you on adventures a few times each year. Plus the honeymoon."

"Tell the truth. You're actually staying for the festivals."

"Now, don't misunderstand me. I'm not about to turn into the patron saint of Friendship's festivals anytime soon but—oh, wait. Wait a second." I pushed a hand through my hair. "Yeah, I might've agreed to host an oyster festival."

"It was only a matter of time."

I laughed, holding her close. "Did you happen to hear the part about me taking you on a honeymoon? Because—"

"Fifteen months, Beck. That's the deal."

"Trust me, I know the terms of this deal. Just as long as you know you'll be taking a significant chunk of time off in fifteen months. For your honeymoon."

"I'm going to need a very elaborate proposal out of you first."

"So, my declaration of undying love and promises of forever in the middle of a hostage situation wasn't elaborate enough for you?" I ran a hand down my face. "Let's grab a book, run a bath, and see if I can change your mind."

She pressed her cheek to my chest. "That sounds good," she said, her tone softening. We weren't playing anymore. "But later, okay? I just want to be with you right now. We have all the time in the world for everything else."

I kissed her hair. "Yes. We do."

epilogue

Beckett

Today's Special:
All You Can Eat Oysters

SPRINGTIME, the next year

"KEEP READING," I warned.

"I'm trying," Sunny snapped back. "You're—you're—"

"I'm doing my part," I said through clenched teeth. God, she felt amazing around me this morning. I loved fucking her from behind while she read out loud. There was something strange and magical about slamming into her while beautiful, indecent words spilled over her lips. "You've repeated the same line three times."

She rocked back against me. Her ass looked good enough to eat. "It's a good line."

"She's been rubbing his cock against her clit for like an hour. It's time for her to take it like a good girl." I moved my hand up her spine, settled between her shoulder blades. Put her focus back on the pages.

"I hope she's had fun playing because he's not going to last much longer."

"I believe what you're saying is you're not going to last much longer."

"Yes, but that's only because you are clenching on my cock so hard that I'm seeing stars. I might be the one in the coma this time."

"No worries. I'll roll you over and finish without you," she said.

"Believe me, storm cloud, I know." I thrust into her hard enough to force a gasp out of her. The shy woman with the sexual history roughly equivalent to loose change was long gone, a memory so distant that I doubted it had ever been real. I gripped her hips, holding her tight to me as I bottomed out. "Keep reading."

"'I felt like I'd belonged to him for a lifetime,'" she started, her words coming apart like a knot frayed down to the threads, "'like everything that was mine had always been his, and I realized I wanted it that way. I wanted to be possessed in every filthy and beautiful and painfully real way I could be, and—'"

She dropped her head to the book when I reached around to stroke her clit. "That's my girl," I growled. "Don't stop now."

"'—I wanted him to be the one possessing me. And the secret I wasn't prepared to share with him—barely with myself—was that I wanted to possess him too.'" She moaned into the mattress as I sped up. "'Every inch of me was hot and sensitive, and my nipples needed so much attention, they hurt.'"

I started to shift my hand away from my clit, but she gripped my wrist and held me in place. "More of this?"

She bobbed her head before reading again. "'I couldn't tear my eyes off him as he stared down at where I was spread around him, as a gulp moved through his throat. "I think I'm watching you kill me with your cunt.'"—oh, god, Beck, yes. Please. Just like that."

"You're definitely killing me," I said through a groan. "Get there, Sunny. Get the fuck there."

Her words turned watery then, all broken sounds and hoarse gasps as the first wave of her release fluttered around me. "'—as the orgasm unfurled from behind my clit and wrapped my center in a brutal throb. As he speared up into me again, again. As he shook with me. As he held me.'"

I lashed both arms around her torso, clinging to her as I chased the explosion waiting for me. Her hand was inside my chest again, her fingers pulsing around my heart with every beat, though I didn't worry about her ripping it out anymore. My lips on her throat, I said, "I fucking love you."

She looped an arm around my neck, nodding in that disconnected way of hers when she was only partially tethered to this world. Her fingers patted my cheek. "Love you too."

My muscles were jelly and I was going to crush Sunny if we didn't move soon. I managed to roll to the side, taking her with me. "And to think," I said, a breath gusting out of me, "I almost let you read that in the bath."

A silly, sated laugh had her vibrating against me. "That would've gotten messy."

Sunny in the bath with a book was one of the absolute best parts of my new life here in Friendship. There was nowhere else I wanted to be than sitting on the bathroom floor and simply observing—and helping, when the moment called for it—while she took my world apart and then put it back together in a perfect, secret way that only we knew.

Though it would've been nice to share that bath with her, we'd tried that and those experiments had failed sensationally. The first time, we'd miscalculated everything and flooded the entire bathroom while slipping and sliding against each other in the tub like a pair of wayward sea lions, desperate to find our way out. The next time, we'd planned everything yet failed to recognize that we didn't actually fit in there together until it was too late and we were those lost sea lions all over again. Not a fun time. No sexy stories read. No orgasms for anyone. We'd ended up wet, naked, and exhausted from the struggle of getting out of there in one piece.

I gave her ass a light slap. "At least I can still have you in the shower."

She shifted to peer up at me, her apple-round cheeks pink as her smile bloomed. "Would you like to have me in there this morning?"

I bounced a shoulder. "Would you like to marry me?"

She snapped her fingers and pointed to the door. "Go home."

We didn't live together.

We also didn't not live together.

Most of my clothes were in Sunny's closet and I kept my contact solution in her bathroom, and I spent nearly every night with her. I couldn't remember the last time I hadn't spent the night with her. But I did not live here. I attempted to renegotiate last summer's agreement at least once a day and though I knew she wouldn't admit it, she was starting to waver.

If I was being honest, I'd admit that I'd expected her to cave sooner. I'd figured we'd play this game for a few months, but that we'd agree it made more sense to live together than for me to straddle two homes indefinitely. Especially after months of straddling two continents. Sunny, however, was steadfast. She wasn't in any rush, as she often reminded me, and I hadn't proven that I'd want to stay in Friendship once the shine of a new relationship had worn off.

If there had ever been a time for the shine to wear off, it was the holiday season when Lance visited. He managed to short-circuit himself every time I touched Sunny—which was often. He didn't say anything but he looked like he was being plucked to death by very small, very vengeful fairies. It only got worse when their mother went a little heavy on the wine and started in on him about why couldn't he meet someone nice the way his sister had? He'd flown back to California a day early and blamed it on an emergency at work.

On his way out the door, he'd pulled us aside and sworn up and down that he wasn't upset about me and Sunny, but that he had a lot of things on his mind. I'd thought he was full of shit, but Sunny insisted we forgive and forget. She wasn't dragging icebergs around these days and neither should I.

Lance and I didn't talk any more or less now that I lived in Friendship and routinely begged his sister to marry me, but it was different between us. He still couldn't believe that I'd chosen a place we'd long-agreed was the worst, and I couldn't believe that he found it necessary to be a moody child so often.

More importantly, I couldn't believe it had been almost a year since meeting Sunny all over again. Of all the things I'd expected to encounter coming back here, the woman who'd change my entire life hadn't been on my list.

I was really fucking thankful for those flowerpots. And her general ability to put me in my place.

Once we'd said goodbye to Sunny's second rainbow cast—the original wasn't stable enough after the beating she'd served Joey—we went to Singapore for ten days. Naked had been under construction and the conversation I'd needed to have with the managing partners at my firm was a face-to-face one. In the end, their desire to keep me on staff outstripped the value of sending me to new corners of the globe every year.

We spent the whole time in Singapore eating, exploring, and enjoying my huge bed. The party-sized shower I'd barely noticed before then too. We'd packed up the last of my suits and the few personal items I'd kept from my travels, and I'd said goodbye to the part of my life that had been all wings and no roots.

I'd be lying if I said I didn't miss elements of it. The shower that was slightly larger than a coffin like the one in Sunny's house came to mind. The huge bed that wasn't shoehorned into the room. But I could deal with the quirks of her 1930s-era hand-me-down home. Just so long as we gave ourselves permission to imagine a future in a place with a bathroom from this century.

There were times when I missed the anonymity of living in big, vibrant cities too, although that was mostly a product of the entire town of Friendship incessantly asking when I was going to propose to Sunny. As if I needed everyone to witness my complete inability to close this deal.

I slapped her ass again. She liked it when I didn't treat her like she was breakable. She was very breakable, I'd seen that firsthand, but I could play along if it made her happy. There wasn't much I wouldn't do if it made her happy. "Instead of going home, why don't I lick your pussy in the shower?"

"Since it's not like I can turn that down," she said, "you might as well start the water."

I'D TRADED my corner office for a rotating collection kitchen tables and I didn't hate it. Most days, I worked from Sunny's place although I also stationed myself at my parents' house if I wanted to check on Parker or Dex. When I didn't have any conference calls on my schedule, I hung out at the newly renovated and expanded Naked Provisions.

The portion of the café lost in the fire had been rebuilt with a one-hundred-and-eighty degree view of Friendship Cove, more seating, and zero dark, narrow hallways. They hosted a grand reopening on the evening of October's full moon and celebrated by dragging out the cauldron. Leary, one of Friendship's newest residents, had started the party by lighting the bonfire. His nephew Mars had told me we were nuts for letting a guy with glaucoma set fire to anything, and, though it had killed me to agree with him, he was right.

Leary helped out in the kitchen at Naked a few afternoons each week. When he wasn't peeling vegetables, he could be found at one of the café tables, devouring every muffin put in front of him and telling stories so outrageous that they were almost believable. There were days when I pulled up a chair beside him just to hear his running commentary on issues such as seaweed, the British monarchy, and the "foxy ladies" who came through with the walking club. It was good to talk to him, even if he grumbled like a box of rocks the whole time.

Dex was still at home, though he frequently made a point of telling us he didn't need to be here and would be moving out soon. I found this amusing as he'd special-ordered a mattress for his room and had a professional batting cage installed in the backyard. All very temporary, of course.

We'd sold his place in Arizona and all the cars he'd forgotten about there too. He'd done some on-air commentary over the winter and survived the whole affair with only a fuckton of drama. He kept himself busy by annoying everyone at SPOC while shucking oysters and inviting himself to practices of the high school baseball and softball teams, where he'd serve up his special blend of complain-coaching. Every swing, every pitch was a personal offense to my brother. For reasons I still did not comprehend, he hadn't been escorted off the field yet. Apparently the teams liked having him around. Something about all those years spent playing in the Major League.

Parker was finishing up his junior year next month and he continued to have no interest in discussing college, which I'd chosen to accept rather than kicking up a conversation that would only give me a headache. Without my knowledge or involvement, he'd signed up for a photography class at the community college last fall. He'd taken to it quickly, and registered for another class this spring. I'd refrained from asking whether this was a hobby or a future career, and I felt like I deserved some credit for that. He didn't keep me updated on the tilt-a-whirl that was teenage love, thank god, but I kept the cookie jar filled with condoms.

As far as my parents went, well, I was still backing dump trucks of cash up to Adrian Pineda's office on a regular basis. That was a work in progress.

The oyster company was in Ayla and Mel's capable hands, and Hale was deep into conversations with the local university to launch a research partnership along with an oyster hatchery. We had many years of work ahead of us, but it seemed like we were closer to making that a reality than I'd imagined.

"Remind me about your schedule for today." Sunny dug in her basket—it was a basket, it was not a bag, and I wouldn't entertain any discussion of this—as I drove down Market Street. "You have things and then other things, and then you're taking me home?"

Jem leaned forward from the back seat and licked the side of my face. "Thanks, buddy," I said. "Yeah, that's pretty much the plan. Are you staying for the yoga and tarot event tonight?"

"No, Beth has that under control." She continued sorting through the basket. "And you're ready for the weekend?"

I turned down Succotash Lane. It was hard to notice things that were gone when so many other, good things crowded in and filled the void, but there were moments when I was aware that I didn't dread coming here anymore. I didn't associate the oyster company—the whole damn town, honestly—with disaster and responsibility. With saving everyone else before I saved myself.

"I am as ready as anyone could be." I pulled into my spot and stole a quick kiss before letting Scout and Jem out. "I will survive this the way I survive most things."

"Oh, wonderful," she murmured, coming around the back of the car. "Am I going to need to rub your neck and shoulders with that salve from the herbalist from Ecuador again?"

"No," I replied, irritable for no good reason. "Maybe. I don't know. It will be fine." I reached for her hand. "Do we have more of that stuff?"

"Yeah, I bought four jars when she visited for her tincture workshop." She smiled up at me. "I know how you get. You squirrel your stress away."

"I do not squirrel anything—"

"Good day, friends!"

We turned to find Ranger and Phil Collins emerging from the path, the walking club in tow. "This guy's timing," I muttered to Sunny.

"It's a gift," she said under her breath. "But he tips like a god so be nice."

"I'm always nice."

"You are contemptuous and intimidating," she said. "Nice is not part of the package."

"Then it's a good thing you're nice enough for both of us." I held up my hand to Ranger and Phil Collins. "Good afternoon."

"And what a fine afternoon it is," Ranger said. "Looking forward to the weekend?"

I swallowed a groan. I'd gotten quite proficient at that over the past few months. "As much as anyone."

"Outstanding," Ranger said. "Mr. Collins and I will be there with bells on."

"Promise?" Sunny asked. "Because I'll wear my bells too, but only if you're doing it with me. Can't be the only one in bells."

"I have a jingly bracelet I got in Portugal that I've always wanted to wear but could never find the right occasion," Phil Collins said.

"Really?" she cried. "Me too! Where in Portugal?"

"Oh, well, this little village at the base of a volcano where—"

"Loew!" Agent Price appeared at the end of the group, waving. He bounded over, dressed in athletic pants and a Friendship High Football hoodie. May was one of those months where it could be summer and winter, all in the same day. Life on the bay was tricky like that. "It's almost time for the First Annual Friendship Oyster Festival!"

"You're perversely excited about this," I said to him.

"This event calls for a considerable amount of excitement," Ranger said. "I believe the agent's excitement is spot-on. Not perverse in the least."

Friendship had claimed another with Agent Price. He'd permanently transferred to the Providence office of the FBI and lived down the street from my parents' house now. When he wasn't traveling on official business, he could be found at every festival, athletic event, and town council meeting on the calendar.

That I was also present at these outings was far less of a hardship than I'd allowed myself to imagine. Especially now that I could stand off to the side with Noah Barden while the women in our lives talked to everyone on the entire planet. The addition of beer at many of these affairs only improved them in my eyes.

Since Agent Price—or Naeem, as he was known to his neighbors—had convinced his bosses that I had no better idea where my mother was than they did, I didn't glare at him anymore. Not here, not around town, not even when he jogged by the house in his FBI t-shirt. Also, he'd broken through a window to save Sunny. I'd never finish thanking him for that. All the oysters in the world for him. Every day.

"I'm ready to see this thing come to life," Agent Price said.

I slipped my hands into my pockets, nodding. The Friendship Oyster Festival was a two-day event featuring food from Small Point and other local oyster companies, shucking demonstrations and contests, games, and—thankfully—a beer garden. Since I was the last person anyone wanted at the helm of a festival, I'd assigned Hale the task of making this idea into a reality. Hale being Hale, he'd turned that directive into a planning committee and convinced Agent Price, Phil Collins, and Mars Murtagh to come along for the ride, among others.

For better or worse, we had most of the FBI agents in this region descending on Friendship this weekend, along with all of Mars's biotech buddies.

"As am I," I said. "It's going to be one hell of a weekend."

With a tip of his hat, Ranger said, "I need to get this crew fed and watered so we can stay on schedule. I'll see you all tomorrow."

I led Sunny and the dogs toward the oyster company to steal a few more minutes with her. They had enough staff working at Naked now that she didn't need to rush over there to help them survive the crush of orders that came with the arrival of the walking club.

Since I wasn't content to ask Sunny to marry me just the one time today, I said, "So, I was thinking we could take the boat out tonight and go down to—"

"Who is that?"

I followed Sunny's stare into the restaurant, to the raw bar where Dex was shucking his way through several dozen oysters at a speed that was frankly concerning, given his wrist and elbow issues. Beside him stood a redhead with teal sunglasses propped on her head and a safety glove on her left hand as she matched him oyster for oyster.

I dropped my hand to Sunny's shoulder as I blinked. I couldn't believe it. Of all the people I'd expected to find at the oyster company today, either of my parents and my dead uncle Buckthorne were higher up on the list than that woman.

"That's Jenn," I said. "Decker's wife."

THANK YOU FOR READING! *I hope you loved Sunny and Beckett! If you'd like to read a super-extended epilogue, get it here!* (https://geni.us/ShuckedEp)

If you want more from the Loew brothers and the Naked girls, as well as the town of Friendship, Rhode Island, join my mailing list (https://geni.us/officememos).

I wouldn't have finished this book without the help of people I've come to consider my book doulas: Jess, Julia, and Erica. These people not only put up with my creative idiosyncrasies but they seem to nod along like "Yep, this is just how we write books around here, don't worry, it's going to be GREAT." The people who, when I tell them I'm very, very sad and I don't think I know how to write love or shenanigans anymore, say, "You'll remember." The ones who, when I tell them it's not there yet, it's not ready, say, "It will be. Just keep going."

I couldn't finish books without them and I am eternally grateful that they have a faith in me that I can't begin to understand.

I couldn't finish books without my husband and my daughter, both of whom keep me sane (mostly), keep me fed, and have adapted to the incredible wonkiness that is living with an author. Special credit goes to my husband for devoting a considerable amount of energy to finding me earbuds small enough to fit my tiny, elfin ears and also strong enough to save me from eavesdropping on every juicy conversation around me in the coffee shop.

It would be crazy of me not to mention some of the other folks who've helped me along the way. Debra, Jodi, Caroline, Melissa, Kim,

Dawn, Lisa, Becca Mysoor, Becca Syme. So many others. I'm so thankful to have you by my side through these journeys.

I'm also thankful to the readers who've been reading my work since the very first Walsh book and who've only just met me and the town of Friendship with *In a Jam*. There is not a day that goes by that I don't marvel at the fact that y'all get lost in my words. Thank you.

Finally: Epilepsy, like oysters, takes many shapes. There is no one, single story of a person living with epilepsy. Sunny's story may ring true for some while sounding foreign to others. My only hope is that this representation sheds a light on one person's experience with epilepsy.

also by kate canterbary

Friendship, Rhode Island

In a Jam — Shay and Noah

Vital Signs

Before Girl — Cal and Stella
The Worst Guy — Sebastian Stremmel and Sara Shapiro

The Walsh Series

Underneath It All – Matt and Lauren
The Space Between – Patrick and Andy
Necessary Restorations – Sam and Tiel
The Cornerstone – Shannon and Will
Restored — Sam and Tiel
The Spire — Erin and Nick
Preservation — Riley and Alexandra
Thresholds — The Walsh Family
Foundations — Matt and Lauren

The Santillian Triplets

The Magnolia Chronicles — Magnolia
Boss in the Bedsheets — Ash and Zelda

The Belle and the Beard — Linden and Jasper-Anne

Talbott's Cove

Fresh Catch — Owen and Cole

Hard Pressed — Jackson and Annette

Far Cry — Brooke and JJ

Rough Sketch — Gus and Neera

Benchmarks Series

Professional Development — Drew and Tara

Orientation — Jory and Max

Brothers In Arms

Missing In Action — Wes and Tom

Coastal Elite — Jordan and April

Get exclusive sneak previews of upcoming releases through Kate's newsletter and private reader group, The Canterbary Tales, on Facebook.

about kate

USA Today Bestseller Kate Canterbary writes smart, steamy contemporary romances loaded with heat, heart, and happy ever afters. Kate lives on the New England coast with her husband and daughter.

You can find Kate at www.katecanterbary.com

facebook.com/kcanterbary

instagram.com/katecanterbary

amazon.com/Kate-Canterbary

bookbub.com/authors/kate-canterbary

goodreads.com/Kate_Canterbary

pinterest.com/katecanterbary

tiktok.com/@katecanterbary

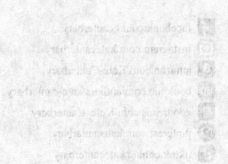